SLEEP TIGHT, WAKE DEAD

A Crag Banyon Mystery

JAMES MULLANEY

James Mullaney Books

Cover art: Scotty Phillips

Cover design/layout: Micah Birchfield

Interior design/layout: Rich Harvey

SLEEP TIGHT, WAKE DEAD

In the beginning, there was Banyon Investigations, Inc. ...

Crag Banyon just wants a little peace and quiet to go along with his bourbon, but as usual his prayers go unanswered. This time trouble comes in the ethereal form of a desperate guardian angel who wings his way through the front door of Banyon Investigations. Banyon's would-be client has been given the slip by a nihilist charge; a human being wholly uninterested in holy intervention, and the sad-sack seraph needs Banyon's help to track the MIA unbeliever down.

Banyon has cracked bigger cases than this, and he thinks he knows the drill chapter and verse. But that's before the arrival on the scene of a heavily armed heavenly host, a mysteriously happy and incredibly well-rested populace, and a delicious-smelling shadow of doom circling the city.

The deeper Banyon digs, the more he regrets not taking that job at the florist shop. In the end, the only great mystery of the universe he wants to solve is how many P.I.'s can pass out on the head of pin or, if a pin is unavailable, the nearest vacant bar stool. Unfortunately for Crag Banyon, P.I., the cosmos, cosmology and probably cosmetology have bigger plans, most seeming to revolve around killing him dead.

... AND IT WAS: "RUDE SERVICE," "INVESTIGATOR APPEARED DRUNK, REPEATEDLY," "OVERALL 'F' RATING."

(Information Courtesy the Better Business Bureau)

For the great Jim Uhls

1

The clock on the wall had been ticking down the minutes to doom ever since I woke up at five that morning. I failed to stop the countdown three times; first in the first few minutes of the newborn, early morning hour with two hurled shoes, then just before half past with a troublingly recently emptied Seagram's bottle.

I recognized the clock that stubbornly continued to keep more-or-less accurate time as my own. I'd picked it up years ago from a seedy street vendor who'd liberated it from PS 38, assuming the faded "property of" sticker on the back could be trusted. I figured that I could probably trust the sticker more than I could the junkie who'd boosted it from a school or the bum — namely me — who'd bought the hot clock from the aforementioned hophead for two bits.

I looked around to make sure that it was my living room the clock was hanging in. This was logical and necessary since it was possible, albeit unlikely, that somebody had busted into my place, stolen my stolen clock and mounted it like a mangy moose head on the wall of their apartment. It was furthermore possible that by some amazingly improbable corkscrew twist of chance, I'd wound up accidentally staggering into and passing out drunk in the new home of my old clock.

After casting a bloodshot eye around the room, I determined that the likelihood of this being someone else's apartment was virtually nil. The burglars not only would have had to swipe my clock, they'd have had to take all my other crummy possessions as well, which would have said a lot about their low self-esteem. Not only that, they'd have had to place my junk in the exact corresponding spots in their sorry dump where everything had been in mine, including my hideous yellowed wallpaper. Not to mention they'd also have somehow figured out how to take down the jagged crack that beautified the otherwise drab ceiling plaster in the corner above my 1982 Magnavox, and which looked amazingly like the profile of character actor M. Emmet Walsh.

That the shithole apartment was mine meant also that the spring in the sofa that was currently burrowing into my back like a vengeful Slinky was my own.

I closed my eyes for a minute which, happily, turned out to be four hours. By the time I woke up for good, the sun was shining and the birds were singing. Or vice versa. I am neither a heliologist nor an ornithologist, so for all I know they do whatever the hell they goddamn want when I'm not looking. For the record, what I am is a private investigator, which means that most days — and this was definitely one — I'd rather be tap dancing on the sun while being pecked apart by flaming birds.

My feet found the floor and I managed vertical on the first attempt. Bully for goddamn me. To celebrate the fact that I hadn't passed out cold, I considered laying back down until the bars opened. Unfortunately, I had just wrapped up a case that had involved a four day stakeout where the only running water was whatever cheap vodka managed to get processed through my bladder.

The spring in my back didn't transfer to my step. It was a last-mile trudge to the bathroom for an overdue shower in water that was alternately hot enough to murder a lobster and freezing enough to preserve my head cryogenically for some future date when science has discovered a cure for pounding hangovers.

I was at the sink dragging a razor across my stubble, and wondering if I shouldn't just draw it across my throat and be done with it all, when I caught sight of a large, shadowy shape directly behind my left shoulder.

At first I figured it was fog. The final burst of water from the showerhead had hilariously decided to flambé my escaping ass, and consequently the bathroom had steamed up as if Enrico Fermi was splitting uranium atoms inside my rusty pipes.

When I wiped away the fog with a sopping wet palm, I caught a glimpse of a brilliant, sincere smile that absolutely wasn't the reflection of my homely, depressed mug.

I wheeled around to find not only nobody crammed into my bathroom with me, but in the process of pirouetting I skidded on my mildewed bathmat and nearly opened my carotid artery, which turned out not to be the laugh riot I'd envisioned just moments before. As it was, I spent the next ten minutes scribbling over the bleeding nick on my cheek with a dried-out styptic pencil that refused to write and tearing off bits of Cottonelle that stuck only to my damp fingertips and not my hemorrhaging face.

I am not the kind of drunk who hallucinates. Imaginary elephants dyed "it's a girl!" pink are the work of more inventive minds than the inert gray loaf that fate had jammed between my ears. The real-world bullshit of my miserable life is more than enough for me to deal with without my subconscious inventing imaginary phantoms to accidentally slit my throat over. Somebody had been there. Now they were gone.

"I would say 'Bloody Mary' into the mirror three times, but I doubt a spectral bartender will arrive with one," I said to my empty bathroom.

I actually said it nearly as a question and with far greater optimism than I usually muster for semi-visible phantasms, as I held out some small hope that the dame in question would appear in reflection in my mirror and offer to take my drink order. As it was, nobody appeared again and so I chalked up whatever I'd seen as a rogue ghost that had accidentally floated through my apartment on its way to scaring the shit out of somebody other than me, since I find ghosts about as terrifying as tying my shoelaces.

I finished my toilette with lethargic gusto and dolled myself up in my wrinkled Sears two-piece suit and Salvation Army necktie. My scuffed Florsheims completed an ensemble that was the perfect combination of functionality and not giving a shit.

I figured I was right and that the bathroom specter of a half hour before had checked a roadmap and found out it had taken a wrong turn at Albuquerque, since I'd finished up in the john and in my bedroom without spying another shadowy peeping Tom hanging over my shoulder like a cheap floozy. That changed when I reached the kitchen.

As it turned out, I glimpsed the figure twice more: once in reflection on my silver toaster when I was lamenting the fact that I had no bread to shove in it and burn, and again upside-down in the doorknob after I'd donned my stylish trench coat and fedora and was exiting my apartment. Both times when I turned around, the indistinct figure with the horrible, charming smile had vanished.

I saw the toothy grin once more in the silver doors of

the elevator.

"Look, if you're following me, you're going to be bored out of your ethereal gourd," I offered without turning around. "There are far more interesting people living in this building. Just one floor up is a gastroenterologist who lost his medical practice for posting patient colonoscopy videos online with accompanying hilarious commentary, all to a *Benny Hill* soundtrack. He now works in a bowling alley delousing sweaty shoes. In fact, I believe this is the second Tuesday of the month. If so, if you hurry you can probably float up there in time to witness his biweekly suicide attempt."

I suddenly didn't see the figure. Not that I had yet seen it clearly. So far, it was nothing but what looked to my tired and increasingly annoyed eyes like a pair of incredibly broad, arched shoulders attached to a benign smile that seemed to be trying to communicate to me that everything was okay. Since nothing was ever remotely okay, I resented any collection of lying teeth that would silently suggest otherwise. But whoever the choppers belonged to, he was gone once more along with his dental work.

The sigh of relief I considered heaving was abandoned aborning when I stepped onto the elevator, the doors slid shut, and I saw once more the reflection of the very large, increasingly irritating figure hovering behind me.

I turned around.

No one there.

I looked forward once more.

Once more, the large, nebulous shape was reflected in the grubby silver doors.

I rode the elevator down to the first floor and, upon exiting, set off in search of my building's property manager. It turned out he hadn't made himself as difficult to find as a lost Incan city of gold or a labor leader whose devotion to honesty had taken a bad turn into the bottom of a New Jersey marsh. The big goon was standing in the hallway two feet from the elevator and attempting to maneuver a paint brush.

For most humans, working a paint brush is pretty much as simple a thing as operating their tooth- or hair- cousins. For Harry "No Thumbs" Hooligan, all three were nearly Sisyphean tasks, which explained why his hair looked like a condor's nest after a New Year's Eve party, why his mouth stunk like an overflowing septic tank, and why half the paint that was supposed to be going on the wall was winding up creating modern art splatter on the copies of the *Gazette* he'd spread out under his huge feet.

In his previous job, No Thumbs had lost a fight with a meat grinder, permanently hampering his ability to approve of motion pictures or to magnanimously spare gladiators. It turned out that nobody wanted hired muscle who could neither cock a gun nor properly clutch garrote wire, and so the eight-fingered goon had tumbled his humiliated way down the ladder of thug success to the very bottom rung, there to shake down widows and P.I.'s for overdue rent.

"Shit," No Thumbs was grousing as I exited the elevator.

He had the paintbrush clapped in both hands the same way you'd capture a fly between your palms if you intended to release it into the wild. With an extraordinarily careful downward stroke he managed to commit only a feeble S shape on the wall. Most of the paint wound up on his feet or drizzled on the newspapers beneath them.

"Shit, shit, shit," No Thumbs snarled.

"I think so as well, but the art world might disagree," I said, admiring the mess he'd made of the sports section underneath his Buster Browns. "Slap some frames around them and you can probably get your own showing at one of those shitty modern art galleries downtown."

No Thumbs squinted one eye hard as he glared at me. "Oh, great," he grunted. "Banyon. This is gonna be a *perfect* morning." He went back to his paint can.

Harry No Thumbs was a huge, hugely muscled monster of a proto-human. The brush in his giant (albeit deficient by one-fifth in the digit department) hands was ridiculously small, and the one gallon can of paint looked like a coffee mug next to the swollen catcher's mitts fastened to the ends of his exceptionally hairy forearms. He managed to thread the needle and got the brush into the can, but delicate precision was beyond the abilities of a lummox whose opposable thumbs had been opposed to remaining attached to his body.

The brush slipped from the fingertips of his clapped-together hands and sank like the *Bismarck* into a bucket of North Atlantic Glidden. It was a miracle of surprising dexterity that he snagged the dorsal fin tip of the handle with a scissor-like snap of his middle and index fingers before the brush could drop down completely to a watery latex grave. When he dragged the brush back up to give it CPR, it was dripping a furious mucus of ugly green paint.

He held the brush carefully between two fingers like a weeping cigarette and dabbed at the handle with an old T-shirt he was using as a rag.

"Whaddaya want, Banyon? Can't you see I'm working here?"

"I'm not entirely certain what I'm seeing, but I confess to dread fascination," I replied, before getting down to business. "I'm going to need an exorcism."

"Why? What're you claiming you got?"

"I don't know. Maybe a ghost. Some kind of phantasm.

I'd point my thumb over my shoulder to where the apparition is more than likely lurking, but I don't want to lord over you the fact that I can stick in a thumb and pull out a plum with both hands."

He continued to mop around the dripping paintbrush with his Colts T-shirt while he peered over my shoulder. "I don't see nothing."

"It comes and goes. It's been there since I got up this morning."

"How do I know you didn't drag it home with you? Your lease covers rats, bedbugs, silverfish, cockroaches, ghostly possessions, chiggers and stuff like that, but only what comes from other apartments. Nobody else around here's complained about a ghost in months. If *you* bring home mice or a poltergeist, *you* gotta foot the bill."

"Look, just get Father O'Flynn's Exorcism Van over here while I'm at work."

No Thumbs Hooligan's scowl deepened. "I'll go up and sprinkle around a little holy water when I get a minute." He aimed the sopping bristles of his sagging paintbrush at my necktie. "*When I get a minute.* If something floats outta the woodwork, I'll call the priest wagon. But if I don't find nothing, we ain't wasting money on no exorcist."

"That's incredibly kind of you, not to mention legally required per the terms of my lease," I said. "I have no idea why every tenant in this fleabag flophouse says you're an asshole. Probably only because you look, sound, act like and also are one."

Whoever's problem the ghostly figure was, it definitely was not mine. I'm not in the habit of dragging home strange phantoms. Before No Thumbs came on the job, a nonagenarian dame down the hallway used to collect a ghost every time she went to the cemetery to make sure her husband was staying put. Nobody knew that for years she'd been collecting deceased members of her old church choir and sneaking them home in her handbag. She had a complete set by the time she keeled over onto her knitting needles.

The old bag wasn't dead on the ratty sofa for two minutes before she'd joined the rest of her wraith pals moaning 1970s pseudo-pop choir loft abominations while floating endlessly around the beeping hallway smoke detector. The old super who'd managed the building before No Thumbs had barely been able to shove the door open from the weight of all the spectral energy pushing back on the other side. That had been serious, Great Beyond bullshit that couldn't be handled with a can of Black Flag Ghost-B-Gone! from Home Depot. A team of Father O'Flynn's Exorcism experts had worked my floor for days, chasing groaning spirits with bible quotes and spray cans loaded with industrially blessed H2O. One old bat ghost in a flowered hat took refuge in my freezer. Believe me, a huge pair of reproachful, vaguely blue, transparent eyeballs isn't something you want to encounter at 3:00 a.m. when you're looking for ice to complete a highball recipe.

Back then it had been an infestation of ghosts. As far as I knew, this time there was just the one. If No Thumbs did his job, the solitary, formless pest that was dogging me around the building like some incorporeal mutt should be gone by the time I staggered back home that evening.

I exited into the street, there to be accosted in broad daylight by a passing stranger.

"Good morning!" announced the chummy bastard. He gave me an unwanted tip of his hat and a menacingly delighted grin.

I don't like the people I know, and I definitely don't like any of the ones I have not yet met. That goes double for the types of strangers who go out of their way to be friendly to people they've never once laid eyes on in their suspiciously cheerful lives.

I didn't have time to string together the proper expletive and second person pronoun combination. The guy wasn't looking for a reciprocal "good morning," which was good because it wasn't one, not least of which due to the new annoying fact that persons unknown to me were now striding up and merrily demanding that I have one. His unsolicited imperative delivered, the SOB marched off.

"Good morning," he blared at another pedestrian a dozen feet away.

"What the hell's wrong with you, asshole?" his next victim asked, restoring my total lack of faith in humanity.

Whatever the reason for his unwarranted good nature, I was an eyewitness to the imminent assault when he approached yet a third subject. I'd swear on a stack of bibles of every denomination that the friendly jerk was asking for a roundhouse to the jaw. The guy he greeted next wasn't a handsome, joyful sort like me. He was portly, but tough looking. A former high school athlete who woke up one day in the middle age of a life that hadn't lived up to teenage promise. He was sour, with black bags under his eyes, a chipped briefcase and a suit that looked like he stored it at night in an empty Pringles can.

When the surly-looking schlubb opened his frowning mouth, I expected verbal fireworks and an eventual, inevitable 911 call.

"Good morning right back atcha," announced sour-appearing Guy #3 who was evidently anything but.

The pair of bastards grinned, nodded, and passed each other by. The first guy headed off down the road, saying good morning to everybody he passed. I would have grabbed the palooka in the rumpled suit — who had just passed me and tossed the second unwanted "good morning" of the day in my direction — but I'd just caught sight of a reflection in the window of an Oldsmobile that was parked on the side of the road.

The amorphous shape with the wide, arching shoulders grinned a row of perfect teeth back at me from the passenger side window.

In the bright sunlight, what I thought were horribly misshapen shoulders might not be shoulders after all. A pair of delighted eyes beamed joy at me. I was unable to duck out of the way, and got blasted with twin barrels of unwanted, unwarranted happiness. I was already worrying about the joy that I'd now be combing of my hair for a week when the shapeless face gave me a big, unnerving, happy wink.

As usual when I glanced over my shoulder, I found the figure that was casting the inchoate reflection nowhere in corporeal sight. There was, however, another pedestrian passing by. This one was a serious looking dame, stuffed hard into a power suit, and whose fat ass threatened the tensile strength of her too-tight skirt.

"Good morning," the business broad commanded through a mouthful of gleaming veneers.

"Up," I suggested with intense sincerity, "yours."

My perfectly reasonable response didn't faze her in the least. She continued on down the sidewalk, issuing the same violently pleasant order to everybody who passed by. I was heartened to see that most of the pedestrians responded as had I, but a handful awarded her reciprocal goddamn kindness. The positive reinforcement seemed to sufficiently satisfy her to cover for any negative replies, and the scary dame continued on her merry way, presumably to viciously accost more strangers with ugly cheerfulness.

"I could go back to bed," I warned the amorphous mass in the Oldsmobile window.

The thing looking back at me shook its head, and for the first time something less than a smile brushed lips which were only lips for lack of a better description of something that wasn't fully there. If the thing had a head, which presumably it must have if for no other reason than to have something into which to shove its eyes and heretofore grinning mouth, it was shaking it imploringly.

I knew now where this was headed, and it was nowhere I wanted to go.

I gave a little jerk of my head, motioning to the shapeless reflection.

"Let's go," I said, adding a resigned sigh to let whatever the thing was know that my heart and every other internal organ with the possible exception of my liver, which needed cash for alcoholic sustenance, wasn't in it.

I caught a slivered glimpse of the figure in reflection on a silver bracket that was lashed to a light post. The floating mouth was smiling once more, and if I didn't know it would be pointless to do so, plus that it would bust every knuckle in my hand, I'd have given the lamppost the right cross each and every mouth that is so happy to be alive so richly deserves.

2

I wasn't alone on the train. Usually that just meant I was crammed in a speeding metal box with a hundred other human dregs who hated the sights, stinks and poking umbrella points of everybody who wasn't them. It was all of that this time, plus one.

The hugely arched shoulders of the big figure who'd dogged me from my apartment were immediately behind me in my reflection in the window across the aisle. I'm a quick study. I'd learned not to bother to turn around, knowing that even though it was standing directly behind me I'd never see it.

I noted that some of the passengers on the train were being as alarmingly nice as had been the three assholes outside my building. Some of the pedestrians I'd met on the way to the subway station had also openly assaulted random innocents with their good moods. I'd say a good, solid five or even ten percent of everybody I saw that morning had taken leave of their senses, abandoned all accepted big city etiquette, and were challenging the orthodoxy by being goddamn nice to their fellow human beings.

I was at least reassured that most of these unfortunate souls who were the recipients of unsolicited geniality weren't having any of it. I saw more yelling, shoving and fistfights on my way to the train that morning than I usually witnessed in a month. Most normal people revel in their God-given right to be miserable. I'm pretty sure it's enshrined in the Bill of Rights. To wit: *It being that we powdered wig-wearing humps just kicked the shit out of the king of England and, frankly, sometimes played kind of dirty in the process, the right of the people to be assholes to everybody no matter his rank or station (especially some inbred maniac named George III wearing a bejeweled Burger King kids' menu chapeau) shall not be goddamn infringed.*

When I got off the train, I deliberately checked my reflection in the glass on a cigarette vending machine. Any hope I had that I'd lost my tail on the train was dashed. The looming shape was still back there. I watched several people walk right through it as if it were no more substantial than my ex-wife's promise of marital fidelity.

I didn't bother to check any reflective surfaces on my hike to my office. I had no sense there was anybody tagging along with me, but I hadn't had that feeling all morning. Whoever or whatever it was, it was going exactly where I was going.

The hundred-year-old brownstone that was home to Banyon Investigations, Inc. revealed itself from the row of equally nondescript buildings in the same manner the guy who doesn't volunteer for the suicide mission gets drafted in old screwball comedies. My approach seemed to make it stand still while all the other buildings took one step back.

An old bastard in a filthy apron was sweeping the sidewalk in front of the open door to the fish market that occupied most of the ground floor. His efforts were pointless for two reasons. First, his doorway was clean enough to operate in since the last customer to venture into the joint was a Mondale for president campaign volunteer who had to be taken out on a stretcher after succumbing to rancid mackerel fumes. Second, the bristles on the broom he was using were worn all the way up to the straw knot on the handle. The broom stub looked more like a giant matchstick that the old, cheap buzzard couldn't get to light, but not for lack of trying.

"If you ever plan on torching that dump of yours with real matches, Vincetti, give me at least a week's warning to rent a truck and rescue the booze I've got stashed upstairs," I warned. "Also, I hope you intend to do the whole neighborhood a favor by climbing up on top of the pyre and incinerating your hirsute guinea ass. We bachelors would thank you if you took along for the ride your hyena-ugly inamorata, Mrs. Vincetti."

The old codger turned on me a set of eyes underlined with layers of bags which made him look like Madame Tussaud had stood him too close to the radiator.

"Hey, mistah! How-a you doin'!"

I was prepared for screaming Italian or a broomstick up the ass. Both would have been typical for my years-long association with the fascist first floor fishmonger. An ear-to-ear smile that revealed the dental horror stubs of Vincetti's rotting teeth was as shocking as what I could only guess was his attempt at a pleasant tone of voice, since a pleasant tone was as impossible for Vincetti's vocal cords as playing a violin concerto on a cement mixer. Still, his tone was different, and given the words and the gingivitis nightmare that accompanied it, I could only conclude that this was Vincetti being nice.

So shocked was I that I actually stopped dead in front of his store which, given the seaside outhouse stench flowing out the open door, was not unusual for passersby.

"Apparently, Vincetti, you've somehow forgotten that you're a choleric asshole and that we hate each other. Why are you being friendly?"

"What?" He held out his broom in one direction, and his one free hand, palm up, in the other, and gave a shrug. "Because you a friendly-a man. You like-a nice-a fish?"

"You don't *have* any nice fish. Clearly you've forgotten that you're Luigi Vincetti, and that you run a fish market that sells only evil fish. That works out fine for you because you are an evil, hairy-eared, Axis Powers-loving bastard. In fact, you and your merchandise would get along swimmingly, if the latter hadn't been out of the water so long it's forgotten how to swim."

His grin never wavered around the stubbed-out butts of his black teeth.

"Ha! You a funny-a guy!" he said. He waved his broom handle in my face in a genially chiding way, then promptly resumed sweeping.

Vincetti and I didn't have a relationship that involved playful back and forth. Our conversations had always been limited to me telling him his stock stunk like a big shit in a small aquarium and him chasing me down the street with a putrid mackerel in each hand while screaming a Mussolini battle cry at the top of his dago lungs.

I backed away from the aged fish seller, expecting the kind of multiple murders during a baptism that his tribe specialized in, but old Vincetti just kept on attacking the dust on the sidewalk with the blunt end of his worthless broom. When I turned and entered the ground floor lobby he had further defied all reason and was actually whistling, apparently unafraid that he risked losing a dozen black, loose teeth in the bargain.

The shadow that had followed me from my crummy

apartment wasn't immediately visible reflected in the ground floor elevator doors, and appeared only after I'd been standing there a few seconds and just before the doors opened.

"If you're losing interest in me, that makes two of us," I said. "I'm stuck with me, but you're welcome to leave at any time."

The big shape shook its uppermost portion, which I was still calling its head. No luck. I was stuck.

The figure was grinning over my shoulder in the dull silver surface of the inner doors as I rode the rattling old car up to the third floor. Only when the doors dinged open was the shapeless form finally gone.

I checked my reflection in the windows of the office doors that I passed on my way down the hallway. It was true. For the first time all morning I was alone.

The opaque glass on the door at the far end of the hallway was decorated with the words **Banyon Investigations**. I trudged wearily up to it and gave a reluctant nudge. As usual, I was disappointed that the door didn't stick or blow up or launch poison darts that would kill me dead before I could step over the threshold.

This day was worse than most, since I already knew someone was waiting for me on the other side. I shoved the door fully open and slogged inside.

"Good morning, Mr. Crag!"

This particular cheerful greeting I at least anticipated.

A grinning elf in a tiny little business suit sat at an adorable little desk filling out what appeared to be delightful goddamn insurance forms.

Mannix was the ace assistant an asshole like me didn't deserve. Kind, dedicated, good-natured, and the all-around swell sort of guy that I'd always thought was the ideal everybody should aspire to. I had reconsidered that opinion now that I'd gotten a large dose of Mannix's optimistic outlook on life spread out amongst the general populace. There can only be one Pavarotti, wisely locked up for eternity in PBS reruns with a remote control "mute" button at the ready to guard uniqueness and eardrums. A hundred Pavarottis out on the street was just some fat slob screaming in your ear at the bus stop.

My elf assistant sensed something evil was afoot. Probably because as soon as I entered the office, I'd quickly shut the door and propped my exhausted back against it in order to keep the world from charging in.

"You're injured," he said, his voice thick with worry as he pointed at my mug.

At first I didn't know what he was talking about. I peered out the corner of my eye and saw with fuzzy, myopic clarity a puff of bright white protruding from my cheek.

"Everybody wants a piece of me, Mannix," I said.

I peeled off the piece of bloodied toilet paper I'd forgotten I'd glued to the nick in my cheek, rolled it into a ball and flicked it in the direction of the trash bucket, naturally missing.

Mannix's brow sank low over his overly large eyes.

"Is something wrong, Mr. Crag?"

"Everything, as usual, Mannix. At the very top of the list is the fact that I have a client meeting this morning."

Mannix frowned confusion. "No one is scheduled," he said. "No one called." He reached for his little day planner, worried that he'd somehow dropped the ball.

"Unscheduled, unplanned, unwanted and unknown," I said.

In fact, I had noticed something that Mannix — his attention directed with concern solely at me — hadn't.

The door to my inner, private office was closed. Through the frosted glass, I could see the outline of a shape sitting at placid attention. Whatever it was that had been dogging me all morning had materialized in the chair before my desk.

I'd concluded that I was dealing with a bashful would-be client once the figure had followed me outside my apartment building. Most ghosts like the familiar, so they generally stay put once they take up residence, and they rarely venture outside their chosen milieu. What I was dealing with here was an eager client who couldn't wait until I got into work and who clearly had no understanding of personal boundaries.

I am never in any great haste to deal with clients. Frankly, my business would be absolutely perfect without them, apart from the crushing poverty. My reluctance to truck with the hoi polloi went double for spectral wannabe clients who were so eager to retain my services that they thought nothing of invading my most private of privacy. I don't need the phantom world laughing that I use the same worn-down nub of Dial soap as shampoo and shaving cream or that my towel is a threadbare Marriott bathmat.

After the pain in the ass morning he'd given me, the bastard could cool his heels (assuming he had heels) in my office for a few minutes.

"What's the latest on Doris?" I asked.

Mannix's little pointed face grew grave. "She's still in the hospital. I spoke to her mother this morning. She said that the doctors are saying poor Miss Doris is lucky to be alive."

Mannix's was one of two desks in the outer office. While his was custom made for his diminutive stature, the second desk was regulation human size. The regulation human to which the bigger desk was assigned was not sitting behind it.

The big desk had been victim of a recent fire. Evidence of the conflagration charred the surface utterly black. The writing on the "World's Greatest Secretary" mug, which the desk's missing occupant had given to herself and was about as prestigious an honor as an MTV movie award and only slightly more difficult to come by, was barely visible. All that had been clearly legible post-fire was "Wor G Secretary," the rest of the original text seemingly lost forever in the inferno. However, some unidentified linguistic archeologist, possibly drunk and exceedingly ticked-off at the time, had used a red Magic Marker to try to piece the original phrase back together by adding an S and a T after the "Wor," and an "oddamn" after the G. The identity of this mysterious language scientist might never be learned, but I deserved about a million points for accuracy.

Three days earlier, Doris had accidentally left her hair dryer running in her drawer while she went out to the movies during that which, in the case of my secretary, can only very loosely and/or humorously be called "work hours." When she got back from the bargain double feature and opened the superheated drawer, she inadvertently ignited the array of crap on the surface of her desk. She might have been okay if she'd stocked it with only paper and pens like a normal secretary. But it was Maybelline inventory week for Doris, so before she'd ducked out for the Adam Sandler movie marathon at the Bijou she had set out a battalion of cosmetics bottles, tubes, brushes and jars that were ordinarily crammed inside her desk drawers.

The resulting flash chemical explosion ignited the desk, charred the ceiling above it, and burned off the last two eyebrow hairs Doris hadn't plucked. She and her purse full of eyebrow pencils might have been able to weather that loss, but the fireball hadn't stopped with those two hairs. In an instant, Doris' bleached bouffant — that thing in life to which she gave more loving attention than work, family, religion, civic responsibility or her goddamn cat stickers — had been burned to black ash. When quick-thinking Mannix had blasted the burning desk with the fire extinguisher I didn't even know we had, the sooty threads that had been Doris' cherished hairdo blew off and scattered to the four corners of the office, leaving a scalp as bald and dimpled as a Titleist. It was three days later and her screams of horror were still echoing along the third floor hallway.

"I'll give Doris credit," I said. "Once she found out her hair was gone, her chemically-scarred lungs didn't prevent her from continuing to hit that sustained A7 high note even as the EMTs were strapping her down."

"Poor Miss Doris," said Mannix, who is a better human being than I will ever be despite the fact that he wasn't human.

"She'll be fine, Mannix. They just have to scrape the burned nail polish from inside her lungs and stick it back in the bottles."

I'd left my waiting client long enough. I was surprised by his/her/its patience. I figured by the way he/she/it/ whatever had tracked me down at home then dogged me all the way to the office, that I wouldn't get two seconds to shoot the shit with my aide-de-elf. But the shape in the next room, which was vaguely human through the frosted glass, remained calmly glued in place, like Doris' eyelashes before they'd been claimed by the inferno.

I headed for the inner door.

"Miss Doris' mother was in a very good mood," Mannix

volunteered.

He was both clearly happy and puzzled.

"Doris' mother is only ever in a good mood when she's sucking down cooking sherry and screaming at Vanna White to flip over the two T's in 'battleaxe.'"

"It's true that she's usually a little...not nice," Mannix agreed in what, for him, were the strongest possible terms. "But I've spoken to her three times since the accident, and she's been much less not nice than usual."

Mannix had been a North Pole Christmas elf in his previous occupation, and he still saw everybody in the very simple groups of naughty or nice. I somehow, beyond all logic and comprehension, fell into his "nice" category.

"There's a lot of that going around," I said. "Just now downstairs Vincetti missed a golden opportunity to shove a broom handle in my mouth and wave me around town like a fascist flag."

"A lot of people do seem much friendlier these days," Mannix concluded.

"I know. Horrible, isn't it?"

I hung my coat and hat on the rack in the corner and shoved open the door to my sanctum sanctorum.

***

It turned out I was dealing with neither ghost nor phantom; not poltergeist, spirit, shadow person or elemental.

What I had thought were huge arched shoulders were actually the majestically curving tips of a pair of brilliant white wings. The back to which the wings were attached was actually pretty ordinary in appearance, as was the rest of the seated figure. He looked like a very placid, very pale middle-aged man. The only variation in pasty pigmentation was around his ruddy red cheeks. He wore a brilliant white robe that failed to cover his bare ankles and feet. A gleaming yellow circle like a radioactive Pfaltzgraff dinner plate with the middle poked out floated above a mane of flowing yellow locks.

The cherubic bastard who'd watched me take a shower that morning was an angel.

I knew it was the same pervert angel when I entered the room and he turned his head. His body had been more insubstantial earlier that morning, but I could have identified that perfect toothy smile in a police lineup packed with Osmonds.

"Hello, Mr. Banyon!" he cried, jumping to his feet. "Face to face at last!" His great wings partially unfolded and they gave an excited, wind tunnel flap that sent all the paperwork on my desk flying to kingdom come.

He grabbed my hand and started pumping my arm like an eager Dust Bowl farmer who expected water to start gushing out of my mouth.

"Can we keep the celestial chorus down to a dull roar? I've got one hell — if you'll pardon the expression — of a goddamn hangover."

"Of course, Mr. Banyon. Of course, of course, of course."

The angel released my hand on its own recognizance and sat right back down before my desk in the plain wooden chair which I had chosen specifically for its lack of comfort in order to discourage extended visits.

Mannix had heard the commotion with the beating wings and the strange voice and had stuck his head into the room to investigate. He was astonished at the luminous figure sitting in the utter crud shack that was my P.I. headquarters.

"Oh, good morning!" Mannix announced.

"Why, good morning to you!" the angel eagerly replied.

"There is a very good chance I am about to upchuck," I said.

I tolerated Mannix because he was the best employee on earth and pretty much the only pal I had, but the waves of enthusiastic niceness rolling off two beings incapable of a harsh word were so powerful that a tsunami force of saccharine was already threatening to blast me out the window and onto the fire escape.

"Mannix, this is the client I told you about," I explained. "Please get the usual forms for him to fill out, and try to be a little bit of an asshole while doing so."

Mannix smiled and nodded twice, once to me and once to the placid creature with the vague celestial glow who was smelling up my office with the stink of frankincense-scented Right Guard. My assistant ducked from the room.

"I apologize for showing up at your apartment this morning, Mr. Banyon," the angel said with breathless haste. "I need to tell you that right off the bat. Completely overstepped all bounds of propriety. But I was anxious, you see. Also, I'm a guardian angel. Maybe I should have said that first? Anyway, no matter. We guardian angels are used to being there at all times, under the most awkward circumstances. You know how your human magicians say 'now you see me, now you don't?' We have our own saying, we guardian angels. We say, 'now you *don't* see us, now you *still* don't.'"

He laughed desperately, like he'd said something funny, which he most certainly had not and probably never had in his life. I had an angelic goddamn Jimmy Fallon in my office.

"But just because you don't see us, that doesn't mean

we aren't always there," he said, abruptly serious. "We are. Always matched up to the fellow we're guarding. On the sidewalk, at the bus stop. In those naughty little places you mortals go off to where you really shouldn't. Always, always there. Well, except in my case right now, of course, which is why I need the services of a private investigator. I checked around with some other guardian angels who watch out for private investigators, and they recommended you and, well, Bob's your uncle, here I am."

He hadn't paused to take a breath. I didn't even know if angels breathed. Probably not, since his head hadn't turned blue and he wasn't keeling over.

I felt like I'd run a marathon just listening to him. Only when his lips stopped flapping did I realize that I hadn't sat down. My ass found my chair behind my desk and slid in to rest up from the verbal assault to which it had just been victim.

"We traditionally start with 'who the hell are you?'" I said.

"Oh, I'm sorry. Invictus."

Invictus shot to his feet and offered me his hand once more.

"Thanks, I'll pass. I'm still trying to shake the circulation back into my fingernails from the last time."

Invictus the angel wasn't insulted. He sat right back down, smiling once more, almost like he didn't realize he was completely goddamn bananas.

"So, I gather from that vocal diarrhea you just excreted all over my office that the guy you're supposed be watching has turned up missing."

His smile vanished, his eyes grew wide, and he nodded somberly. "Yes, indeed," Invictus said. "He's done it before, but I've always managed to track him down. This time, however…poof! Nowhere to be found."

I dragged a notebook and pencil from my desk and started making notes. "You sure he isn't dead? That'd take him off your radar, wouldn't it?"

"Oh, my, my friends were right. You *are* good. That is correct, Mr. Banyon. Guardian angels are for the living. No need for us watching over you if you've gone to the Great Beyond. But I checked records up top and—" A hint of queasiness crept into his chubby cheeks, as if he'd gotten some bad shrimp at an all-you-can-eat manna buffet. "—and I checked the records at the *other* place, too, and no such luck. No, he is most definitely still alive."

"Is there any reason he might not want to be found?"

The nauseous expression grew sicker. "Ah. Well, you see, Mr. Pinder — that's my charge's name, Charles Pinder — is an unbeliever. Always going on about not believing in this, that or the other. Or in *Him*."

He aimed a finger at my ceiling. I was pretty sure he wasn't pointing up the skirt of Madame Carpathia, the dame who ran the top floor dance studio.

"Mr. Pinder spent hours on this…what is it? This Internet thing? I think that's what you call it. He was always yelling at everybody who didn't think like him. It was a switch for me, I can tell you. My last job was a nice little Presbyterian woman who went to services every week, donated to charity, volunteered at a homeless pantry, and finally choked to death on some raisin toast. Wonderful lady. She had faith, but she didn't…well, to be blunt, Mr. Banyon, she didn't yammer on about it all the time. She just *had it*. When she passed on, I got assigned to Mr. Pinder. I have nothing against nonbelievers. Let me make that clear. I'm not prejudiced. I have a job to do no matter what a person's personal beliefs. It's just, well, he could have been a *quiet* unbeliever, couldn't he? I mean, he *could* have just got on with life like my Presbyterian lady before him did, but, well, Mr. Banyon, he was just so angry *all* the time. A man doesn't get that angry all the time at something he doesn't believe in deep down. I thought it would help to give him a little hope, which he seemed to be sorely lacking, to let him know that there was *something*."

It didn't take Hercule Poirot to figure out what happened next.

"You broke the rules and revealed yourself to him," I said.

Invictus looked sheepish. "In a Denny's restroom," he admitted. "Not, perhaps, the best choice for glorious manifestation. But Mr. Pinder had just spent ten minutes berating the waitress for wearing a WWJD bracelet. And they spit in his food *every* time he does it. *Every time*. I've seen them do it. That's the free will of the wait staff, and their transgressions are the problem of forces greater than us guardian angels. But Charles Pinder was my responsibility, and he was, frankly, Mr. Banyon, a bum-hole, and so when he went to go use the restroom I appeared before him and told him to be not afraid."

"What did he have to say to that?"

The angel gave an embarrassed frown and cast his eyes at the floor. "He made a mess in his trousers and passed out. He hit his head on the sink on the way down. They had to call an ambulance. Big hullabaloo. All my fault, of course, and I readily confess that it is. Later that night I appeared before him in the emergency room to offer my apologies, but he wouldn't even look at me. I know he could hear me. I snapped my fingers, made funny faces, everything but stand on my halo. He just pretended I wasn't even there. Which, of course, I shouldn't have been. But I did it the first time I shouldn't have, and now the floodgates were open."

"You said he's disappeared before. Any idea how?"

The angel shrugged the curving tops of his magnificent wings. "I don't know, Mr. Banyon. I should admit right off the bat that I'm, well…I'm naïve. There, I've admitted it. We guardian angels see it all, but we're just silent witnesses. We don't know the nuts-and-bolts 'why' of 'why do they do that?' I guess it's the same with 'how.'"

Invictus had nudged the corners of what I could tell was normally a perpetually grinning mouth into a thoughtful frown.

"He *did* go to church," he volunteered, face suddenly bright once more.

I glanced up from my notebook, where my notes largely consisted of a pretty good stick figure drawing of me climbing down the side of the building to get away from my latest client. "What was he doing at church?"

"After he got out of the hospital, I manifested myself to him a few more times. I thought it was possible he was maybe going blind, which was why he couldn't see me. That would really make my work more challenging. Pulling him back from walking in front of trolley cars, guiding one foot onto the top stair. And *driving*. He still drove. I figured I'd spend half my day in the passenger seat tugging on the steering wheel."

The angel had gotten excited at just the thought of how much more interesting his life would become with a blind charge. The crimson flush of his cheeks had darkened, and the points of his widening grin were threatening to puncture his earlobes. But then he sighed wistfully, and his puffed-out chest deflated.

"Then I realized he'd have to be going deaf at the same time, since by then I was yelling at him to look at me while I waved my hands in front of his face. He saw me. I *know* he saw me. He'd try not to show it, but when I'd stand in front of the TV long enough, he'd slowly lean to one side to see the screen. So that was his life until a few days out of the hospital. He was out for a Sunday morning walk and didn't he take a turn straight through the front doors of Our Lady of Perpetual Bingo? I was beside myself. I'd really made a difference in this fellow's life. Something more meaningful than just getting him to look twice to make sure both shoelaces are tied. But then he vanished. It was like magic. He was gone for days before he came back home that first time. I had no idea where he was. Then, wouldn't you know, the exact same thing happened again that weekend. Gone. Poof. Like he was taken up. The final time it happened…well, Mr. Banyon, it's just been ages, and he never came back. I'm afraid he's gone for good."

"Let me guess. Each time he went to church, you cooled your wings in the park across the street with the rest of your pals," I said. "Then when Mass was over, the rest of them paired off with their charges one-by-one while you stood there waiting for Pinder to exit. He never did, so you went inside looking for him, and that's when you couldn't find him. That pretty much sum it up?"

Invictus seemed amazed. "Yes! How could you possibly know?"

"Guardian angels don't guard inside churches," I said. "It's the one hour a week you guys get off. I remember that from Sunday school, which is pretty lucky it was covered on the first day because I got kicked out on the second. There's a park across the street from Our Lady of Perpetual Bingo that has a good view of the doors, so that's the best place for angels to take a break. And you probably all wait for the bells to ring to let you know Mass is over before heading back across the street. Am I warm?"

"My gosh, Mr. Banyon, that's all true!" he gushed. "So maybe you know this, too. How the heck did Pinder keep disappearing on me?"

"Simple. He left Mass early."

Invictus was one baffled angel. A notch formed between his eyes. His mouth opened and closed silently as he attempted to process my words.

Mannix chose the lull to hustle into the room clutching some paperwork in his tiny little hand. He set the client contracts onto my desk.

"Our information is all filled out, Mr. Crag," the elf said, with typical efficiency. "Mr. Invictus just needs to fill out his lines."

I didn't call attention to the fact that Mannix had obviously been eavesdropping to know the name of the utterly mystified angel sitting in front of my desk.

"*Early?*" Invictus finally managed. "Someone left Mass *early?*"

I shrugged. "I know. Hard to wrap your halo around that one." I spun the paperwork around and nudged it to his side of the desk. "Just fill out these forms. We're mostly a cash only business. You want to go with a check, you've got to wait until it clears. I've been robbed by clients more times than 7-Eleven."

Mannix handed the angel a pen, and Invictus bowed his head in prayer over the line requesting his home address ("no P.O. boxes, please").

"Oh, I don't have any money," the angel said. "On this line that says date of birth, can I just put zero?" He glanced up with hope in his eyes.

I clapped both palms to the surface of my desk and shoved myself to my feet. "Well," I announced happily, "I'm off to get loaded. Mannix, make sure he doesn't swipe your pen."

The angel's confused gaze followed me to the door, after which I had to contend only with a determined elf who'd chased me into the outer office.

"You can't leave, Mr. Crag," Mannix said.

"That's a very negative attitude, Mannix," I replied as I shrugged on my trench coat. "I believe we can do anything we put our minds to. Right now, I have a mind to be sitting on a stool at O'Hale's Bar pouring whatever I need to down my throat to forget this morning ever happened. Visualize, actualize, intoxicize."

The elf's little legs hustled to keep up with me on my way to the door.

"He needs your help," Mannix pleaded.

"We're not running a charity, Mannix. You're the one who's always worrying about paying bills and chasing down deadbeat clients. At least all the other stiffs who haven't paid thus far had the decency to lie up front and claim they would."

I glanced at my open inner office door. Invictus was still sitting before my desk. He was forced to lean over to see the action taking place in the outer office. The angel was grinning that same innocent idiot's grin I'd first seen that morning in my foggy bathroom mirror. He gave me a little wave, and I felt a twinge of guilt in my gut which I prayed could be taken out with a few well-placed shots of alcohol at close range.

"Tell him to stop following me," I instructed Mannix. "We are absolutely, definitely not taking his case. Oh, don't look at me like that. If it makes you feel better, tell him to sit tight at this Charles Pinder's place. A guy doesn't stay missing forever without needing a pair of clean underwear. He'll come back on his own eventually."

Free advice delivered, I slapped on my fedora and

yanked the door open.

"Oh," Invictus called from my inner office. "Are you starting now?"

When Mannix swung his head from the angel's purely innocent mug to my ugly puss, the elf was shooting me a look he generally reserved only for the most naughty individuals who filled the pages of the *Gazette* and crowded the nightly news. For the first time since I'd known him, my pal had silently placed me on the list of murderers, molesters and lawyers who'd be getting a lump of coal in their stockings on December 25.

It was going to take more than my usual ocean of booze to flood the expanding pit of guilt that was swelling in my gut. There was, therefore, no time to lose.

I backed into the hallway and pulled the door shut on the hopeful but increasingly puzzled cherubic face of the angel who wasn't and would definitely never be a client, as well as the deeply disappointed and reproachful little face of my faithful office elf.

3

I can live with guilt. I had lived for years with the woman who was now, blessedly, my ex-wife. If I can live with a screeching piranha in high heels with one hand on my wallet and the other feeling up the mailman, quotidian guilt was a breeze.

I rode my zephyr of hardly noticeable guilt (no kidding, I almost didn't care one goddamn bit) in nearly guiltless silence. I noted that I couldn't see the reflection of the guardian angel's Mary Tyler Moore grin in the window of the cross-town bus in which I'd nestled my guilt-free ass.

Invictus had given up hassling me. Good. A day without clients — especially ones that can only act as counterpoints to my own less than angelic proclivities — is a day very nearly worth living.

The biggest canker sore in this whole affair was going to be dealing with my asshole building superintendent. Harry "No Thumbs" Hooligan was going to have my magnificent hindquarters in a sling for sending him on a wild ghost chase up to my apartment. He takes his life in his hands who makes No Thumbs waste his time, since turning a key in a door lock was half a day's frustrating work for my building's super. No Thumbs' condition made it necessary for him to employ one of those rubber grips the rest of us use to open stuck pickle jars just to get a doorknob to turn. When No Thumbs Hooligan found out there wasn't a ghost in my apartment after all, my building's irate superintendent would upend one of his paint cans onto my head and shove down until the dangling handle reached the tops of my Florsheims.

Before No Thumbs could have my ass, I had other plans for it that involved hours of seeing if it could hatch a chicken from my favorite barstool. So far the many hours I spent each week attempting to do so had been a bust, so I could only reasonably assume that the odds of birthing a fowl from the worn vinyl stool were increasing in my favor.

On the stroll from the bus stop, I did not see Invictus so much as one time in any of the shop windows: from the locksmith's, to the check cashing joint, to the second-hand bread store. I didn't bother to look for the angel's reflection in the grimy window that was set into the door of O'Hale's Bar. The off-center pane was so filthy that the only thing it reflected was the insouciance the proprietor of the boozy establishment displayed for cleanliness. If I ever did see anything moving in that window, I would assume it was a matter for the city health inspector and a can of Raid.

O'Hale's Bar was possessed of a couple of vital, positive attributes that put it head and shoulders above the other dingy speakeasies around town.

First and foremost was the gargantuan tab that I was, in defiance of all sane fiduciary judgment, allowed to keep submerging in liquor (although it was no longer necessary to keep so firm a grip on it, as it had long ago stopped wriggling).

A close second for me was that O'Hale's was such a

shithole that nearly nobody but me ever drank there. Even most of the career neighborhood drunks bypassed its warm hearth on a cold winter's eve for a far more appealing bottle from the corner liquor store shoved inside a brown paper bag. Freezing to death in a cardboard box behind the Gulp 'N' Run was preferable to the risk of contracting dysentery from drinking from an O'Hale's glass or catching hepatitis from using the O'Hale's bathrooms.

I prefer drinking alone. I, in fact, prefer doing everything alone, but until I could find a passing comet on which to stick the other seven billion people who were crowding up my planet, I was stuck with them. But at O'Hale's Bar I was not, generally, bothered by the wretched refuse yearning to annoy me.

When I pushed open the door to my silent inebriate's sanctuary, my eardrums were instantly assaulted with a racket that sounded like it was being piped in directly from the vomit-covered spring break streets of Ft. Lauderdale.

I stopped dead in the doorway and nearly stepped back outside to make sure I hadn't wandered into the wrong bar. I figured the odds of that were pretty unlikely, since I was relatively sober. On the other hand, maybe I had somehow gotten so drunk that I only *thought* I was sober, which is pretty typical thinking for someone who's blitzed.

I ducked back outside.

It was definitely the right skid row neighborhood, which made the Gaza Strip look like Main Street, USA (except here the rats were just eating garbage and spreading plague, not wearing giant red short pants and feeling up kids). I recognized the faded business names over the boarded-up windows of the closed shops across the road. The same derelict cars, which were too old and crummy to steal, shed chunks of corroded rust into the same old parking spaces up and down the street.

The O'Hale's Bar sign hung above my head. That half of the neon which wasn't busted was as silent as the broken half since it was still broad daylight. But, even without the welcoming hornet buzz switched on over my head, I was definitely in the right place.

I stuck my head back into the bar.

So why was O'Hale's, my deserted booze oasis, filled with goddamn people?

At least it wasn't as busy as a successful sports bar on game night. It was the kind of lousy, shit-busy I'd expect from O'Hale's, if I ever expected it to do any kind of real business which, naturally, I never had.

There had to be a couple dozen revelers jammed into the usually empty tables in the middle of the floor, crammed into the dilapidated booths that lined the walls, and crowded along the bar. In point of fact, *my* — since I felt I had spent enough time passed out on it to claim a proprietary interest in it — bar.

I had to elbow my way across the floor.

"Hey, watch it, old man," snarled a balding, white-haired bastard who looked ten years my senior. He'd turned into me and nearly spilled his mug.

The old coot took a tough guy stance, puffing out his chest. Even over the din, I heard his spine crack. He sucked in a gasp of air and slapped his hand over his lower back. He managed to hobble to a chair, and slowly sank his ass into it whilst moaning.

There seemed to be a lot of that going on. Despite the attempted youthful carousing from the decidedly middle-aged crowd, other guys were in as bad a way as the groaning loudmouth who'd just taught me a lesson by throwing out his back.

A chorus of sacroiliac creaks kept time with the 1970s Deep Purple noise that the jukebox had been paid a quarter to vomit into my ear holes. Men hoisted beer mugs, then promptly spilled them because of shoulder bursitis. The usual delightful sleazy bar stink had been replaced with the sharp stench of Ben-Gay.

Still, their painful joints weren't sending them limping out the front door of what had, until two seconds before, been my favorite lousy joint. As I approached the bar, guys continued hobbling up to it.

"A pitcher of beer!"

The shouted order was followed by an enormous whoop of appreciation from the gathered multitude of Generation Asshole booze-hounds.

"*Two* pitchers of beer!"

An even louder whoop from the crowd, with glasses raised around the room in a twenty-one gin salute.

The careworn, half-bald, accountant-looking schlub who was next in line wasn't about to be outdone by the two orders that came before his.

"Whiskey!" the guy yelled, as if ordering one crummy glass of watered-down hard liquor in a bar was an act of twenty-first century courage equivalent to storming the beaches at Normandy.

The piddling little nothing order from the milquetoast loudmouth reaped the biggest "whoop" of all.

Facing the patrons on the other side of the bar was a grubby bastard who had never been as evidently delighted to fill my orders as he was to serve a pack of rowdy stranger SOBs this late morning.

Ed Jaublowski was soaking up the delighted shouting like an Olympic gymnast who'd just performed a perfect routine and dismount which, as similes went, was a real stretch. Jaublowski the gymnast would have gotten stuck between the parallel bars, popped all the mats, and would have hung from the rings until an IOC fire department hook-and-ladder got him down.

Jaublowski slid a glass of whiskey to the brave coward, who knocked the drink back in one gulp and immediately collapsed on the floor, to cheers from the crowd.

The barkeep smiled (which was a silver medal horror show to Vincetti's earlier dental gold) and waved to the hooting and clapping audience. He was still grinning disconcertingly as I sidled up to the bar.

"Please tell me, Ed, that I've not entered some alternative dimension in which you and O'Hale's aren't the failures I find so deeply comforting?" I asked.

"Oh. Hey, Jinx. You're in early today."

His smile faded. He seemed only too happy to let it evaporate. Unlike Vincetti's troublingly sincere grin, Jaublowski's was clearly an effort. The barkeep rubbed his sore jaw as he grabbed a bottle of my favorite varnish from the rack.

He passed me the booze and I downed it in a gulp, sliding the glass back for a second helping.

"Whoa, dude!" cried a far too easily awed skinny guy in a business suit who was nursing half a mug of beer beside me.

I did my best to ignore the nosy bastard.

"First off, Ed, where the hell is my stool?"

Jaublowski reached under the bar and hoisted out the seat in question, handing it over to me. I, in turn, gave it to my ass for safekeeping.

"I knew youse'd bite my head off if somebody else was on it," he said.

"At least you've given some consideration to the guy who, until today, was your one and only customer."

"I know what you're gonna ask next, Jinx," the barkeep

said. A conniving, subdued version of his smile returned. He reached back under the bar.

Jaublowski passed me a stack of yellow Kinko's flyers.

Body Switch Special!

Have U switched boddies with someone?!??!!!
Yuor parent, teecher or camp concillar?
Your about to learn a life lesson about how they got it tuff, just like U, but in difrent ways!!! Before you switch back, take they're ID (that which got you're wearing THEY"RE face on it!!!) and go nuts at O'Hale's Bar!!!!! They got MONEY in the wallets and CREDIT CARDS to!!!!!
Proof of body switch gets 1 drink FREE!!!!!

"I hired a kid to pass 'em out at all the high schools and junior highs around town," the barkeep said, offering a knowing wink of one devious eye.

I riffled through the flyers as I glanced around the room. I saw a bunch more of the yellow papers soaking up spilled liquor stains on tables and sticking out of pockets. I shoved the stack of flyers back across the bar.

"I applaud your audacity, Ed, given that you're nearly completely illiterate, for even attempting to spell 'counselor.' I take it these are all kids in adult bodies."

Jaublowski's greedy grin bloomed full and wide.

"It's genius, Jinx. This is the time of year for body switching. Final exams, last high school sports goin' on. Always happens now. You got your curses, your magic fortune telling machines, your mystical amulets. I saw a story in the paper the other day about some business goomer what body switched with his seventeen-year-old kid. The kid almost cost the old man some big business deal, and the dad nearly blew it with his kid's girlfriend. In the end, the kid's innocent — whatcha call — perspective saved the big business deal, and the dad managed to come in first in the big meet. Both of them learned them real hard lessons about how the other one had it real bad, and that they was better off bein' themselves. Course, that really hit home when the old man got fired when his boss found out he let his kid almost blow a multimillion dollar deal, and the kid got disqualified and lost his college scholarship since it was really his old man what won the big race. But who gives a shit about that? When I read that story, it hit me."

He proudly patted the topmost misspelled flyer.

"I can't fault you for taking advantage of human suffering, Ed," I said. "That's your business, after all. What I am, frankly, is astonished by is the fact that you apparently read an entire newspaper article."

I knocked back the second drink Jaublowski had slid in front of me.

"Dude! Check this guy out!"

I realized now that my appreciative barstool neighbor was a skinny, middle-aged office drone in outward appearance only. Inwardly, he and all the other old coots in O'Hale's were snot-nosed teenagers getting loaded for the first time on dad's liver.

"How long do you intend to keep this going, Ed?" I asked.

Jaublowski shrugged sagging shoulders that were rounded by the weight of years of failure and which weren't about to chiropractically realign over one lousy day of success.

"I figure at best I got a coupla weeks. Once finals and all them seasonal big business deals is done, this'll all be over. In the meantime, cha-ching."

"I don't suppose you consulted with a no-good drunken lawyer first to find out the legal implications of all this?" I asked.

A gruff voice beside me answered before Jaublowski could.

"I told him it's a legal gray area."

The scrawny kid who was hanging on my every boozy breath was to my left. I glanced to my right and found the source of the new voice.

A large sheepdog had just scampered up onto the stool beside me. I'd had a good view of the front door, so the mutt must have come from the toilets out back.

"He's misrepresented that special he's advertising right off the bat," the shaggy fleabag said. "He knows these kids can't prove they're body-switched, so he's lying to get them in here. But they don't care. They're kids." He abruptly offered me his paw. The fur mop was wet and dripping. "Randall Wilkes, Assistant District Attorney."

"Don't take this the wrong way," I said, "but I'd rather have my hand amputated than share whatever you might have contracted from the O'Hale's men's room floor."

The dog appeared not to give a shit. It turned its attention to the bar, where Jaublowski had just slid it a bowl of cheap liquor. The talking dog immediately dropped its snout into the dish and began lapping like it was an ass buffet.

"You sure *he's* old enough to drink, Ed?" I said.

"I'm seven in dog years, which means I've got forty-two years of drinking to catch up to where I am in human years," the mongrel said as it licked the bowl clean.

"He's okay, Jinx," Jaublowski replied. "His license

checks out."

"Gimme another," barked the dog.

Jaublowski tipped a bottle into the mutt's bowl.

"Mr. Wilkes here got some curse that got to do with a magic ring or somethin'," Jaublowski explained. "He saw one of my body switch flyers. It don't all have to be about kids swapping around with their old men. Dames what switched with their daughters, too. I don't know, maybe in some freaky way. Although I ain't got any of them in here so far. Mostly boys." He quickly reversed course strictly for legal (and certainly not for any kind of moral) purposes. "*Men*. Grown, adult men, with I.D.'s to confirm their ages and faces. Of course, animal switchers like Mr. Wilkes here can come on in, too. Everybody's welcome."

The dog paused lapping and stuck its hind foot up next to its ear to scratch. "None of the other bars in town will serve me while I'm a dog," the mutt explained as its foot bounced and its collar jangled. "The bartender at Finnegan's Pub chased me half a block with a broom after I filched half a roast beef sandwich off their bar. Before the curse, I must have blown ten grand a year there on buffalo wings alone. I should have bit that bastard's ankle." He paused to sniff his claws before he resumed scratching. "Yeah, like I really need an assault charge now. I've got that big case I'm about to try that will make or break my career, not to mention my upcoming wedding to the sexy model. Although I think I might be in love with my mousy secretary who is pretty damned sexy herself if she'd just take off those glasses and let her hair down from that bun."

"That's rough, Mr. Wilkes," said Jaublowski, who couldn't fake being genuinely sympathetic if his miserable excuse for a life depended on it.

The dog glanced up, bearing fangs. "Is that supposed

to be funny?" he growled.

Jaublowski clearly had no clue what he'd said, and while I would have enjoyed being witness to the world's first ad homonym attack, I was afraid the mutt D.A. might damage Jaublowski's pouring hand for a stupid, hilarious rough/ruff misunderstanding.

"Ed doesn't do funny," I assured the walking flea motel. "I know what you're thinking, but that rotten comb-over isn't a joke. He plasters each strand down every day with the kind of care somebody else would take building a ship in a bottle. But he's not doing it for humorous effect, he truly thinks it makes him look handsome and youthful."

"Geez, Jinx, c'mon," the barkeep said. He touched careful fingertips to the glued-down streaks of hair to carefully locate the one that must have become misaligned in order to alert me to his great follicular secret.

The dog lawyer seemed mollified. It grunted and went back to lapping from its bowl of booze.

For his part, Jaublowski didn't know what the hell was going on, and was only happy that his beautiful locks were still epoxied down and that he was apparently no longer in danger of getting rabies from one of his customers.

"Oh, I forgot to tell you, you got a call," the barkeep suddenly announced. He found a scrap of yellow paper on the back of the bar. "That elf what works at your office phoned. He said when you got in that I should tell you that."

Jaublowski had scribbled the note on a corner torn from one of his body switch flyers: *He sez hes taking the angle case.*

I couldn't get mad at Mannix any more than I could get angry at Jaublowski's spectacularly appalling spelling.

Getting mad at someone for always doing the right thing would only add another flaw to my extensive heap of personal shortcomings.

I flipped the paper around to see if the barkeep had scribbled anything on the back, but there was nothing there but a public domain cartoon of a deliriously happy drunk pouring liquid down his wide open mouth from a bottle labeled XXX. (Subtlety isn't alive and well, it was murdered by Jaublowski and some underemployed beatnik liberal arts major manning the Kinko's print shop.)

"Did he say anything else?" I asked.

Jaublowski was sliding a fresh pitcher of beer to a kid who was wearing the uniform and face of a local, fifty-something sanitation worker.

"Just that he don't blame you for being naughty. He says it's his fault for always making you collect from your other clients. He says you really should do this one pro boner, but that he understands why you ain't."

The guilt I definitely was not feeling gave a good, solid kick in my gut. Mannix wasn't some manipulating wife trying to get me to repair the kitchen faucet by using reverse psychology. My assistant was the real deal, who said exactly what he meant. If the little guy said he thought he was to blame for hardening my heart to the point where I insisted that a broke angel pay, then he truly thought that me being a bastard was all his fault.

Fido on the next stool was sizing me up.

"You some kind of lawyer?" the dog asked.

"No, I have a conscience," I replied. "Let's see what we can do about killing that part of my brain where said little busybody lives." I snapped my fingers to the barkeep. "Keep them coming, Ed. No pause in between rounds. That's actually P-A-W-S," I informed the mutt next door. "If you want to take offense and rip out my throat, you'd be doing me a real favor."

No such luck. The dog D.A. just grunted before dividing his time between lapping at his bowl of booze and licking his junk.

I would have to rely solely on Jaublowski's watered down hooch to embalm the guilty conscience that I absolutely (honest Native goddamn American) did not feel one tiny little bit. The annoying racket of body-switched bastards continued in the background of my 100% guiltless consciousness as I hunkered down for what was sure to be a long, remorse free afternoon.

4

I was awakened by a hand gently assaulting my shoulder.

"Get up. C'mon, Jinx, it's half past closing time."

My bleary eyes fluttered open on the terrifying close-up image of the cluster of three black hairs that sprouted like miniature porcupine quills from the tip of Jaublowski's rosacea red nose.

The side of my head where it had been resting on the un-soft bar felt like it had melted flat. If I needed a blacksmith with a hammer and an anvil to pound my head back into shape I was in luck, since one had apparently taken up shop between my ears. The village smithy banged a horseshoe symphony on the interior of my cranium as I attempted to sit up straight.

My tongue felt like it had spent the evening pressed inside a waffle iron. I kept my eyelids lowered to half-mast as much to reduce the assault of light on my delicate rods and cones as to obscure the image of Ed Jaublowski, who nobody in their right mind ever wanted to wake up next to. (This went double for Jaublowski's wife, who rumor had it regularly woke up next to every guy in their neighborhood in her successful campaign to never repeat the mistake she'd made on their wedding night.)

I tasted my tongue, which was thick and heavy and definitely something other than tongue flavored.

"You're an evil man, Ed," I said. "You get me in this condition and then you turn me out to fend for myself in a cruel world. A decent human being would let me sleep here all night or die in the attempt. Either would be acceptable."

"Not to me. I got a life outside-a you. Let's go. Up."

He dropped my fedora on my head and grabbed both shoulders to set me up on my stool. I wobbled a little but found that I didn't need the bar for physical support, which only meant that at that moment I was only relying on it for the emotional kind. The barkeep reached under the bar and pulled out my trench coat, which he tossed over my arm.

The D.A. dog was gone, as were the merrymaking bastards who'd swapped bodies with their old men. Beats me where the dog had gone, but the latter were probably home passed out as their fathers — switched into the bodies of their ingrate kids — attempted to sober up their offspring for the big board meeting the next morning.

"I am eternally grateful that I never had kids, Ed," I announced.

"So is they, Jinx," Jaublowski replied.

It was precisely that kind of rare, insightful two a.m. observation for which I kept Ed Jaublowski on the payroll.

I slid off my stool and headed for what I perceived to be the front door.

"Oh, that elf bastard of yours called again," the barkeep called after me.

I turned around.

When I saw the front door ahead of me once more, it

took a fuzzy moment for me to realize that I had, in fact, turned *completely* around.

I turned around a second time, this time being certain to arrest the accidental pirouette I'd flawlessly and unwittingly performed in my first attempt.

Instead of Jaublowski's homely mug, I found myself staring into the face of the jukebox, which I judged to be about forty-five degrees off the mark.

Another attempt which should have absolutely, with no doubt whatsoever aimed me with laser-like precision toward Jaublowski's beady eyes instead resulted in a navigational error that somehow brought me back to facing the front door.

I balanced myself on one Florsheim, placed my right toe firmly on the floor behind me, and turned around again — slowly — this time locking in at only 180 degrees.

Jaublowski could have abandoned his post, locked up O'Hale's, hailed a cab, picked up some flowers for the missus, and been home by now to find his ball-and-chain off at another mysterious all-night pottery lesson with the midget in 23B. But instead of wisely bagging out of the joint, the grubby barkeep was still slouching behind his bar.

I drew myself up in the most dignified manner possible, which proved difficult to manage given the fact that I was caught in that ugly, spider's web no-man's-land between utterly drunk and partially hungover.

"Ed," I informed the bartender, "Mannix is not mine, he is his own person. He is, in fact, a finer person than I or, definitely even more so, *you* will ever be. Taking that into account, if you ever refer to him as a bastard or any other derogatory term again, I will beat the holy living shit out of you. Are we clear?"

There were drunk's threats and there were threats

made while drunk. The former could often be dismissed as inebriated posturing, while the latter — depending on who was doing the threatening — were to be taken seriously. Jaublowski had been in the business long enough to know the difference.

The bartender raised his hands before him, palms out.

"I didn't mean nothin' by it, Jinx," he apologized. "Mannix is okay in my book. It's just...he called again while you was passed out. I tried to wake you, but you was dead to the world." He held up another torn-off scrap of yellow paper.

"I got over here with enough difficulty, I am definitely not traversing the gulf between here and there without a team of Sherpas and a D.A. dog with a barrel of brandy strapped to his throat," I informed him. "What did he have to say?"

Jaublowski glanced at his note. "Mr. Invest-something is in some kind of trouble with...I don't know. I guess work or somethin'. He said somethin' about a 'host.' I couldn't hear with all the yelling here. This Invest client guy of yours work at restaurant? Anyways, Mannix says he tried, but he can't find Pinder, if that means somethin' to you. Says he could really use your help."

The barkeep glanced up from the note, a fervent hope in his eyes that the fact he had taken a message for me would get him off the hook for inadvertently deliberately insulting my world-class assistant.

"Goodnight, Ed," I said.

I did the same toe-to-the-floor precision turn to hopefully set me back in the direction of the door. Thanks to my instinctive, Magellan-like expert navigation I wound up only a few degrees off the mark. I compensated with a leeward stagger that miraculously snagged the door handle on the first attempt, and together the door and I disgorged my sorry carcass into the late night air.

Night held the city in a mugger's grip, one gloved hand clamped over an entire municipality's collective mouth. We urbanites were used to it by now, and knew instinctively that it was best not to struggle. All the weary, aged, lumbering town could manage as proof that it hadn't completely surrendered to the smothering night was an occasional distant car horn yelp and an unimpressive siren bleat.

My footfalls echoed up weeping high rise walls as I scuffed alone down the desolate sidewalk. I walked past the pitch black opening of an alley from which my passing did not go unobserved by a pair of glowing feline eyes. The cat screeched abruptly and the green eyes darted to the right and were gone, leaving me to wonder and worry what kind of utterly silent predator always seemed to be lurking around in the middle of the night with the express purpose of atmospherically pissing off cats.

Steam bled from a manhole into the chill post-midnight air directly in my path. I figured it'd look dramatic for anybody on the other side to see my lonely silhouette stride through it, but it was late and nobody was on the other side to impress. Also, I was worried what the steam might do to the creases in my wrinkled Sears slacks. I realized with horror that it might actually somehow take the rumples out of my suit, and I certainly didn't want to do that for fear that my economical discovery might put out of business my hilariously named Chinaman dry cleaner, Wing Sak Poop.

To avoid the steam I stepped off the curb and into the road…

…and, as it turned out, directly into the brilliant high beams of the utterly silent, speeding bus that had rocketed up out of nowhere behind me.

I was dead. The lights were too close. The bus was right on top of me. All I could do was cower and hope in the split-second I had left to live that my affairs were in order. I had recently been dumped by a dame who worked for a company that made granite headstones. So not only had my most recent affair ended, I had a pretty good chance of getting a big discount on a tombstone, since at our parting the dame in question had suggested in no uncertain terms that she'd pay good money to see me drop dead.

Satisfied that my earthly affairs were, indeed, settled, I awaited the hundred mile an hour Greyhound grille that was about to send me to nirvana, or at least to a damp bench next to a rotting wino in some eternal bus terminal limbo.

The split second became a full second.

One second became five.

I still hadn't heard the sound of the bus engine that was clearly bearing down on me, as evidenced by the brilliant headlights that were warming my back.

I opened my eyes, which I hadn't realized I'd bravely slammed shut.

The headlights had come no closer in those five — now closer to ten — seconds. I saw cast on the ground before me the elongated shadow of my cowardly frame. Surrounding my shadow was a splash of brilliant white light that stretched up the road half a city block. The warm light cast noontime brightness up the sides of buildings which moments before had been gripped in the deepest gloom of darkest night. Streetlights dimmed, their weak glow vanishing utterly before the fresh wash of luminous white. Weak lights in shops surrendered as well to the sudden burst of daylight.

There was a billboard on the side of a building advertising Sleep-Tite Pillows. The caption ordered the masses to "Sleep Your Cares Away." A gigantic photographic dame was curled up with one of the products being promoted, enjoying the night's sleep promised by the Sleep-Tite company. A vandal with a can of spray paint had covered up the "E" in "Tite" and had graphically altered the corresponding portion of the sleeping dame's anatomy to reflect the corrected text. Six bright lights hung out over the billboard, vividly illuminating the defacements. I imagined that the only people who would be pleased that all the lights were winking out on the street were in the promotions department of the newly minted Sleep-Tit corporation.

The half-dozen floodlights that lit up the billboard momentarily phased in and out, dipping from bright white to dull orange specks; back to white, although duller this time; then finally winked out entirely.

With the last of the manmade lamps now gone as if snuffed out by an EM pulse, the only light left on the block came from behind me.

The ominous bus light was not just warming my back. I could feel from it a growing swell of joy and love which, unless you want to get arrested, you don't generally experience from municipal transportation.

I am naturally mistrustful of both joy and love, having been married and, consequently, resolved never to fall for that trick again. I figured it'd be best for all concerned — but especially for me — if I just stood there in the street without turning around or acknowledging the now clearly mysterious light in any way whatsoever.

I was the only dumb bastard out at that time of night, so I had little doubt that the light had to be there for unlucky yours truly. I hoped that whatever was casting those goddamn joyous rays upon me would realize that I wasn't in the market and would move on to some other drunken sap.

"Ahem."

The fake throat clearing was right behind me. Far too close for anything remotely approaching comfort.

I pretended I didn't hear. I was still standing in the middle of the street. Maybe if I waited long enough, an actual bus would come along and do me a favor.

"Ahem."

Whoever it was wasn't going anywhere without my conceding that they did, in fact, exist. Against my better judgment, I turned very carefully around.

And was nearly knocked flat on my ass by the blast of a horn.

I was completely sober in an instant.

It was a bus after all. I'd apparently been caught in that slow-motion amber that people experience in the instant before death. It really had only been a split-second since I'd stepped off the sidewalk and out in front of the city bus.

Except the light wasn't coming from headlights in front of me, but from the sky above me. I glanced up to find a vaguely asexual — tilting toward the effeminate — chubby son of a bitch floating in the air ten feet above and behind me.

The gravity-defying slob had long, flowing yellow hair; a spectacularly white robe; a circle of light plastered in nimbus-level orbit around the crown of his head; and was, indisputably, an angel.

I could handle one angel. As luck would have it I'd already done so within the past twenty-four hours, so the novelty of seeing one of the winged maniacs was long gone for a jaded SOB like me. Unfortunately this guy, unlike Invictus my wannabe client, had not come to the party alone.

My eyes could not wrap themselves around the sheer number of angels crowded in the air behind their tubby leader. It was, as it turned out, an entire heavenly host that had decided to park itself in the air on my eleven o'clock.

There were thousands of them arranged in row upon row up in the sky. They disappeared behind buildings. They reappeared in a chorus line on the other sides. They arced up into the wispy clouds, off into infinity, and circled back around in some kind of eye-twisting angelic Mobius strip.

I realized as my eyes wrestled with the sight that my initial impression was wrong. There weren't thousands. At second glance, there had to be *tens of thousands* of the glowing immortal bastards hovering in the air. The collective racket of a couple hundred thousand wings that were keeping them glued to the sky was like a rushing typhoon wind.

The guy who had blown the horn was in the first row. What I'd thought was a bus horn was in reality a celestial trumpet. The second-string angelic Benny Goodman was tucking up under his arm the magnificent instrument of gleaming gold that had nearly, if not actually, blown a hole through the back of my goddamn head.

"Be not afraid!" commanded the fat angel at the head of the host.

"It's a little late for that," I replied. "I'll be sending you the laundry bill. And if cleaning proves impossible to my skilled Chinese dry cleaner Mr. Wing Sak Poop, which is very nearly likely, you'll be getting a bill for replacement Fruit of the Looms."

"I know not what thou meaneth," the angel announced

(which pretty much summed up my interaction with everything on Earth, above the Earth and under the Earth). "I am Greg," he said, rather anticlimactically. "You are Crag Banyon, correct?"

The SOB knew he was right. Even so, he made a polite show of consulting an endlessly long parchment that another angel had just unfurled before him.

"Last four digits of your Social Security 3-7-8-1?" he asked.

"Yes," I replied. "But I'm only admitting it because I'm afraid if I say no, you'll announce it in its entirety to everybody in the tri-state area who didn't already hear you bellow out the last four numbers."

"Oh. Right. Sorry," announced the Angel Greg. "Is this—" He waved his hand at the multitude of heavenly host. "We're out of practice. Is this all a bit much?"

"Not if you intend to invade Egypt," I informed him.

"Oh, dear. Well *that's* not why we're here. Not yet, anyway." He turned to the angel with the scroll and shot him a very stern look. "*I* thought it might be too much," the Angel Greg informed me as he glared at his fidgeting subordinate.

Greg muttered something I didn't catch to the angel with the trumpet, and with a second burst of his horn that blew my hat off into the street, the entire army of angels disappeared. All that remained behind was the Angel Greg and the unnamed angel to his right, who was in the process of spooling up his enormously long parchment.

The extinguished streetlights all winked back on. The lights on the Sleep-Tite Pillow billboard flashed back to life, illuminating once more the spray painted anatomical enhancements of the sleeping dame on the poster.

"Is that better?" the Angel Greg asked.

"Not entirely. I can also see up your dress."

"Oh, dear," the Angel Greg said.

He and his pal disappeared from the sky with a pop, like a cork launching from a bottle, and in the same instant appeared in the street next to me.

The pair of them looked much more ordinary once they were no longer pinned like giant butterflies to the corkboard sky.

Lights were flicking on in slum apartments up and down the street. Since the angel army had extended from here seemingly to eternity, not to mention the Angel Greg's sonic boom recitation of nearly fifty percent of my Social Security number, I assumed half the city would be hanging its head out the window and looking for someone at whom to fling an old boot.

I snatched my hat up from the road where the trumpet had blasted it and nabbed the Angel Greg by the elbow. I guided the celestial exhibitionist into a hidden alcove beneath the torn awning of an abandoned cash-for-gold store. The second angel tagged along, still spooling up his parchment like a roll of paper towels that had bounced off the kitchen counter and unfurled its ass all the way into the dining room.

"Oh, dear," the Angel Greg said. "We woke people up, didn't we? I forgot that humanity sleeps. We don't do it, you see. This mortal interaction isn't generally in our wheelhouse. We're not the kind of angels who ordinarily involve ourselves with mortals. The last time we did this had to be — sheesh — must be a couple thousand years ago?" he queried his partner, who nodded agreement even as he continued spooling up his roll of parchment Bounty. "I want to say December? It had to be after Thanksgiving, because if memory serves the manger was definitely up."

"What the hell was that racket and goddamn unearthly glow?" an interrupting voice shouted from a fourth story window down the street.

"Oh, my. Sorry," the Angel Greg said quietly to me in our safe space beneath the torn and faded awning. "Sorry!" he repeated much more loudly, and directed to the anonymous shouter above. "Also, you really shouldn't curse, sir!" he added helpfully.

This bit of unsolicited advice succeeded only in opening the four letter floodgates. It was lucky we were under the awning, since we were suddenly caught in a downpour of swearing from every open window. It was a freak verbal storm so intense that it threatened to fill our galoshes with "shits," "goddamns" and enough "ass-holes" to send the Angel Greg's halo spinning off from his helipad pate.

The angel was flustered by the avalanche of rotten language, but undeterred.

"Tsk. Well, *they're* not my responsibility," he said, shrugging his giant wings and waving a hand to our unseen civilian audience hanging from their tenement windows. "They each have their own guardian angel. Speaking of which, that's why I'm here. Did an angel called Invictus manifest to you today?"

I imagined the penalty for lying to an angel was instant smiting followed by an eternity of languid, horrific torture.

I set my bloodshot orbs firmly to Greg's baby blues and spoke absolute truth.

"No," I replied.

The Angel Greg's eyes narrowed, and I got a sense that he wasn't entirely the soft wad of pastry his doughy exterior made him seem.

"You realize, mortal, that we can tell if you are being

untruthful?" the angel said, with not a little hint of menace in his ringing voice.

"I could have used your skills when I was married," I said. "The ex-Mrs. Banyon was unfamiliar with the truth even when it bit her on the ass. Which is literally true, if you are of the persuasion, which I imagine you're not, who believe yogis are possessors of eternal verities. But the hickeys all over her ashram are in the divorce papers."

The Angel Greg frowned. "Oh, dear. The thing is, an elf who says he works for you said that you did, in fact, meet with Invictus. He wasn't lying either. As I said, we can tell. Oh, my, my, my. We *have* gotten our wires crossed somewhere in this fuse box of ours, haven't we. Is that a real thing? A fuse box? We're not really up on all this modern... Anyway, it's lucky you didn't see Invictus. We've got our hands full with him. Guardian angels aren't supposed to manifest to mortals, you see. They're the 'unseen hand of You-Know-Who,' and all that. Oh, dear. If Invictus keeps appearing to mortals, we're going to have to...well, let's just say we haven't had a fallen angel in a *very* long time, but this one is teetering on the edge. He'd just better be keeping that charge of his safe from any funny business, that's all I have to say."

The accompanying angel had finished rolling up his parchment scroll. The Angel Greg gave him a little nod, and the right-hand guy vanished.

The shouting around the neighborhood was already dying down. The heavenly host was long gone, the trumpet blasts had ceased, and people had work in the morning. There was only a little residual grumbling. Lights were switching off one by one.

"Well, it *is* a lovely night," one lone civilian voice in the wilderness called from halfway down the block. The poorly timed optimist was met with a few half-hearted "shut ups" and a "blow it out your ass, Hals" from his neighbors.

The angel's chubby, smiling face looked up in the direction whence Hal had spoken. "It's nice to see that *every* mortal isn't a gloomy Gus."

"Yes, we are," I informed him, lest the optimistic aberration that was invisible asshole Hal give the Angel Greg a false positive view of humanity. "Anybody normal hanging out their window after being blasted out of bed by an angel's horn at three o'clock in the morning would murder a church choir to get back to sleep. If not, he has something seriously wrong with him. Hal up there will be jumping to his death by four, if he's not pushed first."

The Angel Greg turned his attention back to me.

"My, you're just *King* Gloomy Gus, aren't you?"

"I seized power from the previous monarch in a coup d'état," I said. "He wasn't a miserable enough piece of shit for us peasant realists."

It was clear from the look he gave me that he wasn't sure if his infallible truth detector was on the fritz.

"You'll let us know if you *do* hear from Invictus," the Angel Greg slowly said. "We're in the book. You *did* you get what I did there, didn't you? I meant the Bible."

I allowed that his divine wordplay wasn't lost on me. Apparently, angels are morons.

"Good. Excellent." He clapped his hands together and rubbed them for a few seconds as he tried to think of anything he might have forgotten. "No. No, that's it. We likely shall not meet again on this plane." He offered a benign smile. "You should maybe go a little lighter on the drinking, Mr. Banyon," he suggested.

And with that last bit of unsolicited advice delivered,

he was gone.

I cooled my heels a good ten minutes under the awning as the city fell back into deep slumber, or at least was furiously counting sheep with a pillow over its head.

I mulled over my situation.

I hadn't technically lied to the angel about seeing Invictus today. It was well after midnight, so in point of fact I'd seen him yesterday. I guess when a day is like a thousand years and a thousand years are like a day, it gets tricky keeping track of the blurred line between Tuesday and Wednesday on your *Far Side* desk calendar.

I wouldn't have considered lying to Angel Greg at all, but for the fact that I had no idea what Mannix had been up to in the hours since I'd left my office. If the little guy had buried himself in deep, I couldn't abandon him and take off with the shovel.

It sounded like the only thing keeping Invictus from getting his wings clipped was keeping Pinder safe, and the guardian angel had no idea where the bastard was. And now there was a threat that the poor angelic boob might be cast out of paradise for the sin of playing peeka-boo with me in my bathroom mirror.

Probably most disturbing above all else was that I hadn't been lying (but wished I had been) when I'd told hovering Angel Greg that I could see up his skirt. Despite trying to look anywhere but there, I'd inadvertently gotten a good, solid peek.

I hadn't really seen anything, because there was nothing up there to see. I had discovered something that night that would haunt me for the rest of my days. Some things you just want to go to your grave not knowing, and I could add to my list of crap I never wanted to learn the fact that angels had apparently been designed like Ken dolls.

Enough time had passed by this point. Everyone who'd been screaming out their windows was back inside their shitty apartments.

I stepped out from under the awning.

There was a sudden, surprising burst of activity behind me.

I didn't see who it was who threw the pillowcase over my head, pinned my arms behind my back and threw me into the back of a van that had, unlike the bus of my imagination twenty minutes before, actually squealed up to the curb.

Strong hands pinned me to the floor. I felt cold steel against my cheek.

There was a powerfully nauseating scent of cake frosting, which gave me an instant series of horrifying flashbacks back to awkward birthdays, terrifying anniversaries and one gruesome wedding. For some reason the most powerful image was of the dance I was forced to perform at salad forkpoint with my now ex-mother-in-law, a woman of abundant girth who had selected for her reception meal her own personal layer cake rather than starve her diabetes with a plate of beef or chicken.

My arms were pulled back and I felt a plastic zip tie snake around my wrists and draw tight, binding my hands together behind my back.

"You've been a busy flatfoot, Banyon," a rough voice growled in my ear. "Don't think we didn't see the multitude you were just meeting with."

"He wasn't meeting with anyone," another gruff voice insisted, this one behind me and presumably belonging to the bastard who'd just finished tying my hands.

"Oh, right," said the SOB who'd been slobbering in my ear. To me he hissed, "Don't think that we believe in the existence of who or what you think you were just meeting with, because there's no rational scientific basis for us to."

And to punctuate his convoluted self-righteousness, he brought something blunt and unconsciousness-pro-ducing down hard to the back of my head. I saw stars that I was certain weren't there but which were real to me nonetheless, and then I was swallowed up by blackness and finally into, with any luck, a good goddamn night's sleep.

5

I had no idea how many hours later it was when I woke up on the cold stone floor. The shock of the angel's horn had performed the unfortunate and unwanted miracle of blasting the booze out of my system, and so I was pretty sure the pounding in my skull was the exclusive result of being bashed on the head.

I managed to pry my eyes open, which wasn't ordinarily a feat comparable to swimming the English Channel but which this time left me wishing I'd drowned halfway to Calais.

I was in what looked like an old church. The walls were stacked granite slabs, and there were heavy wood beams holding up the ceiling. A vague whiff of coffee filled the air. Probably seeped into the stone from ancient AA meetings.

The room was small. An oversized closet. There was a rack with cleaning supplies arranged on the shelves, on which my fedora had also been placed, hopefully with the loving reverence it deserved. There were a couple of mismatched folding metal chairs. The pillowcase that had been tossed over my head was draped over the back of one chair. Parked in front of the second cheap tin chair was a pair of sneakers.

The sneakers were attached to legs which, when I rolled my head and looked up to get a better view, I found were attached to a bastard with a computer.

He was pasty, in his mid-forties, and his salt and pepper hair was two months past the sell-by date of his last haircut.

My kidnapper had his laptop balanced on his knees. His sunken, sickly eyes were trained on the screen with the kind of cold anger previous generations never directed toward their washing machines, can openers, Whirlpool ranges, or any other appliance.

Slender fingers like fleshy chopsticks pecked furiously away at the keyboard.

"*No*," the wasted SOB said. As he spoke his typed word aloud, he struck the *N* and *O* keys with more venom than a herpetologist can milk from a rattlesnake in a week. "*I* prefer to live in a world grounded in rational thought. Enjoy your field trip to the National Cathedral, students of Mrs. Witulski's St. Anselm's seventh grade class. Say hello to your imaginary sky ruler for me."

The laptop beeped an alert, and the seated bastard opened up a new screen. A tiny spark lit in the depths of his exhausted eyes, and he began speak-typing once more.

"*No*," he announced as he pounded away at the keyboard, "I don't believe in miracles, I believe in what I can see with my own two eyes. The only miracle I see is that in the twenty-first century people like you are still gullible enough to buy into some made-up fantasy that only manages to spread ignorance and misery." He paused as he read a real-time reply, then attacked his keyboard once more. "I have every right to be at the Fabulous Retired Ladies Afghan Knitters Page. This is not Nazi Germany, Adolf. Last time I checked there is still free speech in this country, at least until you backwards Ten Commandments types manage to get it banned as an offense against your imaginary ruler who lives on a cloud in outer space."

Another beep, and he was off to another Web page.

"*No*," he said as his long fingers furiously tapped away at the keys. "I don't see anybody's invisible hand in a sunrise. I see a planet rotating on its axis and I see a star. Morning happened millions of years before humans evolved from primordial slime, and it will happen millions of years after we've gone the way of the dodo. All I *do* see is wars started in the name of some group's supernatural fantasy and the Pope riding around in a brand new Lamborghini."

He paused as he waited for a response from the person holding the tin can on the other end of the Internet. When he read what the sender had written, he sighed. "Yes, I *might* be able to make it home for the Fourth of July," he announced to the four granite walls of the room, as well as to his conscious hostage on the floor. He very carefully typed the words as he spoke them. "Try not to beat dad to death with that cross you've got hanging on your bedroom wall, mother, otherwise the nonexistent judge who lives in the invisible smoke above your head might punish you for being bad. Ooooo."

He held his finger down on the *O* key until the world got the message.

His computer beeped again and he was about to move on when he glanced up and noticed that the poor slob he'd had kidnapped and tossed on his floor was awake.

"Oh," he said.

For a moment he was torn between me and his computer. It was a monumental effort, but he eventually set the laptop to the seat next to him. As he spoke, it continued to beep to him occasional alerts of conversations momentarily abandoned.

"I'm Pinder," my sallow-eyed bastard kidnapper said.

"I hear through tangible, scientifically verifiable sources that you're looking for me."

"You'd better recheck your math, Pythagoras, because I wasn't."

I rolled myself to a sitting position and perp-walked my ass backwards until I could rest my back against the rough granite wall. As I moved, I felt the weight of my gun in its holster under my armpit. I'd apparently been kidnapped on amateur night, although the joke was currently on me since my bound hands prevented me from reaching my piece and permanently aerating Pinder's broad forehead.

Pinder's lips thinned and he hissed an impatient, condescending laugh.

"Mr. Banyon," he said with a disdainful snort, "I can give you a list of perfectly rational, scientifically-based reasons why you were trying to find me."

"Look," I said, "your guardian angel *did* come to my office—"

Pinder was suddenly shouting. "*La-la-la-la-la!*" He clapped his hands so hard over his ears he probably popped his eardrums. "I can see — *la-la!* — I can see you want to say something!" he hollered. "But I can't hear you! *La-la-la!*"

He stopped yelling but left his hands clamped firmly in place. When he was sure I wasn't talking, he lifted his palms with great care.

"As I was saying," the complete psycho lunatic nutbar resumed, as if he hadn't busted into a demented, seasonally inappropriate chorus of Deck the Halls, "I know you're looking for me. I don't know who hired you to find me…"

His eyes grew wide and I could see that his hands were itching to slap the sides of his head once more if I so much as opened my yap. Since I was tied up in a small room with a complete mental patient *fa-la-la-la-la*-ing his lungs out at me, I thought it best at that moment to not bring up the evidently antagonizing existence of the Angel Invictus.

Pinder relaxed and set his hands back to his knees.

"Let us just leave it that I do not wish to be found, Mr. Banyon. By *anyone*. If you agree to drop your investigation right now and forget you ever saw me, I can make it worth your while, financially speaking."

It was as easy as my decision on what to have for supper last night. (FYI: pretzels and beer nuts from bowls that had been carefully selected as ones not slobbered into by mangy district attorneys.)

"Ten thousand bucks," I said. "Cash."

His eyes narrowed. "I'm dealing with a pragmatic man. We are kindred spirits, you and I, Mr. Banyon. Not that I believe in spirits. The only invisible force guiding my destiny is gravity. But clearly you and I see the reality of the physical world as it is presented to us. Good. Excellent." He got to his feet. "The money will be ready for you within the hour. You'll be leaving us the way you came, I'm afraid. I just want to say before we part that it is a pleasure doing business with an equally rational human being."

Having an evident whack-job like Pinder put my sanity in the same bag of feral cats as his own wasn't exactly the psychiatric ego boost he meant it to be. Still, this wasn't the best time to provoke a maniac into murdering me. It was possible I'd gotten myself in dutch earlier that morning with the head of a legion of heavenly angels, and consequently I didn't want to get my skull caved to mush while my final placement in the afterlife was in its current state of flux.

I flashed Pinder my placating pearly whites and, despite the throbbing pain in the back of my head, nodded the crackpot along as he gathered up his computer.

He glanced at his laptop screen.

"I don't believe it. He's going on *again* about some nonexistent omniscient being living in an invisible castle in the sky. The Archbishop of Canterbury is going to rue the day he accepted *my* friend request."

He was already formulating his next hostile Internet post as he pulled the heavy door shut behind him.

The door was made up of thick slabs of wood bound together with metal strips, like staves in a barrel. It was like the wine cellar door in a particularly sinister castle. No light came in from beneath it, and I couldn't hear anything from the other side. I had, however, briefly heard some noise when Pinder had pulled the door open. It had sounded like a hundred sets of fingers clicking madly away at keyboards like Pinder's.

The keyboard racket ceased when the door was shut, and I was left alone with my thoughts, the primary of which was "what an asshole" followed a close second by "escape."

If I'd been dealing with the Leprechaun mafia, I wouldn't have questioned a straightforward meeting like the one I'd just attended: *Drop the case for a pot of gold, or we'll beat you to death with a shillelagh and bury you in a shallow grave on the road to Tipperary.* Threat, payoff. Or, if you prefer, carrot (boiled for ten hours in a pot with cabbage and an inedible lump of stringy meat-like shit), stick. Elegant simplicity.

I hadn't asked Invictus what Pinder did for a living, but by the look of him he wasn't the kind of guy who could so easily part with ten thousand smackers.

There was no money from Charles Pinder that wasn't coming out of a Monopoly box. To get me to drop Invictus as a client, a nut like Pinder would have agreed to shove a camel through a needle's eye. But he didn't have a camel either, and even if he could get his hands on one all he'd wind up doing was confusing an innocent dromedary while going even crazier in the attempt.

Most troubling was that Pinder had accomplices. I hadn't seen their faces, but neither of the two voices in the back of the van had belonged to him. And it wasn't just the two who'd spoken. The van had started driving before the pair in the back had sent me off to my one-man slumber party, courtesy a mallet to the back of the head. That meant there had been a third kidnapper behind the wheel.

At least three more, all working for or with Pinder. Just because Pinder thought he'd made a deal with me, that didn't mean the others wouldn't decide for themselves to row me out into the middle of Lake Tahoe and give me the Fredo special.

I kept my back hard against the wall and braced my shoes on the floor, shoving myself in a slow, shoulder blade crawl up to my feet.

The zip tie bit into my wrists like a starving plastic rat.

I'd seen people on TV more acrobatic than I hop over handcuffs. While it'd be easier if my hands were knotted in front of me rather than behind, I had as much chance of playing jump rope with my own arms as I had of slowly pushing my zip-tied wrists down as far over my ass as I could manage and then trying to haul one leg through at a time: namely, a zero chance in hell. Whatever magic I could manage to perform would have to be accomplished while I was trussed up in what I realized, with no small amount of terrified bladder harmonics, was the traditional firing squad pose.

Except for the two folding chairs, there wasn't anything in the room other than whatever might be stashed on the supply shelf.

First and foremost, I pulled my fedora brim with my teeth so that it was hanging partway off the shelf, and then with determined backwards wriggling managed to replant it back on top of my shivering head.

As for the rest of the contents of the shelf, there were only some cans and jugs of cleaning supplies, as well as an open wooden box with a handful of mismatched tools dumped in it. The box seemed pretty worthless to aid in my great escape. All I could see was a busted tape measure, a hammer head sans handle, some sockets with no wrench, and an assortment of screwdrivers, mostly Phillips head, mostly broken.

I turned around and backed into the shelf to give the box a rattle, hoping to raise from the bottom something that wasn't utterly useless. My hand snaked around a small item just as the handle on my closet door prison rattled.

I darted around the folding chairs and dropped my ass in the nearest one just as the big wooden door swung open.

The door didn't yawn wide. I heard the rat-a-tat of dozens of computer keyboards being pecked away on by unseen fingers. A faceless voice just on the other side of the half-open door instructed, "Close your eyes, Banyon."

I recognized the voice. It was the first bastard from the back of the van.

I did as I was instructed, and a moment later I heard a heavy breather hustling into the room. I was nudged forward, and the pillow case that had been hanging over the back of the chair in which I was sitting was pulled down over my head.

I was pulled to my feet and guided through the door and into the next room.

My captors weren't exactly experienced kidnappers. If

they had been, one of them might have tested on themselves the pillowcase they were using as a blindfold.

The material was thin, and while I couldn't see anything very clearly I did see light pouring through three very large, arched windows. Keeping with the church motif established back in the closet, the sweeping shapes of the windows ended in points at their distant tops. They definitely looked like they might have been in a church. However, I would have been able to see the colors of stained glass through my pillowcase bonnet, and there was only the bright, white light of ordinary glass panes.

The only people I could manage to see in the room were shapeless blobs. In their formlessness, they eerily reminded me of Invictus reflected in my toaster. It was a comparison that I definitely wouldn't have dared mention to any of them.

Most of them were typing in silence, but others were like Pinder, angrily reciting the words their outraged fingers were committing to the electronic ether.

"The next time you need surgery, you can put *your* faith in someone you can't see who isn't real. *I'll* put *mine* in science," one guy snarled. "Say hello to the FSM for me."

Two seats down, another typist was speaking through squeaking, gritted teeth as he swiftly wrote down his spoken words.

"Every war in history has been caused by religion. Incidentally, history didn't start with an apple in some mythical garden. Try reading a science book sometime. Watch out! The FSM is watching you. Moron."

"*Science, science, science!*" a dame shrieked, abusing the same five keys twenty-one times in the space of two seconds.

Those were just the near ones I could hear well. There

were other bellowing loudmouths, apparently scattered amongst the more silent faithful around the large room. The distant shouters were equally determined to straighten out everybody who wasn't marching in lockstep with them, and couldn't manage to keep their goddamn yaps pinned shut while their fingertips screeched "science!" at the tops of their whorls.

I heard "FSM" being repeated by many chirping crickets scattered around the crowd. It was apparently some kind of devastating shorthand, judging from the superior snorts its use elicited. The crowd out here was using the abbreviation far more freely than had Pinder, who had, in fact, not deployed it once in his closeted Internet hit-and-runs.

A rough hand on my bicep directed me out of the room. I was led through an antechamber and out into a burst of sunlight. It was so bright that it must have been somewhere around noon. It was impossible for my retinas to distinguish anything but an explosion of light through the thin cloth.

For a moment I thought it was possible that I'd slept through the entire day, that it was actually night, and that the flash of what I mistakenly thought was sunlight through my pillowcase chapeau was in reality the Angel Greg and his army of sky eunuchs come to smite my ass for not being entirely forthcoming the last time around.

I needn't have worried about anybody loosing the faithful lightning of their terrible swift sword on my posterior. The blockish, black shape of what I gathered was the same van in which I'd been beaten into unconsciousness suddenly loomed two inches from my face, and it became abundantly clear that it was just ordinary daylight and not a vast angelic Aurora Borealis seeping through the cloth.

My guide clapped a hand on the lump on the back of my head and manipulated it like a blindingly painful Atari joystick, negotiating me roughly into the back of the van.

I was forced to sit on the floor. I had a rough idea where all the windows were from the squares of light around me. My back was to the rear doors.

I caught the same smell of frosting from last night, although much stronger in the heat of the day. It was mixed today with the strong smell of coffee that I'd first picked up inside my stone cell. There was also a thick scent of confectioner's sugar and cinnamon which I had not detected the previous evening, possibly because my nose was too busy having its brains bashed in.

"You hear anything yet?" the guy who'd led me outside asked.

A voice in the cab answered. "He's gonna call when he's got it."

Only two men, down from three last night. The engine remained off and my two kidnappers and I sat in the hot van baking like potatoes in a microwave.

Everybody knows the awkward silence that comes when you're crammed in a small metal box with bedroom linen on your head in the company of a pair of insane kidnappers who might or might not be about to murder you. I imagined my nearer captor's sudden attempt at conversation was because he was an anxious guy who hated uncomfortable social situations and felt compelled to fill the silence with asshole bullshit.

"I don't like private detectives," the bastard in the back of the van abruptly announced.

"That makes two billion of us," I said. "Everybody else just hasn't had one peeking through his bedroom window yet."

"*He* says you'll drop it," the SOB continued. "But he's been nothing but trouble lately if you ask me. There's talk. Some people are whispering he's some kind of messiah. '*FSM, FSM, FSM.*' Bullshit. *I'm* rational and scientific. I took an online test that said my I.Q. is 197. That's better than Einstein. As a certified Internet genius, I reject anti-quated theistic ideas of invisible cloud spirits, even when as a term it's only being metaphorically applied to a flesh and blood asswipe like Pinder."

"It's funny," I mused through my hundred thread-count cotton blend muzzle. "Before I met you, I would have said I hated myself more than anybody else."

A ringtone sounded from the cab. John Lennon's "Imagine." Of - goddamn - course.

The driver whispered into his phone for less than five seconds. When he was through, his anxious voice called back, "He's ready."

The engine started and I felt a jolt of movement. We began driving.

From the sounds of traffic and the frequent stops we were forced to make, the bastards hadn't taken me out of the city. I had maybe twenty secularly blessed minutes of perspiring in silence before the nervous driver announced, "There he is."

The wheelman must have spotted their third stooge from down the block, because the van continued to move, albeit more slowly, as if the driver was looking for a parking spot.

I heard the guy in the back with me shifting to get closer to my ear. The sunlight coming in the van's side window was partly obscured by his looming, menacing shape.

"*I* don't have faith in you, Banyon," the SOB quietly informed me. "Faith is a firm belief in something for which there is no proof. If there were a way to measure your word scientifically in a science lab run by scientists, then maybe I'd have faith derived from empirically provable and peer reviewed scientific fact." His voice dropped lower. "I don't care what Pinder worked out with you. I'm going to kill you, and I'm not going to worry about what impact that will have on my eternal soul because the 'soul' is a fairytale concept invented by charlatans to con humankind."

The van had rolled to a stop. The side door popped open, spilling light and a blast of cool air into the hotbox interior of my rolling prison.

"While we're baring our souls," I informed the heavy breathing asshole, "you might find it interesting to know that the small screwdriver I used to push down the tab on the zip tie that was around my wrists was invented by Wolfgang von Screwdriver in the castle von Screwdriver sometime in the late Middle Ages."

I held up in one hand the loose plastic zip tie as well as the alluded to little screwdriver which I'd scrounged from the wooden box back in the church closet where I'd met crackpot Charles Pinder. Sadly, I could only imagine how shocked my captor was by my incredible and brilliantly resourceful plastic handcuff escape, since I didn't have a third hand with which to pull off my pillowcase blindfold in order to see his face, and at that moment I was using my only other hand to sock the bastard in the jaw.

I felt and heard the most satisfying crack that didn't involve ice cubes dropped in liquor, and I knew I'd busted the jawbone of an asshole.

The guy tumbled backwards, a-rockin' the van even as the third member of their kidnapping trio was climbing inside without first a-knockin'.

"I started crossing out 'In God We Trust' on some of the bills," the new arrival was announcing. "He'll have to finish the ones I couldn't get to himse—."

Which pronoun he was unable to finish as he'd just been bowled over by the SOB with the busted chops.

I reached up and yanked off my pillowcase, managing from previous kidnapping experience in my long and miserable P.I. career to leave my fedora perfectly in place like the pot of flowers standing like the last bowling pin in the middle of the dining room table after the tablecloth had been ripped out from under it.

Three faces stared back at me. The bastard with the big mouth and the busted jaw was jammed lengthwise in the side door. The latest arrival, whose voice I recognized from the previous night, was still standing outside the van and looking in over his supine confrere. Up front, the driver was looking back in shock and (I naturally assumed given my astonishing display of derring-do) awe.

Several thrilling things happened simultaneously.

The third kidnapper on the scene dropped something he'd been holding in his hands and lunged forward into the back of the van to try to grab me. With the busted-jaw bastard clogging up the side door, all he managed to do was tumble over his pal, slide across the floor, and possibly break his fingers against the opposite wall.

The scumbag with the broken jaw remained jammed sideways in the door. He twisted like a rung-out facecloth under the heavy weight of the dope who'd just done a jumping belly crawl over him. In a final, intensely satisfying one-two capper, the moron who'd scrambled over him gave him an accidental mule kick in the face. The SOB who'd vowed to murder me a minute before was suddenly too busy howling in pain and futilely trying with both hands to reattach the fleshy hammock in which his detached mandible was taking a relaxing summer snooze to contemplate homicide.

I, now being a free man (but for the obvious fact that I was still trapped in the back of a small metal box with a pack of maniacs), implemented phase two of my daring escape by flinging open the van's rear doors.

There were two final concurrent events that transpired

in that instant, the second of which was the most personally painful for yours truly.

Way up on the other end of the van, the driver realized that their plan had just gone entirely and spectacularly to hell, and in a futile attempt to mitigate the damage he abruptly threw the vehicle into drive and stomped on the gas pedal.

The van lurched forward. I, framed as I was in the back door, did not.

I sailed out into warm air and bright noonday sun, slamming to the pavement in front of a parked Volvo.

I rolled to a sitting position in time to see the van blast through a red light and tear around a corner to an accompanying chorus of blaring car horns, squealing tires and screaming drivers. The kidnapper whose jaw I hadn't busted was hanging out the back and grabbing at the wide open and swinging doors, trying to yank them shut as the van tore out of sight. It vanished, but not before I read the giant words that were plastered in rainbow colors across the side: **Marigold's Bakery**. Alongside the text was a picture of a huge, anthropomorphic, grinning cartoon wedding cake.

All eyes were on the escaping van and the subsequent traffic congestion that immediately clogged the intersection. Nobody cared about the innocent kidnapping victim struggling to get to his feet, with the exception of the Volvo's driver whose car alarm I set off when I pushed off his bumper to haul my battered ass up off the pavement.

"Hey, keep your hands to yourself, asshole!" hollered the future yuppie recipient of the Albert Schweitzer Prize for Humanitarianism.

I was still clutching the zip tie and mini screwdriver in one hand. I shoved them in the pocket of my trench coat so that the appropriate fingers of both hands were free to reply in stereo to the Volvo's owner.

The object that the third kidnapper had dropped when he leapt into the van was sitting in the gutter by a storm drain. It was an old, puke green bowling ball bag that looked like it had been scrounged up from Goodwill. I wandered over and sat my weary ass on the curb, the bag between my ankles.

I dragged the zipper — slowly, because it was more goddamn sexy — up and over. The bowling ball bag blossomed open, revealing stacks of fifty and hundred dollar bills. I pulled out the top stack of hundreds and riffled through it. On all the bills in that one stack a thin blue ink line had been drawn across "In God We Trust."

On the top bill, a double-ended arrow transposed the G and D. The self-appointed lucre editor had scrawled across the bill: *I trust them more, since dogs are real.*

Charles Pinder had defied all of my expectations and had actually managed to pull together the insane amount of cash I'd demanded from him.

My stomach grumbled and I suddenly realized that I hadn't had a proper meal in days outside of whatever stale junk covered in salt Jaublowski dumped into the bowls on his bar in order to trick patrons into flooding the excess sodium out of their systems.

I stuffed the defaced stack of bills back inside the bag, zipped the zipper firmly shut, hauled myself to my feet, and staggered off to find a diner that served the best ten thousand dollar omelet in town.

6

"I'm taking the case," I announced when I made my triumphant, MacArthur-like return to my shitty little office.

It turned out Mannix was out at the post office and Doris was still not back from the ICU at Supercuts, so I had made my grand proclamation to nobody.

Nearly nobody.

"You have a new case, Crag? That's wonderful news. I've never really said this before, but you're a terrific neighbor. You deserve all the success that comes your way."

I turned around to find myself facing the beaming, ferret-like mug of Myron Wasserbaum, D.D.S.

Wasserbaum was the criminally incompetent dentist who drilled and filled down that end of the third floor hallway from which came all the screaming that didn't involve me and a bottle of Jack Daniels lamenting all of my adult life choices.

Wasserbaum had apparently neglected to remember that morning that the two of us had each happily hated the other's guts for a decade. He was standing in the hall in his powder blue, short-sleeved dentist smock and grinning a set of teeth too competently maintained for him to have done the work on himself in a mirror.

"Thank you, Wasserbaum," I replied. "And in this spirit of extended olive branches, may I say that you deserve all the lawsuits that come your way, like the one I read about in the paper last week filed by the little old lady whose tongue you mistakenly drilled instead of her bicuspid."

My D.D.S. mortal enemy was still — infuriatingly — grinning as I slammed the door on his incisors.

I had to cool my heels at my desk for ten minutes before I heard Mannix arrive.

"I'm taking the case," I announced again, finding the proclamation far less dramatically satisfying in rerun.

The elf came hustling into my office, holding a handful of stamps and a little bag of takeout lunch from the corner candy store. His surprise that I was at work two days in a row was exceeded only by his delight at what I'd hollered out to him.

"Good afternoon, Mr. Crag!" he said.

"No, it's not," I informed him. "It is, in point of fact, a crummy afternoon. Have you seen Wasserbaum today? He's in a better mood than Vincetti was yesterday. I want the water in this building checked out. I should be safe, since I don't drink any water that hasn't first been purified with barley, yeast and peat smoke. Still, we need to make sure the landlord isn't making our neighbors compliant in order to sell them to hungry aliens, space or illegal. As a public service to the worthless drunken lawyers downstairs and the bitter hag with the dance studio on the top floor, get the water tested. Use this."

I nudged forward the bowling ball bag which I'd sat in the middle of my desk.

Mannix's already oversized elf eyes bulged from their sockets with Barbara Bush intensity when he unzipped the bag and feasted his peepers on the wads of cash inside.

"I tried to buy a couple of ten thousand dollar scrambled eggs and toast, but they wound up costing only four and a half bucks," I explained. "The rest is yours to figure out how to keep afloat whatever this mess is that we try to pass off as a business."

"Where did all this come from?" Mannix asked, growing suspicious of potential naughty illegality. "Did you get another client?"

"No, but it's going to pay for the one you wanted me to take on. Where is that pain in the ass angel, by the way?"

"Mr. Invictus said yesterday that he thought of somewhere Mr. Charles might be this morning. He was going to look for him, but he said he'll check in with me after."

"No one should be checking in with you," I advised. "You shouldn't have been doing any investigating in the first place. My P.I. license doesn't extend to everybody in my employ. Were that the case, Doris would still be wandering around Dallas trying to figure out who shot J.R."

"*Someone* had to help him," Mannix said, gently chiding. His little face turned sad. "But I'm sorry to say that I couldn't help. I did go to Mr. Charles' apartment, but it looked like he hadn't been there in a long time. All the food in the refrigerator had gone bad and there was dust all over everything."

"Mannix, I was just in my apartment yesterday and it looked just like that. For bachelors, which I assume Pinder is, rotting bologna in the fridge and ten pounds of dust on the rug are comforting. For some of us it reminds us of ex-wives who couldn't find a supermarket or a Hoover if their devotion to infidelity depended on it. By the way, when in the course of your investigation did you run into the other angel?"

He suddenly looked sheepish. "When I was looking through the naughty man's apartment. Someone knocked on the door. Mr. Angel Greg was waiting out in the hallway. He introduced me to his heavenly host, who were standing in the hallway and up and down the stairs. They were also in the apartment of Mrs. Edna, the nice little old lady who lives down the hall from the naughty man. She had a key to his apartment, so she let me in. She said she opened her door to let her cat out and they just materialized all over her living room, down her hallway and out her bathroom window into the sky." He dropped his voice low and confided, "Mrs. Edna used some *very* naughty language that no one should ever use around angels. She said she was going to call the police if they didn't get out of her apartment and stop blowing the trumpet, which was scaring Mr. Dimples, her cat."

"Angels clearly have boundary issues," I agreed. I considered what he'd just told me. "So their chief told you Invictus might get tossed out on his ass, and somewhere in the course of your chat you brought up my name and the fact that Invictus swung by the office yesterday morning, and then you called O'Hale's to warn me. That about it?"

The little elf nodded and bit his lip with his little pointed teeth. "Did I do bad?"

I sighed. "No. They probably would have found me eventually. The semi-good news we can draw from this seems to be that the Angel Greg was loitering around outside Pinder's apartment because he can't directly hone in on Invictus himself. He only got to me because you tipped him, not because of some divine insight. I suppose that's like cheating, which is verboten in a world where everybody's cursed with free will. So he and his host are just blindly snooping around. Advantage, bastards like me."

I took a moment to think, during which the now relieved Mannix's amazed eyes were drawn back to the bowling ball bag in the middle of my desk.

"Where did you get all this *money*, Mr. Crag?" he asked, redirecting the conversation and my concussed gaze to the bag stuffed with dough sitting on my blotter.

I told him about my kidnapping and the deal I'd struck with nutball Charles Pinder, who'd sent kidnappers to bring me to him for the express purpose of telling me not to find him, which was like bringing an arsonist to a match factory just to show him the closet where the gasoline is stored.

"The Pinder deal was made under considerable duress, Mannix," I cautioned. "Which gives me every morally tortured reason under the sun to take the payola and to use it for the exact opposite reason for which my abductors, which included at least one would-be murderer, had agreed to give it to me."

I expected some kind of argument from my ethically pure assistant, which I intended to vigorously oppose. If necessary, I planned to call up an overpriced fat drunken attorney — which I could now afford — from the downstairs law firm of Shyster, Pilfer & Fraud. I figured I could let said boozebag lawyer lay out my case for keeping the loot while I retired to my chambers at O'Hale's Bar.

It turned out that hiring a thieving, drunken, degenerate lawyer to plead my case for me wasn't necessary. I was surprised when the elf nodded emphatic agreement.

"Absolutely," Mannix said. "He gave the money to you to get you to do a bad thing. *And* he had those other bad men kidnap you and hit you on the head, which could have very seriously injured you."

"Hopefully it did and I'm dying in a hospital some-where and all of this is just my brain shutting down on the last day of business," I offered optimistically.

"Mr. Charles is a *very* naughty man," Mannix con-cluded emphatically. "If this is his money, and if he didn't steal it, then it's not bad at all to keep it."

"And if it isn't his money and he *did* steal it, we'll keep it all the same just to teach whoever it belongs to not to leave ten grand lying around the bowling alley," I insisted just as emphatically. "In the meantime, get it to the bank before someone less morally high-minded than me busts in here and swipes the first real cash we've had in this dump in months."

Mannix's eyes sprung open wide. "I forgot in all the excitement," the elf announced, suddenly breathless. "Someone *did* break in here last night."

He spun around and hustled out of my office, which I reluctantly recognized as the universal sign that I needed to haul my ass up out of my chair and follow him.

When I joined the elf in the outer room, he was swing-ing the front door open.

"There are scratches on the lock," he said, pointing to the doorknob. "See? Someone must have picked it. The door was wide open when I came in this morning."

I looked around the outer office. The file cabinet drawers were all closed. Doris' charred desk was still a Revlon fire sale. Nothing looked out of place.

"Was anything missing?" I asked.

"I don't think so," Mannix said. "I checked everywhere, and nothing looked different from last night. None of the files were taken, and everything is still in all our desks. I thought maybe it was Miss Doris, but I called the hospital and she's still there."

"No, Mannix, Doris is nearly too stupid to turn an *unlocked* doorknob. She certainly couldn't muster the brain power to pick a lock. And need I point out that she's burned all her hair off? Yes, she ordinarily has five pounds of bobby pins clamping down that bleached tornado mess to keep it from escaping. But with nothing to fasten them to, her bobby pins are all currently at home on her bureau taking a well-earned vacation. She'd have nothing on her with which to pick the lock."

Mannix's face grew sympathetic, and he nodded somberly. "They were taking Miss Doris down this morning to perform an MRI on her follicles," he informed me.

Just in case my facial expression and body language didn't convey my total lack of interest in my secretary's hair problems, I verbally informed Mannix that I gave not a solitary shit.

I glanced around the outer office.

"Well, if nothing's gone, I suppose for a change we should thank whatever neat freak busted in here. My asshole clients or the SOBs they hire me to tail usually just put a brick through the window and tear the whole joint apart."

Mannix, who always had to clean up the mess, nodded agreement. "I didn't call the police," he said.

"Good call. I don't need a bunch of flatfoots rooting around my underwear drawer."

As long as I was standing again — albeit against my better judgment — I figured it was as miserable a time as any to put my Florsheims to use. I collected my hat and coat from the rack in the corner.

"If Invictus comes back, get him out of here as fast as you can. Arrange for a meeting at a neutral spot. The heavenly hostess with the mostest is probably hiding out in the broom closet down the hall waiting to jump out the minute he materializes here."

"Yes, sir, Mr. Crag!"

"You don't have to be quite so excited that I'm on the case, Mannix," I said. "Invictus might be getting the boot out of his condo in the clouds no matter what you and I do. In the meantime, I've got a lead on Pinder to follow up on."

"You said you didn't see where they brought you," the puzzled elf said.

"Yes, but that just means I have to order a wedding cake," I informed him, which non sequitur I hoped was sufficient to keep him from ever trying to play P.I. again.

The little guy was clearly sufficiently baffled, so I pulled the knob with the picked lock shut on his puss. I headed down the hallway in the direction of the elevators. Screams muffled by a mouth packed with cotton emanated from the offices of Dr. Myron Wasserbaum, D.D.S., accompanied by the lethal humming of his antique dental drill.

I had no idea why Wasserbaum and, before him, Vincetti the fishmonger had decided to go against their bastard instincts and were suddenly being nice to me. However, if it kept up much longer, it might become necessary to set fire to the building. For now, I had a case and a client. Contemplating that ugly reality, I climbed aboard the elevator and stabbed the ground floor button. Unfortunately, the wiring wasn't faulty and I didn't get electrocuted. Just my shit luck.

7

Merely joking to an elf about ordering a wedding cake was enough to give me PTSD flashbacks on the bus ride across town, where the *P* stood for the agony of the proposal and the acronym ended in the salvation *D* of divorce. The *TS* in the middle was, naturally, "tough shit," which pretty much summed up my end of the spear catching Olympics that was the version of wedded bliss lethally practiced against me in the happy household of Mr. and Mrs. Crag Banyon.

I had looked up the address of Marigold's Bakery while I waited for Mannix to return to the office. The cupcake palace was just on the edge of downtown, parked in an upscale strip mall alongside a Subway Platinum, an Irregular Tiffany's Outlet Store and a Five Thousand Dollar General.

It wouldn't have been hard to figure out which one was Marigold's Bakery, even if the name hadn't been plastered on the sign out front and that goddamn trademarked googly-eyeball cartoon cake hadn't been painted on the window. Marigold's was the joint surrounded by cruisers, cops and miles of yellow police tape.

If the bus had stopped out front I probably would have stayed in my seat and kept on riding until my quarter ran out of gas. But the bus stop was down the other end of the block, and so I'd hoofed it up to Marigold's Bakery's front stoop.

I was standing at the edge of a crowd of onlookers wondering what I should do next (and invariably coming up with an intoxication-level event) when a voice as unwelcome as a Harley in a hospital zone hollered from the other side of the Maginot Line of yellow tape.

"Well, well. Crag Banyon. I should've known the minute my day turned to hell that you'd wind up showing up. You're the icing on the cake."

No one laughed, which restored a sliver of the non-existent faith I had in humanity.

From the crowd of uniformed cops surrounding the open front door of the bakery emerged an off-the-rack, shit-brown suit. The bastard's white shirt was yellowed, and his ugly red tie was wide enough to flip a pancake. He held a notebook and pencil in a futile attempt to look like he had a clue what the hell he was doing.

"Personal perspective is a funny thing, Detective Jenkins," I called across the narrow parking lot that separated us. "For instance, I was kidnapped last night, bashed over the head, threatened by both bad guys and, allegedly, good, and dumped out in the street this morning like a bundle of soggy newspapers, yet my last twenty-four hours only turned to shit when I laid my peepers on your ugly mug. Also, everybody here knows you've been waiting to use that 'icing on the cake' line ever since you found out you were coming to a bakery. In fact, I assume you've already used it five times, with similar Vaudevillian flop-sweat results."

I'd deduced the hell out of that one, judging by the sour look on the plainclothes cop's mug.

Jenkins was my nemesis on the force from back in my

cop days. He'd been an asshole then, and his great, innate asshole-ness had only expanded to more epic assholic dimensions over the past decade. He would eventually collapse into a black asshole and drag us all in, a metaphor over which even the NAACP wouldn't picket once they were forced to spend two minutes clawing futilely at Jenkins' assholian event horizon.

Jenkins waved at a uniform standing near the crowd into which I had so unsuccessfully managed to blend that the worst detective on earth had detected me.

"Let him in," the tin badge in the ugly necktie droned.

The uniformed cop dutifully hiked up the yellow tape and I limboed under.

The cocktail party clutch of chatting uniforms outside the entrance parted like the Red Sea before me, and Jenkins led me inside the bakery.

There were three tiny tables near the front windows, each with a pair of attendant little metal chairs that looked like they'd been fashioned from coat hangers. A plump, shell-shocked woman of about sixty sat in one creaking chair, staring blankly out the window. A couple of wet napkins that she'd used as Kleenex were crumpled on the little glass-topped table. There was a fresh, dry napkin clutched in her hand.

"Bakery employee Letta McAllen," Jenkins, the prince of compassion, explained absently as we passed the dame, as if he were a museum tour guide and she were nothing more than an exhibit on grief. "She came back from lunch to find this."

He led me past the glass case in which lived a terrarium of pies, and through a curtained door behind the counter.

The dead guy was lying next to an oven rack just inside

the door. The cops had used a pastry bag to outline the body in frosting, presumably since it was more hilarious than the traditional chalk.

"Shot in the face at close range," Jenkins announced. "Killer used the pillow to muffle the shot."

Jenkins was stupid, but even he wasn't dumb enough to confuse a macaroon with a bed pillow. There was, indeed, an entirely incongruous example of the bedroom accessory in question at the scene of the crime.

The pillow looked like one of the perfectly ordinary Woolworth's variety, but for the burn hole blasted through the middle. It was parked on the deceased bastard's face, thoughtfully covering the gruesome plate of spaghetti and meatballs that was the exploded human head stuffed under-neath it. Tufts of feathers jutted from the opening that had been torn by the fired slug, looking like a miniature choir of razzing avian tongues. More feathers had made it out to the floor. The heavy traffic of cops through the joint as well as the bakery's constantly blowing fan had propelled the feathers to the far edges of the room. They formed a frail, shivering chorus line of white under the stainless-steel tables and sinks.

Jenkins fished a wallet from an evidence bag and held out what I assumed was the dead slob's driver's license. William Grasse. His asse certainly was that, although who had been the lawnmower was an open question. Grasse had been the driver of the van in which I'd spent much of my leisure time the past day. I noted that his license was due to be renewed next month. I couldn't decide if that was ironic. At least there was one less getaway driver in the world for the DMV to send a notice out to.

"Now," Jenkins said, hiking up his belt and jutting out his sunken chest. "I've got to wonder why you showed up here, Banyon. You know the stiff?"

My instinct was to lie. My other instinct was, as always, to sock Jenkins in the nose. As instincts went, the two of them were easily in my personal top five all-time favorites. But prison is hell on pretty boys like me, so Jenkins' deserving conk got a pass. As for lying about knowing Grasse, even though it was technically true, since we hadn't been formally introduced while his partners were beating the shit out of me, there was the pesky matter of my fingerprints all over the back of his van.

"I never made his formal acquaintance," I admitted. "He was, however, the driver of the van in which I was shuttled to and from my kidnapping last night and this morning."

"You were kidnapped?" Jenkins said, cocking a dubious eyebrow.

"I just told you out front not two minutes ago. Do you only listen to the sound of your own voice? It's not necessary, Jenkins. The rest of us never do."

Jenkins, seething, led me through the back of the bakery to an open delivery entrance. Parked outside was the aforementioned Marigold's Bakery van.

The cab doors, side door and rear doors yawned open wide. I could see two more corpses lined up in the back even before we reached the van. Unlike the schmuck in the bakery, these two were relatively unblemished in eternal repose. I couldn't say I was too busted up over the ghastly purple broken jaw of the bastard who'd vowed to kill me.

"Suffocated," Jenkins explained. "Both of them. Forensics team say it could be with the same pillow. My guess is victim *A* inside killed victims *B* and *C*, then got killed himself by an unknown perp, who we *were* calling unsub *D*. Or maybe we should switch those letters around now that you're here, Mr. 'B' for Banyon."

Mr. A for Asshole flashed a superior smirk. He deserved getting it socked off his kisser for using "unsub" unmockingly.

"It's a good thing there weren't more than twenty-six people involved," I said. "Once you ran out of letters and fingers, you'd have your shoes off counting suspects. In the meantime, back on earth, check with a guy who owns a silver Volvo with the vanity plates BABLVR. This deeply compassionate greasy lover of babs will tell you he saw me get tossed out of this very van by these very bastards. You've got security cameras at the intersection of Hanover Street and Frank Zappa Boulevard which may have caught the whole thing. Even if not, these assholes blew through the lights, so they'll be getting an automatic ticket in the mail. Minimally, you've got the headless driver on camera. Maybe all three, since the back doors were open. Next, talk to a waitress named Carol at a greasy spoon called, unironically, The Greasy Spoon over on 122nd. She served me runny eggs and burned toast five minutes after that. Then you can discuss my whereabouts with the driver of the #17 bus. He picked me up on the corner down the street after I left the diner. He'll remember me, since I didn't have exact change so I bribed him with a fifty to let me ride for free."

Jenkins had attempted at the start to take notes, but his pencil ran out of steam halfway through my monologue. "*You,*" he accused. "*You* had a fifty dollar bill?"

His ordinarily completely accurate insulting tone wasn't enough to deter me.

"The bus dropped me off two blocks from work. I went straight there. Mannix can vouch for me."

The dumb flatfoot got a triumphant, aha! look on his mug.

"Right. How stupid do you think I am, Banyon?"

"That's difficult to measure, detective. Every time I think the depth gauges have reached the ocean floor, you inadvertently offer up a soft target like that and I suddenly find a vast new sea trench of brainlessness yawning open before me."

He was still holding his pencil to his pad, and for a moment he considered planting it in my eye socket. Instead he tapped it until the graphite snapped.

"I'm supposed to believe your employee," he said.

"You would if you were smart, which you're not. Mannix would never lie, even to cover for me. But you don't have to ask just him. Myron Wasserbaum, the war criminal dentist down the hall, talked to me for some reason that I pray never recurs. He had an appointment right after, judging from the barn owl shrieks coming from his dental abattoir, so he'll have an exact time for you. The upshot, detective, is that there has not been one unaccounted for minute since these assholes dumped me out of the back of their van during which I would have had time to get clear across town to punch their tickets."

It was an amazingly lucky morning for me, since I generally can't vouch for my own whereabouts, let alone get anybody else to do so. For a change of pace in my rotten life I had an alibi so airtight that it was currently clutching its throat and asphyxiating on the dirty pavement between me and the increasingly frustrated Detective Daniel Jenkins.

The flatfoot let out a stale coffee sigh and reluctantly altered course.

"Why did they kidnap you?" he asked. "Is it connected to some client? You bilking the wife of some deranged husband? What happened, Banyon? You get hubby mad tailing him like a low-rent Sherlock, he snaps and does all this?"

"I didn't have a case or a client last night," I replied which, while a vague non-answer to his five specific, rapid-fire, questions, worked as the literal truth.

"Past case then," Jenkins speculated.

"Possibly," I said. "Someone did bust into my offices last night. I didn't report it because I know how hard you detectives work to avoid protecting and serving. I was afraid I might call at nap time and wake up the whole station."

"Oh, I can get a team over there," Jenkins insisted darkly.

"Make sure they bring a warrant with them, Detective Jenkins," I said. "My files are privileged. I don't need everybody downtown laughing at how bad my business is."

Jenkins was stuck. I had successfully eliminated myself as a suspect, which was a major disappointment to a cop with the worst batting average on the force. Jenkins could watch the first half-hour of a forty year old *Columbo* rerun and still be surprised an hour later when Johnny Cash gets arrested.

No judge in town would grant him a warrant to turn out my office. I was a victim here as well, although with an outcome thus far happier than that of the bastard with the hole through his head inside by a rack of bear claws.

It killed Jenkins to speak his next words. The constipated look on his face was worth the price of admission, and I only wished I had a camera on me to forever immortalize the Kodak moment of a lifetime. I would have hung it on the fridge. I would have made it into a Walgreens calendar. I would have built a mantle over which to hang it. It would have been a merry Christmas card photo for the next hundred years.

I suddenly remember that I was a private investigator

and that as a vital tool of my trade I did, in fact, sometimes lug a camera around with me. Like, fortunately, today.

"If you think of anything," Jenkins said, "give me a call."

The high-pitched squeak from his gritted teeth set dogs barking a mile away.

"Perfect," I said, snapping a sixth and seventh photo, and gliding around him like a less masculine Annie Leibovitz. "I particularly like the way the light bounces off the frothing spittle at the corner of your mouth."

"Get the hell out of here, Banyon."

I intended to. I was actually only taking pictures to get a good shot of the faces of the two dead guys in the van, which mission I had successfully accomplished. Moron Jenkins had, naturally, completely failed to detect that the lens wasn't even pointed at him for ninety percent of the shots and that I was, in fact, shooting photos all over his crime scene, for which negligence he could get busted back down to patrolman.

In the process of taking pictures, I noticed something through my camera lens that I hadn't spotted with my naked eyeballs.

"If you need an eight-by-ten for your desk, let me know," I told the worthless detective as I pocketed my camera. "Just don't mistake it for a mirror and try to shave by it."

I turned to go.

"*Banyon.*"

For an instant I thought the worst cop in the universe had figured out what I'd just done. Maybe holding the camera high over his head to get the best possible angled-down shot of the two stiffs in the back of the van had been a bridge too far.

I turned back to face the flatfoot.

"Don't leave town," Jenkins commanded.

"Although you have no authority or reason to order me to stay put, in the spirit of détente I will definitely consider not doing that," I said. "Unless vacation, business, whim, or another kidnapping comes along."

Leaving the cop and his cheap brown suit to screw up yet another investigation, I headed around the side of the building and back out front.

The one thing I had to hand to Jenkins was that he at least wasn't showing signs of uncharacteristic congeniality. I'd had more of that in the past twenty-four hours than I could deal with from Vincetti the fishmonger and Wasserbaum the dentist. The bastard sands might be shifting underfoot, but Jenkins remained my Gibraltar of assholes.

A fresh blue suit with a badge, who looked all of fourteen, lifted the police tape and allowed me to pass back into the crowd of gawkers. I had never been as young as the kids they were recruiting for the force these days, and seeing yet another infant in uniform was sufficient provocation to my joints to suddenly remind me through various snaps, crackles and pops that I was a middle aged wreck with Rice Krispies cartilage, and that the excitement of the past day had dumped milk all over my antique ass.

Once I was through the crowd, I banked left and headed down the sidewalk in the direction my helpful camera had suggested. I hadn't gone more than eighty feet when I was assaulted by a flash of light so brilliant that it momentarily eclipsed the noonday sun.

The light receded with an audible sucking noise, and in its wake I was unsurprised to find that I'd been joined by an hermaphroditic seraph.

"Hello, Mr. Banyon," the Angel Greg said. "Be not

afraid, for I am Greg." He offered a weak, hopeful smile. "You remember? You and I met last night over on Pike Street? I was the rather tall one with the wings." He shook out his wings to their magnificent length to jog my memory, succeeding only in clotheslining a bicyclist who was peddling by, presumably racing to the Spandex store to pick out another gay-ass Halloween costume. "Sorry," the Angel Greg said to the bicyclist, who'd been yanked hard from his Schwinn seat, slammed to the pavement, and now lay rolling around in agony on the road, hugging a bloody knee to his chest.

"Watch where you unfurl those things, asshole!" the dethroned bicyclist snarled.

The Angel Greg seemed to suddenly notice for the first time since he had been miraculously summoned into being countless eons ago that he had massive wings, and that one of them was currently blocking traffic while the other was preventing pedestrians in both directions from passing us on the sidewalk.

A dame in a Dodge who'd had to screech on her brakes to avoid both a wing and the guy tumbling off his bike was inching forward and laying on her horn.

"Move it! I'm late for Pilates!" she screamed out her half-open window.

The shadow of Angel Greg's great wing shaded her windshield. She was bent practically in half at the waist and was peering up through her steering wheel in an attempt to see under the swooping tips of his primary feathers.

The Angel Greg quickly spooled his wings back in. "Sorry," he told the dame in the car, who yelled a reply richly supplied with four-letter bombs as she stomped on the gas.

So angry was she about the incommoding wing that

she forgot about the battered bastard bike rider in the road. She swerved like a maniac and came within an inch of not flattening him. The biker had been spared, but she did manage to crush his bike into a ten-speed boomerang before she raced off down the road.

The traffic that had stalled behind her resumed, more careful than had been the Jazzercise dame to avoid both bike and bicyclist.

"Ohhhh," the bicyclist moaned as he hauled his ass to the curb.

"Oh, should I—" the Angel Greg began. He glanced around nervously from the flowing traffic to the disinterested pedestrians who were no longer impeded by his other wing. "You'll be all right," he assured the bike rider. "Go in peace, and all that."

He took my arm and quickly led me down the sidewalk, relying on the appearance of a mythical good Samaritan in this hellhole of a city to sort out the problem of the injured and abandoned bicyclist on the side of the road.

At least this time Greg hadn't brought his multitude with him. As we walked, two more angels popped into existence behind us. His entourage today consisted only of the angel with the parchment scroll and the Louis Armstrong wannabe with the golden trumpet tucked up under the armpit of his Clorox-white bathrobe.

"Bit of a mess, that," the Angel Greg said. "As I was saying, we met last night."

"Yeah, I remember," I said. "As much as I wish that the SOBs who bashed me on the head two seconds after you flapped away had knocked the memory of you out of my hippocampus."

"Yes. Tsk-tsk. I saw. It looked terribly painful. Is that the word? 'Painful?'"

I stopped dead. "Thanks for the intervention. It does

the heart good to know that ordinary citizens such as yourself don't just stand by and let somebody get their head caved in by maniacs."

"I can't get directly involved in that way," the Angel Greg said. He glanced nervously at the bicyclist down the street. "I'm…that is, *we're*…that is, my heavenly host and I…we aren't that kind of angel. *Angels.* I thought I told you, direct intervention in human affairs is more or less the domain of guardian angels. Oh, and archangels, of course. Hoo, golly! You don't want to get on the bad side of one of *those* fellas."

I was not interested in angelology or the hierarchical urinating contest that the different classes of flapping bastards engaged in, so long as I wasn't standing underneath them without an umbrella when they did it.

"Have you been following me since last night?" I asked.

(If so, it was a good thing I hadn't bumped into Invictus in my office that morning, or he'd be facing his own personal Apocalypse now.)

"No, no," Greg promised, happy that I had suddenly resumed walking away from the bicyclist, who had hauled his boomeranged bike to the sidewalk and was now on his cell phone. "I had just departed when I heard the noise of that horseless chariot stopping. I want to say it's a 'wan?' A 'van?' Something with an 'an.' Anyway, it really is ingenious what you people have done over the eons with your wheel invention. I mean, coating them with rubber from trees? I never would have come up with that in a million years. It took me my first million just to get my VCR to stop blinking twelve o'clock. Anyway, I heard the noise and I looked back down and saw them throwing you into the chariot with the cake painted on the side. If I'm not mistaken, it's the same one back there behind that building with all the people out front, isn't it?"

He tipped his halo in the direction of Marigold's Bakery.

I nodded that it was, in fact, the same goddamn bakery chariot.

"Ah. Very sad about those men," Greg said. "But that's free will for you."

"If you get a vote in where they get sent, I know where I want them to go."

"Well, all of that is determined entirely absent us, of course," the Angel Greg said. He was suddenly interested in his own feet. "Oh, my, this sidewalk is warm, isn't it?"

He glanced back to his equally barefoot companions, who remained stone-faced.

"Whatever you want, can we get on with it?" I asked. "My kidneys have a long, demanding evening of turning wine into water ahead of them."

"I want to *hire* you, Mr. Banyon," the Angel Greg said. "It's just, well, we've had no luck finding Invictus on our own, and that *is* what you do, isn't it?"

"Why didn't you say so?" I asked. "No."

He and his pals continued dogging me down the sidewalk.

"We can't offer you money, exactly," the winged bastard insisted, torpedoing completely any infinitesimally slight shot he might still have had at employing me. "You humans do still use money? I'm right about that, right?"

"Only if we want to drink to excess, which all sensible humans do. Also eat, have roofs over our heads, and not have to stitch together leaves for underwear."

"Well, as I say, I can't offer money, but I can offer — oh, my isn't this sidewalk hot?" He was lifting each foot in turn. Even though his bright red soles were a mile from his mouth, he tried with a few sorry breaths to blow out the candles on the birthday cake. "Oh, dear. Where was I? Oh, yes. What I *can* offer is..."

The Angel Greg waved one robed arm and we were suddenly no longer on the sidewalk half-a-block from Marigold's Bakery.

We didn't transport in a flash. There wasn't any kind of warning whatsoever. A nice bright flash of light would have been nice. Or maybe a crack of thunder. Or even a referee whistle or any other goddamn sign that my two shoes were going to vanish from the sidewalk and that they, with me still stuffed down inside them, were going to be abruptly standing at what at first glance appeared to be the top of the world.

Wind buffeted my middle aged carcass. The first terrifying gust nearly flung me to my untimely, long overdue death. In a blind panic I somehow managed to grab onto a buttress with both sweaty hands and stay my execution. It was while I was clutching the granite in a desperate bear hug that I realized I was seeing close-up something I had heretofore only observed from afar. The lunatic angel had transported me against my will to the topmost spire of St. Regent's Drive-Thru Cathedral.

Most of the old lights that illuminated the steeple were burned out. Crows who, unlike me, didn't suffer from acrophobia had built nests behind the rusted fixtures. It was too bad for them that they weren't scared of heights, since something had apparently eaten them and tossed their bones and wet black feathers back into their nests. In addition to the crow remains, there appeared to be the skeletons of every rat and cat that had made the mistake of taking up residence in the neighborhood far below.

Some of the avian ossuaries were doubling as kitchen cupboards. Tucked in with the animal skeletons were several takeout food containers filled with maggots and, even more revolting, a half-dozen unopened bottles of Mountain Dew.

The Angel Greg and his two angelic companions weren't paying attention to the nests, nor did they see the figure I'd just spied through the wide-open portals built into the arching sides of the spire. The very large shape hidden away inside the highest attic in the church opened its very large, yellow eyes and scurried back into the shadows from his bed of pigeon shit. Over the howling wind — which hadn't even been a light breeze in the dead calm down on terra firma — I heard the squeaking hinges and thud of a trapdoor opening and closing.

The Angel Greg was pretty much as infuriatingly calm as I goddamn wasn't, which I imagined came from the fact that if he was swept off the steeple he could fly off into a glorious sunset while I was being prosecuted to the full extent of the law of gravity in the parking lot a million miles straight down. Greg and his two pals stared out at the gleaming office buildings and crumbling tenements laid out before them.

The angel held out a delicate hand to encompass the city. "I have no money, but I *can* offer you all of this," Angel Greg said dramatically.

"Ah, well, yes, good," I said, as I continued to grip for dear life to my buttress new best friend. "We could have handled this down on the sidewalk, actually. Which, if memory serves, I did when I told you goddamn 'no.' As for offering me the city as payment, I don't want it. It's used. I like that new city smell. I only accept recently constructed cities, towns or villages — Tudor or newer — in payment for services rendered. Or goddamn cash, which you people don't have."

A gust of wind kicked me in the gut and I felt myself

being lifted off my feet like a Kleenex caught in an updraft. No one was more surprised than me when I managed to wrestle the forces of nature to a standstill. I slammed my feet back to the ledge on which I was precariously perched. It became a hell of a lot more precarious when half the bricks under my feet gave way. Eternity yawned open beneath me, my stomach did a jellyfish belly-flop in my abdomen, and I nearly plunged twenty thousand feet to my death.

I somehow managed to swing my buffeted corpse around the buttress as if the pair of us were the central characters in some Elizabethan PBS period drama, with me cast in the role of the pallid, limey dame, which was more apt a description than I'd have liked since all the blood had drained from my face, as well as — as far as my suddenly woozy head and tingling legs could tell — from the rest of my entire body. Fortunately, my buttress dance partner took the lead, and when I swung desperately around to its other side, my Florsheims landed on a row of brick that didn't surrender to my dainty touch.

I glanced down to see the bricks I'd busted loose sliding down a tile roof about three stories down. They zipped out into open air one at a time and vanished down the infinitely long side of the cathedral. Seconds later rose the shriek of a car alarm.

"If that's the archbishop's Yugo, I hope your insurance is paid up," I said. "In the meantime, no still means no. So unless you plan on leaving me up here, I'd appreciate it if you put me the hell back where you found me."

The Angel Greg tore his eyes away from the panoramic view. I could see the poor slob's worried gears turning inside his head.

"Well, you probably know that I couldn't actually *give* you the city," he said. "That's true. But I — that is we

— could move things around a little. Small things add up over time. You could be mayor. That's a thing, right? Mayor? Not right away. These things take time. But in ten years. Fifteen at most. The world is yours."

"I don't want it. I don't like it. Take me back."

"But why?"

I risked loosening my grip so that I could count off the whys on my fingers.

"For one thing, there's the fact that you left me to possibly be killed by three lunatics who were themselves murdered ten hours later."

"Again, free will—" the Angel Greg began.

"For another," I interrupted, "I don't like being spied on day and night."

"Oh, but I told you we weren't watching you all this time," he insisted. "After we left you we directed our beatific gaze on Mr. Pinder's apartment all night from the fire escape across the street. We thought Invictus might be with him again, but Mr. Pinder didn't show. We only fixed celestial eyes on your office this morning after we wasted the whole night. Honestly, Mr. Banyon, we only beheld you getting off the bus down the street from where you work about an hour ago."

"I recognized your hat," volunteered the angel with the trumpet, whose voice was less the song sung at the birth of the universe than it was a 1940s B-movie thug.

The Angel Greg beamed and nodded and pointed at empyrean Chuck Mangione, as if one of his staff being able to make out my fedora from the troposphere was some kind of significant game changer in my decision not to take him on as a client.

"Still no," I said. "Just exercising my free will like those assholes you allowed to beat me senseless and cart me away. By the way, at least one of them was planning to kill me, so thanks for that as well. And if you need another reason why I'll never take you on as a client in a billion years, *this* is goddamn it."

I nodded around to the decaying spire on which the four of us were impossibly parked. The Angel Greg finally got the message.

This time he didn't even wave an arm. For all I could tell, he didn't bat an eye. One moment I was one loose brick away from doing a high dive into the shallow end of an empty swimming pool, the next we were back at the exact spot on the sidewalk from which we'd departed, halfway down the block from Marigold's Bakery.

"I really rather thought you'd say yes, Mr. Banyon," the Angel Greg said, his slightly effeminate voice laced with disappointment.

"I couldn't be happier to break your heart. In the meantime, I'm delighted to report that you have another problem."

He was freshly confused as he followed my nod back down the street.

A police cruiser was parked at the side of the road. A uniformed cop was talking to the injured bicyclist. The bike rider kicked at the wobbly front tire of his U-shaped bike and pointed in the direction Pilates Lady had gone, waving his hands over his head as he explained. When he turned and aimed a finger directly at the Angel Greg, the bastard in the halo suddenly remembered he had a pressing appointment on the other side of the Horsehead Nebula.

"Ahhh, well," Greg said, turning abruptly from the uniformed cop. "Thank you all the same, Mr. Banyon. I'll just…that is, we— *Goodbye.*"

He and his two pals were there one instant and gone the next, like Paul Lynde vanishing from Samantha Stevens' living room but without the benefit of a piped-in laugh track to let me know just how hilarious their abrupt departure was.

I caught sight of a few incredibly bright somethings floating down to the pavement.

A handful of feathers had become detached when the angels disappeared. They were like glass reflecting midday sun. The glow came off the feathers themselves, more brilliant than the sunlight. The feathers floated down to the pavement and were blown away like autumn leaves by the wind shed from passing cars.

Down the road, the cop nudged his hat visor back with the tips of his fingers and offered the bicyclist a "whaddaya expect me to do about it?" shrug.

I figured I'd better get out of there before they started playing pin the wings on the P.I. Angels, I was quickly discovering, were almost as big a pain in the ass as flesh and blood clients. When it came to clients I already had a strict no ghosts, no gods policy. I was a strand of angel hair away from amending that to include monotheistic messengers.

I hustled away from cop and bicyclist, off for the destination I'd been aimed at before the Angel Greg and his posse manifested their sorry asses unto me.

8

I'd gotten a clear view through my camera lens from the small parking lot behind Marigold's Bakery. The distant sign was neatly framed between a pair of nearby brick buildings. It was a given that the cops on the scene of the triple homicide hadn't noticed it. Not that I'm the world's greatest goddamn sleuth, it was just that their investigation was preordained to fail the minute Detective Daniel Jenkins was put on the case.

I'd never grow broke betting against Jenkins. I rounded the corner and saw not a single cruiser parked in the big lot in front of the anchor store that took up half the corner mall. The sign I'd seen from Marigold's Bakery's back lot bellowed down at me in huge block letters: **Salome and Sam's Mattress Emporium**.

If Jenkins had seen the sign he'd have dismissed it. It wouldn't have occurred to the moron flatfoot what traditionally went along with mattresses (although if my marriage was any indication, the answer to what goes hand-in-hand with a mattress is "betrayal," so maybe I could cut Jenkins a little slack in this one instance).

A sign in the window of the mattress door hollered: *Yes! We Sell Sleep-Tite Pillows! Sleep Your Cares Away With Sleep-Tite!*

I looked both ways and, satisfied I wouldn't get knocked on my ass by an incautiously unfurled angelic appendage, hustled across the busy street to see if I couldn't scrounge up the purchase of a murder weapon and, with luck, a triple murderer.

I'm not in the habit of doing the work of the police for them.

Check that. I am *constantly* doing the work of the police for them. Most of the time I've already solved the case when the boys in blue finally come plodding over the hill like the exhausted cavalry on half-dead nags that are two weeks past their sell-by date to the glue factory. And the thanks I get, naturally, is an asshole like Jenkins sticking me in jail or trying to get my P.I. license yanked for interfering in a police investigation. Three times in the previous ten years I'd ended up before the licensing board where I was forced to explain, in the sweetest possible way, that I can't help it if the cops are shit at their jobs. Each time the board sided with me which, *naturellement*, has resulted in a pile of heart-shaped chocolate boxes on my doorstep and sloppy wet air kisses blown in the direction of yours truly's derriere every February 14 from the direction of police HQ.

Truth is an absolute defense, and Detective Daniel Jenkins truly was the absolute worst representative of a profession which, to the dismay of any taxpaying citizen relying on him to crack the big case, he had audaciously selected.

Not that I had the whole affair figured out. It might not be Charles Pinder who'd murdered the three stiffs back at the bakery, but it was at least reasonable to suspect my ringleader kidnapper was involved in some way. And a mattress store that also sold pillows that was right around the corner from the bakery where two dead bastards had been suffocated under a pillow and where a third had gotten a face full of silenced lead through, again, a goddamn pillow seemed a pretty logical stop to the Nancy Drew in me.

I wasn't sure exactly where my deceased kidnappers had brought me (although I had some ideas on where I might start looking). But if the goose-down murder weapon had been purchased at Salome and Sam's Mattress Emporium, a casual comment by Pinder to a store clerk while the sale was being rung up or a second address that wasn't his apartment could deliver me the missing SOB's location within the hour.

The front door of the mattress store was open wide on the warm afternoon. I noted when I entered that the main storeroom floor had that new mattress smell, which was to say that it stunk like neither failing bladders nor marriages.

Back when I was on the force, I worked a case that started out as a simple board of health issue. Neighbors were complaining about a stink coming from the house next door. The entire *Better Homes and Gardens* editorial board would have committed ritual seppuku if they'd laid eyes on the dump. Junk all over the front yard. A cat sitting on a rotted fiddle, a rusted water tank, an old Ford up on blocks, one of those magic beanstalks that looked like it was growing clear up to Giant Land, Glad bags loaded with rotting garbage dating back to the bicentennial. You couldn't even see the driveway from all the weeds growing up through the cracks in the ancient asphalt.

The house was in even worse shape than the yard. The front porch had collapsed. Judging from the bricks scattered over the remains, it looked like it had been taken out by the missing chimney. Santa would have no problem shinnying down the gaping hole in the shingles, assuming he didn't mind getting mugged by raccoons when he exited the hearth. For some reason there was old dinnerware scattered around the roof, as if a picnic in the park had gotten hit by a tornado. It looked like the dishes were running away with the spoons, or had at least climbed out a window to yell an SOS to any Coast Guard gravy boats that might be sailing by.

The dump was going to be condemned. Hell, it was already halfway to tearing itself down. The city health department just needed me and my partner present to keep the peace while they served the eviction.

The owner was a male Caucasian. At least I guessed that's what he was under all that dirt. The guy was filthier than a magazine rack at dirty book shop. When we entered through the kitchen door, he was in the middle of constructing a huge pie out of stitched-together Pillsbury crusts and two dozen flapping blackbirds he'd caught in the backyard. Bastard claimed "four and twenty pie" was an old family recipe. "Just like mother used to make," he told us. Yeah, the dame hadn't screwed up junior one bit.

My partner and I both saw that the guy was acting hinky, so we poked around. (*Con* his *permiso*, for any legal-scholar ACLU bastards looking to put your shitty law practice on the map.) Why the genius let us search the dump, I'll never know.

The guy slept on the ratty living room couch, which you could barely see over the mountains of dirty birdhouses, stacks of corrugated boxes and dozens of busted lawnmower engines. There were four bedrooms. One bed in each. Each bed was piled with mattresses, stacked one on top of the other, from floor to ceiling. Wedged between the topmost mattress and the ceiling, pinning the stacks in place and keeping them from so much as wobbling, were cases of Safeway canned peas.

I thought my marriage and *Crocodile Dundee II* stunk, but the smell coming from those bedrooms surpassed the latter and nearly gave the former a run for its alimony.

We found the deceased dames in various stages of decomposition at the bottoms of each of the four stacks of mattresses. Sick bastard had dressed each one of them in a pink princess Halloween costume. A real twisted SOB, this psycho. After we arrested him, we swept through the place and found hundreds of old photos of the maniac as a kid decked out in the same homemade pink Lady Di number. Just like mother used to make.

The *Gazette* headline the next day screamed "**Princesses and the Peas!**" The article started, "Once upon a mattress…" Nothing shocks anybody anymore. Four dames dead under stacks of Sealys and Libby's registers as barely a blip on the radar. John Q. Public doesn't take serial killers seriously any longer, thank you very much Jonathan Demme, fava beans and the CBS primetime shit-tacular *CSI Hooterville* lineup.

Ever since that case I've had to concentrate to keep from breaking out in a cold sweat whenever I'm surrounded by mattresses. Thanks to my largely unsuccessful love life, it usually registers in negative digits on my personal concern-o-meter. Still, I kept a wary eye out for cans of peas as I scoped out the merchandise in Salome and Sam's.

"Can I help you, sir?" a pouncing salesman in a dress shirt and tie, sans suit jacket, inquired the instant I stepped over the threshold.

I flashed my business card too fast for him to see that it was a worn out scrap of yellowed cardboard and not a tin police badge.

"I want to question your staff about a customer who might have been in here earlier today," I said in my best Joe Friday voice.

He was clearly relieved that I wasn't a customer. He let his phony smile droop, his weary shoulders sank, and he exhaled exhaustion along with the gaseous remains of a rancid tuna fish sandwich.

"*One* guy?" he snorted. "Good luck. We had about a million customers today. It was a madhouse in here until about an hour ago."

He pointed at a promotional standee at the end of a nearby aisle. On it, a cardboard jerk in a dark blue suit was holding a cardboard pillow. Inside a cardboard dialogue balloon, the sallow-eyed cardboard man hollered in blue Magic Marker: "*Today only! Meet Mr. M. Sandan!*"

The sales clerk offered a knowing, simultaneous roll of bloodshot eyes and sagging shoulders. Clearly I was supposed to know who the bastard in the life-size photo was, and why his presence today was explanation for why the store had been swamped.

"Just for fun," I said, "let's pretend that I haven't got a goddamn clue who this Sandan is, and you just tell me."

The clerk looked back and forth from the standee to me, apparently engaging in a telepathic tête-à-tête with the motionless cardboard cutout. When his gaze finally settled fully on me, it was evident that he had erroneously concluded that between the two of us, I was the one who was the maniac.

"*M. Sandan,*" the clerk said. "*The* M. Sandan?" He very slowly stressed the name, as if enunciation and repetition would clear up my ignorance.

"Let me save you a little time," I said. "You can say

that name in slow motion, you can holler it through a bullhorn or get a biplane to skywrite it over my head, you can buy a star, name it 'M. Sandan,' and give it to me for Christmas, you can tattoo it on my forehead when I'm passed out drunk (which, incidentally, I hope to be before nightfall, and with a blood alcohol level high enough to sterilize the dirtiest tattoo parlor needle) and I still wouldn't have a clue who the hell that sunken-eyed bastard is."

The clerk was evidently deeply offended that I didn't know his cardboard pal, but was too tired from his busy morning at the mattress casa to punch me in the throat.

"M. Sandan is only the *inventor* of the Sleep-Tite Pillow," he said, with the same kind of thin patience you get from sports-loving assholes when you inform them that you don't give two shits about the batting order of the 1942 Schenectady Hedgehogs.

Clearly his friends, family or clergyman had never told him where manufacturers of cloth bags stuffed with polyester rate in the grand scheme of human existence. As usual, it was up to unremunerated me to explain the facts of life.

"Okay," I said. I held my hand high in the air. "Up here are the Pyramids and penicillin. Also planes, indoor plumbing and the A-bomb. In here," I said, waving my hand up and down in the wide area between the high of the Wright Brothers and a low of roughly a foot off the floor, "is TV, the internal combustion engine and home computers." I brought my palm down to an inch off the floor. "Down here is the Earl of Sandwich and the first guy to stuff hay inside a small rag sack before bedtime. I admit, it's nice to know enough to put the bologna between two slices of bread and not vice versa when you're sprawled drunk on the couch with your head on a throw pillow while watching a sixty year old rerun of

The Untouchables, but neither sandwiches nor pillows rate as so much as a blip on the scale of human invention when measured against, say, Apollo 11. And this Sandan hero of yours didn't even invent the pillow, he only found a way to make suckers pay more money for one. Kudos to him for that — fools need to be parted from their money with relentless ruthlessness, or else they might accidentally blow it on food, clothing or shelter — but some guy with a sewing machine and a pile of foam isn't the goddamn wizard of Menlo Park."

By the time I was done, the sales clerk was as frosty as my last date when I informed her that I found her endless stories about the Machiavellian machinations at the insurance company where she worked more boring than a 1988 Toshiba VCR instruction manual.

"Well, everyone is entitled to his opinion, *sir*," the clerk sniffed. "But a million satisfied customers can't be wrong. Maybe you should buy one. Sleep-Tites are famous for improving sour dispositions. I only wish *I* could use one, but I'm allergic. When I tried one, I woke up sneezing with my eyes so itchy I wanted to tear them out. But it was the best ten minutes of sleep I ever had."

Some cultists are happier not being deprogrammed.

I gave the Tom Cruise of asshole mattress salesmen a description of Charles Pinder. For the hell of it, I described William Grasse, the dead van driver. Both faces and names came up empty. Same with the other staff he collected for me to question.

Pretty much all the employees of Salome and Sam's Mattress Emporium were still coming down off the high of meeting the celebrity pillow pitchman who'd been hawking his product and autographing register receipts all morning.

I'd only ever seen Salome and Sam, the owners of

the eponymous dump, on TV. Contrary to what their names indicated, he was the she and she was the he. Salome was Raphael Salome, and his wife and partner was Samantha Salome.

I had no idea what the two elderly monsters looked like in the mattress Dark Ages a thousand years before, back when the first mattress they sold was a pile of mouse-filled straw and a good night's sleep meant dying of plague before breakfast.

Salome and Sam were in their eighties, overweight, and desperately unattractive. In a dirty, post-menopausal trick, what was left of their hormones had reconfigured their lumpish bodies so as to trap them in a hermaphroditic limbo in which neither of them was fully man nor woman, the upshot of which was that they were both utterly repulsive to each sex. However, not, apparently, to one another.

After interviewing the rest of the staff I had been invited up to the office of the owners, which offered a panoramic view of the store's showroom. The pair of them sat with knees touching on a brand new faux leather couch that squeaked beneath their gigantic asses as if it was stuffed with rabbits. All four of their hands were piled up like a hero sandwich in which the main ingredients were arthritis and liver spots.

They were the kind of people who opened their mouths far too wide when they talked, as if they were angry at air and wanted to chew as much of it to death as possible.

"It was a *huge* coup getting Mr. Sandan," the ugly husband confided to me, as if he'd managed to score a guest appearance by the last surviving Beatle that wasn't Ringo. He nodded across the room where a second standee stood in the corner.

Sandan's features looked like he might be Middle Eastern, which matched his exotic, Arab-sounding name. I assumed he wasn't, however, since he was still holding a pillow in his hand and not a smoking cartoon bomb.

"All the other mattress stores in town wanted him first," the ugly wife agreed. They both seemed exhausted. She more than he. She used the back of one hand to cover a yawn so massive the highway department should have surrounded it with orange cones.

"But *we* got him, didn't we, sweetikins?" the ugly, weary mattress dealer said. He let loose a yawn that surpassed hers in size and duration.

"I can see I'm boring you," I said. "And the two of you are, quite frankly, nauseating me. One more time: *Charles Pinder*." It was the second time I'd mentioned my bastard kidnapper's name since they'd welcomed me into their shared office.

"Ah, yes," Raphael Salome said.

He disengaged his hands from his wife's and proceeded to struggled against the sofa and gravity, winning a surprising upset victory against both. Once he managed to haul his enormous ass to its feet, he waddled over to a big mahogany desk and crash-landed in the creaking seat behind it.

"P-I-N-D-E-R?" he asked, hunting and pecking the letters on his keyboard. I gave him a nod, and he struck "enter." "I have a dozen Pinders in the system. 'Charles,' you said? Here's one. We sold a mattress and box spring set to Pinder, Charles six years ago. No wonder the staff didn't know him. No one down on the floor has been here that long. That's the professional mattress game. Chews them up and spits them out."

He gave me an address, which I jotted down in my brain since I'd neglected to bring anything with which or on which to write. I did, however, turn up a hip flask while frisking my trench coat, a hit from which I felt I'd earned for being forced to bear witness to the pair of octogenarian mattress vendors' horrifying display of affection.

The two of them were back happily holding hands and yawning on the couch as I left the room. There was not enough booze in my pockets to erase the image when they started making out before I could yank the door shut. I felt bad for the cardboard standee that was trapped inside bearing terrible mute witness, but I wasn't about to venture back in to scribble a Magic Marker blindfold on Sandan the pillow king.

The original sales clerk was still hanging around by the door on my way out.

"I'm sorry, but you missed him," he was announcing with great sympathy to a young couple, who were themselves holding hands but with nowhere near the savage unattractiveness of the brace of mattress hawkers currently going at it in the room above all our heads which, for the sake of maintaining a vomit-free showroom, had been wisely constructed with one-way glass pointed 100% in the right direction.

The salesman and the two customers were standing in a respectful semicircle around the standee of Mr. M. Sandan, who was apparently a huge name in pillows that had somehow failed entirely to be noticed by me. I didn't care how goddamn famous he was, the bastard still looked like a vulture in a cardboard suit.

I had to sneak silently around the three of them, lest the salesman suddenly emerge from his trance, remember that he was a retail asshole working on commission, and rally the rest of the staff to tackle an escaping mark. The last thing I needed was somebody forcing a queen size mattress down my credit card's throat. But the three of them — clerk and customers — failed to break eye contact with the cardboard photograph.

They were still paying unsettling homage to the standee as I slipped through the open front doors and back out into the warm afternoon.

9

I called Mannix from a pay phone.

The address the randy antediluvian mattress pushers had given me turned out, unsurprisingly, to be Charles Pinder's apartment.

"I didn't find anything when I was there, Mr. Crag," the elf said.

"That's why I get paid big bucks to go through people's rubbish barrels," I told him. "My keen eye might see something the average elf's missed. Speaking of money, did you take care of that ten grand?"

"It's in the bank," Mannix replied. "But it wasn't ten thousand, it came to nine thousand, nine hundred and twenty-five dollars and forty-five cents."

"Twenty went in my wallet, fifty for a bus ride, four-fifty for eggs, and a nickel tip to the waitress for giving me the stink eye when I sweetened my orange juice from my flask. If I wanted to be judged, sentenced and executed over breakfast I'd have stayed married. Have you heard anything from our client?"

"No, sir."

"If you do, tell him to steer clear of Pinder's place. The joint is hot as hell, which is me being delightfully ironic. The creepy, eunuch Angel Greg and his host of heavenly voyeurs are keeping tabs on the joint. In the meantime, I need you to run down a name for me. William Grasse. Spelled like what dogs shit on at the park, but with an E on the end. Grasse is one of the bastards who kidnapped me last night. He's dead this morning, so somebody up there likes him less than me. Rah-rah, team. See if you can find out anything about him, especially anything that connects him to Pinder."

The phone booth was suddenly rattling apart at the seams and I noted through the dirty glass a trailer truck driving by in the heavy afternoon traffic. Plastered hugely on the side was the same billboard with the snoozing dame I'd seen the previous night. She was still enjoying the best night's sleep of her life which, from billboard to truck, had thus far lasted a minimum of eleven hours, courtesy the Sleep-Tite Pillow jammed under her head.

A drunk, four-legged assistant district attorney was chasing the noise behind the truck, alternately barking and hollering and basically enjoying the inebriated hell out of a sunny afternoon out of court.

"It truly is a dog's life, Mannix," I grumbled. "Even the mutts are loaded before me today. Did Invictus mention where or if Pinder works?"

It was a question I hadn't asked Invictus since I hadn't intended to take his case. I had forgotten to ask Mannix that morning since I was still recovering from being kidnapped and being paid, the latter being the greater of the two shocks.

"He told me the naughty man used to work at the aquarium until they sold all the fish to Long John Silver's. He hasn't worked in almost two years."

"Okay. No catching him at that job."

"Wouldn't Mr. Invictus have thought to look there?"
"I wouldn't make any assumptions about these angels,
Mannix. They have the innocence of babies and are just
as likely to crawl around sticking their fingers in all the
outlets. Besides, it's possible Pinder could have gotten
himself transferred if he worked for a company that
had another location. Write that down if you're ever
going to play detective again. In the meantime, if you
need me I'll be checking out Pinder's place."

"Be careful there, Mr. Crag."

"I am careful everywhere, Mannix. I want to risk
neither life nor limb. Actually, the former isn't so important to me, but I'm stuck with it for the time being,
which makes the latter vitally important for walking
me to bars and lifting drinks."

"Please, Mr. Crag, I mean it," Mannix insisted. "I
thought I heard something funny there. It sounded like
it was moving around in the walls. When I worked at
the North Pole I didn't see Mr. Santa much, but there
was one time when he came down the chimney in the
elf quarters. He never visited there before, at least not
when I was there. The pipe was very narrow, but he
uses Christmas magic. Before he appeared I heard a
funny, squishy noise and then he was suddenly in the
room. I heard something like that in the apartment of
the mean man who had you kidnapped. Then all those
angels showed up and started asking about Mr. Invictus.
I didn't hear the noise anymore over the trumpet."

"It was probably the angels," I said. "They can't
find Invictus on their own, so they're hiding behind the
nearest molecule just waiting to pounce."

"Maybe," Mannix said. "Just, please, be careful,
Mr. Crag."

"I will, or I'll die trying," I promised.

I caught a glint of something bright in the sky, and I ducked down to look out the windows of the booth. A low flying 747 had just taken off from the airport at the edge of town. Sunlight flashed off its silver wings as it slowly climbed into the blue sky.

"You know something, Mannix? Why don't you shutter up the office for now and move HQ to your place? I don't like the way these angels are spying on me, and I don't want them moving over to you. Whatever you do, don't leave a note for Doris. If by some bizarre fluke she somehow stumbles in to work, the Angel Greg and his host can go nuts trailing her from one wig manufacturer to the next. I'll check back in later."

I hung up the phone and departed the upright glass AT&T coffin.

The D.A. dog was tearing back up the street, this time in barking pursuit of a shitbox car with a Domino's Pizza delivery sign attached to the roof.

"Oh, hey, Banyon," the mongrel D.A. panted as he raced by.

The canine district attorney nearly got flattened by a dozen cars on the busy street, paused at the corner of an intersection to hike his leg on a fire hydrant, gobbled up some blob of garbage somebody heaved at him from a speeding minivan, then booked it like a maniac after a Best Buy Geek Squad car that made the mistake of, in the drunken mutt's bleary, black-and-white eyes, resembling either a shot of Jim Beam or a Milk-Bone.

I noted that if the various cars had been secretaries, all of his behavior would be exactly like that of every other sloppy inebriate law school graduate, and for the first time all day I felt a little better knowing there was at least one goddamn profession out there worse than the one I'd idiotically selected for myself.

I headed off in the direction in which the D.A. stray had disappeared, in search of a subway seat with my weary ass's name on it.

10

Charles Pinder's apartment building was in a nicer part of town than my own, which was damning the armpit neighborhood in which the slouching, six story dump rotted with praise too faint to see even under an electron microscope.

It had one of those old wire cage elevators that I thought only existed in James Bond or Blake Edwards 1960s European shithole buildings. I didn't enjoy my ride up to the fourth floor by trading sexy quips with Ursula Andress or Elke Sommer but, rather, by being repeatedly stabbed in the gut by a loose wire that jutted like an angry unicorn horn from the busted corner of the enormous cheap plastic purse of an old bat who smelled like mothballs and looked like Ed Asner in drag.

We got off at the same floor. The wheels of the two-wheeled grocery cart she was schlepping along behind her got stuck on the way out. I gallantly refused to help her in her struggle since she looked like she could use the exercise.

I made a beeline for Pinder's apartment door and listened with my ear to the wood. It was hard to hear at first, but once the hag stopped bouncing her shopping cart around like a mechanical bull full of Metamucil, I managed to not hear anything inside.

I tested the knob. Locked.

"You want to get in there?" a wrinkled prune of a voice called from down the hall.

The old lady had wheeled her cart to what I presumed was her apartment, since she was standing before a closed door and had produced a key ring loaded down with several billion keys. She performed the major miracle of locating the correct one from the maddening, jangling crowd and jammed it in her lock, shoving open her door.

"I was just going to break in," I informed her. "I assume that nobody in this crummy neighborhood has a problem with that. If you do, be forewarned that the average police response time is about two hours, which means I'll be long gone and they'll be pestering you to identify my blurry cataract features during *Judge Judy*."

"Just hold on," she said, releasing a prolonged, impatient sigh that nobody but she had forced out of her.

One wheel of her cart squeaked as she bounced it into her apartment. She reemerged a moment later without her cart but still clutching her massive ring of keys.

"I've had it with him," she announced as she wobbled up the worn hallway carpet. "We all have. Knocking on our doors all the time, passing out them nihilist pamphlets. I tell him all the time, I say, 'I'm a Zurvanist.' Nonpracticing, but that's none of his bee's wax. I swear, he's worse than them Jehovah's Witnesses my daddy chased up that tree in the front yard and set fire to when I was a little girl. Here. Get out of the way."

She had produced another key and a second miracle in a row, since it managed to fit the lock of Pinder's apartment.

I figured this was "Mrs. Edna," the dame who'd let Mannix into Pinder's place the previous day, a deduction confirmed in the next instant by the old bat herself.

"I let an elf in here yesterday," Edna said. "You with him?"

She seemed lonely and wanted to talk. I wasn't and didn't.

"No," I said.

"Hmph," she said. "Them angels showing up yesterday finished Pinder off for me," she concluded as she shoved the door open. "Then my place gets busted into when I'm bringing my pennies to the bank. It's sure been a week around here, let me tell you."

Edna followed me into Pinder's apartment, creating a series of hilarious fart jokes along the way.

It was hot inside, and stuffy. All the windows that I could see from the front hall were buttoned up tight on the warm day. Pinder had painted the panes black.

I stuck my head back out into the hallway. The window at the near end of the hall offered an unobstructed view of the fire escape on the building across the street. The Angel Greg would have had a clear shot at Pinder's front door if my bastard kidnapper had returned home, his MIA guardian angel in tow. For all I knew, he and his buddies with the scroll and horn were lurking there now. Just in case, I gave the fire escape the sign of the cross with my middle finger before I ducked back inside Pinder's place.

Back inside the apartment, I flicked the switch next to the door. The lights stayed dead. By this point, the old bat had settled into a living room chair.

"Electric got cut off," she explained. "Pinder's been missing for ages. Before that he was only here off and on for that last month. Don't know why he painted all the windows. It's like he was hiding from something. I asked, but he claimed he wasn't hiding from nothing. What he actually said was, 'There is nothing from which I am hiding because what I am hiding from doesn't exist.' Or some falderal like that. More of his horse hockey, pardon my French. I'm supposed to get what the nut means by that?"

"Don't let me keep you," I said. "You must have a lot of phone calls to make to equally ancient old bags who similarly stink of mothballs to remind each other that things were better back in the days when everybody you knew was dying of influenza."

"No, I'm good. You a cop?"

I didn't feel I owed her any kind of answer at all since she'd just obviated the need for me to break and enter. I left her alone to heavily breathe the thick air and dust of the living room. I wandered deeper into Pinder's apartment.

I wasn't sure what I was looking for, but when you're a P.I. that's the case half the time.

Frankly, I still had hope that, as cases went, this wouldn't be too hard. Invictus wanted me to find Charles Pinder. For his part, Pinder had stupidly not lammed out to Atlantic City or Las Vegas, as would anybody with sense who didn't want to be caught by his guardian angel. The dumb bastard had stayed right here in town, so at worst it'd cost me a couple of days of shoe leather to run him down. Once Invictus was back at work quietly doing his guardian angelic shtick on behalf of ungrateful Pinder, Greg and the other angels would hopefully let him off the hook, with the proviso that he no longer appear in full angelic splendor in Pinder's living room during *Jeopardy!* trying to convince the inconvincible nonbeliever by the very act of his manifestation that — like the ottoman or Alex Trebek's mustache — the ethereal was real.

Not that I hoped Pinder would get out of this unscathed.

I hadn't forgotten that he'd arranged my kidnapping and near death experience, and I planned to bring it up as much as necessary in front of Dan Jenkins, as well as my new pal the barking assistant D.A. For good measure I'd also squeal to a dame I sometimes dated who worked at the *Gazette* and any judge in town that I could find either sober or drunk enough to listen to the likes of me. As a bonus to my client, Invictus' work as a guardian angel would be infinitely easier if Pinder the asshole was rotting behind bars.

The windows were painted black in the bedroom, too.

I assumed the bed-shaped object that the gloom was failing to fully illuminate was the mattress he'd picked up at Salome and Sam's Mattress Emporium six years ago.

Pinder's bed was unmade, but didn't appear to be chronically so. My sheets always look like they've been snagged in the gears of a Tour de France contestant and pedaled the two thousand miles from Mont de Kraut to the Arc de Surrender. Pinder's looked like he'd slipped neatly out from under them the last day he occupied the joint. Could have meant he hadn't intended to leave when he did or just that he was a neat slob.

"You know where Pinder works?" I hollered out to the old dame in the living room as I poked around the bureau.

According to Mannix, Invictus said the answer was nowhere, but how reliable was a guardian angel who kept losing the guy from whom he was supposed to stand three inches from cradle to grave? Not to mention, Invictus' source would have been Pinder himself, a guy who clearly wouldn't want Invictus to know where he was employed. I figured my erstwhile kidnapper had already committed at least one major felony without breaking a sweat, what was a little Caucasian lie to a guardian angel? It was the kidnapping I wanted to get the bastard on. Lying alone wasn't against the law, which was good for my ex-wife who would have gotten the electric chair for the many and varied answers to my weekly Monday morning question, "where were you all weekend?" (Not to mention that the only one lying alone in our marriage was me.)

"He worked at the shaving cream factory for a little while after the aquarium shut down," the old bag called back from the living room. "He complained about the foam sometimes. He didn't talk much about work except to complain. Said he hated the place and everybody he worked with. That didn't last. I don't think he had a job in years."

There was something off about the bedroom. Something missing. Something that I couldn't quite place my finger on, probably because it wasn't there.

I stood in the middle of the room for a moment trying to see where the missing something should go in order to determine what exactly it theoretically was and why it wasn't there. Unfortunately, my brain had been fried by a trumpet blast at three a.m. that had burned out all the booze that helps me do my best thinking.

There was a small closet in the corner. The two lou-vered doors were closed, but I noticed the soft glow of a light source battling through the shuttered slats.

My first thought was halo. Those things glowed like a son of a bitch, and I'd had angels leaping out from behind every floating dust particle yelling "boo!" at me all week. I approached the closet with trepidation, fully expecting the doors to burst open and a million and one angels to come tumbling out like Groucho, Harpo and Chico carried on a tidal wave of waiters with trays of hardboiled eggs.

It turned out the glow from inside the closet was not unearthly in nature, but came courtesy the good, corporeal folks at Duracell.

Charles Pinder had built a shrine inside the little chamber. A hundred battery-powered votive candles were the source of the glow, although more than half of them had burned out. Pinder had cut a dozen articles out of various newspapers and magazines, and had printed out a bunch of stories from sites all over the Internet. All of these scraps of paper were framed and hanging on the walls. I noted some bylined pieces by Richard Dawkins and Christopher Hitchens.

In an act of Norman Bates-level creepiness, it looked as if Pinder had applied lipstick to his kisser and slobbered all over the articles. The sheets of glass on the framed pieces were adorned with hundreds of rosebud smackeroos. Any hope that he had a dame friend kiss his pictures for him vanished when I spotted the tube of ruby red lipstick sitting — presumably deeply ashamed — next to one of the burned-out candles.

As I was perusing the incredibly disturbing contents of my asshole kidnapper's closet, I heard a noise on the other side of the wall. A soft, prolonged whoosh. I figured the old dame had gotten up and hobbled to the bathroom. I hoped that she wasn't stealing all of Pinder's towels since I'd planned on helping myself to one to replace the bathmat I'd been using to pinch-hit in my bathroom back home (the painful lump Pinder's lackeys had planted on my head was justification enough for any and all petty theft of any toiletries and liquor I could cram in my trench coat pockets on my way out the door).

The articles which Pinder had feverishly molested had been mostly relegated to nail hooks on the side walls of the closet in order to accommodate the main attraction.

An entire front page from the *Gazette* had been framed and hung in the place of highest honor on the main wall in the creepy dead center of the shrine.

Wholly Moses! screamed the headline, in a hysterical font usually reserved for atomic wars and Moon Men invasions.

I remembered the story from a decade ago.

When the Old Courthouse was built just after 1900, our innocent forebears — who did not foresee a world populated entirely by seven billion thin-skinned assholes — had hung in the lobby a granite slab on which were chiseled the Ten Commandments. (That would be the biblical Decalogue and not my personal denary catalog which starts with I: Thou Shalt Not Pay Thine Alimony On Time and ends with numbers nine and ten, IX: Thou Shalt Drink To Forget, X: Thou Shalt Not Forget To Drink.)

Apparently Pinder had been part of the group of chronic whingers who'd screeched from their fainting couches for the city to remove the granite slab, lest it offend thieves, coveters and liars on their way upstairs for their murder, rape and arson trials.

The city had first tried covering the rock with a sheet. Pinder's group found this unacceptable, claiming the risk too high that the sheet might fall off and consequently upset some drug dealer or paralegal who'd just spent the weekend obliviously indulging in what they didn't know at the time was the kind of adultery that was unsanctioned by a deity that Pinder and his pals didn't believe in in the first place.

Eventually the city had been forced to remove the granite slab. However, it had been hanging for over a century and so had left such a noticeable, permanent mark in the wall that, even after it was gone from the lobby, employees saw it as a landmark in absentia and would give directions to visitors along the line of, "turn left where the Ten Commandments used to be."

Pinder's group was enraged by this as well, and so had forced the city to blow up the building and build a new courthouse untainted by religion, but for the daily oaths sworn on Bibles, to the flag, etc. in pretty much every room in the joint. Cost to taxpayers: $42,000,000. A more elegant solution to the trumped-up controversy might have been for anybody who didn't like a bearded sky king telling them they couldn't covet their neighbor's ass to ignore the Ten Commandments as they rode into the lobby on their hot donkeys. It certainly would have been cheaper.

The framed copy of the *Gazette* was from the day of the controlled detonation that wiped out the original court-house. Pinder was standing front and center with a half-dozen other bastards. I spotted William Grasse, the getaway driver who'd been plugged in the puss in the backroom of the bakery. The other five I didn't recognize, but the *Gazette* had thoughtfully captioned their names underneath the photo.

I was going to take down the big frame and smash the glass in order to swipe the newspaper, but then I had a thought about the kind of asshole who'd take the time to frame something so worthless in the first place.

The flickering electronic candles sat on a short chest with a couple of drawers in it, and I found a stack of yel-lowed duplicate copies of the same old issue of the *Gazette* piled up inside the topmost drawer. I stuffed one in my trench coat pocket.

When I reemerged from the bedroom, I found the old bag carefully examining me from way the hell down the length of the hallway and across to the far side of the living room. She was decomposing in the same soft, dusty armchair in which I'd left her. Her eyesight apparently wasn't as crummy as my ageism had assumed. Her observational skills would have put any P.I. to shame, if P.I.s were capable of that or any other emotions besides avarice and not giving a shit.

"That's all you took?" old lady Edna hollered up the hall at me. "What's that, a newspaper?"

Clearly she could see in the dark, since the black paint on the living room windows made it nearly impossible for me to make out anything but the rough outlines of furniture. She'd spotted the *Gazette* sticking from my pocket from a hundred miles down the hall and knew it wasn't on me when she'd let me in Pinder's apartment.

Ancient Edna squinted in the dark, the better to see me.

"You never said if you was a cop," she said. "If you're a crook, do you mind some constructive criticism? You're not good at it. You're as bad as the one that busted into my joint. They didn't take anything either. In fact, it looked to me like they cleaned the place. I called my son to see if it was him who come and cleaned. I forgot, he's my daughter now. What am I supposed to make of that? Me, a decent woman."

"Don't ask me," I said absently as I poked around the linen closet at the opposite end of the hall. "I'm a slightly annoyed heterosexual trapped in the body of a deeply irritated heterosexual. I looked into reassignment to fit my perceived body image, but I was told by my personal M.D., Dr. Charlotte Cheese, that there's such a fine line difference between the two that there isn't a surgical solution."

"Yeah, well…" the old bat said. "My he-she son said he didn't clean my place. I called the cops, but they didn't do anything. What can they do? I mean, what do you say about some crook busting in and not even taking nothing?"

"I say there's a lot of that going around," I informed her.

I'd completed my perusal of the linen closet, coming to the conclusion that Pinder wasn't hiding between the facecloths. The old dame hadn't swiped the towels. I took a good size cotton bath towel and managed to stuff it into an inner pocket of my coat.

As I shut the linen closet door, I heard the same soft whoosh I'd heard coming through the wall of Pinder's closet, but this time seemingly from Pinder's bedroom.

I looked down the hall. The old dame was still sitting out in the chair. She hadn't used the crapper after all. I suddenly remembered Mannix mentioning how he'd heard something eerie and St. Nicholas-like when he'd been in here playing junior detective.

"Do you have plumbing problems in this dump?" I asked.

Sudden movement. I glanced back at the bedroom door. I thought I saw a shadow cross the ceiling in the flickering light cast by the battery-powered votive candles.

"Mister, it'd be easier to list the things we don't got trouble with."

The muffled whoosh that I knew now definitely wasn't a toilet flushing crossed under the cheap wallpaper at my back, moving in the direction of the living room. Like Mannix had said, it seemed to be traveling through the walls.

I glanced back down the hall at the old broad in the dusty chair.

She'd indicated there were myriad problems with the

old building. I wondered if she was aware of the existence of the current one, which was the giant, incorporeal mass that was rapidly hissing up from between the spreading wings of the chair at her back.

For an instant I hoped Invictus was back. The shape was huge enough to encompass the guardian angel's wings. It was more or less the same blob-like silhouette I'd seen reflected in my toaster and bathroom mirror the previous morning. But I had none of the sense of irritating warmth and unwanted happiness that the guardian angel radiated. And it definitely was not smiling. I felt a sudden wash of cold menace.

Unlike Invictus or the Angel Greg or any of the cast of thousands of manifesting heavenly bastards I'd had to endure the past two days, the thing didn't stop when it reached the size of an average human. It continued to expand behind the unaware old bag, spreading wider and wider and without a limited, defined shape.

"Get up, lady," I commanded from the safety (I sincerely hoped) of the hallway, which only five seconds into the materialization was already far too narrow for the still-expanding creature to fit into. "Run calmly and rapidly this way."

I spoke in a relaxed, soothing tone, and remained perfectly still so as not to antagonize the amorphous whatever-the-hell-it-was, all of which I imagined was exactly what Siegfried and Roy were doing just before the tiger decided to floss its fangs with one of their rhinestone-studded thongs.

"What?" the old dame said with a squinting scowl from the chair from which she refused to budge. "Why? What are you doing hiding up there?"

She craned her wattled neck to get a better view of me and my stolen towel on one end of the apartment, and thus completely missed out on seeing the slavering fangs of the creature that suddenly lunged down and snapped her head off.

There might have been blood. Usually there is in decapitations, although the woman was old enough that there might not have been all that much left in her collapsing body. Whether it was an Old Faithful geyser or a puff of plasma dust with an IOU from the Red Cross, I had no idea, since the instant the old dame's head vanished inside the creature's drooling mouth, I heroically turned tail and ran. Or tried to. Unfortunately for me, there was nowhere for a retreating coward to flee.

A bedroom, a bathroom and a linen closet. The thing had already been in the bedroom. I'd just seen its shadow. I'd heard it moments before that in the bathroom, jiggling the handle and rooting through old copies of *Mother Jones*. It had moved inside the goddamn hallway wall seconds before it had taken on corporeal form.

In my moment of hesitation, trying to decide which useless door to enter, I felt a massive rush of displayed air accompanying by a deafening, flapping roar.

I spun around in time to feel the hot rush of a hurricane wind pulverize my face with the kind of G-forces that make fighter pilots pass out. Every stick of furniture in the living room was suddenly airborne, flipping end-over-end in a crazed, cyclone swirl.

End tables cracked to kindling against walls. The upended sofa rocketed towards me at a thousand miles an hour, only catching a fresh current at the last instant, ripping off to the left and vanishing from sight in the direction of the dining nook. The monstrous crash of the couch busting into a million pieces took place off-camera.

A headless body soared up the hallway past me, splatting hard against the wall at my back. I assumed it was that of the old bag who had probably in her last second of life regretted letting me in Pinder's joint. On the other hand, I hadn't had time to investigate the kitchen, and the world inside the apartment had gotten so chaotic so rapidly that it was possible the body that flew by me might have belonged to some other decapitated neighbor lady that Pinder had stored in a Tupperware container under the sink.

A mirror shattered, promising seven years of bad luck to somebody other than me, since I was reasonably certain I'd be dead in about two seconds.

I was caught in a NASA wind tunnel, battling like a goddamn street mime against a typhoon.

And just as suddenly as it had begun, the wind cut off. A huge, dark form dropped down from the living room ceiling, and a mouth filled with a nightmare of savage dental work suddenly appeared at the end of the hallway.

I figured in some lucid part of my brain that hadn't checked out with the rest of my terrified wits that the ceilings of Pinder's old apartment were about nine feet high, with a seven foot arch leading into the hall. Which meant the gigantic mouth that was currently staring me down was taller than me when I stood on my toes.

The mouth tipped to one side and part of an evil eye as big as a beach ball appeared in the uppermost corner of the archway.

"Look, you're hungry," I said. "I can appreciate that. I've got nearly ten grand I can blow on lunch. Just let me find a whip and a chair and we'll go to Red Lobster."

I still couldn't see clearly thanks to goddamn Charles Pinder and his black-painted windows, so I still wasn't clear on what it was I was dealing with. There appeared to be three rows of jagged fangs for each jaw. Each row looked to have about a hundred individual choppers. The longest teeth were fifteen inches, and the shortest about six. The apartment wasn't dark enough to keep them from gleaming at me. If I'd had a bucket of black paint I would have slathered the windows with the second coat Pinder had obviously neglected to give them to keep from seeing any of the creature, and if there was any left over I would have dabbed my eyes out for good measure.

The one eyeball of the massive beast that I was able to see disappeared from view. The mouth leveled off once more. The rows of slavering fangs stared me down like the grille of a dragster. The invisible bastard behind the wheel revved his engine. In the pause before I became road kill, I felt the exhale of warm breath.

The only door out of the dump was beyond the gaping mouth. Pinder's bedroom door was back three feet. The obscene phone call breathing heavily before me could turn into a ghost and travel through walls. Right now, however, it was in solid form.

If I could get to the bedroom, smash a window and jump, maybe the thing would stay put in Pinder's apartment. Maybe it would return to the plaster from whence it had come, from where my poking around had awakened it, and where it had apparently been happily dwelling for Mannix the day before. Maybe I'd only bust both my legs in the goddamn four story plunge. A jump which, if I survived, I fully intended to remind Mannix until my dying day I wouldn't have needed to even consider taking had my elf assistant not guilted me into taking on an angel as a client.

I kept one eye on the furiously hungry mouth, and the other on the open bedroom door — which was no mean feat since they were in opposite directions — and I took one, sliding, cockeyed, half-step back.

The instant I moved, the mouth yawned impossibly

wider, and one long, slimy white tendril shot out of it with a whip-sharp crack, encircling my ankle. A quick yank, and I was off my feet. I landed hard on my ass, smashing the back of my head on the leg of an overturned phone table that had been blown around in the maelstrom and had landed on its side in the hall. I heard two simultaneous cracks: one from the leg busting off the table, the other from my skull splitting in two.

There was a horrible roar, louder and nearly as terrifying as that which issued from my ex-wife when I informed her that I'd emptied our savings account to pay the rent with the dough she'd planned to use on a Bahamian cruise with our butcher. The eruption of hot air from the creature's gaping mouth was like a blast of sulfur mixed with a stench of Chef Boyardee. The latter was, frankly, absurdly incongruous enough to merit a good, long evening of puzzled contemplation in a comfortable easy chair, and I fully intended to purchase said hunk of living room furniture in which to do so. However, surviving the next five seconds would be crucial in order to make the acquisition, and I figured the odds of that happening were pretty much zero.

The odds dropped lower when the thing's tongue lashed out and took a good, long lick of the entire front of my sinuous body.

"*GRRAAAAWW!*" screamed the creature's gaping mouth.

My gaping mouth screamed something as well, but more high-pitched and girlish than I'm willing to admit. Fortunately, my sissy screech was covered by the sudden sharp blasts from the handgun which my much braver hand had, unbeknownst to me, yanked from my shoulder holster.

If the thing had a uvula, I aimed for it. Six shots, one

after the other.

Blam! Blam! Blam! Times two.

The slithering tendril that encircled my right ankle went slack and slapped to the floor. I got a look at the appendage as the thing screamed. White, with a blunt end.

For the first time I noticed that five more of the things had shot out of the creature's mouth. The gunshots had arrested their forward momentum before the slithering snakes could latch onto me and drag me home for dinner. In the frightening pause that descended on the hallway in the split-second after I'd unloaded my gat, the five serpent arms flapped wildly around Pinder's ugly carpet.

"*GRAAAAWWWW!*" the thing screamed.

I got another Beefaroni blast of stink breath.

This time it was a wounded yell, and the ugly shadow and its mouthful of jagged teeth abruptly fled the opening to the hallway.

Another massive burst of wind threw the shattered remains of living room furniture back against the walls, and suddenly there was a blast of light as if a supernova had just gone off somewhere in the vicinity of Pinder's *la sala* radiator.

The brilliant eruption of daylight came simultaneous with a massive crash that shook the building to its foundation.

I reloaded my piece as quickly as my courageous, violently shaking hands would permit. I wondered when I was through if I should stay hiding out in Pinder's hallway for the rest of my life, just to play it safe. When no more noise issued from the living room, I threw caution and common sense to the wind and took a peek around the corner.

A fresh hole had been blown through the living room wall to the outside world. From ceiling to floor, the entire wall was gone. From the crumbling, jagged bricks on the left side, to the exposed corridor outside Pinder's apartment on the right, my best guess put the hole the creature had made to about fifteen feet.

I saw a very large shadow pass over the building across the street. Whatever it had been, a pair of apparently very sturdy wings were carrying it away.

The flying thing with the ugly mouth and the canned-goods halitosis was a son of bitch, but it definitely had the right idea. Escape at that moment seemed the wisest course of action for all concerned, as dealing with endless questions from the cops about a trashed apartment, an escaped monster, and a headless old lady corpse was more than my precariously balanced sanity could manage right now.

I took one last look around the living room. The destruction was near total, with furniture blasted back into a massive debris pile. I realized now that the violent wind had been caused by the beating of the wings of the huge, unidentified beast.

Even in the ruins of Pinder's place I got the nagging feeling that something was missing. It was the same sense I'd had back in the bastard's bedroom.

A pile of bricks that had managed to hold on after the creature had blown out the wall suddenly decided they'd had enough. They collapsed all at once, a stack of red dominoes plummeting down to the street.

The falling bricks reminded me of the fall I'd nearly taken from the top of St. Regent's Drive-Thru Cathedral. For an instant they also terrified me into thinking the flying whatzit was already back home after a brief spin around the neighborhood, hungrier from the workout.

I forgot all about whatever it was that my subconscious thought was missing, and I booked it out of what was left of Pinder's apartment. I took one step into the hallway and I was almost decapitated for the second time in less than five minutes when I nearly walked into the buzz saw of a bobbing, brightly glowing halo.

"Hello, Mr. Banyon!" announced Invictus, my no-longer-missing client, his face beaming nearly as brightly as the divine Frisbee that was parked over his thinning yellow hair. "I understand you've decided to take my case after all! What joyful news!"

That was his opinion, and I didn't have time to tell him how wrong he was.

There was a sudden burst of light that filled the hallway around us.

It was far more brilliant than the sunlight that had exploded in Pinder's living room when the escaping crea-ture had busted out the wall. Invictus and I were suddenly surrounded on all sides by a million guys in glowing robes. A goddamn trumpet blasted a triumphant version of Taps at my right eardrum.

A benign, yet somehow simultaneously slightly men-acing and entirely victorious pasty face was suddenly parked uncomfortably close to my own. The pale blue eyes of the Angel Greg were looking beyond my shoulder, at my angel client.

"You are in a lot of trouble, Invictus," Greg announced.

The Angel Greg suddenly noticed me standing there like the last wallflower next to the punchbowl at the junior prom.

"Oh," the asshole angel said. "*You, too*, Mr. Banyon."

And with another trumpet blast that would be the basis of my future tinnitus lawsuit if I got out of this alive, the Angel Greg suddenly held in his soft hands the most viciously long and sharp sword my neck had ever seen.

11

I had twice avoided having my head lopped off that afternoon, once by monstrous fangs, and again by nearly walking into the sharpened edge of a happily nodding halo. When the sword of righteous goddamn heavenly retribution appeared in the Angel Greg's hands, I was up to time number three, and anybody with a lick of common sense would have concluded at that point that the unseen forces that guided events throughout the universe were determined to mount my noggin over their cosmic mantle.

Invictus seemed oblivious to the calamity that was about to befall both of our pretty little necks. My angel client continued to smile that infuriating "everything is fine, we appreciate your business, an operator will be with you shortly" smile of his as he looked from the Angel Greg, to the nameless angel with the parchment scroll, to the unnamed bastard with the horn who'd just nearly blasted my hat into the next state to herald their arrival, since there was no way we'd have noticed a thousand angels clogging up the path to the elevator without goddamn Doc Severinsen playing them onstage.

"Ah, hello there," Invictus said. He seemed to suddenly notice the other hundred million angels who were crammed into the shitty apartment hallway.

The corridor wasn't big enough to hold them all. Through the window at the end of the hall, some angels were visible hanging out on the fire escape across the street, where the Angel Greg had presumably been keeping silent watch over Charles Pinder's apartment door for Invictus to return. Many more hovered in the air between both buildings, giving an eyeful to any unfortunate passing FedEx drivers and milkmen who might be wondering why the sun was suddenly blotted out, and who might justifiably but erroneously conclude after a glance up that Judgment Day was pretty damn nigh.

The end of the world was at hand for only two of us, and the one of us whose fault it entirely was had just finished taking a good, long look at the celestial posse that had arrived to take him to the last golden roundup. Invictus finished his unperturbed perusal of the immediate vicinity with a slow glance along the entire length of the gleaming gold sword that the Angel Greg had just unsheathed from out of nowhere.

The point of the sword caught a wayward beam of sunlight that had somehow battled its way past the solar eclipse caused by the otherworldly mob. I was momentarily blinded by the glint off its horrifyingly sharp tip.

"Oh, dear," Invictus said, calmly understating the hell out of the sword and the mob that was there to back it up. "Is something wrong? Can I help?"

The Angel Greg held his sword straight up in one hand. If he'd been a man I'd have been surprised that a wimp like him could hold something so obviously heavy without any strain on his soft features. But he was no man. He was a celestial being of immeasurable power with uncountable centuries of violence against iniquitous humans under his belt. The sword held steady as he snapped the fingers of his free hand. The angel with the scroll muscled his way through the crowd to Greg's side.

"Invictus, guardian angel, 87th Battalion, serial number thirty-four, plus pi, plus 2-B, " intoned the angel with the scroll. "You are charged with willfully manifesting yourself to the human Charles Pinder, whom you are meant to guard from such-and-such a date (on record at the home office), until the date of his mortal death. You are suspected of manifesting as well to one Crag Banyon, private investigator—"

The scroll angel looked up at me, then at the Angel Greg.

"Fix it later," Greg instructed.

Scroll Angel nodded and started to return his attention to his parchment.

"Before you hack us into strips of bacon," I interrupted, "would you mind telling me what the hell did this?" I stabbed a thumb at the open door of Pinder's apartment.

The garbage dump of shattered furniture was brightly lit thanks to the hole that had been blown through the living room wall. I noticed for the first time that there were drizzles of red across the floor from the hallway where the creature had Frenched me with it's scabby tongue, over to the newly formed opening in the wall.

Nonagenarian Edna had just had her body amputated in there, but the reddish stains were tinged with too much orange to be blood.

"We didn't see anything," the Angel Greg firmly and quickly stated, before I'd even finished spitting out my question.

Their leader apparently spoke for the blind eyeballs of every angel in the crowd. At my question, the rest of the heavenly horde was suddenly nonchalantly fascinated by the hallway ceiling.

"So, all of you were on the fire escape but not one of you saw a thing?" I said. "And by *a* thing, I mean *the* thing. You know, the thing that blew out the wall about seventy feet away from you, and which flew off directly in front of you. I just want to be clear here that you are claiming to have seen nothing at all of the exploding wall. So you didn't see any of that, but a minute later you *did* see my client through a hallway window that looks like it was washed with oatmeal? A window so dirty, it is only slightly less opaque than the ones that Pinder painted black in his apartment to keep people — and possibly angels — from seeing inside. That's the story you're all sticking to?"

Everyone in the throng was suddenly looking at absolutely everything other than me: ceiling, walls, floor, fire hose, doormats, exit sign. They stuck their hands deep in the pockets of their robes, adjusted their halos, and scuffed their bare toes on the worn carpet. Many of the desperately nonchalant angels suddenly attempted a little nonchalant whistling until the angel with the scroll hissed at them to shut the hell up.

"Like I said," the Angel Greg said. "We saw nothing. *Was* there something?" He made a show of looking in the apartment and pretending to see the hole in the wall for the very first time. "Oh. Yes. Oh, my. But, see, we were distracted by the dust mite we were hiding behind. Fascinating creatures, mites. It must have happened in that tiny little fraction of a second when we weren't looking."

He waved his free hand to spur the scroll angel along. Before the SOB could open his yap again, I interrupted.

"Is there something in there about bearing false witness?" I asked. The scroll angel pulled the parchment to his chest to keep the words from my prying eyes, so I turned to Invictus. "I think I read that somewhere. I could check the lobby of the courthouse, but Pinder, who nobody seems to be able to find, had it blown up. I'd ask our local archbishop, but after being zapped to the top of the steeple of St. Regent's — where I was offered the city as a bribe, by the way — I'd have PTSD just getting near the rectory door, so there's no way I'm going near that place again until my own funeral. So, Invictus, would angels lying their halos off in order to act as judge, jury and executioner of another angel still be considered bad these modern days?"

"Oh, yes, bearing false witness *is* bad," Invictus said, sounding remarkably like an elf office manager I knew. "We're all quite firm on that."

The light was dawning for Invictus. He gave the Angel Greg, who was obviously lying his halo off, a suspicious look through narrowed eyelids.

"I'm stuck here in the real world," I told my client. "I can't zap my ass away from getting my skull split in half. But if I were you, I'd pop over to the office of a good lawyer. 'Good,' in this context means competent. All lawyers are evil bottom feeding alcoholics, even good ones. You need somebody to defend you, because there's something bigger going on here than you not obeying the rules."

"Now you just hold on there," the Angel Greg said, waving an angry finger in my face. "That's quite enough from *you*, Mr. Banyon."

He raised his sword like an angry Hank Aaron. A dozen nearby angels stumbled and dropped out of the path of the sweeping blade.

In the moment before my death, I realized I'd forfeited my Constitutional right to be judged by a jury of my peers. It was just as well, as the thought of twelve drunk P.I.'s stumbling around the jury box or getting lost on the way back from deliberations would have been too depressing a reminder in the two seconds I had left on earth that I probably should have taken that job in my brother-in-law's florist shop.

Blinding sunlight glinted off the tip once more. And then all the violence of the horrifically sharp heavenly sword was loosed.

There was a whoosh of air. My imminent murder became a slow-motion peep show. The stereocilia in my ear holes itched from the vibrations that emanated from the rapidly approaching sword. The gleaming edge of the blade leveled out and raced forward for a bottom-of-the-ninth home run.

The split-second before the sword completed its lethal journey towards my ring around the collar, I felt a gentle tug at the elbow of my trench coat.

In the blink of an eye, the hallway, the thousand angels, Pinder's wrecked apartment, and asshole Angel Greg and his killer sword abruptly winked out of existence.

Every molecule in my body was disassembled, and I was rocketing backwards through a kaleidoscopic jumble of bright colors and blurred images. The feeling of being torn apart down to my basic building blocks — which I got the firm sense consisted solely of barley, beer nuts and resentment — lasted less than a second.

The unreality through which I was traveling reached its destination. I was vomited back out into the real world, reconstructed instantaneously into myself like one of those Lego kits that can only be assembled into the Star Wars Death Star, thus obviating the need for boring creativity and fun that kids used to waste so much time on.

I did a quick inventory with my hands to make certain all my parts — starting with my vitally important fedora

— were where they were supposed to be. Only when I was satisfied that my spleen wasn't on my forehead and my feet weren't in Las Cruces did I finally look around to see where the hell I was.

I had been transported to a familiar little apartment in which everything was scaled down to elf size.

Mannix was waiting up for us. The elf had moved some of his work down from my third floor offices to the corner of the basement where the building superintendent allowed him to maintain a little place in exchange for doing side work around the dump. There was always work around the building that could benefit from the tiny, skilled craftsman's hands of a former North Pole elf.

"Mister Crag!" the elf cried jumping to his feet. "Mister Invictus found you!"

The angel stood in the middle of Mannix's parlor, his wings folded in tight to his back to accommodate the narrow walls.

"And only ten minutes too late," I said, with no small amount of urgency. "There's a lying bastard angel with a sword hot on our heels, Mannix." I wheeled on Invictus. "Can he follow us through that wormhole you just yanked me through?"

Invictus shook his halo. "No," he replied, lost in thought. "He *was* lying just then, wasn't he, Mr. Banyon? I could see it. Those kinds of angels don't have experience with people like we guardian angels do. They aren't as worldly."

"Yes, you're a real cynical SOB," I said. "Remind me how many times Pinder has given you the slip by sneaking out the back door of the confessional?"

"But that's my point, you see," Invictus said. "We guardian angels witness lying from humans all the time. Mr. Pinder is, to my eternal shame, quite good at it. But some humans are very bad at it, like that angel back there. He wasn't telling the truth to you about not knowing who made that awful mess in Mr. Pinder's apartment."

"Yes, he was definitely lying through his flawless teeth," I said. "And it wasn't a *who* at Pinder's place, it was the most terrifying *what* I've ever met that wasn't standing at an altar in a hilariously unironic white wedding gown. So you're saying you didn't ever see a huge, multi-fanged, tentacled flying horror show flapping around the forty-watt bulb when Pinder would stay up late underlining jokes in Kafka?"

"No, I'm sorry," Invictus said.

"I thought I heard something moving in the walls yesterday," Mannix volunteered. "The nice lady with the keys who let me in said she didn't hear anything, but then she said she had to go back to her apartment to rub liniment on her cat's, um, private things."

"Well, the good news for her cat is that its unmentionable areas will remain its own private domain from here on out," I said.

I began unloading my pockets onto Mannix's exquisitely handcrafted, tiny little dining room table.

"Have you had any luck tracking down William Grasse?" I asked.

"Not yet," the elf said. "There are four in the phone book. I think I've found him on the Internet, but I haven't figured out which address belongs to him."

"This might help you narrow it down," I said, slapping down the yellowed newspaper I'd swiped from Pinder's bedroom shrine. "See what you can do about tracking down the other five guys in the photo with Pinder and Grasse, as well." I found the end of the towel I'd filched from Pinder's linen closet and pulled it from the recesses of my trench coat like a cheap magician yanking a bunch of tied-together handkerchiefs from my sleeve. "This is going in my bathroom at my apartment. I can finally retire my soggy bathmat, which I'll hoist to the rafters with the rest of the mold stains if I ever get home again. Thanks to the events of the past half-hour, that won't be happening soon." I took out my camera and popped out the roll of film. "Get this developed when you have a minute. There are pictures of two of the dead guys on there. The photos probably won't do us any good but I at least have some good shots of Dan Jenkins unwittingly letting me take pictures of a crime scene. I can use them as leverage the next time he tries to lock me up for the crime of not being as stupid as him."

"Yes, sir, Mr. Crag," the elf announced. He collected all the gifts I'd laid out before him and began hustling around his little joint, starting with stuffing the roll of film into a handy Kodak envelope from his little corner desk.

"I wasn't able to find Mr. Pinder anywhere," Invictus said as Mannix worked. "I searched all the churches where I last saw him each time he disappeared. I even checked the aquarium where he used to work two years ago. It's a petting zoo now."

"Yes, they had problems on the news when they opened. Eight sheep drowned before they finally figured out how to attach the little air tanks."

"He was nowhere I looked," Invictus said. "I finally sat on a park bench the whole rest of the day and had a good, long cry."

His eyes were welling up and he looked like he was about to add to the discomfort I was already feeling from being sober and hunched in Mannix's little apartment.

The elf offered a look of deep sympathy and patted the crybaby angel's hand.

"It will be all right, Mr. Invictus," Mannix promised. "Mr. Crag is a wonderful private investigator."

I wished that Invictus had been able to detect a lie in Mannix's tone, but there wasn't one. The elf was maddeningly sincere in his erroneous conviction that I wasn't as completely worthless as I am.

"The guy shouldn't be all that hard to find," I sighed. "It'll just take a little time. In the meantime our big problem will be avoiding Greg and those other angels. I do my best detecting work with my head attached to my body, and I'm not sure I can bring my A-game if I have to fish it out of a storm drain with a piece of gum on a stick."

In truth, I wasn't all that worried about the Angel Greg. The guy might have a scary sword that could slice down to my chewy nougat center, but he was a complete ass-hat when it came to navigating the mortal plane. Greg was like a tourist in a sidewalk Paris café. His pattern so far was to sit and wait for the world to come to him. At least for the short term, as long as I steered clear of anywhere he was most likely to set up an ethereal duck blind, I'd be all set.

Invictus sniffled and wiped his nose on the sleeve of his sparkling white robe.

"You people are very good," the angel insisted.

"Mannix already sees me through rose colored glasses despite my most debauched efforts to set him straight, I don't need you getting in on the act," I warned. "Do you have somewhere you can stay that'll keep you off Angel Greg's radar?"

"He can stay here," Mannix offered.

"Oh, that would be fine," Invictus said, suddenly beaming a smile so bright I could have used Mannix's aforementioned rose tinted spectacles to block the UV glare. "Do you have a toast crumb on the kitchen counter

or dust ball under the bed? I'll be quite comfortable set-
tling in behind anything like that."

"Mannix is disgustingly fastidious, but there's all kinds
of tiny little shit out in the basement you can hide
behind."

The angel nodded, and in the next instant he'd vanished
from our sight.

"You're welcome to stay here too, Mr. Crag," Mannix
offered.

"Thanks, Mannix, but the buzz from his halo would
keep me up all night. I've got to be somewhere I can think.
I saw something at Pinder's apartment that I think might
be crucially important. The problem is that I didn't see it,
and I haven't been able to figure out what I saw that I
didn't see. I'll let you know what fleabag I settle on."

Mannix saw me to the door, which angels apparently
didn't know was the accepted route of ingress and egress
in polite society.

"I know you told me to tell Mr. Invictus to stay away
from the naughty man's apartment," Mannix whispered,
"but he wouldn't listen. He thought he could help."

"In this case he was right, Mannix. He kept me from
being kebabbed. On the other hand, I wouldn't have been
staring down the ugly end of a sword if he hadn't popped
over there in the first place, so we'll call it a wash."

"Wash!" Mannix cried. He spun from the door and
hustled over to his little desk where he'd set up the annex
to Banyon Investigations, Inc. "I almost forgot. I had the
water tested like you wanted."

He hustled back over and handed me an official looking
printout that he'd collected from the desk. It was from an
outfit called Aqua Solutions, Ltd., which had set up shop
halfway down the block five years ago.

"They say the water in the building is fine," Mannix

offered brightly.

He was so excited that I didn't have the heart to tell him I'd been pulling his leg about checking the water. If it were anybody else, I'd have crumpled up the paper, tossed it aside and told them I didn't give a shit. But this was Mannix, and so I glanced down at the sheet.

From the looks of it, the water being pumped into the building that was home to my world headquarters met the minimum quality standards of the city's water department. There were the usual trace amounts of arsenic and iodine. The fluoride level was still high from when the Crest mill exploded the previous year. (Goddamn Cavity Creeps.) If I was in the habit of drinking water and not cheap varnish from the corner package store, I would be concerned about the level of raccoon shit, but according to the conclusions of Aqua Solutions it was within acceptable levels, the level of raccoon shit that was acceptable in drinking water somehow being more than "none."

If there was a reason that both Wasserbaum the asshole dentist and Vincetti the asshole fishmonger weren't acting their usual asshole selves, the answer wasn't swimming around in the reservoir and splashing out into spit sinks.

"Thanks, Mannix," I said, handing him back the report. "File this mystery under 'who the hell knows?'"

I had to duck low to get through Mannix's door. The elf had carved out a little corner of heaven for himself in the otherwise typically hellish office building basement. Hidden somewhere among the busted furniture, dusty canning jars, and rotting stacks of thousand year old wicker laundry baskets, Invictus was safely tucked away for the night.

Mannix didn't seem to care that we were no doubt being ogled by a pair of angelic peepers. The elf offered me a typically cheery adieu, heralded me on my way with a joyful wave of the worthless water report, and clicked the door shut at my back.

"Just in case it never occurred to you," I announced to the empty room. "We humans find being spied on twenty-four hours a day creepy. Trust me, I'm in the same business. If your job is supposed to give mortals comfort, it doesn't."

"Goodnight, Mr. Banyon," an infuriatingly contented and oblivious voice replied from behind a dust mote on top of the old, unused oil furnace.

I sighed. At least for now there was only one of the bastards. Hopefully the rest weren't waiting to kill me with kindness or, failing that, a broadsword the minute I stepped back outside.

I headed past the angel's invisible, ever watchful eyes and over to the rickety old staircase at the back of the cellar which, if the universe had any love for me at all, would collapse under my ass before I reached the top.

12

As poor luck would have it, the ancient basement stairs didn't collapse and kill me. Another goddamn testament to early twentieth century American craftsmanship. Neither did the building drop on my head and crush me to death in the short corridor to the back door, and so I was stuck with life for the time being, which meant avoiding a legion of potentially extraordinarily pissed off angels.

Even the most useless P.I. should be able to shake a tail like a Pekinese, and as stalkers went the Angel Greg wasn't the most brightly twinkling star in the heavens. I weighed my options and decided on the best disguise at hand to outwit him.

Before exiting the building, I took off my hat.

If Greg and company were observing from on high, they had their eyes trained on the front door, not the rusted back door to the alley. Just to play it safe, I hugged walls and slipped under awnings and was four blocks away before I reasoned that, since I hadn't been vaporized by a bolt from the blue, I was safe.

My apartment was currently off limits, but there was no lack of sleazy motels from which to choose. I opted for the Paradise Motel on Bleeker Street for the sheer audacious irony of the name.

The Paradise was the kind of dump that relied on repeat business, much of it taking place during the same depressingly busy overnight hours. It was fast food accommodations, with low lights, lowlifes, and prorated rooms.

Cars arrived and departed in an endless stream.

Ladies of the evening, filles de joie of the wee morning hours and — caffeine and meth permitting — skanks of the entire rest of the day strutted through the manager's front door on stiletto heels. The men were far less daring than their rent-a-dates. The johns all looked like Mafia stoolies on the way into court, hiding their faces behind anything at hand on the mad dash from cars to motel doors. A stoned hooker octopus in six fishnets staggered across the parking lot on all eights, searching for a five-minute boyfriend in order to scrounge up the cost of a dime bag of Gorton's bread crumbs.

Underneath the sporadically flashing neon parking lot sign was fastened a piece of cardboard on which was written in Magic Marker: **Our Rooms Now Have Sleep-Tite Pillows!** Apparently the management of the Paradise Motel had grossly misunderstood the ephemeral nature of their clientele's relationship with their facilities.

In a small building separate from the main strip motel, the grubby manager was a nonjudgmental sentinel keeping simultaneous watch over Paradise proceedings as well as a black and white rerun of *NCIS*. The manager wore a muscle T-shirt that displayed no discernable muscle whatsoever, unless the President's Council on Physical Fitness had surrendered to the reality of modern America and redefined flab, back hair and pizza grease as muscle, in which case he was Mr. Goddamn Universe.

It occurred to me that I should have stuffed more than twenty bucks from my ten grand bowling ball bag lottery winnings into my wallet, but it turned out the two tens I had on me were more than enough to help me make it through the night.

"Two bucks back, Romeo," the manager said, sliding a pair of singles across the counter. The bills stuck at the midpoint and had to be peeled off the Formica like Chiquita Banana stickers.

"Wherefore art thou, syphilis," I said.

I denied his hepatitis and refused his change, leaving the sticky bills in his hairy hand. I picked up my room key between two careful fingers, which I intended to amputate by slamming them in a bureau drawer the minute I got to my room.

The Paradise was the last place I imagined I'd bump into the Angel Greg and his buddies. However, the fact that it was so far on the other end of the scale from virtuous made it come as no surprise that I spotted a familiar figure lurking with a mop and a pail on a bench that was positioned between the manager's seedy office and the first floor doors of the main strip motel.

"I would feel immeasurably better," I said, "if I even thought you might know which end of the mop to use to clean the sheets."

The huge, seated figure with the leathery black skin was so tall that even with his vast ass planted on the groaning bench he didn't have to glance up to look me in the eye. When he saw who it was who had spoken to him, his ridiculously small, worthless black wings retracted and his brow sank low over his giant yellow eyes.

"Banyon," grunted the demon, pretty much as unhappy to see me as was possible without taking the mop out of his slop bucket and beating me to death with the handle.

His name was Molokai. He was a bastard so treacherous that even Hell didn't want him, at least not badly enough to spend much effort looking for him. He liked to keep off their radar so as not to remind those down below of his defection to the upper realm. He frequently took low-key odd jobs around town to make ends meet, which apparently included the odious task of mucking out rooms at the Paradise.

"I'm gonna start thinking you're following me around," the demon said.

"For the record, it wasn't my idea to materialize outside your bedroom," I said. "And thanks for helping save my life. I only hope I can return the favor someday."

Molokai worked for room and board at St. Regent's Drive-Thru Cathedral. I'm the one who'd gotten him that job, a fact for which the ungrateful bastard had yet to thank me. When he was home, the demon hid out amongst the stone gargoyles, just another ugly face in the crowd. In addition to chasing rats and mice, he apparently also dined on crow and neighborhood cats, which I'd only learned earlier that afternoon.

Molokai was the figure whose shadow I'd glimpsed beyond the nests of bones in the tallest spire of the church after the Angel Greg had beamed me off the sidewalk where I had been happily not almost falling to my death. The demon was the same bastard who'd failed to toss me a rope to keep me from pitching off the Gothic cathedral, and instead had ducked quietly down a trapdoor while the SOB angel just outside his window was offering to gift wrap for me a city that wasn't his to give.

"If you're looking for an apology, you can keep right on walking," Molokai said, gesturing me along with his mop. "I've got a long memory. The Fall might be ancient history that predates all extant human communication, written or spoken, but I remember it like it was yesterday. Being lined up on a cloud, made to walk the plank, dropping millions of miles over thousands of years, landing on jagged rock or, worse, splashing down in boiling lava. They even cancelled our insurance. You pay all those premiums all those millennia and never use the stuff; not so much as a tetanus shot, because in the perfection of early creation there's no such goddamn thing as tetanus yet. But slam into an active volcano at a million miles an hours and break every bone in your body? All of a sudden Aetna ain't glad they met ya. And all of it thanks to jokers like your buddies there. You didn't bring them with you?" he added, glancing around.

"Yes," I said, "the heavenly host is currently scoring nose candy in room nine."

For an instant he thought I might be telling the truth. He half-stood, eyeing the ninth door down. Molokai wasn't a dope, but he wasn't somebody inclined to take chances. If he actually believed me, I figured he'd take off like a rabbit in the direction opposite the angels; expelled yet again, this time from an altogether different Paradise. But instead of booking it away from the motel as fast as his cloven hooves would carry him, a strange, almost hungry look crossed his ugly mug.

The door to room nine happened to open at that precise moment, and a wingless nebbish in a rumpled suit stuck his face out into the parking lot to see if the coast was clear. When he saw the demon and me looking straight at him, he darted back inside and slammed the door so hard that his nine somersaulted into a six.

When the distinctly non-angelic wife-cheat disappeared back into room six, née nine, Molokai finally got that I wasn't being serious.

"Yeah, well," the demon grunted, tearing his eyes from the door and crossing his long arms over his barrel chest. "What are you doing hanging out with *them* anyway?"

"You know," I said, tipping my head in thought, "I'm disinclined to share that with you."

I bypassed the demon and headed for my room, which according to the tag on my key had been room six, which meant I was in for an evening of hilarious French farce to go along with my chiggers.

"I had a halo once too, you know, Banyon," Molokai snarled after me. "I have no idea where it went. It fell off in the Fall. I think I saw it roll away into a lava flow when I was busy getting pummeled flat, but at that point I wasn't exactly keeping track of the change that had fallen out of my pockets on the way down. But get this one. At creation *He* made us all sign a contract. If our halos were lost or stolen, *we* were out the dough. Of course we all signed. This was *pre-original sin*. Paradise wasn't lost yet and nobody understood the concept of 'stolen' back then. Except *Somebody* did."

I'd paused en route to one or the other of room sixes. When I glanced back I saw the demon pointing one long, crooked index fingers toward the evening heavens.

"Hell, even we couldn't see a revolt that was still millions of years off. We were all still playing our harps along with the rest of them and having a grand Old Testament time. But *Somebody* knew the future, and He eventually made a bundle off the forfeited security deposits of a bunch of dumb schmucks' who'd lost, bent, folded or mutilated their halos, only because a bunch of His own angels left them on us rather than collect them in a box before they tossed us overboard. But *I'm* the evil one. Isn't misuse of omniscience just a *little* evil? Noooo, not if you're the One making bank bending Your own rules. Good isn't always so good, Banyon. I'd watch my back if I were you."

As bitter tirades went, it didn't merit an Oscar nod.

Maybe a Golden Globe. But it did give me a thought.

"You're always hard up for cash," I said, "and as you've just reminded me, you're evil, so this is right up your alley. What do you know about a monster that's apparently been living in the walls of an apartment in the Fleckner Building? Wraithlike, but can take physical shape. Last seen heading east. At least that's the last I saw of its shadow."

The demon on the bench had been staring into the sour mists of his idyllic, horrific youth. His eyes came back into focus and he suddenly got all cagey like.

"What's it worth to you?"

I excused myself and ducked back inside the manager's office. The hairball in the deceitfully labeled muscle T-shirt had managed to peel one of my abandoned bucks off his pudgy hand, but was still in the process of carefully removing the second.

"Thanks," I said, as I nabbed the first bill from the counter and tugged the bill that was still glued to his hand in sharp, Band-Aid fashion, removing only one fingerprint in the process. I returned to Molokai and dangled the two bucks before his pointed snout.

The demon eyeballed the pair of Washingtons greedily. He reached for the bills, but I held them back out of reach of his sharp, clicking claws.

"I don't know what it is," Molokai reluctantly admitted. "But a guy hears things, you know? Like, I heard there was maybe something like what you're talking about that showed up on the roof of one of those old warehouses near the waterfront." He held up both leathery palms to yank back the reins on any exuberance on my part. "I only overheard that from a gangster ghost, Banyon, so it's not the most reliable source."

I gave him a tense moment to wonder if the information was worth the price of admission. I finally forked over the bills.

"Keep your ears open," I instructed. "Find out the building."

"Yeah, I'll do that, Banyon," the demon grumbled, "because you're such a swell guy." He stuffed the bills away inside his tattered rags. "Duty calls."

He got to his hooves and glumly wheeled his watery slop bucket off the curb with a malodrous splash. As I entered my room, he was wearily mopping away at an ink stain in the parking lot and loudly complaining to a stoned dame with eight legs who was denying all responsibility. I closed the door on the racket.

As sleazy dumps went, I could have done worse than the Paradise. The bed was made and the carpet, while stained, had been recently vacuumed. An air conditioner was trying to escape the bathroom window through a series of violent chugs and rattles, but although the wall around it shook like a sheet of simulated thunder in an old radio mystery, imprisoning screws and brackets held the bucking AC fast in place.

It was still early evening. I couldn't go home, and likewise I couldn't go to my home away from home. If the Angel Greg had a malicious eye out for me, O'Hale's Bar was almost certainly at the top of his list of my favorite haunts.

Still, I am nothing if not an optimist at heart, and there were a billion other watering holes in town from which to purchase liquid depressants. In particular, there was a joint over on the corner of Twelfth and Orchard that I'd been softening up with occasional visits during which I actually paid for my booze, and which consequently had recently foolishly decided that I wasn't a horrible default risk. With my last folding dough having gone to pay for my luxurious lodgings and demon stoolie, tonight would be the night that the good folks at the Iron Maiden Pub would rue the day they were stupid enough to run me a tab.

The drapes were drawn on the activity in the parking lot, and the rumbling air conditioner functioned as a white noise machine to dull the racket of cars arriving, doors slamming, and deadly sins being both joyfully and shamefully committed. I figured it would teach my anxious liver an important lesson in delaying gratification if I took a few minutes to rest my fatigued bones before I struck off to bankrupt the Iron Maiden.

I lay down on the bed, rested my hat over my face, rested my head on a trademarked Sleep-Tite Pillow, and in two minutes, despite the frantic shaking and muffled shouts of my increasingly panicked liver, I was sound asleep.

13

I didn't know at first how long I'd slept. When I climbed into bed, there had been weak parking lot light mixed with the fading pink of a post-sunset sky battling through the long fiberglass drapes. When I opened my eyes and removed my hat from my face, there was brilliant light fighting through the crap-brown curtains.

I hadn't noticed the lovely feces shade of the drapes the night before. Several of the clips that fastened the left-hand drapery to the rod had become detached in the middle, and the curtain sagged like a hammock at the midpoint. It sagged so remarkably that I couldn't help lying there for a few minutes admiring the perfect nature of the sagging.

In fact, I noticed that the round hoop fasteners that were meant to hold the drapes in place were rusted in the most spectacular fashion. I had seen rust before, but never rust so admirable. And the fact that rust could find purchase in so high a location, seemingly so far from anything damp that could have caused it to form was testament to the tenacity of this most wonderful and vigorous rust.

I spotted a huge, dripping water stain on the ceiling just above the curtain rod. Peculiar, since I ordinarily spotted something like that right away and would have immediately associated it with the rusty curtain rod hoops that were getting doused directly below it. But I hadn't, and now that I had I recognized it as the most magnificent mildewed water stain I had ever before seen in my life.

The air conditioner continued this morning to viciously assault the bathroom window in which it had been trapped. It was fighting much more violently to escape than it had the night before, and I could smell a faint whiff of smoke. The AC was like a grizzly bear caught inside a Ford Fiesta who was trying to get out through the glove compartment. Chunks of ice shot out and pinged around the bathroom. The racket was unendurable. Yet, it was somehow the sweetest music my ears had ever heard.

I was reluctant to get up. The morning was already so gloriously perfect that I was afraid that anything I might do to move it along might bring it to early ruin.

Drip-drip-drip, went the water spot.

Clunk-clunk-clunk, went the air conditioner.

Zing-zing-zing, went my gosh-darn heart strings.

I swung my feet around and sat up on the edge of the bed.

A piece of air-conditioned ice fired like a rocket from the belly of the busted AC, ricocheted off the bathroom sink, and bounced to a wonderful stop between the toes of my Florsheims. I picked it up, and immediately noted that it was the most perfect hunk of filthy ice ever puked out of a broken air conditioner.

The piece of ice melted almost immediately to a tiny puddle of dirty water in the palm of my hand, and I could not help but see that it was the most perfect puddle of dirty water ever to be transformed from the most perfect hunk of dirty ice.

I could have sat staring at the water in my hand all morning. It was, frankly, just that G.D. fascinating. But I decided that sitting there would make me a big old lazy-bones, and I didn't want that on my conscience. I wiped the water on the bed, which had surely seen more wonderful and varied stains than a little dot of H2O, and hopped to my feet.

I threw open the motel door on the most glorious early morning sun I had ever had the privilege to witness.

Light cascaded off the windows of the higher buildings that surrounded the Paradise Motel. Brilliant yellow streams of sunlight played amongst the oil stains and bedewed fast food wrappers that decorated the parking lot. In fact, the sparkling effect of sunlight-on-refuse was not unlike a gaily decorated, horizontal Christmas tree, an observation that I shared with the cherubic manager in the muscle T-shirt whose shift had ended with the break of dawn and who was passing me on the way to his car.

"Up yours, freak," the manager suggested.

"Duly noted," I replied. "Not everyone is a morning person. I can only hope that once you're home and have properly rested, that you'll awaken to an afternoon as splendid as this most perfect morning."

He tried to run me over with his Pontiac Bonneville, which I noted as I ran back inside the temporary shelter of my motel room, was decorated with falling chunks of rust almost as exquisite as those that adorned the curtain rod rings of superb room six.

I would have loved to have said good morning to Molokai, who wasn't half as bad a demon as people seemed to think he was, but apparently he'd gone home for the day to his steeple apartment at St. Regent's. I glimpsed his abandoned mop and wheeled pail inside the open door of the Paradise's office.

I agreed with the neon sign out front, which had been shut off with the breaking dawn: the motel was, indeed,

Paradise.

I figured that the vast cloud of oil smoke that had disgorged from the tailpipe of the manager's classic car afforded me sufficient cover from any angelic observers who might be in the vicinity. I whistled while I walked, surprised that I was capable of producing such a mellifluous sound and embarrassed that I might be showing up any passersby who were not so musically inclined.

"Take heart," I offered to a scowling pedestrian; a careworn office type. "I'm sure you're blessed with many unseen talents."

I was right, as his aptitude for stringing together four letter words in a run-on sentence without pausing to draw a breath was surely unmatched.

I traveled back over the route I'd taken the previous night, offering salutations to all passersby who seemed in need of a friendly hello and a hearty suggestion that they endeavor to have a nice day. A few returned the encouragement in kind. The vast majority didn't, which I took as silent approval of a shared sentiment. A small number were less accepting, to the point of threatening to shove me in front of garbage trucks or to disembowel me with whatever they could dig out of lunch pails or briefcases.

"Better luck next time," I encouraged a tenacious little fellow who broke his plastic spork on a parking meter when he waved it around at me.

I rapped out a friendly few taps of Shave and a Haircut on the back basement door of the building that housed my offices. It took a little while, but after a couple of minutes the door opened cautiously and a curious little face peered out.

"Good morning, Mannix!" I announced, sweeping past my assistant.

The elf was wearing a puzzled expression and a pair

of little pajamas decorated with cartoon panda bears.

"Is something wrong, Mr. Crag?" Mannix asked worriedly.

As he cautiously closed the door, his tennis ball eyes were aimed up at the strip of bright blue sky that separated my building from its neighbor across the alley.

"Nothing is wrong whatsoever," I replied.

We were safely entombed in the gloom of the short hallway that led into the main basement. I'd snuck out the back way many times over the years, and had somehow failed to realized that my building was possessed of the most lovely dank basement corridor I had ever seen in my entire wonderful life. When I, quite naturally, mentioned this indisputable fact to Mannix, the elf didn't seem for a moment to know what to say.

At last, he asked, "Did someone hit you on the head again, Mr. Crag?"

"Not in the past twenty-four hours," I replied. "I'm lucky to be alive, aren't I? But then, aren't we all? Life is grand. Something is desperately, desperately wrong with me."

I turned and marched up the hallway, down the stairs, and into the basement proper. Mannix hustled to keep up with me.

"What's the matter?" the elf asked. "Mr. Crag, the office doesn't even open for another two hours. You aren't usually in for another three hours after that at the earliest. And since you were here yesterday, I didn't expect to see you until next week."

"Yes, that's lamentably true. I need to remedy my poor work habits, among all my other bad life habits."

The dank of the basement smelled like roses, which sparked a thought as well as a grin that caused the gener-ally unused muscles in my face necessary for the expression to rebel by aching like heck.

"We should send Doris some flowers," I insisted.

"I already did, Mr. Crag," Mannix pleaded, seemingly worried for some reason that I couldn't fathom. After all, everything was so absolutely, exquisitely perfect, what was there to possibly worry about?

"Yes, but this time I want to pay my share. I don't know why I told you before that I'd only chip in to send a swarm of bees to her hospital room. I vaguely recall saying something about pollination and flowers growing out of her bedpan if she waited long enough. Also that she could keep the honey. But that's silly. The hospital staff wouldn't allow enough time to pass for flowers to grow in a dirty bedpan. Well, *maybe* if she was staying at the VA, but she's at Holy Guacamole, isn't she?"

"Yes, sir," the elf in the panda pajamas replied, his concern growing only deeper.

"Excellent," I said. "Cancel the bees and send the most wonderful secretary in the world a giant bushel of posies with a card offering her my sincere best wishes and a heartfelt hope for the speedy recovery of her ailing hairdo. Also, I have very clearly somehow been drugged. I will need my personal physician, Dr. Charlotte Cheese, to come over and take a gallon of my blood and whatever else she needs to harvest for immediate testing. In the meantime, I will be lying down and possibly dying behind this stack of 1980s pornographic magazines."

I noted the growing fear on the face of my able assistant, but didn't much worry about it as I dropped down onto the cement floor, settled my head on Bo Derek's impressive rack, and promptly passed out.

14

I awoke in surroundings much more pleasant than the damp, grimy floor of my office building's basement; the damp, grubby sheets of the Paradise Motel; or the embryonic Hazmat site that was my apartment. I was still on a floor, but I now had soft cushions beneath me. Someone had thoughtfully tossed a blanket over me.

My arm hurt like hell and a worried elf in a little business suit was staring down at me. Mannix didn't seem to be much relieved when my eyes fluttered open.

"Do you feel any better, Mr. Crag?"

"I was wondering the same thing, Mannix," I said. "Let me see."

I paused for a moment before answering to get a really firm sense of myself physically and mentally, as well as of my greater place in the larger world. I cast a broad net to drag in any and all emotions, not wishing to leave anything to chance.

"In every imaginable way," I replied, "I feel like shit."

The elf was heaving a sigh of relief as I pushed myself up to my elbows.

I was in Mannix's remarkable little apartment in the corner of the basement. Neither sofa nor bed were large enough to accommodate my average human length, and so my host had dragged his mattress and all the cushions he could plunder out into the middle of his living room carpet and set me up like the king of goddamn Siam.

I glanced around at the cushions beneath me. "Hold on, Mannix," I announced in a deeply somber tone. "There's something here that I believe is desperately important."

Mannix waited for me to say more, but when I didn't, he ventured, "Yes?"

"Oh," I said, more than a little deflated. "You expect *me* to know what it is? That's disappointing, because I haven't got a goddamn clue."

I dragged my back up against his sofa, which was stripped of cushions, and examined my aching arm.

My trench coat and suit jacket were gone. My shirt sleeve was rolled up. A piece of tape held a wad of cotton gauze over a black and blue bruise on my right forearm.

"Dr. Charlotte came for your blood," Mannix explained. "She also took some saliva and hair. She called with the first results a little while ago. She said that she couldn't find anything so far." (Here he consulted a scrap of paper in his little hand.) "'There is nothing to indicate that he...'" He looked up. "That's you," he explained.

"Got it," I said. Just for a moment, I very carefully partially collapsed from the sheer exhaustion of having to listen to the jotted-down opinion of my pain in the ass physician.

Mannix was back at the scrap of paper. "'There is nothing to indicate that he has swallowed, inhaled, injected or absorbed anything worse than the...*stuff* he regularly pours down his throat every day.'" Mannix looked up and shook his head. "Dr. Charlotte said something naughtier than 'stuff,' but I couldn't write *that* down."

"No problem. I'm a shitty stenographer too. How long

have I been out?"

Mannix checked his watch. "Two days. At first it sounded like you were having some very nice dreams. You were talking in your sleep a lot. You were having lots of nice and happy conversations with people. Then yesterday you weren't so friendly. Just a little while ago, you changed. You were still talking sometimes, but you weren't very cheerful any longer. I hoped that meant you were getting better."

He didn't say it as an insult, since Mannix had no idea how to hurt anybody's feelings. He was actually genuinely optimistic that my increasingly nasty nocturnal blathering meant that I was reverting back to my regular asshole self.

"I'm better than I was, that's for goddamn sure," I said. "If I'm ever that nice to anybody again, hit me in the back of the head with a shovel."

I can't generally remember my dreams. I imagined it was an act of self-preservation from a mind that knew only too well the horrible reality of my daily life. If I unwittingly spent my nights merrily sailing a shot glass boat on a distillery sea only to awaken to a middle aged life, the great achievements of which were a faded P.I. license and two dress shirts to my name, it was likely that Waking Me would toddle out to the garage and attempt to permanently jumpstart my REM cycle by hooking it up to the tailpipe of my car. This day, however, was different.

I had vague memories of shapes and a few flashes of faces from what had apparently been a two-day coma. One of the faces that suddenly hopped out pretty clearly belonged to the overly friendly business dame I'd encountered on the sidewalk outside my apartment on the morning I first saw the shadow of Invictus in my toaster. She was smiling and chatting, although I couldn't recall what my dream dame had said.

"That is exceedingly strange," I said, after the image of the woman had scattered like a puff of smoke.

It was as if a dream had intruded on reality. Indeed, the ugly puss of the dame had momentarily superimposed itself over the face of my elf assistant.

"What's wrong now?" asked Mannix, clearly worried that he wasn't going to be able to keep track of the mounting list of my unknown troubles.

"Wait right here," I said. "Let me try something."

I closed my eyes. Two more shapes immediately rocketed up from the dancing floaters on my eyelids, coalescing into Myron Wasserbaum, D.D.S. and Luigi Vincetti, evil fascist fishmonger. It disturbed me to think that the forces that controlled my dreams might have been shoving this pair of assholes into my unsuspecting unconscious for years. On the other hand, at least I had the pleasure of telling the two of them off during both my waking and sleeping hours.

Except my vague memory told me this wasn't the case.

I suddenly had a very clear image of the dentist and the fishmonger, as well as several other SOBs from the neighborhood, all standing around, chatting and laughing and enjoying the hell out of one another's scintillating company. And since this was clearly the worst nightmare in human history, I was standing in their midst. And for some unfathomable reason I was not pointing out their hilarious flaws and foibles and hating them and enjoying the fact that they hated me back, I was actually conversing with these evil morons and reprobates. I saw my hands gesturing, and I heard a sound coming out of my throat which I could only assume was laughter, since it was a noise hitherto alien to my mouth hole. And it was one big giant joyful cocktail party, without the only thing that made cocktail parties bearable: namely, goddamn cocktails. Also without the second thing that made a cocktail party perfect: namely, nobody there to get drunk but me.

I detested these people in the real world. What's more, they rightly detested me back. Even more than that, they all hated the hell out of each other with great determination, vigor, and in the case of one party attendee in particular, pickerels jammed up a tailpipe.

"Something is definitely very wrong here, Mannix," I announced.

The ominous dread in my voice couldn't possibly convey my horror at the thought of enjoying Vincetti's company, even if only in a nighttime hallucination. I was sure my sleeping mind didn't hate itself so much that it would willingly inflict upon the both of us something so masochistic.

In my memory of my dream, the nightmare version of Vincetti said something impossible for my waking deaf ears to hear. Instantly, the familiar, repulsive faces of my horrible neighbors erupted in laughter. So vivid was the memory that I could smell the stink of rotting fish from Vincetti; a whiff of Midnight in Chechnya perfume off of Madame Carpathia, the top floor dance instructor; B.O. from Olaf the bespectacled Viking corner locksmith; and the stench of failure, prosecution and mint dental floss off of Wasserbaum the malpracticing third floor dentist.

I was about to open my eyes and hopefully scatter the visions of my memory, but all at once something new appeared. A ghostly black shadow was suddenly gliding silently and pretty goddamned ominously along the back of the crowd.

It kept its distance, this unknown entity, hugging walls

that I was hitherto unaware were present. Something about it felt important, although I hadn't a clue if it was anything more than my dreaming mind conjuring some version of the recent memory of smoke pouring from the tailpipe of the Paradise Motel night manager's Bonneville, which had chased me back into my crummy motel room like a charging Pamplona bull. Still, it felt like it could be important, so I kept my eyes clamped shut.

The vision of neighborhood assholes dancing in my head vanished, each SOB exploding in a puff of smoke, and I was suddenly transported to another memory.

The smoke that had been Vincetti and the others drew back in on itself and reformed into a pair of nearly identical shapes. I had suddenly been thrust back three days before to my visit with the asexual mattress salesmen Salome and Sam.

He still looked like a transitioning she, she like half-a-he, both were deliriously happy and each was groping the hell out of the other. If this was the sort of thing I usually dreamt about, I couldn't offer enough thanks to my conscious mind for suppressing, repressing or murdering the hell out of my dreams.

The mattress peddlers were on a bed on their showroom floor, and I thanked the camera in my mind for panning off the memory of what should have been a nightmare but, bizarrely, didn't give me the sense of the horror my waking mind knew it to be.

Another image came into view. It had the shape of a man but it was difficult to focus on since Mannix suddenly chimed in, breaking my concentration.

"Who's Mr. Sandan?" the elf asked, his voice strangely distant and dreamlike.

Or maybe Mannix asked the exact right question at the exact right time.

The unknown figure that my mind's eye was trying to recapture from my two day slumber came into sharp focus.

In the memory of my dream, I was standing nose to nose with one of the cardboard standees from Salome and Sam's Mattress Emporium. The guy in the photo in my mind was wearing the same dark blue suit he'd been wearing in the promotional picture. He had a long beak and a pair of dark eyes rimmed with black bags.

I looked deeply into the eyes of the standee.

Staring into the limpid pools of another guy isn't something I'm in the habit of doing unless it's a bookie and I'm pleading for my life, but there was something warmly inviting in the depths of the standee's freezing cold, incredibly dark black eyes. Besides, I figured as a cartoon cutout in a photograph in the memory of a dream I wasn't quite sure I remembered having, Sandan wouldn't really give a shit if I took a moment to ogle him.

Except it turned out that maybe he did.

I became aware of the same eavesdropping black cloud that had been swirling at the periphery of my previous dream memory. It sat there hovering for a moment, spinning in on itself like a flushed toilet filled with soot and glitter.

All at once, the high-tech 1960s *Star Trek* special effect rocketed forward, slamming the back of the standee and causing it to rock in place.

The cardboard face leaned toward my own mug and the brow of the photo was suddenly drawn into a furious V. The eyes that had been staring off into the distance in photographic blankness snapped to one side and glared hard into what I could only assume was my soul, since I'd never before met the inchoate spirit that allegedly lived inside my wearily — suddenly frantically — beating heart.

Fortunately, my eyes snapped open before I required a change of underwear which, since I apparently hadn't been home in three days, was an outcome imperative to avoid.

I thought I had been awake the entire time, but now that I was back in the land of the living I had the sense that I had been half-asleep and was only now fully awake. In fact, I came back around in mid-snore, which indicated to the genius detective in me that I'd drifted off for at least a moment. A weird, lingering, logy sense of a dozing mind remained even as I snapped back to reality.

I had awakened for the second time in the span of ten minutes staring into the worried face of my elf assistant.

"Who's Mr. Sandan?" Mannix repeated, this time much more clearly.

"Pillows," I announced.

The non sequitur apparently didn't give my assistant the same frisson of exuberant discovery as it did me. In fact, as I pawed around at the stuffed bundles on which my ass had been thoughtfully propped, Mannix took a cautious step back.

I held up a small pillow and waved it around in triumph.

"*That's* what was missing in Pinder's apartment," I said. "There were no pillows on his bed or on the living room couch and chairs. Not one pillow in his whole dump. I knew *something* was missing, but I couldn't put my finger on it. In my defense, the windows were painted over and the walls had just given birth to a ravenous, man-eating monster, but even as I was pissing my pants in terror I knew there was something that I didn't see flying around in the hurricane in his living room. Pinder didn't have a single pillow in his whole joint."

I tossed the little throw pillow onto Mannix's cushion-less couch.

"Is that important?" the elf asked.

"Monumentally," I said. "I have no idea why," I added, lest he expect these genius epiphanic moments to go on all afternoon. "Wait, yes I do. The standee. You asked about that pillow bastard Sandan. Why?"

"You were just saying his name," Mannix replied. "Didn't you hear yourself?"

"No, I was apparently asleep again. Besides, nobody else ever listens to me, why should I? Did I say anything else?"

Mannix shook his head.

"Too bad," I said. "I could have used some free assistance from the greatest private eye on earth. Okay, so Sandan is a pillow peddler, and Pinder had no pillows in his apartment. Why does that matter? Beats the hell out of me. Not to mention, although I will, that two of Pinder's pals who kidnapped me were smothered under a pillow while the third, Grasse got his brains blown out under one. So there's that as well."

I stopped deducing for a moment, since being brilliant had triggered what I suddenly realized was an incredibly full bladder that had been patient for two days of unconsciousness but would await evacuation no longer.

When I returned to Mannix's living room minutes later, I had a vitally important announcement to make.

"Cancel any flowers that I may have told you to order for Doris while I was out of my mind," I said. "She's the worst secretary since the dawn of time. Neanderthals would still be ruling this planet if the *homo sapiens* had put that dingbat in charge of getting out the memo to be fruitful and multiply."

It was clear from the look on his face he'd already followed through on the batshit crazy command I'd made while stoned.

"I sent them two days ago," Mannix said. "Miss Doris' mother already called to thank you for the nice flowers."

A monstrous face suddenly appeared out of the ether, covered in pancake makeup and with its mouth silently yapping. It zoomed in on me, and I had to duck to keep it from slamming into my puss. The hideous monstrosity in giant plastic curlers flashed by my shoulder and vanished before it could splatter like a paintball against the wall.

When I straightened up, Mannix was staring at me with the same look of deep concern that had taken over for his normally boundless joviality. The wall behind me was as clean as ever, with no sign of the exploded head.

"I'm fine, Mannix. It was just a hyper-realistic dream flashback. You said the other day that Doris' mother was being uncharacteristically pleasant."

"She was again today," Mannix said. "She's been very nice lately."

"There's far too much of that going around. I hadn't assumed when you first told me that you meant pleasant for a normal person. I just figured you meant nice for Doris' ratbag old lady. Pleasant for her is not hurling that alopecia-afflicted cat she wears to bed at the mailman for undressing her with his eyes. Mind you, I was dating Doris then. I told her that men, in fact, *dress* her with their eyes. I got a feral cat in the face, too. It was worth it. But apparently Doris' battleaxe mother was at the party in my head as well. Mannix, everybody I hate has apparently become my best friend between sundown and sunup. That can't be allowed to go on. But we now have what seems to be a clear link between Pinder and whatever happened to me these past two days."

"Miss Dr. Charlotte said you weren't drugged," Mannix pointed out. "And I was at the naughty man's apartment before you, and nothing happened to me."

"Oh, I didn't tell you that part?" I said. "I didn't get anything from Pinder's place except almost eaten and beheaded. It was the motel pillow. Whatever happened to me last night — which, yes, I realize was several days ago — was the result of me resting my unsuspecting head on a poisoned Sleep-Tite Pillow."

15

"Good morning," the receptionist threatened into the phone, "Myron Wasserbaum, D.D.S. If you're a cop, a Fed or if you're with the American Dental Association Task Force on Gross Oral Incompetence, you have to tell me."

"None of the above," I replied. "Let me talk to Wasserbaum."

"Wait a minute, I know that voice. That's you, isn't it, Banyon? You son of a bitch, you still owe me for dinner. *Plus* that extra twenty you conned out of me."

While Wasserbaum's office and Banyon Investigations were on either end of the No Man's Land that was our shared hallway, I may have once or twice staged a successful incursion into enemy territory and fraternized the hell out of the evil dentist's knockout receptionist, all for the noble purpose of establishing a lasting peace, or at least one night of vigorous détente. I hadn't seen her in the hall for a few months and I'd hoped she'd quit to pursue her absurd dream of being the first dame ever to work for Wasserbaum not to be indicted as a coconspirator.

I thought I'd have to mount a defense of the indefensible acts I'd committed against the receptionist, which would prove difficult since I didn't remember them, but at the mention of my name I heard another voice chime in from the background.

"Banyon?" called the distant voice of Wasserbaum, whose crimes against dentistry would one day give a whole new meaning to the term "oral arguments" in a dock at The Hague. "*Crag* Banyon? Gimme! Gimme!"

The phone clunked. Clearly his annoyed receptionist had let it drop from her fingers onto her counter. It was fumbled up by Wasserbaum.

"Crag, old friend, how are you?" Wasserbaum cried. "Why are you calling? Not that I mind, it's always good to hear from you. But you could have come over to see me. You're right down the hall."

"No, Wasserbaum, I'm not. Which is good news for you at the moment because you're being excessively nice again and I have a loaded gun. Also, we're not old friends, we are new friends, and currently only one of us mistakenly thinks that. I think I know why. Did you buy a new pillow recently?"

"Why, yes," Wasserbaum replied. "You really are a great detective, aren't you? I picked up one of those new Sleep-Tites. I saw one of their infomercials on late night TV. Promised me a good night's sleep. I could use it with the trial coming up."

For Wasserbaum there was always a trial coming up, from selling watered-down nitrous oxide to an undercover cop, to accidentally filling in a patient's right nostril rather than his mandibular second molar while stoned on nitrous oxide.

"Since I bought a Sleep-Tite, I've been getting the best sleep I ever had," Wasserbaum said. "It's made me a new man."

"The good news is that I don't think it has," I said.

"Not permanently, anyway. Which is good because I can't take much more of Wasserbaum 2.0. Underneath, you're still the same incompetent asshole you've been since you flunked out of the first three Caribbean dental schools you attended. Yes, I've known for a long time. I was saving it for a rainy day. I also know how you finally got your degree from Haiti School of the Mouth, which is nothing but a van with a dental chair parked in a Port-au-Prince Subway parking lot. I even found your graduation ceremony on YouTube. Very moving. You and that other guy getting a five buck coupon for a foot-long sub before they shoved you out of the van. So, do you still not want to kill me?"

"What, for that? I wouldn't be much of a friend if I did. And you wouldn't be much of a detective if you couldn't find something like that out. And you're a *great* private investigator, Crag. The best in the business."

"Your diploma is printed on a meatball sub wrapper."

"Well, we make do, Crag old friend," Wasserbaum said. "You can't see me, but I'm winking right now. Tell Crag I'm winking, Beverly."

"Screw you, Banyon," snarled the echoing voice of his receptionist from somewhere in the depths of Wasserbaum's dental slaughterhouse.

"You wouldn't happen to know if Vincetti bought a Sleep-Tite, too?" I asked.

At first, I thought my theory was shot to hell aborning.

"No, sir, he didn't," Wasserbaum began. "*I* bought one for him. The poor fellow was always in such a sour mood. I *tried* to tell him how mine changed my life, but he wouldn't listen. He even dumped a bucket of fish guts on my car. Well, that was just a *cry* for help, poor fellow.

When he did that, I drove right over to Salome and Sam's and picked him up a Sleep-Tite. He agrees with me now. He says he hasn't slept this well or felt this good in years. He's a changed man. Say, do you want to join us for lunch? We're going out today with a few other folks from the building."

I was lost in thought. "No, I hate all of you," I said, absently.

"Well, if you change your mind," the dentist said. "By the way, there were some fellas asking about you yesterday. One of them had a trumpet. We tried your office door, but it was locked. I hope you're not going out of business. I know I speak for everybody in the building when I say we certainly don't want to lose you."

"That's just pillow talk, Wasserbaum," I said. "Deep down, you still think I'm an asshole. You're not wrong. As proof, I offer the fact that I was certain your receptionist with the enormous rack's name was Betty."

I hung up the phone on the old-fashioned cradle. The telephone sat on the coffee table that was parked in front of Mannix's reassembled sofa, three stories and a basement down from Wasserbaum's practice. The elf was in his bedroom. I could hear him talking on the other side of the closed door.

"Yes, ma'am, thank you. Please give her our best wishes. It was very nice talking to you, too. You're welcome."

Mannix came hustling out into the living room a moment later, a cell phone clutched tight in his little hand.

"You were right, Mr. Crag," the elf said, out of breath and typically exuberant. "Miss Doris' mother bought a Sleep-Tite Pillow last week."

"Wasserbaum and Vincetti are confirmed as well," I

said. "That's the common thread. Those pillows are somehow convincing complete jerks that they're actual human beings." I had a sudden, terrible thought. "You don't have a Sleep-Tite, do you?"

"Oh, no, sir," Mannix said, shaking his head. "I always make my own pillows."

"That's good. I'd hate to find out after all this time that the only reason you're not as horrible as the rest of us is because you're being brainwashed every night. Speaking of which, I feel compelled to point out to everyone who's ever gently nagged me about my intemperance—" I shot my occasionally mildly hectoring elf assistant a look. "—that submerging my brain in a cleansing nightly alcohol bath has the opposite effect of these Sleep-Tite Pillows. From what I can tell, they produce nothing but hypocrites. Give me a sincere angry drunk any day of the week. Booze might turn the consumer into a surly SOB, but at least we're being honest when we're yelling at you in the aspirin aisle at Walgreens. Hell is a world where some nefarious bastard has robbed the Wasserbaums and Vincettis the right to their innate asshole-ness."

"But Mr. Crag," Mannix said, dragging me back to our on-topic disaster, "I don't understand how this connects to the naughty man who had you kidnapped or why he'd want to hide from his own guardian angel."

"That makes two of us," I said. "But Pinder's pals were killed by or under pillows, and Pinder didn't have a single pillow in his apartment. There's a connection " I stood up, portentously announcing,. "I've got some shopping to do. And for a change this time, mostly not for booze."

"Mr. Crag, you should rest. You haven't had anything to eat in at least two days, and there are still some things we have to go over."

"Are they work related?" I asked as I shrugged on my suit jacket and trench coat, both of which my efficient, indispensable elf assistant had cleaned and carefully draped on wooden hangers which he'd hung over pegs by his front door.

"Yes, sir."

"Good. Maybe I'll get murdered and I won't have to deal with them."

"*Please*, Mr. Crag."

I had made it out his front door and into the cellar. Sweet freedom, quite possibly from breathing, lay tantalizingly close. But in that one word "please" it was clear the little guy was actually begging for my life, which even I wouldn't have done out of fear that getting down on my knees would ruin the creases in the rumpled Sears trousers in which I'd just taken a two day siesta. With a sigh, I turned back around.

"I'll give you *one* thing, Mannix," I said. "Prioritize, and give me the first thing that comes to mind."

There were apparently several vital things he was thinking of at the same time. It looked like his brain would overload as his huge eyes darted back and forth in desperate, two-second contemplation. At last he turned on the heel of his highly polished little shoe and flew back inside his apartment. He returned with an envelope.

"I ran out and picked them up when Dr. Charlotte was here," the elf explained breathlessly. He handed over the package from the CVS photo center.

I'd forgotten about the pictures I'd taken of the dead men in the van behind Marigold's Bakery. They were certainly worth examining, preferably with a warm bar stool under my ass, but now wasn't really the time. Still, I'd given Mannix a choice of which irritating, business-related issue he thought I needed to address on my way out the door. I was just grateful that it didn't have to do with pension plans or his ridiculous annual assertion that the IRS was interested in my business any more than I was interested in its affairs, both of which were the usual sort of things my assistant thought should merit the attention of the busy CEO of Banyon Investigations, Inc. Purely for the sake of not disappointing an assistant who I couldn't afford to lose to another P.I. firm — since he was the only one who ever put in a goddamn day's work around here — I tipped the photos out of the envelope and quickly leafed through them.

I held up a photo of Dan Jenkins with his eyes at half mast. "This is a must for the photo album. It proves that the camera adds ten pounds of stupid."

There were pictures of the two dead men lying in the back of the van.

Both had been suffocated under the pillow that had then been used to muffle the shot that had finished off William Grasse. I noticed something lying on the floor of the van next to the body of the bastard whose jaw I'd busted. Some kind of pill bottle had dropped out of his pocket, but I couldn't read the small print on the label.

I didn't have a shot of Grasse's body from inside the bakery. Not that it would have done me much good. His face had been scrambled eggs under the torn and charred pillow. I had a momentary flashback of goose feathers vomiting out of a ripped hole and blowing all around the bakery's backroom. The mental image was enough to put me off tarts for the rest of my life which, had it arrived twenty years earlier, would have saved me a bundle in alimony payments.

I shifted through the remaining photos rapidly. The last one was a long distance shot of Salome and Sam's Mattress Emporium, which I'd glimpsed through my lens.

I hadn't realized my itchy trigger finger had snapped the image. A worthless shot.

I was about to slide the final photo back inside the envelope along with the rest, when I noticed something above the roof of the mattress store.

"What the hell is this?" I asked.

When I looked up, Mannix was no longer standing in his doorway. Alone, I ducked back into his place, fishing in my pocket as I charged across the living room.

There was a good, strong reading lamp on an end table, along with the most recent issue of *Magnetic North: The Periodical for the Modern Elf.* I switched on the lamp and set the picture down on the magazine, which featured a cover photo of a bunch of elves standing next to a Formula One racecar, their little arms crossed arrogantly over their skinny chests. Behind the pit crew a pair of gloved hands stretched up to grip for dear life onto the steering wheel, the only evidence of a driver in the cockpit of the car. One turn of the wheel would result in a spectacular crash, and I took a second to wonder why nobody had informed me of the existence of elf NASCAR or where I could place a bet.

Mannix was making a racket hustling around in his kitchen. I was glad he wasn't present to witness the embarrassing stereotype of my P.I. magnifying glass that I pulled from my pocket. I hunched over the table to examine the photo.

It had been a perfect summer day three days before (if you were the kind of asshole who went for that sort of thing). The sky had been nearly entirely free of clouds and there hadn't been so much as a hint of inclement weather. So why was there a dark cloud hovering over Salome and Sam's Mattress Emporium?

The cloud was small. Easily missed. Clearly, in fact,

missed by me the first time around, since I hadn't seen the it through my camera lens when I'd taken the shot. Before I confirmed it was a cloud with the aid of my magnifying glass I thought it could be a swarm of bees, which would have been terrific luck if I could have rounded them up and delivered them to Doris' hospital room to make up for the appalling error of the flowers.

It wasn't bees or a swarm of any other insects. Nor was it a storm cloud or even a signal to parking lot pilgrims that the mattress store had elected a new pope. What the black cloud in the photo clearly was, much to my regrettably sober surprise, was the exact same swirling black mist I'd seen in my dreams.

I only had the hazy memories from my multi-day coma to go on, since the greater details had evaporated from my waking mind. But I knew with certainty that this was the same cloud I'd seen gliding along at the far distant edge of the amiably chatting crowd of horrible fishmongers and malefactor dentists. It was the same swirling black mist that had attacked the cardboard promotional standee in the mattress store in my dream. And here it was in real life, hovering over the exact same goddamn retail outlet where I'd first seen the standee of pillow maker Sandan.

I left the other pictures I'd taken on Mannix's end table and shoved the shot of the black cloud into my pocket along with my magnifying glass.

I was heading back for the door when Mannix came charging out of the kitchen carrying a little brown paper bag, which he shoved into my hands.

"You *need* something to eat, Mr. Crag," he insisted.

My rumbling stomach agreed, and voiced its deafening opinion on the subject.

"Be careful while I'm gone, Mannix," I warned. "Don't open the door for any clouds of black smoke you don't already know. And Wasserbaum says the angels were upstairs rattling our doorknob yesterday. They won't be letting up anytime soon."

"They could still see you leaving," Mannix warned. "*Please* let me go do whatever you need to do."

"No. For all I know they were peeking in our office windows when you were still upstairs filing the rubbish in triplicate. They may have made you, too. Stay out of sight here. I'll be back as fast as my curvaceous pins will carry me. Hopefully they'll be more wobbly by then. And for a good reason, not because I staggered in here like a chicken — which in the cowardly sense I am — with my head angelically amputated."

16

I snuck out the basement door and down the alley without alerting the heavenly host to my presence. As I walked, I stuffed into a pocket of my trench coat a pair of heavy ancient work gloves that I'd filched off a cellar work-bench.

My head was frustratingly clear now, and I was amazed that the la-la version of me who'd practically (and, I suddenly recalled, for one embarrassing half-block *actually*) skipped back from the Paradise Motel hadn't gotten the smiting to end all smotes. I was much more cautious this day than I had been on my return to Mannix's place, especially given Wasserbaum's report that a bunch of angels armed with a trumpet had been peeking through my office keyhole. They were out there, they were watching, and they were — risks of both sacrilege and to eternal ass duly noted — goddamn SOBs.

Mannix had packed me a lunch of a couple of ham and cheese sandwiches, a tinfoil-wrapped dill pickle, a little bag of potato chips, and a pair of sacrificial Twinkies, all of which I devoured greedily en route to my final destination. I even downed the two cans of carbonated crap he'd wrapped in foil in the paper bag he'd supplied for my field trip, as I had discovered to my horror that I'd bled my main flask as well as my three emergency backups dry. I would need to recharge my alcohol batteries soon or risk a complete catastrophic system collapse or, worse, sobriety.

Fortunately, the place I was heading wasn't too far away as the bus flies. I was sure it would be a quick trip in and out, followed by a merry jaunt to the nearest package store, an hour after which, provided the wind was at my back, I'd be blissfully passed out under the nearest park bench until next Thursday.

The bus vomited me out onto sticky pavement, and I hoofed it to a large mall that sprawled over half the block. Several small stores were bracketed by a pair of anchor outlets. On one end was a Hole Foods, the hipster supermarket chain that only sold items that had been chewed through the center by the bugs and rats that weren't killed like they sensibly should have been because the goddamn hippie owners refused to spray for pests. On the other end was the store for which I made a beeline.

Bed, Bath & Barn was a retail chain that specialized in items for upscale homes and rural farms. If you wanted an appliance to help milk a cow or juice an orange, they had what you needed in aisle twelve, at only a two hundred percent markup over the same exact item at Target or the local general store.

I passed stacks of $450 Armani hay bales and boxes of four $200 Caterpillar napkin rings on my way over to the "Bed" 1/3 of the store. On my way, I nabbed a good, sturdy pair of $150 Christian Dior barbecue tongs that were hanging conveniently on a rack in the middle of the main aisle near the cash registers. I tore the cardboard backing from the tongs as I fished in my pocket for the work gloves I'd swiped from the basement of my office building. It was a tough fit to get the fingers of the gloves through the holes, but as I walked I managed to get a couple of good maraca clicks out of the tongs.

The number of shoppers grew thicker over in the bed department, but I didn't realize anything was amiss until I followed the arrows to the pillow section, turned a corner, and came abruptly face-to-face with the man of my goddamn dreams.

Another day, another retail outlet, another cardboard standee.

Today Only! Meet M. Sandan, Inventor of the Sleep-Tite Pillow!

The black-rimmed eyes of Sandan stared coldly at me from the photograph. However, they were not quite so cold as the actual peepers that were set into the actual skull of the real-life version of Sandan himself.

The bastard just happened to be sitting at a table five feet away from my justifiably shocked mug. When I stumbled upon the scene, Sandan was in the middle of schmoozing up a portly, middle-aged dame while autographing her pillow.

"'Gladys,' you say?" he was asking. "What a lovely name." While he droned, his hand was already at work on its own independent business, scribbling with great élan on the clean, white polyester.

A crowd of ecstatic admirers jammed the aisle, forming a line behind the dame at the table. All were waiting for a stranger to make weird stains on their pillows, which could cost upwards of ten bucks at the Paradise Motel but here came free with the $65 purchase of a Sleep-Tite Pillow. There were silver posts and velvet ropes, a no fly zone that was enforced by a couple of drowsy-looking bodyguards.

Sandan was aware that I'd crashed the party, either alerted by my abrupt appearance or by the fact that I immediately threw my transmission into tiptoe reverse.

The guest of honor didn't glance up right away. He was apparently used to people popping up at his elbow in the Bed, Bath & Barn pillow aisle, and used to his bodyguards keeping the riffraff at bay. He wore the kind of practiced bored expression you'd expect from a celebrity who'd dealt with gate crashers a hundred times already that afternoon.

"I'm grateful for your enthusiasm for my wonderful product," he said, glancing up at me with exhausted eyes, "but all these nice people were here fir—"

When he saw who it was making a slow-motion escape, the bastard did a comic double-take so over the top it would have embarrassed Sid Caesar.

Even though I'd never before met the pillow pimp outside my horribly pleasant nightmares, Sandan gave me a look that started with shock, then flashed to a deeply disturbing, sinister recognition. His eyes locked firmly on my own and he froze in place, his autograph hand stock-still over the pillow on his table.

Giggling hausfrau Gladys, still standing at the head of the line, was oblivious to the fact that she had stumbled in between Brian Dennehy and Kevin Kline at the end of *Silverado*, or maybe more accurately judging by the hungry fury Sandan was directing my way, between Kirstie Alley and a fatally understocked all-you-can-eat Chinese buffet.

"Could you write on that, 'To sleep, purchased to dream?'" Glady prodded. (Judging solely by her plastic curlers, the sic flirted with wit purely by accident.)

Sandan, still staring at me, finally blinked. "Of course, my dear," he replied, forcing a soothing Perry Como tone.

The pillow maker was autographing with a long, quivering feather quill. He was suddenly gripping it hard enough between the tips of his pale, bony fingers that somewhere in Canada the donor goose was rubbing its ass and squawking to Celine Dion about a phantom pinch. The blob of ink which he'd dragged over from an inkwell at his elbow clung to the quill's nib like the last drop of blood from a rapidly dehydrating corpse. When he spoke, the fat drop of ink detached from the quill and splattered a deep blueberry stain on the pure white canvas.

"Look, we both see this is awkward," I said, taking another step back. "Frankly, my real beef at the moment isn't with you, it's with the store manager for not posting a warning out front that they were hosting the psycho who's been invading the dreams of everybody in town. I'll register a complaint from Guam, where I plan to mail myself if I'm not too dead to flag down the first US Postal Service truck I see."

I'd backed up to the end of the aisle. I had smooth sailing from there at breakneck speed to the front of the store, from which point there was a better than fifty percent chance that I'd follow through with my vow to tackle a passing mail truck. Unfortunately, my federal crime spree ended before it began when I walked backwards into a solid brick wall.

I glanced back to find that a rogue mason had not, in fact, silently built a maximum security prison behind me at the end of the aisle. I was staring at a very large shoulder. If I had to guess, my first instinct was to assume someone had cut the tusks off a mastodon and shoved the poor extinct bastard into an ugly, rumpled suit.

I looked up from the shoulder. More shoulder. I hadn't looked up enough.

I looked up a little more. There wasn't a neck, which missing anatomical feature on the behemoth made the strain on my own craning neck less severe.

I saw a chin surmounted by a pair of cavernous black nostrils.

"There were some Versace nose clippers down front," I informed the mountain, who was obviously one of Sandan's bodyguards. "If I'm not back with them in ten years, feel free to drop dead."

I tried to jam past the SOB, but he dropped a hand like a cartoon anvil on my shoulder. The sheer weight of the furry mitt nearly brought me to my knees.

"Oh, you won't be escaping, Mr. Banyon," Sandan menaced behind me. "Not this time. I had you at the Paradise Motel, but you got away from me."

"As creepy challenges to my masculinity go, I've had worse," I replied.

There was no getting out the way I'd gotten in. The mountain of muscle blocked my path. I did a "Niagara Falls" slow turn back around, dragging my eyes across shelves jammed with Sleep-Tite Pillows, until I was once more facing Sandan.

He was the picture of calm behind his table. Hands folded. Smug look on his gray bastard's face.

I wasn't surprised to see that the crowd had stopped its excited chattering. I'd heard the hush fall the instant my back was turned. A shared, far-off look had descended on the faces of the autograph hounds. I saw a whole lot of euphoric smiles and unblinking eyes partially obscured by drooping lids. Whatever happy waking coma they'd been experiencing when they'd come out in force to get their pillows signed, the mob was now clearly sound asleep and wide open to their hypnotist's suggestion, which I had diminishing hope would be a whole lot of hilarious goddamn chicken clucks.

The velvet ropes were down. Pillows that had been

hanging at sides or clutched to chests like babies were stretched out in both hands in the universal sign for suffocation. Even though their eyes were partly open, several of the murderous bastards were snoring like chainsaws and drooling on their pillows.

"I don't know how much you've learned, but I obviously can't let you go," Sandan said. He was flanked at his table by the two nearer, dozing guards.

"You probably only think that because you haven't tried," I helpfully suggested. "What say we give it a whirl? I bet you're good at it. Hell, if it doesn't work, we can always reconvene tomorrow and you can let me go again until you get it right."

The snoring giant with his hand on my shoulder twitched in his sleep like a dreaming dog and nearly drove me like a fence post through the Bed, Bath & Barn floor.

I yanked off one work glove and shoved my arm at a ninety-degree angle from the floor, snapping my fingers in front of the dumb bastard's face.

"Hey, Mount McKinley, wakey-wakey!"

Judging from the size of him, there had to be at least two people inside: one to wear the ugly head, the other shoved in the ass. The pantomime horse kept on snoring.

"It won't work, Mr. Banyon," Sandan said, rising to his feet. He rested his sickly knuckles on the edge of the table. "He's sound asleep. He was already partway there, my will has just put him under completely. And while he's under, he's mine. They are *all* mine. I'm afraid I have an appointment at a Kmart on the other side of town. I mustn't keep my growing fan base waiting. In the meantime, I'm afraid it's the big sleep for you here, Mr. Banyon. Good night. And pleasant, *pleasant* dreams."

I would have done a little halfhearted begging for my life since, like an old pair of skis stuffed for decades in the back of a closet, I'd always held off throwing it out myself because I figured that one day somebody other than me might find a use for it. However, I didn't even get a chance to begin a semi-sincere plea for clemency for my miserable ass before the pillow king, in a twist that M. Night Shama-Lama-Ding-Dong wouldn't have seen coming, suddenly started to melt away before my eyes.

It was as if some unseen hand were shaking the Etch-A-Sketch that held Sandan in human form.

It started at the top of his head. His slicked-down black hair disappeared, like the world was nothing but a dry erase board and he was being wiped from existence. The haunting eyes were quick to follow, then the bags below them. Rich dames in New York and Los Angeles would have shelled out a fortune to a plastic surgeon who could make major league eye bags like Sandan's disappear that fast.

His pulverized self was being dragged in one direction, like dust being sucked into a vacuum cleaner. When the grains that comprised his body began to quickly reform into a new shape, I was unsurprised to find that the form he was assuming was the same swirling black cloud I'd seen in my dreams and which I'd inadvertently snapped a photo of in the sky above Salome and Sam's Mattress Emporium.

As the black cloud expanded, tiny flashes of light within it popped like a miniature thunderstorm. The cloud was the red carpet at the Oscars, and the disintegrating B-list bastard was being hailed with flashbulbs by insect paparazzi.

Sandan's head was nearly completely gone. His lips moved one last time on the flat mushroom cap of his neck.

"Nighty-night, Mr. Banyon," the vanishing SOB threatened in soothing, horrible, sepulchral tones as his mouth danced off to join the rest of his disintegrated head inside the Aqua Net hairspray cloud that was parked in traffic off his left shoulder.

All at once, the slow-motion fizz that had evaporated his head became a silent dynamite blast that exploded his entire body from existence.

The Sandan supernova roared out in every direction. I would have covered my face from the stinging grains in the hurricane gust if not for the fact that one of my hands still clenched tight to the barbecue tongs while the other was suddenly somehow holding onto my gat.

Lucky for me my instincts worked faster than my brain. When I felt the weight of the behemoth bodyguard's hand begin to crush my shoulder I was already spinning around and pistol-whipping the SOB hard in the side of his primordial skull.

The bigger they are, the more bastards they can pin underneath them when the fall, an axiom simultaneously coined and proved when the meatheaded lummox with the .38 caliber knockout drop wiped out the first two surging bastards who were charging me, armed with fully loaded and unlicensed pillows. Pinned arms and legs bounced and slapped and were otherwise useless beneath the massive, snoring bodyguard.

I planted my foot on a shoulder like a muscled mesa and launched myself out into the main aisle.

Such dramatic bursts of histrionics might work to score Meryl Streep her eightieth Academy Award nomination, but all I managed to do was slam into a table display of copper pots and get my head wedged inside a rack of refrigerator magnets. Magnetized watermelon slices, cartoon turtles and overstuffed hamburgers showered me in plastic kitsch.

I was flat on my back and yanking the rack off my hat when the first of my would-be murderers came charging out into the main aisle, a pillow clutched like a garrote in white-knuckled hands. Gladys, the dame in curlers who'd been first in line at the autograph table, came at me in a spectacular housewife dive.

"ZZZZZZ!" she snored triumphantly. The ink blot Sandan had dripped on the pillow clenched in her fingers zoomed down at my face.

Before she could plant the pillow on my kisser with *Cuckoo's Nest* finality, I jammed a foot into her sagging belly. She hit my heel with an *oomph* of escaping wind, and for an instant it looked as if her sleepy eyes might wake up. The sole of my Florsheim was firmly planted, so in lieu of a "good morning" I gave the fatso a shove for the ages. She flew backwards, hands flapping like an out-of-control windmill, straight into two maniacs who were bringing up her rear. All three went down for the count.

A second slumber party wave flew from the aisle in a stampede and promptly tripped over the three that were already on the floor. Pillows flew out of hands as the next four went down on top of the growing pile.

Oreo magnets fell from the brim of my fedora as I scrambled to my feet, and with lightning reflexes honed from years of catching drinks slid down bars, I snatched one of the soaring pillows from the air with the Tyrannosaurus jaws of my tongs.

Prize in hand, I spun on one victorious heel.

Naturally, I immediately slipped on a plastic banana peel magnet, because life loves nothing more than to point at me and laugh its ass off. I twirled, tipped, wobbled, yet somehow managed not only to not wind up sprawled back on the floor, but somehow found that I was running like a madman for the front doors.

I'd barely made it eight feet when a swirl of black dust burst from the mouth of aisle 21. The Sandan cloud was followed by a mob of pillow-wielding lunatics.

I had a head of steam behind me by this point, not to mention the incentive of avoiding the comical obituary that would result from being murdered in such a ludicrous albeit humorous manner, and so when two guys in suits and a fatty Goth dame jumped forward to bar my path, I just kept right on running.

I sent an elbow at the bridge of one guy's nose and a shoulder into the other guy's chest, and with a leap like a pre-murderer O.J. at the airport, I was jumping over the collapsing bodies of the men and steamrollering straight over the squealing dame.

The black cloud dogged me, swirling furiously around my head as I ran.

I don't have the greatest willpower. I keep most of my vices on speed dial for easier access. But one thing I absolutely did not want to do at that moment was fall asleep. Yet as hard as I could fight it, it wasn't enough. Against my will I felt a strong tug of sudden exhaustion, and for an instant I was no longer in Bed, Bath & Barn.

It was a waking dream. I saw a landscape this time, much more than I'd recalled of the dreamscape back at Mannix's place. Beds with warm quilts and soft blankets populated a limitless field, like comfortably stuffed and inviting cattle. There were palm trees with fronds of feathers ruffling in the soft "zzzzzzzzz" purr that filled the air. Cotton clouds gently brushed a serene, twilight sky, and the giant crescent moon didn't threaten the infidel with slaughter, but invited the world-weary traveler to kick off his shoes and enjoy the view on the inside of his eyelids for the next eight hours.

An uncountable number of sheep jumped limitless fences into a muzzy twilight. Peppered throughout the landscape, as far as the eye could see, were the happiest, most relaxed people I'd ever seen not lying on their backs in a morgue. They stood in groups both large and small, chatting quietly in their pajamas. Some yawned, stretched, and climbed into one of the billion available, warm and comfortable beds.

The image had rocketed into my suddenly sleepy mind courtesy the Sandan cloud. This time, however, unlike the mugging at the Paradise Motel that had put me into a two day coma, I knew what to expect.

An entire adult lifetime of training like an Olympic marathoner to shake off alcohol-induced blackouts at a moment's notice in order to climb out bathroom windows to avoid angry creditors, landlords and current and/or ex-wives, suddenly asserted itself. With a whiplash snap of my head, I forced myself through the dream veil and back out into the real world. I awoke to see the black haze of the Sandan dust cloud drawing apart. Also, just in time to see a charging crazy man with a pillow tackle me to the floor.

I went down backwards, slamming my elbow hard and nearly dropping my piece, to which I still tightly clung. My attacker scrambled to sit on my chest. A plump pillow ambushed my face, and the noise of the busy store was abruptly muffled to a soft din beyond the suffocating lump of polyester.

My breath was gone. My lungs were suddenly bursting in my chest. Worst of all was the rush of total relaxation and utter peace that I could feel wash over my entire body from the Sleep-Tite Pillow that was enveloping my head.

Lucky for me, the SOB who'd blindsided me was a

scrawny little hipster jerk with retro glasses, skinny leg pants, no socks, and wrists like toothpicks. I lashed out blindly with my gun and was rewarded with the solid one-note symphony crack of Roscoe on Skull in D Major. The pillow fell from my face and my beanpole assailant slipped semiconscious off my chest.

I kept a firm grip on my trusty gat as I clambered back to my feet behind a stack of Prada lawn chairs.

Aside from the bastard on the floor, there was nobody else around. Sandan's cloud had escaped up a nearby aisle. I caught my breath as I considered my next move.

The front of the store was a million miles away. Instinct sharpened by years of cowardice was screaming at me to blast everything that moved between me and the front doors. But my attackers weren't zombies, they were just regular assholes stoned on sleep, courtesy Sandan and his Sleep-Tite Pillows. I was in enough trouble today without a hundred murder raps piled on top of the tottering shit heap that was my life.

The bastard on the floor groaned from behind one of those perfectly groomed beards-of-bees that hipsters glue to their goddamn chins like the decapitated tops of hairy cacti. Suddenly a bony hand launched out and grabbed my ankle and, more for his choice of lifestyle than for the fact that he wanted to murder me, I gave him a second whack to the temple. He went out like a light, hopefully to dream of a nightmare world without purple pork pie hats and goddamn man buns.

I screwed up my courage as best as I was able to without at least a .10% blood alcohol level, and stepped out from behind the stack of lawn furniture.

My appearance drew a sudden somnolent roar, like an angry lion yawning while in the middle of declaring himself king of the jungle. I wheeled around to see the Sandan cloud racing towards me at a hundred miles an hour. The desert sandstorm of directed fury was followed be a charging horde of exceedingly pissed off Sleep-Tite consumers.

Sandan redirected himself at the last instant, rocketing up and exploded against, and ultimately through, the ceiling, presumably late for his engagement at Kmart.

Tiny grains of glistering dandruff caught the air conditioning and blew off to the four corners of the store. At least I assumed they did. I wasn't present to see exactly where they ended up, as I was at that moment courageously running for the nearest exit like a French soldier from the opposite direction of "le charge!"

As I ran, Sandan's troops were pouring from the mouth of every aisle. Clearly the line for the autograph table must have wrapped around half the goddamn store.

My lungs burned like fire, my aching legs felt like they would collapse beneath me, and my wildly trilling bladder was a constant reminder of my official 1997 induction into the international cowards hall of fame.

Sleep-Tite bastards surged out in front of me, flooding the front of the store. At first dozens, then hundreds.

More continued to spill from the mouths of aisles like quarters from a one-armed bandit. Pleasantly napping, furious in their induced somnambulism, they crammed the main aisle, flipping display tables, advancing sleepily, smothering pillows at the ready. A few wore nightcaps, evidently mistaking the 21st century for a 1940s screwball comedy.

The thunder of hundreds of feet stampeded after me. Shelves collapsed from the earthquake vibrations. Can openers, toilet brushes and pie plates crashed to the floor.

I ducked arms, socked jaws, tripped bastards, and

somehow managed to weave through the mob of pillows with the nimbleness of an NFL Fanny Hill.

I was surprised as anyone to suddenly find myself running past the cash registers at a breakneck sprint, which would have been necessary even without a murderous mob on my tail, since I happened to be stealing the tongs and pillow to which I still desperately clutched.

Terrified cashiers dived for cover beneath cash registers. A hapless store greeter ordered me to have a nice day as I flashed by him at a hundred miles an hour. An instant later, I heard him being crushed by the stampeding mob.

I flew through the front doors. Behind me, store windows shattered. Boxes of crock pots and electric mixers soared through the panes, bouncing across the asphalt.

The air was broiling as I ran like a madman through the parking lot.

I am never lucky, so a lifetime of grabbing onto the shit end of the stick had earned me my one and only decent break, which appeared in the form of a city bus on its regular route that happened at that moment to pull to the curb at the edge of the parking lot. The door yawned open before me and I bounded up the stairs.

I was doubly lucky, as it was the same driver to whom I'd given fifty bucks earlier in the week to forget the fact that I had no coins to drop in his box.

"Drive!" I hollered.

"Exact change," the driver demanded.

"Fine, we can discuss your lack of gratitude or your short term memory loss as we're both being crushed inside your shit-smelling city bus."

I hopped aside and gave the ingrate bastard an unobstructed view outside.

The store was in ruins. A massive fire was burning out

of control, since union rules dictate that spontaneous fires must erupt at scenes of civil unrest. Smoke and flames rose from Bed, Bath & Barn. Overturned cars blazed in the parking lot, sending clouds of choking black fumes pirouetting into the air. Through the lot swarmed the silent mob, pillows held aloft, charging like Apaches for the parked bus.

The first sleepwalking killer reached the bus before the panicked driver could snap the doors shut. I mule-kicked the bastard onto his ass on the sidewalk.

A large wave of pillow-wielding psychos reached us all at once, crashing into the side of the bus and lifting the sidewalk side tires off the ground. The driver managed to yank the doors closed on a couple of grabbing arms. He threw us into drive.

The bus lurched forward, slowly picking up steam as it went, shedding the bulk of the mob in seconds. Only the pounding fists of a few of the most determined members of the horde echoed inside the bus, and even these gave up after half a block.

The bus driver was panting, wild-eyed.

"What the hell was that?" he demanded.

"Sadly," I replied, finally shoving my gun back in its holster, "a typical work day. Is it any wonder why most days I choose not to work?"

I headed down the aisle, rocking back and forth and tipping my hat to any of the scattered passengers who scowled at me, while being sure to scowl at any of the SOBs who nodded approval at the Sleep-Tite Pillow I still gripped in my stolen tongs.

Through the rear windshield, far back up the road, I saw that the mob had given up chase. Many had decided that a busy public street was the perfect spot for a nap. They were laid out in the street, heads resting on their

Sleep-Tites, oblivious to honking horns, the burning retail store they'd just demolished, or the fact that the toxic pillows on which they were blissfully slumbering were why two of them had just been run over by a Toyota Land Cruiser without even waking up long enough to die right.

The bus took a corner and the slumbering, splattered bastards vanished from sight.

The back seat on the bus was empty. I dropped into it both the pillow and my ass, with what I hoped was a safe enough distance between the pair of them.

I'd had the forethought to stuff my second work glove into my pocket at some point during my blind panic back in the store. I shoved it onto my hitherto naked gun hand, after first retrieving a pocket knife from the depths of my trench coat. Armed with the necessary tools, I proceeded to autopsy the Sleep-Tite Pillow.

There were no feathers, which hadn't been the case with the pillow that had been used to murder William Grasse and his pals. Inside were layers of ordinary spongy, poly-fiber foam you'd expect to find in any pillow for which a shivering goose hadn't been forced to perform a striptease at gunpoint.

I cut deeper, separating the foam with the makeshift rib spreaders that were my oily work gloves. As soon as I'd shifted the foam to either side, I saw a gleam emanating from the dead center of the pillow. It was like a lone, shining pearl parked in a loud-mouthed clam's wide open pie hole. I reached in very carefully with the barbecue tongs, and a moment later I was holding the prize from the box of Cracker Jacks at arm's length.

It dazzled like the explosive birth of a tiny universe. It was its own light source, the glow from within it burning brighter than the brilliant sunlight that spilled in through the grimy bus windows.

A week ago I might have been confounded by the mesmerizing little object, but as it so happened I had recently seen a whole bunch of the exact same tiny little glow worms glimmer, glimmering. They had been all over the road near Marigold's Bakery after the Angel Greg and his pals had disappeared, right after he'd brought me to the top of St. Regent's and attempted to bribe me by offering me a city that nobody in his right mind would have wanted, especially those of us who were stuck living in it.

"Holy—" I mused.

"—shit," I added.

I replaced the tiny glowing angel feather back in the open orifice of the Sleep-Tite Pillow from whence I'd extracted it. I left the dead bedding to hog the back seat of the bus alone while I and my stolen tongs retreated a la Rosa Parks to the safest distance away from it as was possible on a speeding bus, whereupon I hollered in the driver's racist ear to step the hell on it.

17

This time I only had to knock once on the basement door before it shot open wide, its creaking hinges shedding flakes of rust on the grimy asphalt. The great relief on the face of the little elf that greeted me washed away the couple hours of anxiety that I was sure he'd been wearing the whole time I was out nearly getting killed.

"Don't get too relieved," I warned before my assistant could herald my triumphant return with a goddamn brass band. "The category six shit storm hasn't reached landfall yet. Invictus," I announced as I marched inside. "Is he still in there somewhere?"

I noted as I headed up the hallway that Mannix had moved his desk and laptop out near the cellar door so that he could worry me home faster. He snatched up the laptop as I marched past the desk, snapping it shut as he fell in beside me.

"I haven't seen him in several days," Mannix said, hustling to keep up.

I led my calamitous Pickett's Charge from the building's back door and down the stairs into the crummy main basement area. The carved wood door to Mannix's charming little apartment, which he had fashioned in the old, abandoned coal bin, was open. My angel client wasn't visible in either the main basement or in the visible slice of Mannix's living room.

I knew Invictus could be anywhere as I cast a narrowed eye across the heap of busted desk lamps on the right wall, sliding it all the way over to the half-naked lady mannequin on the left that sometimes came to life and scared the shit out of every guy in the building asking us for a date. (Goddamn horny mannequins.)

"I can't regret what happens next any more than I already regret taking him on as a client, which I blame entirely on you, Mannix," I said. "Invictus," I hollered. "Get your feathered ass out here."

I'd had no reason to summon him before now, and I frankly wasn't sure if in the two days I'd been incommunicado the guardian angel hadn't been dragged off to have his head, halo and stupid happy grin chopped off by the Angel Greg and his sword of godDamocles, which at this point would have been fine by me.

Invictus wasn't MIA. I was utterly creeped out when a crisp, anxious voice called out from, as near as I could tell, a half-open shoebox that appeared to be full of plastic yo-yos, straight clothespins, and a handful of mismatched wire nuts.

"Hello. Yes? Have you found Mr. Pinder?"

There was a total absence of anything to herald his arrival, but suddenly Invictus was standing in our midst. The angel had a slight hunch to go along with his pleasant, if somewhat strained, smile. The weight of his wings and his current dilemma were apparently getting to him. I noted and ignored with the appropriate level of masculine discomfort that he had clearly been crying his eyes out again.

"No, I don't know where Pinder is yet," I informed him.

His wings sagged at the news, and a few small feathers fluttered to the floor where they fell in amongst the oil and paint stains.

Despite the fact that every part of the cellar other than

Mannix's cozy corner residence was shadowed and gloomy, I noted that the feathers shone like fiery glass, as if possessed of their own internal light source.

"How much of that do you people do?" I demanded.

"Do?" Invictus asked with a confused sniffle. "What do we do?"

"That," I said, pointing at the glowing feathers on the floor. "Molt. Just exactly how many feathers do you lose every time you appear and disappear?"

Mannix, in his hyper-efficiency, already somehow had a dustpan and brush in his little hands. He took a step for the feathers, but I held him back.

"Stay away from them, Mannix," I commanded. "You're high enough on life already as it is, and I don't need you trying to kill me in my sleep."

Invictus looked at the feathers on the floor and shrugged, which knocked a few more little white feathers loose. "I don't know," the angel said. "I guess I never really knew that we did it at all. I don't think it happens when we're not on this plane."

"But you've been popping out all over the place lately," I pointed out. "A lot more than you're supposed to, since you're not supposed to make yourself visible at all. So you're saying every time you materialized in front of Pinder, you *could* have been leaving some of those behind and you didn't even know it?"

"I suppose. Is it important?"

"Only in the sense that it's probably at the root of everything," I said.

"There *were* some feathers on the floor after your first client meeting with Mr. Invictus," Mannix volunteered. "I threw them away that day. In fact, before you left on your errand a little while ago you mentioned something about filing rubbish, which got me thinking. I remembered after you left—"

"That the rubbish was the only thing that was stolen from the office by whoever broke in," I finished for him.

The elf was far more impressed than he should have been. "Yes, sir," he said. "I didn't notice they took it because I was looking at files and in our desk drawers. It didn't occur to me that someone would break in to steal our trash. That's odd, isn't it?"

"More common than you think," I said. "I know a little old lady without a head whose apartment was broken into and mercilessly cleaned. Unlike us, she didn't just have one angel in her place, she had dozens of them crammed into every corner. Whoever busted into her place after the angels had scrammed made sure they vacuumed the place clean. Now we know what they were after. I'm assuming that the same cleaning crew, whoever they are, arrived to clean up the hallway outside Pinder's trashed apartment right after the Angel Greg and co. left."

"Someone is collecting angel feathers?" Invictus asked.

"Whatever for?"

"For the best goddamn night's sleep of your life," I replied. "You angels have been marinating in love and happiness and everlasting peace from one end of eternity to the other. You constantly give it off, like stoner phero-mones. Even now, after you've been blubbing in a shoebox for two days, I don't want to punch you in the face. That's remarkable, since I always want to punch *everyone* in the face. Your feathers have that same *je ne sais merde* the rest of you does. The good folks at Sleep-Tite have been sticking one solitary angel feather in the middle of each of their pillows. That's why so many people in town aren't acting like the bastards they truly are. Every night when they go to bed, they're being bombarded with eternal goddamn joy."

I had just described the greatest nightmare scenario that could possibly grip any major metropolis, but I'd picked the wrong audience at which to bug my eyes, wave my arms and foam at the mouth. Neither Invictus nor Mannix seemed terribly disturbed.

"Okay, since both of you are irredeemably nice, neither of you is seeing this clearly," I told the pair of blank faces. "One of the greatest motivators we humans have is the drive to out-asshole assholes who are bigger assholes than ourselves. If enough angel-infected pillows get out there and everybody winds up happy, all motivation stops. Personally, I don't have any motivation, which explains my choice of profession. But I rely on other people to take up the slack for me. If the doers can't mount enough enthusiasm to prop up my slacker ass, society collapses."

"That *would* be bad, Mr. Invictus," Mannix informed the angel.

"Goddamn right," I said. "It would be catastrophic. Society is where they keep all the good liquor. I don't want to have to try to make gin in my bathtub. Yes, it would make bath time spectacularly fun, but I might choke on all the olives. Not to mention if you can't bring yourselves to panic about what's been making everyone around town so happy lately, maybe you can lose a little sleep worrying why the Sandman is behind it."

The Sandman was the ruler of night, the king of dreams, the undisputed high emperor of everything from the moment you closed your eyes at night until you opened them in the morning. He was also the baggy-eyed bastard who'd been running around town autographing pillows, not to mention rousing an unholy army of sleepwalkers in broad daylight to put me to permanent bed without supper or so much as one postprandial snort.

"M. Sandan of Sleep-Tite Pillows is the Sandman," I said. "Not a lot of effort went into that anagram. He was probably really tired when he came up with it and, frankly, it's gone discouragingly unnoticed until now."

"Mr. Sandman?" Mannix asked. "He just helps us all to sleep."

"He's apparently branching out from harmless slumber into organizing homicidal, noctambulating flash mobs," I said.

The angel in our midst was having a hard time stuffing all this data down inside his halo.

"But why?" Invictus asked. "All you mortals sleep already without any help." He immediately contradicted himself. "Well, except Mr. Pinder, of course, now that I think of it. He was at one of those devices all the time, the ones with the naked women on them." He pointed at Mannix's laptop, which the elf had set down on an old wooden soda case, and which was probably the only computer in the world that had never had a single naked dame sexy-ing up its browser history. "Mr. Pinder didn't sleep very much. Sometimes not for days, and even then he'd only lay down for a little while. He'd be very angry at himself for sleeping at all when he'd wake up. He would say some very bad words, and then go right back to his naked lady device. But everyone else besides Mr. Pinder sleeps. I mean, don't you? I don't understand why the Sandman would need to bother with helping to relax people by hiding angel feathers in pillows."

"That is the sixty-five dollar question," I replied. "Which is the price of one of his pillows if you don't steal one and leave it on the bus, which I did. That reminds me." I pulled the pair of hot tongs I'd boosted from Bed, Bath & Barn out of my pocket and handed them to Mannix.

"Doris' Christmas bonus this year, but only if she promises never to come back to work again."

"I simply don't understand any of this, Mr. Banyon," the angel said.

"I suspect we'll learn more if and when we find Pinder," I told him. "Hopefully we can track him down through the three dead bastards who tossed me in that van, once we find out who they all are. Any luck with Grasse and the other two, Mannix?"

The elf's face brightened. "Oh, I know exactly who *all* the naughty men who kidnapped you are, Mr. Crag," the elf replied.

"Okay, there's that," I informed the angel. "A lot happens when you're in a coma for two days. I can start by questioning the families."

Mannix's face fell. "Oh, dear."

Clearly the good news was bad.

Mannix ducked through the ornately carved door of his little luxury suite and returned with a newspaper and a manila file folder. The paper was a copy of the previous day's *Gazette*, which he unfolded for me to the main page as he forked it over.

WAKE 'N' BAKE! screamed the headline.

"This was one of the things I wanted to talk with you about before you left," my devoted assistant informed me.

There had apparently been a service for William Grasse, the bastard getaway driver whose body had turned up amongst the raspberry tarts and splattered bits of asshole brain in the backroom of Marigold's Bakery.

Careful to respect his wishes as a devout atheist, his family had booked the Sectarian Nondenominational Secular Humanist Chapel at Gorilla View Cemetery. During the service, which had consisted of nonbeliever friends taking the pulpit to tell everyone else how stupid they were, the chapel had been attacked by an as-yet unidentified creature that had smashed it to pieces, burned it to the ground with its fire breath, bit the heads off of everybody in attendance, and had flown off with Grasse's body.

"I found out that he lived with his father," Mannix said. "I got the address and I thought you could start there. But then you were unconscious for two days, and his poor father was killed along with everyone else by that awful flying thing."

"It *is* an awful flying thing, Mannix," I said. "It is also awful in a hell of a lot of other ways, including the way it tried to eat me, the way it savagely bit the head off an old lady, and the pants-pissing way that it can turn poltergeist and travel through walls. It apparently can also breathe fire, because having multiple rows of huge spiked teeth wasn't quite savage enough."

There was no doubt in my mind that the creature that had trashed the Gorilla View Cemetery chapel and flown off with Grasse's body was the same evil asshole entity that had escaped from behind the cheap wallpaper that held up the bathroom walls in the apartment of missing bastard Charles Pinder.

"Were my other two SOB kidnappers waked yet?" I asked.

"No, sir," Mannix said. "Their obituaries were in the day before." He reached in the pocket of his little suit coat and handed over two newspaper clippings. "One of them will be waked—" He checked his watch. "—starting in an hour at Pierson's Funeral Parlor. The other one is scheduled to be waked at Happy Trails Cowboy Funeral Home tomorrow, followed by a Mass at Holy Shmoly Church."

I had the names of the two other bastards. Carl Young and Manny Wescott. Their pictures accompanied their respective obits. Young was the SOB with the bowling ball bag of cash. Wescott was the bum who'd been gung-ho to murder me and whose jaw I'd happily busted during my thrilling escape from the back of the cupcake delivery van.

Young's family mentioned seventeen times in the first paragraph of his obituary that the deceased bastard was an atheist, just in case any old neighbors or spinster aunts were thinking of revving up the rosary beads to waste a perfectly good prayer on him. Wescott's family only obliquely slid past his non-belief by saying that he "was on a spiritual path of personal identity and exploration," which grotesque misrepresentation of reality had earned the guy who'd planned to murder me a high Mass at Holy Shmoly followed by entombment in the family crypt at Sacred Pancreas Cemetery.

"These two will need to be seriously monitored," I said, flapping the obits like newsprint birds before bringing them in for a landing in the pocket of my trench coat.

"I found all three of them online," Mannix said. "The obituaries made it easy to narrow them down from all the people who have the same names. I'm almost certain, Mr. Crag, that I've found that other naughty man, as well."

At this news, the angel in the room brightened.

"*You* found Mr. Pinder?" Invictus asked, turning to Mannix as his salvation since I had already crapped the bed with the same question.

Mannix bit his lip with his pointy teeth. "Only sort of. I don't know where he is exactly, but he and the other three bad men are all friends on Faceplate."

The elf instantly reconsidered, taking into account the

fact that three of the friends were fresh corpses, and thus no longer able to log onto the big social media Web site where assholes screamed about politics and shared pictures of kitty cats.

"They *were* all friends on there," the elf amended. "Until three of them became dead."

"Excellent work, as always, Mannix," I said. "And we now have real pictures of them with their obituaries, which is better than the ones I took of them dead in the back of the van. You'd be surprised how many people don't like to look at photographs of upside-down dead bodies with waxy corpse mugs and busted purple jaws."

"I made you copies of their obituary photos, just in case you needed them," said Mannix, who was more prepared than a goddamn Eagle Scout. He reached into the file in his hand and handed over some glossy eight-by-ten shots of all three dead men. "Also, I noticed something about one of the pictures you left on my table, the ones you took at the bakery." He pulled out another photo and handed it over.

Mannix had blown up a photo of the pill bottle that I'd noticed next to the body of the kidnapper whose jaw I'd busted and whose name I now knew, thanks to the *Gazette*, was Manny Wescott. I hadn't been able to read the tiny print on the bottle, but it was now clearly visible in giant letters: No-Snooz. The caffeine pills were used by college kids and truck drivers to keep from falling asleep. They were basically the exact same thing as No-Doz, but with a slightly amusing and non-trademarked name.

"So they're trying to stay awake," I said. "I can't say I blame them. The blood-curdling affliction known as polite social interaction is happening to people who fall asleep." I held up the blowup photo of the pill bottle to Invictus. "You ever see one of these before?"

The angel's eyes widened in recognition. "Oh, yes," he said, nodding enthusiastically. "Mr. Pinder had one of those with him all the time. They're candy, right? He must enjoy them immensely. Although Mr. Pinder never really seems to get anything you'd really call 'joy' out of anything in life. But he had to like those very much, because he used to eat them all day and night."

So Pinder and his pals were forcing themselves to stay awake with caffeine pills, and not just to get into relentless online arguments at three a.m. with total strangers who committed the unspeakable sin of saying they would pray for typhoon victims in the comments section of a CNN article. Whatever the Sandman was up to Pinder knew because he and his buddies were working for the narcoleptic bastard.

"Okay, first off," I said, "I need you, Mannix, to get online and find out where the factory is where Sleep-Tite Pillows are made. The feathers Pinder and the rest of them are gathering up are all winding up there. And, yes, I am one hundred percent certain that it's Pinder, Grasse and the rest who busted into our offices and that old lady Edna's apartment to collect dropped angel feathers." I held up a warning finger to the angel. "Not that I give a shit about finding Pinder anymore, because this has become much bigger than him. But we *can* track him back through there, which gets you and hopefully that multitude of heavenly pains in my ass out of my hair."

The angel was so delighted at the prospect of having his nonbeliever ward returned to him that he burst out crying.

"I hope your flood insurance is paid up, Mannix," I said to the elf, who had sat down on an overturned bucket and was already typing away at his laptop.

I offered a sigh, since the worst was about to come

and it had nothing to do with whatever nefarious scheme the Sandman had brewing, flying creatures with fire breath, armies of wannabe killer angels, or exhausted somnambulant mobs armed with bed cushions laced with Xanax and LSD.

"In the meantime, I have less than one hour to prevent a probable mass slaughter, and to do so I'll somehow have to convince a complete and utter moron to abandon over forty-five years of unremitting stupidity."

18

It took ten minutes just to get Detective Daniel Jenkins on the phone, then another five to convey to him that in just about a half-hour from now dozens, perhaps hundreds, of people — depending on the popularity in life of the deceased rat bastard Carl Young — would be lining up for a wake in which they were the unwitting appetizers, soup, salad, main course and, if there was any room left at the end of the massacre, dessert and mint.

All I got out of the asshole flatfoot by the end of my humanitarian spiel was a snarling, "I *might* send some uniforms to look into it. You just better not be sending us on a wild goose chase, Banyon."

"Forcing you to match wits with geese wouldn't be an exciting spectator sport, Detective Jenkins," I said. "You'd be no match for their superior bird brains. In the meantime, goddamn tick-tock on the bloodbath that's about to take place at Pierson's Funeral Parlor."

I slammed down the phone in Mannix's living room.

The elf had moved his computer inside. I could see by the worried set of his jaw and the deep furrow in his brow that the little guy had come up with bupkis on the location of the Sandman's pillow factory.

"Nothing?" I asked. "Not domestic? No overseas sweatshop working tiny Third World fingers to the bone stitching on 'Made in the USA' tags?"

Mannix raised his hands from his keyboard in a gesture of frustrated surrender.

"I can't find the Sleep-Tite factory *anywhere*, Mr. Crag," he said.

"Okay, I'm going to have to attack from a different angle. The next wake is in less than a half hour. It's in the hands of the boys in blue now. You're going to have to go on Faceplate, Mannix. Check out all the personal photos Pinder and the three dead assholes have posted. Look for local landmarks at which you can place any or all of them. Buildings, signs on businesses in the background, street signs, anything that could pin them down to a recurring spot or spots."

It was a boon to private eyes how people shared intimate photographs with the world online these days. The level of embarrassing revelations willingly given up for Faceplate approval was the polar opposite of the olden days when people used to keep appendix scars and beach shots of their sagging asses locked away in photo albums on living room shelves, only deploying them to scare away guests who'd overstayed their welcome around the holidays. It was a long shot, but it was possible Pinder or the others had posted an online photo that would be helpful in tracking the missing bastard down.

Before Mannix could drop his swift little fingers back to his keyboard, we both heard a snotty nose honking outside.

"Hold that thought," I instructed.

When we exited back into the main basement, we found Invictus sitting on a plastic milk crate and gently sobbing. The tips of his wings were bent against the cement floor, and he had shed a few more glowing feathers.

Mannix hustled over to pat the sniffling angel's robed forearm, which in the absence of a visible handkerchief was a more repellent proposition than he'd probably bargained for.

"There, there," the elf cooed. "Mr. Crag will straighten everything out."

"I wouldn't bet on me," I said. "From what we've pieced together so far, we'd all be better off if the whole mess stayed crooked. But since I'm cursed with being amazing at what I do, I'm going to have to trouble you for a ride."

The angel looked around for an obliging horse before he suddenly realized that I meant him. He sniffled and got to his feet.

"And don't chastise me for that 'amazing' crack," I warned. "I know all about 'pride goeth before a fall.' I'm a P.I. I have no pride. And where we're going I don't need to put up with your goddamn ironic foreshadowing on my way to the ground."

***

The reality-warping journey took all of an instant, but in that single moment it was like someone had strapped a Trident missile to a roller coaster car and sent me on a mushroom cloud rocket ride through a crooked key hole.

I was tugged through unreality like an infinite string of taffy, then vomited back out into the real world on the far end. In a flash, the limited scope of my office building's shitty basement had been replaced by a panoramic view of the entire shithole city.

I was once more at the top of St. Regent's Drive-Thru Cathedral.

Although the spire was exposed to any eyes that might be looking down on it, I felt fairly confident I was safe. I'd told the Angel Greg in the hallway outside Pinder's destroyed apartment that I had no intention of returning to the church after he'd dragged me up to the roof to offer me the shit job of mayor (assuming he and his pals could nudge circumstances just right over the course of the next hundred goddamn years). Plus I figured if he was keeping a lookout, my torso would already be waving bye-bye to my head as it tumbled its screaming way down to the archbishop's overgrown azaleas.

Instead of standing on the crumbling brick outside the steeple, Invictus had materialized us in the tower room inside.

The floor consisted of rotting bare timbers that reeked of oil. A half dozen, ten-foot high arched openings devoid of glass panes exposed us directly to the world outside. At some point in the ancient history of the cathedral, a custodian had affixed wire mesh to the openings to try to keep the pigeons out. The wire had long ago rusted and rotted until only a few gnarled and withered square inch pieces remained, barely holding on to spikes drilled between the bricks.

The room itself was larger than it appeared on the outside, but it was made to seem much smaller by the hulking presence of the enormous figure of Molokai, the church's demon in residence. The raggedy bastard was sprawled on a crummy paisley chair that he'd evidently picked up on trash day out in front of the house of an elderly spinster with shit taste.

When we popped into existence before him, the hideous, gnarled beast from the fiery pits of the netherworld nearly jumped out of his leather skin as if his pointed tail had been plugged into a wall socket, and comically dumped

out half the contents of the bag of Cheetos he was clutching in his massive hands.

"Geez! What the hell?"

Molokai's giant yellow eyes did a little sitcom kaleidoscopic spinning before he saw that it was I standing on
the pigeon shit carpet in the middle of his windswept
parlor.

"Oh. *Banyon*. If you're here to get your two bucks
back, too bad. Spent it." He rattled the now half-empty
bag of Cheetos in which he'd invested my hard-earned
dough.

The demon hadn't missed the angel standing beside
me. Molokai seemed to be struggling to feign indifference
to the presence of my fine feathered client. It was the same
forced blasé look he'd plastered on his puss at the Paradise
Motel when I'd made a hilarious joke about a multitude
of angels having a coke orgy in room nine. Just like back
at the Paradise, a trace of greed brushed the demon's
ghastly face.

Molokai grabbed a mittful of Cheetos that had landed
on his belly and tossed them at his pair of unwanted house
guests.

"Down in front," he said, with forced blandness.

One of those shitty little black and white TVs that car
dealerships used to give away with every Model T test
drive sat on a piece of plywood balanced on top of two
cinderblocks. An extension cord ran out one window and
presumably connected up to five hundred more extension
cords; an electrical python that slithered down the side of
the cathedral until it sank its fangs in a sparking outlet a
million miles below. On the tiny little screen played the
famous banned Peckinpah-directed show where Gilligan
had finally gotten fed up with getting hit on the head with
a hat every week and kicked the shit out the Skipper for

thirty minutes, minus commercials, in slow motion.

Molokai was making a show of watching the action on the TV screen, but his eyes betrayed his true interest. They darted only once to the floor beyond my feet to where the angel stood. Just one glance was all I needed to confirm my suspicion.

Invictus wasn't crying any longer. The angel was peeking nervously out the high brick arches and jumping at every sinister cloud that passed by.

"If we could just do this quickly, please, Mr. Banyon," Invictus said. "They could see me up here and, to be absolutely truthful, I'd be lucky if they only beheaded me. I don't want to be cast out. Angels who are cast out wind up looking like..." He searched around for an example that my mortal brain could understand, and was delighted to see the demon Exhibit A conveniently sitting on the moldy stuffed chair. "Well, like *him*. No offense," he told Molokai. "I'm sure you're a very nice man."

"Shove it up your ass," Molokai said.

"Like goddamn Hope and Crosby," I said. "You must have perfected this act before Molokai got tossed out on his ass a billion years ago."

"No, I don't think I've ever had the pleasure," Invictus said. Right on cue, his wings spread open and he offered the demon a polite bow of his halo.

Molokai tried desperately to look anywhere but the floor at the angel's feet.

"Heaven is like Texas, Banyon," Molokai grunted. "At least what I can remember of it all these millennia later. You can walk from one end to the other for a million years and still not meet everybody there. Besides, all angels look alike. And don't jump down my throat. That's not racist, it's true. They've all got that same stupid goddamn smirk. Bastards." With a long, viciously sharp fingernail, he flicked a Cheeto from his gut. "Why are you here, Banyon?"

"I want the information for which I paid two good American dollars. Did you find out the building that the flying monster landed on?"

The demon suddenly became a cornered rat. "Oh. That."

"You were going to check around," I reminded him.

Molokai's eyes darted around their sockets. "Yeah, well, you see, that was a bust," he said. He picked a dropped Cheeto from the tattered remains of a size XXXX L.L. Bean casual Henley shirt, and tossed it back to his greedy molars. "It turns out my source? That gangster ghost I told you about? Full of shit. Nobody else I talked to has seen anything like what you're talking about."

"Except for the paper," I said.

I got the king of dumb looks in lieu of a smart-ass reply.

"That wake that got eaten at Gorilla View Cemetery," I prodded. "You must have heard about it. It was all over the *Gazette*. Front page news."

To further prod his lying memory, I held out the photo of William Grasse that Mannix had pulled from the Internet. Also, because Molokai was an arrogant bastard in addition to being the worst liar in the history of creation, he must have figured I wouldn't notice that the exact goddamn issue of the *Gazette* in question was lying face-up on the floor three inches from his demon hooves.

I picked up the paper, which featured a splashy photo of the smoking ruins of the cemetery chapel. There was a little insert in one corner of Grasse's obituary photo, a miniature of the same photograph I'd just showed him. I held out both hands: *Gazette* in the left, picture of my SOB kidnapper in the right.

The demon narrowed his eyes as if seeing a newspaper for the first time in his life.

"Oh, yeah, yeah, yeah," Molokai said, auditioning sixty years too late for the goddamn Beatles. "I thought you meant…no…yeah, of course I heard about *that*. *That's* the same thing you had me asking about? Well, like I said, no one's seen it. That is, outside of the people at the cemetery. They sure as hell got a good eyeful." He snorted at the thought of a hundred people slaughtered in the collapsed and burning ruins of the cemetery chapel, then instantly thought better and pulled a horribly phony look of sympathy. "Poor bastards. But, hey, at least they were in the right place for it, right?"

"When the whole world loses hope, we can be drawn like moths to the ever-burning lantern of your bright and shining optimism," I said. "Keep your bloodshot eyes and pointed ears open. You hear anything at all, give the elf at my office a call."

"Yeah, I'll do that," Molokai said. He hopped to his cloven hooves, simultaneously rolling down the top of his Cheetos bag and tossing it onto the crummy, threadbare chair. He was suddenly the polite host, seeing his unwanted guests to the door, which was actually a window a hundred stories up, out of which I got the distinct sense he'd push me if he could find a banana peel magnet to pin it on when the cops arrived.

I caught him casting another greedy glimpse at the floor. He quickly pulled his eyes from our feet and plastered on a grin.

The cityscape stretched out through the openings all around the steeple. Blue collar tenements to the north, upscale Yuppie apartments to the west, and directly before us the gleaming office and civic buildings of downtown.

"Just imagine," I said, surveying the domain that could

have been mine. "Those angels offered me the position of lord high mayor of this entire cesspool town. In fifteen years I could've had zoning power over all lesser mortals."

By now Molokai was beyond idle chitchat. His blackened, cracked lips were straining in an approximation of a smile, and he nodded his horns in agreement.

"You'll let me know if you find out anything," I said. And, having dragged out the demon torture as long as possible, I turned to my angel client. "Let's go."

"You've got a lovely place here," Invictus told the demon, nodding politely to the pigeon shit, rat bones and the 1970s poster of high beams Farrah Fawcett in the red bathing suit that I'd just noticed creepily framed behind a dorm room mini-fridge.

The angel touched my forearm.

It immediately felt like somebody had clamped my head in a vise and squeezed it down to fit into a plastic drinking straw which some fat kid was sucking the life out of like it was midnight on March 17 and my brains were the last goddamn Shamrock Shake of the year. The rest of my body was equally compressed, and I was suddenly rocketing back through the invisible pneumatic tube system used by the Deity's heavenly representatives on Earth to mail themselves from point A to point Z and all twenty-four letters in between.

This time, however, we took a detour on the way back to my building's basement.

For only one moment I was a strand of spaghetti stretched from one end of the universe to the next. In the following instant I was exploding back into my reconstructed self, but this time parked behind a single strand of spider web in a corner of Molokai's round steeple room.

What I was suddenly witnessing was impossible to reconcile with human understanding, at least not sober. I could see atoms dancing, molecules mooing, and the entire microscopic fabric of creation shrunk down to such impossible size that I half-expected a giant rubber gorilla hand to reach in and grab Fay Wray.

I wasn't alone. Invictus had shrunk down and sidestepped reality with me. The angel was sitting in an Adirondack chair he'd conjured out of nothingness. There was an empty seat beside him that I presumed wasn't for Godot. I sat down.

While my nearby world had shrunk down to impossible miniature size, just a few feet away from where we sat reality was going about its normal full-sized humdrum. It was like peering down the wrong end of a telescope while simultaneously looking right in a window, and the distortion was so great that I figured it'd be best to ignore it since I didn't have time at that moment to go completely off my rocker.

Molokai thought he was alone inside his spire room. Invictus and I had only just popped out a second ago, and so the demon stood there for a moment waiting for the doorbell to ring again just in case we'd dropped a cufflink. When he finally decided we were gone for good, he shook his head.

"You're a stupid son of bitch, Banyon," he grunted to what he perceived as an empty room.

Just to be sure Molokai's piquantly accurate observation was not, in fact, aimed squarely at the living, breathing me who was watching his every move like a goddamn pervert, I whispered over to Invictus lounging in his Adirondack chair.

"You're sure he definitely can't see me or hear us?"

"No, we're fine," Invictus said.

Although the angel spoke at a perfectly normal volume, the demon was so close to the two of us it sounded to me like the holy bastard was shouting through a megaphone.

I looked over at Molokai. He hadn't heard a thing.

The demon hustled over to a rickety old bureau and extracted from the bottom drawer a couple of thick green gloves. They looked like the rubberized asbestos numbers you'd wear to protect your hands while juggling uranium rods at a nuclear power plant. Molokai pulled on the oversized gloves and hustled back across the room, where he knelt down at the spot where Invictus had been standing.

A dozen brilliantly glowing feathers clung to the oily wood floor.

Molokai picked up each of the feathers and placed them carefully inside an old plastic I Can't Believe It's Not Brimstone! container.

A sudden wind gust nearly blew the last feather away, but the demon clapped his hand down hard and held it safe under his palm until the breeze died. After, he peeled up the last feather, dropped it in the plastic container, and clamped on the lid.

The demon straightened up, container clutched in his gloved hands.

He tipped a disdainful chin in the direction in which he presumed I'd left and not at the spider web where I was currently parked and watching the entire floorshow.

"Moron," he snarled, which, I'm the first to admit, is generally a more than fair assessment, but perhaps just this once wasn't totally accurate.

The demon yanked up the trapdoor and hastily descended the ladder below.

19

In a list of the hundred worst things about being a P.I., surveillance easily ranks in the top five (the number one worst thing about being a P.I. is, obviously, the fact that you *are* a P.I., a mental disorder that has somehow thus far flown under the radar of the American Psychiatric Association's annual report "From Soup to Nuts: Wacky in the Workplace").

Watching somebody for days on end with only the thin hope of a payoff is the kind of sexy tedium they don't show on TV private eye shows. Imagine an episode of *Magnum, P.I.* that lasts four days, during which Tom Selleck's mustache can't bathe, booze, eat a decent meal or go to the bathroom without having to be resourceful and worrisomely unhygienic. The ratings for such a realistic program would understandably be in the toilet, which in the surveillance game is an old, two liter Fanta bottle in the back seat.

Angels, on the other hand, had the whole surveillance thing down cold. When Molokai left his room at the top of the cathedral, Invictus and I were somehow going with him. When he exited a back door of the church five minutes, six ladders and ten narrow staircases later, the two of us continued to go along for the ride.

I checked my legs to see if they were moving. My feet were planted on the H in a water molecule. Invictus and I both still had our asses planted in our chairs.

"If you ever decide to quit being a guardian angel there is definitely an opening for you at Banyon Investigations," I said. "I just have to kill my secretary first." Invictus shook his halo. "I just want to find Mr. Pinder," the angel insisted. "If I can just get him back maybe those other angels will find it in their hearts to forgive me my trespasses."

The last time we'd encounter the Angel Greg it was pretty clear he was past the point of forgiveness, but I figured there was no sense torturing Invictus with reality on what might be his last few hours with a functioning head.

Molokai was hustling down the sidewalk, plastic container clutched tight. Some friendly pedestrians here and there offered cheerful hellos to the demon. They were drifting along in deliriously happy fugue states, clearly high as goddamn kites on the excellent, poisoned sleep that only a Sleep-Tite™ pillow could provide. Molokai, to his credit, flipped them all off and kept right on going.

We moved along with the demon. So, too, I noticed, did a faint yellow patch of light between the shriveled, vestigial wings at his back.

I had seen the light up in the spire of St. Regent's, but I'd assumed it was a reflection of sunlight since the perilously high point of the cathedral put us within about eight goddamn feet of Sol. But now that we were down on the street and the little light dot was still there, it was clear that it was not of earthly origin.

I hadn't seen the yellow splotch at the Paradise Motel or any other time out in the world when I was face-to-ugly-face with the bastard demon. It had only appeared after I'd been sucked into Invictus' angelic deer blind.

"So, who's that tagging along behind the scabrous bastard?" I asked, pointing at the single point of light.

"Oh, that's his guardian angel," Invictus said. "We can't see each other as anything other than patches of light when we're on duty. You know, you get distracted, caught up in a conversation about a lovely cloud you saw the other day, the next thing you know — whammo! — a grand piano falls on your charge's head."

"Molokai has a guardian angel," I said. "Molokai, the donkey-footed rat bastard who got thrown out of heaven for participating in a revolt against management. Molokai, the towering, iniquitous demon SOB who lied to me over two bucks and who is currently on his way to sell your feathers to the evil bastards who are brainwashing people into being nice, which goes against all human instincts. Are you sure there wasn't a clerical error somewhere up the chain of command, because it seems to layman me that assigning a guardian angel to Molokai is pointless on the same level as assigning salads to the McDonald's menu. If he accidentally starts to wander out in front of a bus, so what? Let him. Hell, if I were in charge I'd assign an angel to watch over the bus, not him, and stomp on the gas the minute it saw the treacherous asshole step off the curb."

"Everyone has the choice to be good, Mr. Banyon," Invictus said. "And everyone deserves to have a watchful eye trained on them. Even if it's just to be there on the day that inevitably comes to all mortal creatures."

The insanely naïve, matter-of-fact sincerity with which the angel said it made me want to lock his wallet in the safe back in my office for safekeeping, since there was no way a sap like him would last five minutes in the real world without getting mugged of every last feather on his MasterCard. On the other hand, he'd been at his job watching over a succession of humans for what I assumed was thousands of years, and his library card was still safely tucked away in his pocket, so what the hell did I know about the insane decisions made by Heaven's human resources department?

Molokai clip-clopped down to the corner. I was hoping he'd lead me straight to the Sandman's pillow factory and, presumably, to missing son of a bitch Pinder, but instead he ducked his head, turned his horns sideways for better ingress, and slipped through the front door of a goddamn Starbucks.

The weird, otherworldly bubble in which we'd tailed him from the cathedral didn't pass through the glass door behind the demon. We bounced away from the entrance like a billiard ball before floating up to a parking meter, which from my perspective looked like the North Face of Mount Everest with an appropriate "EXPIRED" announcement where George Mallory was found. Our tiny bubble came to a Don Ho hovering stop.

"Why," I asked, "can't guardian angels go in Starbucks?"

It was clearly the case. The sidewalk in front of the dump was crammed full of patches of light identical to the one that had been trailing Molokai like a lost puppy or a future ex-wife before marital reality sets in. Each blob of light contained, I assumed, a frustrated guardian angel sitting in an Adirondack chair like Invictus and me. When the demon had passed inside the coffee shop, the forty-watt Sylvania light bulb that had been on his tail had bounced off as we had, eventually parking its ass at the front window.

There had to be fifty similar splotches of light cooling

their heels on the sidewalk. Presumably there was one for each of the hopeless cases who was inside sucking down gallons of overpriced, ethically sourced, 8.5 percent fair trade caffeine shit.

"It can't be the dress code," I said, "since there isn't one at Starbucks. They are completely egalitarian. Even the counter help are utter slobs behind their green aprons.

Park a powerful enough magnet out front and two seconds after you switched it on it'd be covered in bloody barista ears, noses and, I assume, all those parts you've had to cover your eyes for every time Pinder turned on his laptop."

Invictus offered a deeply troubled frown. "There are places on Earth that even we guardian angels cannot go, Mr. Banyon," the heavenly bastard somberly intoned. "Places where the collective evil is so strong it repels us." He began counting down on his fingers. "Black masses, Pyongyang, Congress, Tallahassee, Rosie O'Donnell's house, Starbucks. That last place — this place before us — is particularly bad. Everyone in there is on one of those things…what are they again? Oh, you just mentioned Mr. Pinder's. The abaci with the dirty television pictures on them?"

"Computers," I said. "Or phones," I added. "Or tablets," I postscripted. "Or a goddamn Cuisinart with an LED screen, if that's what Microsoft tells them is fashionable to stuff down their Dockers today."

"Yes, any of those," Invictus said. "They're in there right now, typing away, telling everyone around the world how to live their lives while at the same time complaining every second about people who tell people how to live their lives."

He didn't shake his head hard enough for his halo to

fall off, but he clearly didn't approve of the anonymous scrotum-kicking that constituted the remaining 2% of the Internet that wasn't evenly divided between porn and cat photographs.

"Can you float us a little closer to the front window?" I asked.

Molokai had been inside for about twenty seconds already. There was no telling what the scaly bastard was getting up to unobserved.

The will of the angel glided us forward. At least I assumed it was his will that sent us drifting across the sidewalk. His chair could have been a recumbent bike the way in which he was slumped in it, but I didn't see him furiously peddling his bare feet. Or maybe the sadly relaxed posture of the angel was just my perception of reality. It was hard to tell what was real and what my dishonest eyes were lying to me, given the fact that we were currently wafting into the ear hole of a passing wino.

For an instant we were in a terrifying forest of gray ear hair and thick wax deposits before we abruptly passed inside the alky's skull. I got a close-up look at a garbage dump of deceased brain cells, which I assumed was my personal goddamn Ghost of Christmas Future, before we rapidly passed out of the scalp and through the mottled thinning white hair at the back of the drunk's head. The boozebag staggered off down the road, oblivious to the fact that we'd just used his hippocampus as a Slip'n Slide.

Our floating bubble didn't get much farther. The dozens of flickering fireflies that were Invictus' fellow guardian angels were a solid barricade that instantly bounced us back out to our parking meter.

The java Starbucks stink had managed to permeate the angelic membrane in which Invictus and I floated.

Molokai was evil even when he wasn't trying to be. The fact that he hadn't chosen to stop at a sweet-smelling distillery was only further proof of the pointlessness of George and Ira Gershwin assigning someone to watch over him.

"I've got to get out there," I informed the angel.

"Why, Mr. Banyon? He'll come out eventually. We can follow him then."

"That's the same theory you subscribed to when Pinder was climbing out a stained glass bathroom window," I pointed out.

"Oh, I see," Invictus said, nodding as if he got it which, given the fact that I was pretty sure I could have sold him the Brooklyn, Golden Gate and George Washington bridges as an exclusive Time-Life set, I wasn't entirely sure he did.

Whatever hocus pocus he needed to perform to vomit me back out into the real world became unnecessary, since Molokai came clomping back out onto the sidewalk before the angel could blink me back to full size.

"Hold on," I quickly commanded.

The demon was clutching a super-size coffee cup as big as a KFC bucket, which looked like a thimble in his giant mitt. In his other hand he was still holding on tight to the plastic I Can't Believe It's Not Brimstone! container.

The glowing patches of yellow that crowded the front of the dump scattered as he passed through them. One glum spark separated from the rest and trailed after Molokai. I could almost hear the sigh of the guardian angel inside it, who was the only poor bastard in town with lower job satisfaction than yours truly.

The demon had gone only a few feet down the sidewalk when a blissed-out maniac walking in the opposite direction sidestepped left instead of right and accidentally plowed straight into the demon. Molokai managed to hold onto his coffee, but the plastic container flipped out of his other hand and busted open on the sidewalk.

"So sorry, but isn't it a wonderful day?" said the dozy pedestrian, whose empty head was crammed so full of fuzzy warmth from his Sleep-Tite Pillow that he was unaware he was an inch away from being beaten to death with his own detached arms.

Molokai's instinct should have been to murder the guy right then and there. Hell, I would have testified on his behalf based on the pedestrian's stupid, lopsided smirk alone. However, Molokai needed to keep off Hell's radar, and no small part of that effort included not slaughtering innocents in public. Still, I expected at least a dose of perfectly justifiable four-letter verbal abuse. Instead, Molokai, completely against asshole type, flashed his own hideous, horrifying grin.

"Hey, not a problem there, pal," the demon assured the beaming bastard. "It's definitely a beautiful day in the goddamn neighborhood."

For a couple of brainless bastards, the two of them had certainly reached a suspiciously courteous meeting of the minds, and I saw why when the grinning clod reached down and politely retrieved Molokai's I Can't Believe It's Not Brimstone! container and lid, both of which he handed over to the demon.

As Molokai was slapping the cap back on the plastic container, I saw for the first time that it was empty. The demon had sold the angel feathers to somebody in the coffee shop.

Molokai was marching off down the sidewalk, a morose glowing blob of useless guardian angel trailing after him, as I spun to Invictus.

"Get me the hell out of here *now*," I snapped.

In a completely metaphorical flash — as it was absent anything like an actual flash or, indeed, any warning at all — I went from standing inside the angelic observation bubble to standing on the hot sidewalk in front of Starbucks.

A constant stream of Yuppie, hipster, and Occupy Wall Street bastards were parading in and out the front door. Any one of the half-dozen worthless dregs who'd scuttled out of the dump in the last two minutes might have been the asshole to whom Molokai had sold Invictus' feathers.

I threw caution to the wind and hustled inside, hoping that at some point my personal physician, Dr. Charlotte Cheese, had jabbed me with all the necessary shots to survive a trip to goddamn Starbucks.

The tables were filled with neatly trimmed Grizzly Adams beards and nonprescription glasses worn only for trendy and not ocular necessity.

A couple of baristas with two hundred grand in liberal arts degree debt and dazzlingly bright futures (provided they were okay with hairnets and nametags) manned the java cauldrons at the main altar. The embarrassment they should have been feeling for every major life choice they had made thus far was heroically masked behind an air of insufferable smugness. Or maybe they honestly had no idea that quoting Shelley all day long wouldn't change the fact that for the previous hundred years the job of pouring coffee had been handled better in diners across the country by high school dropouts named Mabel with pencils in their beehives and a pot of Maxwell House.

It was a whispered battle over which one wouldn't wait on me.

"Relax, I'm only here for the ambiance," I informed

them. "If I were you, I'd take the free time to calculate how many times an annual salary of twenty grand goes into a worthless, quarter million buck theater degree. If you can't do the math, which is likely since you're under thirty, the answer is 'parents' basement.'"

Having done more than any of their professors to educate the younger generation — and nearly getting a jar of sugar hurled at the back of my head for the public service — I turned my full attention to the crowd.

I was surrounded by cups of coffee, photos of coffee and worshipers of coffee. The stink of coffee hung in the air. I'm mistrustful of the beverage, as is any career drunk who has ever been victim of some do-gooder dastard pouring a bucketful of the stuff down his throat to undo an entire night's hard work of getting shit-faced. This crowd, on the other hand, had willingly submerged themselves in the dirty brown ocean like Krauts in a U-Boat, and as I scanned their pasty faces I knew there was no way to tell at a glance to whom Molokai had sold his ill-gotten angel feathers.

The purchaser might still be in the shop, but I had no way of singling out one flake in the blizzard. Or he could have left already, since there was still a steady trickle heading out the door and through the invisible swarm of guardian angels who were waiting patiently outside.

I was prepared to abandon this futile hunt in favor of stalking a less elusive prey, namely a dirty glass with my name on it at O'Hale's Bar, when a fragment of one-sided conversation at the nearest table caught my disinterested ear.

"You *do* realize that every war in history has been fought because somebody thought their imaginary sky being was waving a bigger celestial hammer than the other guy's, don't you? No, you don't. Maybe you should pray on *that*, you backwards hick."

The scrawny Starbucks customer, who had hired himself to loudly narrate his own big-mouthed life because no one else wanted the job, sat alone at a table for two. He wore a blue flannel shirt fresh from the dry cleaner and a pair of ironed jeans with creases sharp enough to bisect a metaphor. He was an ersatz lumberjack who would have phoned 911 in a panic and hightailed it on his designer boots to the nearest safe space if he ever encountered a real ax that wasn't a bottle of body spray.

I glanced at the screen of the laptop on which he had just finished furiously striking keys like a tin-eared twenty-first century Mozart.

May B U shud prayon THAT, U bckwords hic!!

Clearly his fingers weren't as smart as his pie hole. Still, he snorted satisfaction at the word fragments he'd just incompleted, and grabbed up his steaming cardboard cup of joe for a victory slurp. Ten more empties littered the surface of the table.

Someone on the "Fans of *Blossom*" message board posted a reply, and the well-pressed warrior slammed down his coffee and launched his fingers back at his keyboard like ten ballistic missiles. Before he detonated a single stroke, he noticed the silhouette on his screen and glanced over his shoulder to find yours truly casting a long shadow across his Internet flame war.

"Do you *mind*," the Gucci lumberjack sneered.

"As a matter of fact, yes," I replied. "Unfortunately, I don't have enough bullets to take out everybody in here unless some of you agree to share."

My roving and suddenly interested ear caught another snippet of one-sided conversation at the next table.

"*X*-mas trees started with druids worshiping oak trees. How does it feel to find out you're nothing but a pagan who's traded in one cult for another? Will you be mixing baby blood in your eggnog next *X*-mas? Instead of a star, you should put the FSM on top of your pagan tree, pagan. All hail the FSM, god of all imaginary gods. Idiot."

The keyboard soldier at the adjoining table was fatter than the first hero who, once my attention had shifted, was back to flaming fans on message boards dedicated to 1990s sitcoms. The second bastard was clad in flannel as well, but evidently neither laundry nor hygiene were priorities for him.

"God, shmod! God, shmod! God, shmod!"

Another oral typist, this one a dame sitting one more table over. She was screaming like a maniac as she assaulted her laptop. She was heavily tattooed and pierced, with only a few ghostly white patches of unclaimed virgin real estate. From what I could see of the clean spots, Sir Walter Raleigh would have turned his boat around and headed right back out to sea before planting a flag on them.

As I passed her table on my way to the door, I saw that the tattooed pincushion was posting in the product comments section on the Web site of a swimming pool filter wholesaler. A symphony of likeminded digits all around the coffee shop clattered me back out the front door into daylight.

Invictus was waiting for me under the shade of an anemic city tree that had been strategically planted so that its growing roots would rip up the sidewalk all around it. Although they were pulled in tight, the angel's wings still glowed bright enough in daylight to dissolve the small shadow cast by the pathetic tree.

As I hustled over to him, I glanced at the sky for any sign of an attacking heavenly host which, for all blithely oblivious Invictus knew, could have been hiding behind the nearest rusty old rooftop TV antenna.

"I'm beginning to agree with asshole Angel Greg about you not staying out of sight," I said. "It can't be that you're genetically incapable of it, since genetics doesn't have anything to do with your kewpie doll physiology."

"What's the point?" Invictus asked, posing the big question that had confounded human philosophers ever since the first proto human aimed a hairy finger skyward at something other than a hungry pterodactyl.

"You're in luck, because I know the answer to that," I said. "There *isn't* one. You're born. At some point after that you die. Everything that happens in between is meaningless. That's assuming you're doing it right. It's the people who insist on finding meaning to meaningless existence who keep getting the rest of us in trouble. That's how we ended up with Hitler and Jared from Subway."

I could see that the angel was on the verge of turning on the water works yet again. His bloodshot eyes were wet, but the tears had not yet began to cascade down his flushed, pudgy cheeks. He shook his halo woefully, and when he spoke again the words came rushing out in a breathless, hopeless torrent.

"We tricked that awful demon into taking my feathers, and he managed to sell them right under our noses, and — heck, Mr. Banyon...I mean it...*heck* — we're right where we were at the start and, well, oh, gosh, I'm afraid we'll *never* find Mr. Pinder, and we're both going to get our heads cut off, and maybe it's the fate we deserve."

He grabbed up the voluminous sleeve of his robe and honked a massive, wet blow into the brilliant white fabric.

"Okay," I said, "first off, *we* don't deserve anything. *I'm* just a hired hand. All my moving parts need to remain firmly attached, at least until FedEx brings the bionic liver I ordered from Japan. Second, ye of little faith. You hired the best P.I. in the biz for a reason. It so happens that I've figured out exactly where Charles Pinder is."

His tears miraculously burned away in an instant, and his hitherto sopping eyes were suddenly bright with angelic optimism. His chubby face beamed pure, radiant joy.

"Truly?" the annoying cherub practically sang.

"Absolutely," I replied. "Everything except for the part about knowing exactly where Pinder is. But lucky for me, I've got an elf up my sleeve."

20

Holy Jumping Jehoshaphat Reformed Orthodox Temple was one of the oldest religious institutions in town. It had been built by Presbyterian-Jewish settlers with nothing but faith, sweat, and the proceeds of a hardscrabble frivolous buckboard lawsuit.

The church had thrived for more than a century and a half, deriving most of its operating capital from slip-and-fall claims made by Jehoshaphat parishioners at potluck suppers at other churches around town. Creeping secularism coupled with allegations in the *Gazette* of decades of rigged fundraisers in the parish's basement rec room had resulted in a dwindling congregation in the latter half of the twentieth century. The last minister-rabbi to run the joint had fled the authorities like a thief in the night with just the shirt on his back, his eighteen-year-old sexpot Methodist housekeeper, a suitcase full of cash and 144 solid gold mahjong tiles.

By the time I walked up the sidewalk that afternoon and spotted its red slate roof winking coquettishly at me around the rooftops and alleyways of the surrounding buildings, I was glimpsing a huge stone church that had been vacant for over two decades. There was periodic talk of repurposing the deserted dump into condos or some other renovated blight on the landscape, but its proximity to a crumbling, abandoned highway overpass over a slum on one side and, worse, a Papa Gino's on the other was a real estate development even the most foolhardy investor wouldn't pull the trigger on.

No one with half a brain would enter that neighborhood without a platoon to back him up, and since I was strolling along without an armed escort it was clear that my tank of gray matter must have finally slipped below half-full. I wouldn't have been there at all but for a call from a sidewalk pay phone a half hour before to my tireless elf assistant.

"Hey, Mannix, are you going over the Faceplate photos that Pinder and the other assholes posted?" I'd said to my assistant.

"I've gone through them all just like you asked, Mr. Crag. *Three times*, " Mannix stressed. "I haven't been able to find *anything* that might help."

"You probably have, you just don't know it," I said.

I heard a sudden soft commotion issuing from the earpiece, like somebody who was a better housekeeper than I am gently shaking out a blanket.

"Oh, hello, Mr. Invictus!" the elf announced off the phone.

I heard the angel, who I'd just ordered back to H.Q. and whose robes were presumably making the blanket-shaking racket, reply with equal unwelcome enthusiasm.

"Ah, hello there, mister elf!" the voice of Invictus cried. "*Very* good news on the investigation, I suspect, according to our shared friend. Is that who you're speaking to now? Excellent. I shan't interrupt you good people at your hard work. I'll just wait behind this dust mite. Carry on, good sir elf."

The aggravatingly cheerful voice of Invictus shut up, having, I assumed, vanished from Mannix's basement living room.

"Make him stay put, Mannix," I instructed. "The guy is getting reckless with all the materializing he's doing, and I can't have him getting his ass smote — and possibly my taut hindquarters, as well — now that we're finally in the home stretch. And he and I are definitely not friends. We're not quite the opposite yet, but we will be if the dumb bastard gets me killed."

"Speaking of that, Mr. Crag, Officer Dan called. He said that flying thing showed up at Pierson's Funeral Parlor, just like you said it would. It tried to attack everyone, but the police shot at it and it flew away. No one died, thank goodness, but it took that poor man's body with it when it flew off."

"We're changing around definitions so that 'poor man' now takes the place of 'bastard who wanted to murder me?'" I said. "That'll be good to know if I live long enough to ever do another crossword puzzle. Did the cops follow it?"

"They tried, but Officer Dan said they lost it."

"Officer Dan Jenkins loses his socks every time he puts on his shoes," I pointed out. "They'll have another chance at Wescott's funeral tomorrow, either at church or at Sacred Pancreas Cemetery after the comically inappropriate and pointless Mass. I told Jenkins about it when I told him about today's potential bloodbath. It's in the hands of the most incompetent cop in Christendom now. In the meantime, get on your laptop and take a look at those Faceplate pictures again. How many look like they were taken in, around, outside or on top of a Starbucks or any other java joint? Look through Pinder's photos, as well as the pictures of the three dead SOBs who kidnapped me. I'll wait."

I didn't even get a minute to take a well-earned break, since Mannix is better at his job than I am at mine.

"It's funny you ask, Mr. Crag," the elf instantly replied. "I noticed that there were hundreds of photos taken in coffee shops. I thought it was odd. Those naughty men seemed to spend a lot of time drinking coffee."

"They'd be coffee drinkers no matter what," I said. "Their fingers need to remain vigilant to defend the Internet against total strangers who've committed the mortal sin of having opinions they don't share. I don't know if they started drinking gallons of coffee for fun way back when, but at some point they switched from pleasure to business. They know they *have* to stay awake now. They're all up to their humanist eyeballs in the goddamn Sandman's angel feather racket."

"You haven't seen Mr. Sandman, have you?" Mannix asked, concerned.

"No, and let's forget M. Sandan, for now, Mannix, other than to point out that he's clearly as bad at coming up with anagrams as the rest of us are at solving them. Right now, let's stay focused on coffee shops. We need to narrow down our search to a single shop. It'll be near an abandoned church. Take a look back through the Faceplate pictures and see if there are any taken outside a Starbucks that shows a big old stone church in the background. Keep a careful eye out for any shots taken inside the coffee shops as well, where said old stone church might be visible through the window."

It hadn't taken my dependable assistant long.

There were photos taken at a billion coffee shops around town, but only one abandoned house of worship kept cropping up in dozens of my kidnappers' photographs.

The Holy Jumping Jehoshaphat Reformed Orthodox Temple had shut down before Mannix moved to town, so he didn't know the name of the joint., but based on his description of the Crucifix of David chiseled into the belfry, my destination was clear.

I never would have found the place without the online photos posted by Pinder and his three dead pals. I generally know my way around town, sober, drunk, or in that delightful, hazy in-between state when the world doesn't quite hate you as much as usual and you hate it back with somewhat less ferocity than always. The problem was there were too many Starbucks locations to search them all on foot. If Earth had a 5,800 hour day like Venus I still wouldn't have been able to sift through every goddamn store. They were as countless as grains of sand on a beach, which I would rather drink a boiled cup of — medical waste included — than a cup of Starbucks crappuccino.

But it was coffee that was key to tracking Pinder down.

The building my kidnappers had dragged me to and from had stunk of coffee. At the time, I'd chalked it up as a smelly remnant of countless PTA or AA meetings. It was Molokai who'd inadvertently straightened me out. The fact that the demon had dropped off his ill-gotten feathers at a Starbucks had finally clued me in that it wasn't an ancient odor soaked into granite I'd smelled through my pillowcase mask, the coffee stink at my kidnappers' church headquarters had been freshly brewed.

A church made sense, in a smug asshole way. Pinder and crew must have loved the sledgehammer subtle irony of using a decommissioned cathedral for home base.

I'd hung up on Mannix after another warning to keep Invictus under wraps, as well as instructions to inform the angel in no uncertain terms that he was a client and definitely wasn't my goddamn friend, before I headed for church.

Thirty minutes later, I perambulated around a corner and at last came face to face with the old Holy Jumping Jehoshaphat Reformed Orthodox Temple, the parking lot where I'd been dumped inside the Marigold's Bakery van, and the brand new Starbucks that had apparently opened in the past five minutes in a building that had housed an old yarn shop that had been open for business for forty years across from the church.

I noted that my eyeballs had been correct, even with a pillowcase obscuring them. The reason I had only seen clear light coming through the windows on the day of my kidnapping was because all the old stained glass had been removed, presumably sold off to a congregation that hadn't yet hit the skids, and replaced with clear panes.

I had no way of knowing if Pinder was still inside, and I wasn't loaded enough to storm the Bastille solo. I hung back near the corner to await the apocalypse.

I was only three minutes into my stakeout when up the sidewalk on the other side of the street shuffled the same beardo bastard whose loudmouth fingers had been yelling their cuticles off on a laptop at the Starbucks across town. He was currently thumbing an angry text one-handed while slurping from a cardboard coffee cup as big as a bathtub, which was delicately clutched in the crook of his arm.

The main front doors of Holy Jumping Jehoshaphat Reformed Orthodox Temple were a couple of slabs of painted oak that would have withstood the Second Coming. Rather than cease drinking or texting in order to politely knock, Beardy McFlannel-Shirt gave the church a swift kick in the apse.

"What's the password!" somebody hollered through

the thick door.

"Science is golden!" the bearded James Bond yelled back.

The door opened a crack and Beardy tried to fork over, without spilling a drop of coffee, a Glad sandwich bag he'd pulled from his pocket. Even in full daylight, the feathers he'd bought from Molokai glowed brightly. Presumably to counteract the utter peace and joy, the delivery boy took a heavy pull from his coffee cup.

"Not here!" snapped the pasty face at the door.

The new son of a bitch had a pair of bags under his eyes so big you could have packed a week's worth of dirty underwear in them and still had room enough left for the hotel towels. He, of course, because he was another asshole, wore a slide-rule perfect hipster beard. Nuevo Beard at the door popped back inside, reappearing in an instant with an overstuffed pillowcase, which he yanked open like a kid on Halloween.

When the church door slammed shut a moment later, Beardy was still standing out on the stoop, now in possession of the pillowcase full of angel feathers, including his own Glad bag he'd bought from the demon.

I really wasn't there for the angel feather racket, the Sandman, or the collection of coffee club bastards. I was technically there for my client just to locate Charles Pinder. Good sense and self-preservation told me very loudly that I was staying put. However, my legs apparently had a different opinion on the subject, and made it clear that I'd been outvoted two to one when they began following the bearded bastard down the sidewalk.

I stayed on the opposite side of the street, although I imagined the only way he would have spotted me was if I marched across the screen on his goddamn phone.

I was sure the feathers were on their way to a Sleep-

Tite Pillow factory, which could have been anywhere in the world. Beardy might have just been on his way to UPS, and I informed my nosy legs that a mailbox would be the end of the line for us all.

Three minutes down the block and around the corner, Beardy stopped at the gates of a factory on the front of which hung a sign that read: Sleep-Tite Pillow, LLC.

I knew the building when it manufactured the little plastic bits on the ends of shoelaces. Shoelace Tip Things, Inc. had gone out of business fifteen years ago, and as far as I knew the factory had been vacant ever since.

The joint looked brand new. The brick had been sand-blasted, the parking lot resurfaced, and a gleaming new, eight-foot chain link fence encircled the grounds. The rotted window frames had been repaired and the panes replaced.

Despite the new windows, the drunks who lived in the street out front couldn't see inside. Just as in Charles Pinder's apartment, all the panes had been painted black. In Pinder's case it was probably as much to keep a guardian angel he didn't believe in from seeing in as it was to keep anybody from spying the creature that had eaten the head off his old lady next-door neighbor. Here, the Sandman was simply protecting his privacy — a sensible precaution for any maniacal supervillian with a nefarious plot to protect.

Lucky for me the armed guard at the gate was product loyal. The uniformed slob was sound asleep on the floor of the guard booth, his head buried in a drool-soaked Sleep-Tite Pillow. He waved me inside with a sudden apnea snort.

The bearded bastard was already on the grounds and headed for the front door. I hadn't been shot in the face on my way inside, which was probably a good thing, even though I wasn't able to come up with a really solid reason why off the top of my head. Still, I had probably pushed my luck close enough to the abyss. When Beardy made for the main door, I slipped around the side to the fire escape.

The factory was three stories tall, and as I climbed the side of the building I checked on each floor for the slightest gap in the black paint on the windows. Whoever had painted the glass was definitely more skilled with a brush than No Thumbs Hooligan, my useless building superintendent who a week later was probably still chasing a sopping paintbrush around the lobby of my apartment building, guided only by unwarranted optimism and out-and-out stupidity.

There was a moment before I reached the roof that I questioned whether I shouldn't turn around, collect Pinder at the church, deliver him to Invictus, and hopefully end my role in this tragicomedy, pending the approval of trigger-happy Angel Greg and his .44 caliber sword. There was, however, my concern of the near one hundred percent likelihood that I would be blissfully unconscious on the sidewalk in front of O'Hale's an hour after I'd closed that part of the case, and I couldn't risk the chance that some do-gooder might drag me to a flophouse and slip a Sleep-Tite Pillow under my head.

My ass end continued to ascend.

When I crested the roof ledge, I saw that there were new skylights on the roof. From the top of the fire escape, they appeared not to have been slathered with black paint like the windows below. A few new, gleaming silver vent fans blew lazily in the breeze. Unfortunately, what blew even greater was the fact that I'd just stuck my gopher-like head straight up into a goddamn ambush.

Several very sleepy but very large men in pajamas and

bathrobes were waiting for me on the roof, all aiming wide awake handguns at my pretty little skull.

I heard clattering footsteps on the fire escape below me, and when I glanced down I saw a somnambulant swarm shuffling up on slippers from below. Up on the roof, the distant door to the stairwell was open. Beside the yawning roof door, the bearded bastard I'd followed from church stood beside an ominously swirling black cloud.

"That's him," Beardy said to the storm cloud in which whirled the personification of sleep itself. "He must've followed me here."

From the hand that still clutched his giant coffee cup, Beardy unfurled in my direction an index finger so slender, crooked, and pasty I felt like a homicidal logger who'd just been picked out of a lineup by an angry birch.

The black cloud rose to a menacing height. It wasn't really necessary to pull out all the stops threatening me since anybody with sense would've already voided his bladder. (I have buckets of sense, but I avoided voiding since I didn't want to risk rusting any flasks that might have settled in my trench coat below waist level.)

The upturned faces that were currently pounding up the fire escape below me hadn't a clue the downpour I'd courteously forestalled, although I regretted my generous nature when I felt the first hand clap onto my ankle.

"*Mr. Banyon*," the exhausted, soothing voice of the Sandman boomed from the center of the swirling cloud. "*You're a man who doesn't know when to quit.*"

"A thousand court appointed AA sponsors would agree with you," I said.

If it had been the kind of black cloud from which lightning shot, I had the distinct impression that my smile could have lit up Broadway, provided Con Edison had an extension cord adapter that could plug into the human ass.

"Take his gun and bring him below," the voice of the Sandman commanded.

The cloud swirled in on itself and slipped down the toilet drain that was the darkened roof stairwell. Bastard Beardy hustled down behind the Sandman.

There was a chance I could make a run for it. Only one hand was currently encircling my ankle. A swift kick to the face would knock that bastard loose. I could see that the SOBs in the pajamas on the roof were in the same shape as my attackers at Bed, Bath & Barn. Their eyes might have been open slightly, but they were all sound asleep. Grab one by the gun arm, swing him into another, use them as cover as I leapt heroically down the fire escape into the bulk of the shuffling throng that had just reached the landing below me. Real heroic, Errol Flynn stuff.

Except my knees aren't much for heroic leaps, and at my age I trusted my ankles, hips and heart about as much as I trusted Doris with my company checkbook. Not to mention the fact that while it might have been satisfying to shove a couple of them off the roof, it might still also be considered murder by a pedantic asshole like Detective Daniel Jenkins, since my attackers were zonked on angel feathers and thus not in control of their own actions.

I reluctantly put up my hands, and my gat was pulled from under my armpit.

"Move," the nearest gunman sleepily yawned. I took the final step onto the roof and we all began shuffling for the door.

The lead gunman let out an infectious, lion-like yawn that spread amongst his cohort. Even sound asleep the bastards were still highly suggestible.

Simultaneous to the yawn, the gunman's cell phone

started ringing in the pocket of his flannel bathrobe.

The dozing bastard seemed puzzled by the sound, as if it almost succeeded in penetrating the haze of deep sleep induced by his Sleep-Tite Pillow. The other rooftop gunman as well as the sons of bitches who'd just reached the top of the fire escape and were piling in behind me were similarly distressed by the sound of the ringing phone. Phones, particularly cell phones, were ubiquitous in the lives of human beings, and the instinct to answer a ringing phone was so great that even men deep in artificially-induced slumber felt an unconscious, Pavlovian need to find out if they qualified for a free trip to the Bahamas or a Medicare-supplemented knee brace.

And, just like that, the crummiest escape plan in the history of the universe was born.

"Relax," I offered magnanimously as the whole herd of us shuffled closer to the inevitable catastrophe that existed beyond the wide open roof door, "I'll get it."

21

The sleepwalking goons with the wide-awake roscoes led me down to a second-floor office.

The room was luxurious and lethargic. The lights were flying at half-mast. Instead of office chairs, giant pillows in deep drowsy colors were scattered all around. It was a harem multiplied by a dream divided by an opium den.

A half-dozen dozing bastards in suits and ties snoozed and drooled on the massive pillows. None of them had taken the time to kick off their dress shoes before curling up for their business siesta. They'd each schlepped a briefcase in with them. One attaché case had dropped open and spilled its contents onto the floor. The sleeping suit beside the briefcase was apparently a hitman from OSHA, at least according to the pile of menacing government paperwork that had vomited onto the floor.

Two of the bastards from the roof nudged me further into the room. The rest remained behind in the hallway. I glanced back to find them leaning against walls, eyes closed, breathing rhythmically, not a care in the world.

As far as caring was concerned, it was clear that I was taking up the slack for the entire goddamn room. My deep concern wasn't for whales, glaciers, or owls with measles, but for my own ass, whose days were currently numbered in minutes.

One wall of the office was made entirely of glass, which afforded a spectacular view of the sweatshop ground floor production facility of Sleep-Tite Pillows.

Happy, fluffy white squares of naked polyester lumps were relentlessly shit out of a thumping and grinding cutting machine. They slid down on a conveyer belt to the main floor. There, the newly born pillows were murdered with one swift stab to the bloated abdomen by the first group of at least a hundred assembly line workers.

Next up, plastic metal rods were inserted in the freshly made gashes by the next round of workers.

The hollow rods reached into the centers of the pillows, assuming the Sleep-Tite I'd vivisected on the bus was any indication. It was down this tube that the subsequent gaggle of factory workers inserted a special fortune deep inside the cookie.

Great pains had been taken to shield the workers from the effects of the angel feathers. The feathers were kept in special sealed boxes. Only one was released at a time, and only when yet another group of workers who stood behind and at the ready were given a signal by those at the conveyer belt. A nod released a single, glowing feather, which was lifted with tongs and placed inside the plastic tubes that were jutting from each of the pillows like the single quill on an albino porcupine.

Once the feathers were in place, the pillows moved down the line where nozzles were slapped to the mouths of the plastic tubes. I couldn't hear the whooshes from my side of the glass, but I assumed they were coming hot and heavy. Compressed air launched the feathers, one after another, deep into the guts of the pillows.

The next set of workers pulled out the plastic tubes, and the final group used some kind of modified heat gun to seal up the hole in each gut-stabbed pillow.

From start to finish, a single pillow made it through the line in less than twenty seconds. They rolled further down the line, there to be stuffed into cloth sacks, stitched up, boxed and shipped to Bed, Bath & Barn, Salome and Sam's Mattress Emporia, and every other retail outlet in the tri-state area.

The workers were wearing masks, which they only slipped down to take an occasional slug from two-liter bottles of Jolt Cola that were set in equidistant modified cup holders all along both sides of the conveyer belt. They all wore ear buds, which I guessed weren't for protection from machinery noise. Even through the thick glass I could hear the sound of the eighties hair metal that was blasting into every auditory canal below. The caffeine, the racket, and an occasional pin to the ass from one of a dozen passing semi-sleeping foremen worked in concert to prevent any of the assembly line workers from nodding off on the job.

A sign on the factory wall altered by two ominous extra words the slogan I'd seen in the outside world: **Sleep Your Cares Away** *Or Else!*

Up in the office with me, the emperor of naptime had retaken human form. The Sandman's back was to me as I was stopped by my escort just inside the door. His tired gaze was directed at the factory floor below.

In the corner of the room sat the bastard responsible for an entire city's nightmare.

Charles Pinder was hammering away at his laptop, just as he had been when I'd first met him in a closet in what I now knew was the old abandoned Jehoshaphat Temple around the corner. My kidnapper's brow was furrowed, and there was a massive cup of coffee on the floor near his ankle. He continued to punch away at his keyboard, seemingly oblivious to the presence of anybody else in the office.

The Beardy bastard who'd led me to the pillow factory was in the process of genuflecting before Pinder. He was a humble cleric, awed in the presence of his Holy Internet Father. Beardy maintained a subservient bow all the way out the door until he reached the hallway, whereupon he beat a hasty retreat.

Pinder remained behind, indifferent to the reverence.

The Sandman seemed as unaware of the action as Pinder was of all of us.

"You could have taken the money to drop this," the droopy-eyed Sandman said to me without turning. "Oh, yes, Mr. Banyon, the ten thousand dollars came from me. I'm not a monster, after all."

"Well, in point of fact, I did take the dough, and you are, in fact, a monster by pretty much any goddamn definition of the word," I said.

I got just the glimpse of a profile and an arched eyebrow. "They told me they lost the money. I assumed they kept it for themselves."

"Just to be clear, we're talking about the three dead assholes who kidnapped me," I said. "And for further clarification, you're the one who killed them?"

The Sandman nodded. "I do not brook incompetence or theft," he said.

"And you made sure you didn't use one of your own products for the job, so the triple homicide wouldn't impact sales," I said. "So, what did you do? Told Salome and Sam that you had to use the bathroom, picked up a Brand X pillow off the rack, turned into a sandstorm in the stall and slipped out the window over to Marigold's Bakery, killed all three of them, and got back just in time to flush?

Perfect alibi. A hundred people saw you go into the crapper there, and since none of them knows who you really are, nobody had a clue you ever left the building. Am I warm?"

"You are much too clever for your own good, Mr. Banyon."

"My current situation unquestionably belies that observation," I pointed out.

The Sandman sighed. Hundred of grains of fine sand were expelled from his mouth and scratched against the window pane at which he stood.

"Do you know how much sleep Americans get on average these days, Mr. Banyon?" the saggy-eyed bastard asked.

"No, but I can go find out. I'll be back in sixty years. Seventy, tops."

"Six point eight hours of sleep per night," the man of sand said as if I wasn't there, which I assumed was just him getting in practice for after my imminent murder. "Seven to nine hours is what's recommended. You people worry about cheating death, worrying about glucose and gluten, whatever the hell that is. You worry yourselves to death about exercise and nicotine, but you don't give a damn about cheating *me*."

"In all fairness to me, I'm not like other people," I informed him. "I *do*, in fact, spend as much of my time unconscious as humanly possible. And that goes double if it's my birthday, New Year's Day or Rosh Chodesh."

Over in the corner, Pinder exhaled angrily. It had nothing to do with the exciting life-and-death action going on in the middle of the office. He spoke aloud, but the words were directed at some anonymous somebody online.

"'Did a supernatural being living up in the stars build

the machine you're spouting your unscientific mumbo-jumbo on? No, a *scientist* who studied *science* did. You better watch out, or the FSM will get you!'" His fingers typed furiously, spurred to angry swiftness by his furrowed brow and a healthy spray of thick saliva.

The Sandman finally tore his eyes off the glass and looked to Pinder. The Internet troll was oblivious to the interest he'd drawn, continuing to clatter away at his laptop. The Sandman released a protracted sigh, then turned slowly to me.

"What *am* I going to do with you, Mr. Banyon?"

"You're taking suggestions?" I said. "I'm surprised, albeit delighted. Well, for starters, I say you should let me go, pay me some more hush money — a couple hundred grand should do it — and shut this dump down. Are burning the building to the ground and killing yourself options, or are you only asking about me specifically?"

"People don't even take naps anymore," the Sandman continued, not even considering my suicide suggestion, the rude bastard. "Don't get me wrong. I like a good nap. Who *doesn't* like a good nap? A nice sunny day on the sofa. But biphasic sleep can ruin your real sleep like a candy bar can ruin your dinner. I *need* longer sleep out of you people. Your go-go lifestyle and Red Bull energy drinks might be keeping you going, but nobody cares about *my* kingdom. I'm the king of dreams, Mr. Banyon. I'm the ruler of the night, and no one is giving me the obeisance that I deserve anymore."

"Are you sure you have the right dimension?" I asked. "Maybe you're talking about a different America. These days we're mostly morbidly obese slackasses who only go-go from fridge to couch. Half the time I don't think most of us get-get to the bathroom on time. Rosie O'Donnell alone has to be sleeping twenty-five hours a day. They only wake her long enough every few hours to drop a roast pig down her throat."

"Six point eight hours on average, Mr. Banyon," the Sandman insisted. He smiled the kind of creepy grin perverts in rusty vans parked outside elementary schools specialize in. "But not anymore, at least not in this city. Seven point two hours. That's what we're up to now. All thanks to Mr. Charles Pinder's guardian angel."

These were the words that finally pierced Pinder's protective bubble of willful ignorance. His head snapped up. A second later, the impulse from his brain reached his fingers, like a secondary brain sashaying a dinosaur's ass, and he ceased typing.

"Whoa. Just, whoa there," Pinder said. "I don't know what you think you're talking about, but there's a rational, scientific explanation for that guy with the wings. Not that I'm conceding he exists," he quickly added. "For the record, I'm agnostic on his existence and I absolutely disagree with any religious nut who claims he's an angel. Again, if he even exists in the first place, which I doubt. It's more likely I'm crazy."

"One does not automatically exclude the other," I informed him.

"Thank you," Pinder said. He nodded firmly to me, then to the Sandman.

"While you've stopped here for a minute on planet Earth," I said, "would you mind telling me what that thing is that trashed your apartment, ate the little old lady next door, and demolished the funerals of your asshole buddies?"

Pinder clapped his hands to his ears and started yelling "*la-la-la!*" at full volume. He whacked himself so hard on the sides of the head that the solid construction of his empty skull was the only thing that kept his palms from praying directly behind his eyeballs. Panicked yelling and blocked ears was clearly his go-to response when confronted with anything that challenged his worldview. This time, however, unlike in the church storage room where I'd awakened from my midnight kidnapping, the raving loon's stream of "*la*'s" was broken up by an occasional muttered "*F-S-M.*"

"La-la-la! F-S-M! La-la-la! F-S-M! F-S-M, F-S-M, la-la-la-la-la-la. Shit."

Whatever the flying thing was, Pinder clearly linked it to the "FSM" bullshit that the army of angry typists at his church and in Starbucks unleashed on anybody online who made the mistake of saying "thank God" when someone wasn't killed in a car crash.

FSM. The stink of Ragu that accompanied the beast. A sudden memory of long, pale, wet tentacles grabbing for me in the hallway of Pinder's apartment.

And just like that, in a Chef Boyardee flash, I knew exactly what Charles Pinder and his unwitting pals had unleashed on the world.

The Sandman wasn't interested in my personal book of revelations, as he was at the moment busy being peeved at *la-la*-ing Charles Pinder.

"My associate's belief system—" the Sandman began.

"I don't believe in anything!" Pinder hollered over the sound of his own hands.

"Notwithstanding his *un*belief," amended the king of dreams, "his guardian angel's revealing of himself to Mr. Pinder was, for me, a godsend."

At the mention of the dreaded G word, Pinder let out a pained yelp and *la-la*-ed harder than a Teletubby in an Australian bathhouse.

"Of course, the properties of angel feathers have always

been known to me," the Sandman continued. "After all, I've been ruling the world of slumber for eons. But angels have made themselves scarce for the past couple thousand years. I only found out Mr. Pinder's guardian angel had appeared to him when Mr. Pinder went to sleep that night and visited my realm of dreams. At first, I didn't believe it. People think all kinds of crazy thoughts when they're asleep. In the 1980s, every post-pubescent was dating Christie Brinkley. But Mr. Pinder was so adamant telling his story to me that he nearly woke himself up. A delicious irony. Imagine, Mr. Banyon, a man like our Mr. Pinder confronted by something he can't reconcile with his beliefs. He tried desperately to block it out, but as soon as he went to sleep that night he was tormented in his dreams by the angel his waking mind insisted it didn't see."

Pinder stopped his serenade yet again. "I *didn't*," he insisted. "There is a logical scientific explanation. Maybe it was swamp gas. *La-la-la*!"

"If you really don't want to hear us, you clearly need to shove your fingers a lot deeper into your ear holes," I said.

"I *can't* hear you," Pinder replied. "*La-la-la-la-la!*"

The Sandman continued.

"I questioned Mr. Pinder while he was asleep, and then I exited my realm of slumber and went to the Denny's toilet where he said the first angelic manifestation took place. Sure enough, I found a dozen feathers. Some janitor had swept them up and tossed them in the trash, then fell asleep on the toilet floor. He was so relaxed when the manager fired him. Nobody at Denny's knew what they had. No one except me. I collected those feathers and hatched a plan. I introduced myself to Mr. Pinder in the real world. He had no job. He needed the money. I let him come up with whatever comforting scenario he needed to invent in order to explain the existence of his angel."

"Pigeons somehow keep getting into my apartment," Pinder yelled, fingers still plugged in his ears. He shrugged blasé helplessness and in the process nearly punctured both eardrums. "Probably up through the toilet. Snakes do that down in Florida sometimes. You see it on the news all the time. I've never actually seen the pigeons, but they obviously go out the same way. They nest in the reactor of a nuclear power plant, which is why their feathers glow. It's the only rational explanation." He nodded agreement with his own insane, molting shit-bird scenario. "Science," he added, deploying the word with the same faith-based certainty that priests use when discussing transubstantiation. He finished up with yet another, "La-la-la-la."

"Yessss," the Sandman said, dragging the S into a resigned, protracted hiss. "Anyway, imagine my delight when an entire horde of angels started appearing over this fine city looking for the guardian angel who started it all. Mr. Pinder's heavily caffeinated associates have been going out after each appearance and gathering enough angel feathers to fill twelve baskets. I've got enough now to take Sleep-Tite international. I've made arrangements with a factory in the Philippines to mass produce my pillows on a scale that will dwarf this operation. Soon, my Kingdom of Dreams will rise to glory once more. Think of it, Mr. Banyon. People will be sleeping somewhere other than college lecture halls and Mexico. Once more, the king of the night will get the respect he deserves."

"Kudos on turning a city full of assholes into docile sheep," I said. "Your customers can count each other if they can't fall asleep, so you've saved a lot of wear and tear on the shanks of the imaginary ovine population. Well, now that you've explained your entire batshit plan, I guess

I can go."

"Oh, no, no, no," the Sandman said. "First, you're going to tell me who hired you to uncover my foolproof scheme. It was that son of a bitch Juan Valdez, wasn't it?"

"I don't divulge the names of my clients," I informed him. "Yes, they are all horrible in their own unique ways, but even they don't deserve the whole world finding out they were stupid enough to hire a private investigator. But in this case, Pinder already knows I was hired by Invictus to find him."

The Sandman turned to the crazy Internet message board troll sitting in the corner of the office with his laptop. "Is this true?" he demanded.

Pinder's downcast eyes and aggressive *la-la*-ing confirmed the whole ridiculous story.

"Do you know what, Mr. Banyon?" the Sandman said. "I believe you."

"Terrific. I know I can't get to sleep at night until I know my sincerity has gotten a five-star review from a raving lunatic."

"Yet, you now know everything that I have planned. We can't really let that stand, now can we?"

"Well, we *could*," I said, "if we didn't want to be an asshole about it."

He did something. I couldn't really attest to what. It was definitely, probably, possibly something. It might have involved a hand. I wasn't sure. Maybe his big, flapping mouth was in on it as well. I didn't know for certain about that either.

The office was already gloomy, but for an instant it got very dark. A moment later and it had lightened back up again, like the electric burp of a minor power outage.

Pinder was still sitting in the corner. He'd finally

stopped shouting his toneless chorus of *la-la*s. As I watched the bastard who'd started this whole mess, I blandly noted that his laptop was beginning to shiver like a wet dog in a cold bath.

The two open computer halves turned into wings. The fat body of a cooing pigeon suddenly sprang up from the hinges.

I was stone sober, unfortunately, so for some reason completely unrelated to alcohol (booze being my usual go-to explanation for this kind of hallucinatory hilarity) none of this baffled me.

The pigeon poked around at the chair on which Pinder sat. I saw that the flying rat was distinctly phosphorescent. The chair, which had been standard office fare a moment before, was suddenly one of those orange plastic potato chip-shaped numbers from the groovy 1970s. Pinder was still in the chair, but he was now represented as nothing but a miniscule brain no larger than a peanut. An instant later, the gray, wrinkled clump of gray matter turned into an actual peanut, which the glowing pigeon ate just before flying down a toilet that I hadn't seen sitting smack-dab in the middle of the office. The john was invisible to me a minute before, but must have been there all along.

"Hello, are you from the government, too?"

I glanced to the voice and found the previously unconscious OSHA representative, who had been snoring and drooling into a pillow when I entered the office, standing off to one side of the room. The pillow on which he'd been sprawled was gone. In fact, all of the pillows that had been there a moment before were nowhere to be seen. The men in suits who had been sleeping on the pillows were all upright and alert. Most were still in their suits, but one was wearing a suit of armor, while the OSHA bastard who'd spoken was wearing a polo shirt and a pair of ugly plaid slacks. He was holding a five iron, which he aimed across the room to the wall that had somehow turned into a vast field.

"The rhinoceros is taking drink orders," he offered brightly.

An anthropomorphic rhino with ruby red lipstick and a gigantic tutu batted her eyelashes at me and offered a coquettish wave.

"Oh, excrement," I said. "I'm a-goddamn-sleep."

22

The vast dream world kingdom of the madman Sandman spread out limitlessly around me in every direction.

My sleeping brain only vaguely remembered my last waking moments in the king of night's pillow company office.

I remembered him doing something, but at first I could not recall exactly what. It was plain as day now. He'd blown onto his palm and, before I could duck out of the way, a blast of pure, concentrated Sandman sleep dust had hit me square in the mug.

Right now, my physical self was back in the real world. I only hoped that I'd fallen onto one of the empty pillows in the room and not cracked my skull open on the desk. If I was currently bleeding out on his office floor, the maniac Sandman was unlikely to call 911. Charles Pinder, the bastard I was truly after and who, unfortunately, was not actually a brain-size peanut who'd been swallowed by a radioactive pigeon, would've been back on his laptop the moment I lapsed into blissful slumber.

"This place is loaded with violations," the OSHA guy informed me. He consulted an official government clipboard that was suddenly in his free hand, tapping at it with the grip end of his golf club, which for the sake of convenience obediently transformed into a solid gold ballpoint pen. "Two urinals half an inch too far apart in one men's room, two of them a quarter inch too close together in another, several fire extinguishers painted a hue that's a shade too light, all exits clearly labeled but in a font that, while conforming to official guidelines, I personal don't care much for. Violation after violation. The government really should close it down."

Out in the real world, the government bastard would have flexed his petty authoritarian muscles to harass Sleep-Tite Pillows with every arcane and contradictory infraction in the book. In fact, I assume that was exactly what he'd tried to do with the list he'd just spouted off. The Sandman had received his threats, as well as those of the other sleeping bureaucrats, with a mush-full of naptime sand and a private pillow of their own from which to inspect the interiors of their eyelids for all eternity.

In the dream realm, the OSHA SOB might have been remembering Sleep-Tite's real-world violations, but they were only forming a platform from which his slumbering flights of fancy were prepping for takeoff. Literally, as it turned out, when the clipboard and pen abruptly turned into a couple of solid rocket boosters.

"Funny, I don't remember seeing this space shuttle in Mr. Sandan's office," he said, before rocketing off spectacularly for parts unknown.

The evaporating contrails turned into stardust which rained gently down, fading to twinkling nothingness in the perpetual twilight sky.

"A dream is a wish your heart makes," an asshole voice said beside me.

I glanced over to find the smug Sandman standing there, hangdog eyes directed at the spot in the soothing gray sky where the OSHA agent's shuttle had disappeared.

"No, a dream is a nuisance that my thirsty liver forces on me and that my bladder wakes me up from twice a night," I said.

"Oh, there will be no waking up from this dream for you, Mr. Banyon," the Sandman assured me. "You are asleep back at my factory right now, surrounded by my armed foot soldiers. They are asleep as well, but highly suggestible. Even if you were to wake up — which, I assure you, you will not — they have been instructed to shoot you. No, you'll stay asleep here forever. Or, rather, until you die of starvation and dehydration in the real world. Goodbye, Mr. Banyon. Pleasant dreams."

A whirlpool opened up in the air beside him, and the Sandman stepped into the shimmering vortex. He promptly exploded like a clod of dry dirt. The whirlpool swallowed every last grain of sand before collapsing in on itself.

"Giddyap!" someone nearby hollered.

I turned to find the remaining G-men perched atop saddled horses that I was reasonably certain hadn't been parked under their asses an instant ago. They charged off after their rhinoceros cocktail waitress through a forest that suddenly became the main floor of a casino whose midget manager was evidently Hervé Villechaize.

I vaguely recalled having dreams in which I was aware I was dreaming. I wondered as I turned and headed across the gently sloping landscape how many people in the dream realm knew that they weren't dreaming anything like the natural dreams they were used to, and that they were home and zonked out like zombies on a Sleep-Tite brand pillow? Would they care even if I told them?

It sounded like the Sandman was only holding onto them for one good night's sleep at a time. He wasn't imprisoning them forever, and was allowing most everybody to wake up and go about their daily lives. That is, until nightfall when he got his bony clutches on them again. But me, the government bastards currently orbiting the moon or charging around the baccarat tables on Secretariat, and anybody else who crossed the Sandman out in the real world wouldn't have the option of ever waking up again.

I could take the thought of starvation. Solids aren't all they're cracked up to be, and, other than the occasional bologna sandwich or bowl of pretzels, just take up valuable abdominal real estate that would be put to better use for temporary alcohol storage. Speaking of which, I had already been practically dying of dehydration even before the goddamn slumber king had put me under. It was the Sandman's threat of a parched and sober end that propelled me forward.

So, too, it seemed, did a goddamn Segway, on which I was suddenly and inexplicably perched and racing along at a breakneck half-mile an hour.

My vague memories from my hotel night in Sleep-Tite slumberland were of an enormous party populated not just by Vincetti and Wasserbaum, but likely by everybody in the tri-state area who owned a Sleep-Tite Pillow.

The party was where I needed to be. Unfortunately, it was becoming abundantly clear to me that even though I was aware that I was asleep and dreaming, it was very easy in this hazy, suggestive state to be distracted by the slightest...

I spent the next ten minutes, or possibly ten hours, running around as a six year old version of myself at the circus that an old spinster neighbor took all the kids on the block to when I was a kid. She was a decent old bag who, when she bought us all an armload of cotton candy, suddenly turned into Rosalind Carter and began hectoring us on the importance of switching over to the metric system. I was reasonably certain the neighbor dame hadn't been the former first lady, and that my shit-pit childhood apartment wasn't next door to the White House. The goddamn Sandman and his dream kingdom had successfully corrupted the one good memory from an otherwise rotten childhood.

"Metrification is the future!" Rosalind Carter bellowed.

She was abruptly twenty feet tall, belching sulfurous ash, and stomping all over the circus tents. I avoided a hurled clown and ran like mad from the big top.

When I retook my Segway, I was suddenly the grown-up version of myself. The cotton candy that I was still holding suddenly turned into deca-minutes or millipedes or some kind of goddamn submultiples of units in a decimal pattern and began swirling around me in swarms of perfectly measured tens. I swatted frantically at the cloud as I raced as fast from the ruins of the circus as my camel would carry me. (I was also suddenly on a goddamn camel, which almost as rapidly became a giant wheeled cigarette.)

I realized first what it must be like to be Keith Richards, and second, that apparently this dreamland was trying to impede my progress.

I concentrated on the cocktail party that I recalled from the fractured memory of my multi-day coma back at the Paradise Motel, and for an instant I swore I heard the gentle tinkling of glasses.

As soon as the sound brushed my eardrums, my speeding cigarette-mobile was suddenly gone from underneath me and I was in the crow's nest of a ship in the middle of a storm at sea. I was holding on for dear life. Lightning pierced the sky. Deckhands raced around like sopping wet rats far below me. The cold spray of violent rain stung my baby soft skin. A space shuttle blasted in out of nowhere and buzzed the mizzen mast, its OSHA pilot waving at me from the cockpit window before it blasted back off again into the winking eye of the ferocious storm.

I could feel my stomach lurch and my head spin.

But this wasn't real. It was just a dream. And no matter what horror movies tell you, if you die in dreams you don't die in real life. If you did, everybody who's ever had a dream in which they're falling would wake up splattered like a stomped-on jelly doughnut on their Sealy Posturepedics.

I was pretty sure I was right, but I only had one option available to me to test my hypothesis. I climbed up onto the slippery rim of the crow's nest, tested the direction of the wind with one damp finger, and hurled myself overboard.

I had the aforementioned sense of falling. Wind whipped at the tails of my trench coat. The endless black ocean raced at me like a salt water sucker punch. I held fast to my fedora for fear of losing it and having nothing with which to cover the road kill remains of my mush if it turned out I was wrong about the lethal effects of dream falling. A single twenty-foot high whitecap — which was precisely eighty million and a half milliwangers translated into goddamn metric language — jabbed up out of the surface of the tumultuous sea like the dorsal fin of some extinct leviathan.

In my dreaming mind the wave sharpened into a lethal knife blade. The boat became a massive salad bowl and I was a P.I.-shaped cucumber ready for dicing.

And then storm and sea and knife, as well as a deadly mile-high crouton, disappeared and I was standing at the edge of a vast plain.

Groups of men and women mingled in nightclothes.

Others were tucked away in comfortable beds that were arranged with graveyard efficiency across the endless field. The same benign cartoon moon I'd seen in a flash of memory back at Bed, Bath & Barn kept a watchful eye over the slumbering horde, offering a soothing smile and a ready wink to anybody who glanced up into the warm twilight heavens.

I had made it to the nightly party. The all-night soiree was more than likely lasting most of the day now. If the Sandman had his way, the poor bastards trapped in this dream world would eventually be in here most of their lives, leaving just long enough to tramp to the bathroom or to an increasingly empty fridge, since shopping, work and anything else that might take them more than twenty feet from their addictive Sleep-Tite Pillows would ultimately become a thing of the waking past.

I generally wasn't inclined to save the day. In point of fact, I had very little use for the day, what with the noisy traffic, the infernal sunshine, and everybody going around living horribly productive lives. But on the other hand I couldn't bear the thought of living in a city where the package store owners neglected to stock their shelves because they were spending all their waking hours asleep on lobotomizing pillows.

If I was going to save the saps at the slumber party, I figured I didn't have a lot of time to do so, as I'd already set my own brilliant escape plan — assuming it worked — in motion before the Sandman had knocked me out.

There were dozens of people gathered in small groups nearby. Hundreds more were beyond them. At the darkest fringes of night, I could just make out the shadows of thousands more. A constant trickle of men and women peeled away from the little groups, donning nightcaps, scratching asses, stretching like contented housecats, and climbing into the ever-expanding number of beds that continued to multiply to infinity like randy rabbits under the ever watchful soft moonlight.

A familiar face grinned rotten teeth in a nearby group of contented revelers. Vincetti the fascist fishmonger was laughing at something hilarious Madame Carpathia, the commie dance instructor, had said about torture chambers, gulags or ethnic cleansing. I headed straight for my building's assembled group of chuckling assholes.

Before I managed to walk two feet, some bastard with burn scars all over his face and an ugly, red-striped sweater jumped out from inside a large hallway mirror that hadn't been there a moment before and threatened me with his razor-fingered gloves.

"You're not too *sharp*, are ya, pal?" he rasped, clicking his Lady Schick fingertips together menacingly.

"A., if you're going to quip don't suck at it," I informed the grinning creep, who was obviously the Sandman's last line of defense, "and B., I was married." I pulled out my gat and plugged the SOB in the band of his fedora. The bullet slapped my would-be dream assassin in the forehead and he dropped like a sack of lead nails. "Nightmares can't compete with ten years of wedded bliss," I informed the ghoulish goddamn corpse.

I marched straight up to Vincetti.

The fishmonger spotted me approaching, and his ghastly grin widened.

"Hey, it's-a Mistah Banyon! 'Ow's-a ya doin', my good-a friend?"

I disabused him of the false notion that we ever had been or ever would be friends by the judicious application of a sharp fist to his crooked guinea conk.

Vincetti grabbed his nose, which was suddenly spouting blood and then, because this was still a goddamn dream, sprouting chrysanthemums.

"Why you do-a that?" the fishmonger demanded, tugging at the flowers that were clogging his hairy nostrils.

"Aside from a satisfying act of elder abuse which I'd never get away with out in the real world, I need you to realize, Vincetti, that you are both asleep and an asshole." To motivate him in that direction, I popped him another one.

A flash of his choleric old fish peddler self crossed his ugly mug.

"You stop-a doin' that!" he demanded.

"Okay," I said. Instead, I turned to the fishmonger's left and socked one of the fat, drunken junior partners from the law firm of Shyster, Pilfer & Fraud.

The lawyer was holding a drink, of course, since he was a lawyer and thus couldn't pass a bar since he'd passed the bar. When I nailed his jowly mug, his drink splashed back into the puss of Madame Carpathia. The dance instructor was quicker to anger than were the men, probably due to a pent-up rage from having to stand on her toes so many years propping up a shit political system of centralized planners who couldn't build a decent tractor, amusement park or pair of goddamn blue jeans.

Madame Carpathia screamed like Russian bear and launched proud Soviet fingernails into jugular of decadent Western lawyer.

It was amazing how quickly a couple of strategically delivered punches could unravel an entire empire. Even I didn't anticipate the catastrophic Archduke Ferdinand effect my act of uncivil disobedience would have on the Sandman's kingdom of dreams.

Vincetti the unrepentant, Mussolini-loving fascist fishmonger was clearly still holding a grudge against the

Allies. Rather than turn against me, a guy who might fight back, he promptly began strangling Madame Carpathia, the Russian expat who, clearly in his demented brain, was a greater threat to the Axis powers than Churchill.

The barroom brawl spread like wildfire from one group to another. It was clear that the Sandman and his Sleep-Tite Pillows with their narcoleptic angel feather cores were only effective to suppress, not eliminate, natural instincts. It warmed my heart to find that there was some innate human desire to kick the shit out of one's fellow man after all.

Half of the many distant shadows seemed to vanish, clashing silhouettes disappearing, presumably back to reality, moments after the melee began.

Nearby, Wasserbaum the dentist was curled up in a fetal position and screaming for his hygienist to save him. I don't know if it was an invention of his dreams or if the hygienist herself was sleeping it off somewhere close by and had heard the call to arms, but a version of the heroic dame arrived in a jiffy with a dental drill as big as a how-itzer. She promptly corkscrewed the chests of two of the nearest brawlers. Instead of drawing blood from punctured thoraxes, the heads of the two bastards snapped back, their sleepy eyes went wide, and they vanished from sight.

I was certain now that wherever the two men had been zonked out on their respective Sleep-Tite Pillows in the real world, they had just woken up.

The same assuredly went for every shadow that was disappearing from the horizon, and for every bed in which a previously gently slumbering figure had sat bolt upright, awakened in sleep from the noise. Waking *in* sleep clearly caused waking *from* sleep. Bedrooms all over town were currently overloading with the groggy and confused diaspora population of the Sandman's sleepy kingdom.

I felt a whoosh of air beside me, felt a brush of fine grains of sand rake across my face, and heard the sucking pop of the dream king himself materializing out of thin air.

The Sandman surveyed the hair-pulling, knee-kicking, eye-gouging slapstick battle that was taking place on the Agincourt Field of his otherworldly realm.

"*What on earth is going on here?*" the Sandman demanded.

"As near as I can tell, a lot of pent-up natural instinct," I said. "You've had them all far too relaxed in the real world for too long. The lid blew off the pot."

He gave me a saggy-eyed glare of pure hatred before wheeling around.

"Stop it right now!" he shouted.

His magnified voice boomed out of every corner of the kingdom over which he ruled, the practical and unintentional effect being that the soundest sleepers who'd managed to snore through the worst of the brawl promptly woke up and disappeared.

Vincetti, Madame Carpathia, the drunken asshole downstairs lawyer, Wasserbaum and his hygienist and a million other soundly sleeping bastards vanished from sight, reemerging in their own bedrooms, boardrooms, bathrooms, cockpits, sleeping bags, mistresses' boudoirs, widow's walks, elevator cars, mayor's mansions, Dumpsters, drain pipes, floor boards, roach motels, and behind the steering wheels of a million vehicles throughout the tri-state area. I was left alone on a barren countryside with hundreds of thousands of empty beds and one royally pissed off dream king.

"*You* did this," accused the Sandman.

"I wish I could stick around and soak up the praise, but I've got to be going, too."

I heard the sound of revelry behind me. The casino was just over my shoulder, and I was somehow suddenly partially in the lobby. The G-men were the only ones other than myself who hadn't vanished from the dream world. They were currently on horseback and playing polo around the slot machines using Mel Torme's head as a ball. In an eye twisting display audacious for the fabulous impossibility of it, the OSHA SOB was doing doughnuts in his space shuttle around a ceiling security camera.

"Oh, *you're* staying," the Sandman said. "Those government agents, too. I don't know what victory you think you've won here, Banyon, but you've lost. I gave you and those Washington bastards a direct blast of sand in your eyes. I don't need any of you snooping around. You're all in it for the big sleep. As for all the rest of them—" He waved a sickly hand toward the field of empty beds, "they'll all be back. An afternoon nap, a dozing daydream at their desks at work, falling asleep in front of the TV, turning in for the night." He leveled an angry, crooked finger at my chest. "Every one of them will be back in less than twenty-four hours. And before that happens, you're going to rue the day that you—"

BAP! BAP! BAP! BAP! BAP! BAP! BAP!

It came from everywhere and nowhere at once.

The noise pierced the blanket of night and punctured every cell in my brain. The hitherto smiling, benevolent moon that sat like a low-hanging Christmas bulb, bending the Yule branch of night over the swollen twilight sky, was suddenly a scowling yellow blob vomiting daylight into every nook and cranny of the Sandman's realm.

"Hold that thought," I said to his royal ass-ness. At least I think I said it. Against all of its mighty resolve to the contrary, night had very promptly and quite spectacularly become day, and the pull to wake up was so great that, frankly, I wasn't sure if I had time to get out so much as the *H* in "hold" or, for that matter, any *F*s, *S*s or any other letters of the alphabet that were near and dear to my self-satisfied lips.

Before the third *BAP!* screamed in my head, the dreamscape abruptly vanished and I was awake and marginally alert back in the Sandman's factory office.

I was on the floor and staring up at the ceiling tiles. There was a fat pillow underneath me. I could hear the clattering of Charles Pinder — who was definitely not a peanut — religiously wringing religion from the Internet in the corner of the room.

The moment I regained consciousness, I started scampering to my feet.

I realized immediately that my odometer had racked up far too many miles to realistically accomplish anything remotely close to scampering. Likewise, frolicking and gamboling were probably out of the question as well, and I figured if I tried cavorting that I'd most likely bust a hip. I stopped in mid-scamper, and instead performed a very careful middle-aged crawl to my uncertain Florsheims.

Bap! Bap! Bap!

The noise was softer here in the real world, muffled as it was by a bathrobe pocket. One of my erstwhile guards, a participant in the bench-clearing brawl off in dreamland, was yawning himself awake. He didn't even noticed the gun that the Sandman had stuffed in his hand while he was sleepwalking. He simply let the heavy gat slide from his fingers and began scrounging around in the pocket of his flannel dressing gown. He located and retrieved the source of the nuisance noise.

When his cell phone had started ringing up on the roof pretty much precisely twenty minutes before, I'd thoughtfully answered it. Judging from the nasty tone of the dame on the other end, I assumed it was the poor sap's wife. I told her my opinion of marriage (strongly against), hung up in her screeching ear, and — brilliantly, as it turned out — set the gadget's alarm to go off in twenty minutes. For the sound, I selected the universal clock radio *bap-bap!* which was the bane of the early morning hours of everybody from brick mansions to wood Cape Cods to grass huts to goddamn Eskimo ice cube log cabins. No matter how much sand the sleepy bastard had blasted in my eyes, I'd correctly assumed that the noise of a clock radio going off like a stick of stuttering dynamite in one's ear was enough to make the entire planet reach out one-handed in the dark in search of the snooze bar.

As the world around me was reluctantly awakening, I quickly grabbed some paperwork off the desk, lit the corner with the lighter in my pocket, and dropped it into the trash barrel I'd seen underneath the desk when I'd been dragged down from the roof.

The rest of the hired guns who'd herded me downstairs were yawning themselves wide awake and wondering how the hell they'd gotten to the pillow factory. Like me, the government men had needed the extra push of the clock radio sound to get them out of their dream-world casino and space shuttle cockpit. They were all awake now, pushing their bed-sore asses off of the harem pillows that were tossed around the room. Their bureaucrat hands went straight for their abandoned briefcases.

"Time to get up already?" my nearby former sleeping prison guard groaned to himself as he shut off the alarm on his phone.

"Long past," I informed him. "Apparently your wife has been waiting for over a week for you to get home from a business conference at the airport Ramada. You were supposed to bring pizza home for her and the kids last

Tuesday. She screamed at me a little while up on the roof in that frequency that can only be heard by dogs and emasculated husbands. If you need the name of a good divorce attorney, I can give you mine. He was terrible, but if you have his name you can at least make sure to steer clear of the most incompetent ambulance chaser on the planet."

The poor henpecked SOB didn't believe me until he checked the date on his phone.

"Oh, shit," he said, eyes wide. He dropped the phone back in his pocket. It landed with a muffled clunk on something that shouldn't be there.

"I believe you'll find that's mine," I said.

With a puzzled look on his tired puss he pulled out the alien object. Even though he'd just dropped a gun, which he'd used to gently threaten me down from the roof, he seemed surprised to find yet another piece in his hand. I liberated from his sweaty palm my gat, which he'd taken from me upstairs. Just in time.

A minor sand storm erupted in front of the plate glass windows that looked out over the Sleep-Tite factory floor, and from the swirling cyclone emerged the furious mug of the Sandman. This time even after his body fully formed, there remained a Saturn's ring of sand swirling around him. He directed his angry gaze at the assembly line below.

The foremen had been indentured sleepwalkers as well, but they'd been awakened from their slumber by the brawl. Their constant threats and physical abuse were all that had been keeping the assembly line workers on the job. Now that the confused foremen were awake, order had broken down on the factory floor. Men and women were pulling off hairnets and masks. Some had already abandoned ship. The front door was wide open on the parking lot. Sunlight streamed in and slave labor streamed out.

The Sandman wheeled on me, eyes gleaming red-hot rage.

I've never been to the desert. When I was a kid, the little chick next door had a sandbox, but the landlord made her parents get it out of the living room when the rest of the tenement complained that the neighborhood cats were burying their shit in it. I distinctly remember my adorable little childhood playmate getting mad at me for pointing out that her mother was a nasty slag, matched only in her utter worthlessness by her old man, whose only source of income was losing on the ponies. The little dame had hauled off and whacked me on the coconut with a pail full of beach sand. My memory of the look of fury on my ancient playmate's cherubic face and the accompanying tin bucket of cat-shit beach sand came rocketing back to me in a single glare from the king of night.

"*Banyon!*" the Sandman bellowed.

I was staring in the face of a swelling sandstorm. A category one-hundred sandstorm. An extinction level sandstorm, and I was the goddamn dinosaurs.

Even Charles Pinder couldn't blot out the distraction. The color drained from his already pasty face, and he clapped his laptop shut, hugging it to his chest.

Lights flickered. Fine grains of sand swirled around the office, audibly pelting desk, chairs, and tin file cabinets. Pinder turned his face away from the sand that raked his pale kisser. At the center of the storm, the Sandman raised his arms.

The OSHA bastard and the other G-men fled the room in the company of my pajama-wearing captors. I inched in the same direction. A gust of violent wind slammed the door so hard that the reverberations shattered the high glass panes at the Sandman's back. Swirling sand instantly ground the glass to dust, and the sparkling newborn sand joined the whirling maelstrom.

"Look," I said, edging further back towards the closed door. I kept an eye trained on the footwell of the Sandman's desk. "I can see why you'd be a little put off. I'd be too, if a moron like me so effectively undid an evil plan I'd obviously worked so hard on. But you pointed out yourself that you can reset your diabolical scheme. At least I think you did. You said it in my dream and, unfortunately, it being a dream, I've already forgotten pretty much all of it. But what should be vitally important to you right now is that I noticed the fire inspection certification you've got hanging out in the hallway."

Unseen by the Sandman as his temper flared, the blaze I'd set in the trash bucket had continued to roast the bottom of his desk. At that precise moment, the flames leapt up from the underside of the desk and raced across the surface. Fanned by the wind of the Sandman's own storm, crackling streaks of fire leapt from desk to pillows.

Apparently, the Sleep-Tite Pillow company used the same material for their products that was once very popular in kids' pajamas and filling station rags.

The Sleep-Tite Pillows that were scattered around the periphery of the office flashed to flaming life, one after another, flooding the room with noxious smoke.

I had bet, correctly it turned out, when I saw the fire inspection certificate that the one thing the OSHA bastard didn't have to trouble himself with was the fire suppression system. The instant the smoke reached the ceiling, a dozen silver nozzles burst to life.

Water exploded in every corner of the office.

The Sandman was standing directly below one of the nozzles. He looked up in horror as the geyser poured down.

"No!" he yelled as his face turned to streaks of mud.

He was wrong to the end, as the correct answer, it quickly became obvious, was, in fact, a resounding "yes." His melting voice box didn't have time to change its mind.

It was like watching time-lapse film of a chocolate Easter rabbit dissolving in a saucepan. His head melted away, streaking his shoulders and chest, which quickly softened and joined the dripping candle wax sludge that was pouring down his waist. For a moment he was nothing but a pair of legs supporting a couple of royally pissed-off hips. Those soon followed the rest of the body, transforming into a massive puddle of gritty brownie batter that spread across the 9 x 13 pan of the drab office carpet.

The last grain of sand was cleansed from the air, the crackling flames on the burning pillows spit a few final feeble sparking raspberries, and the howling wind, which had by this point dissolved into a desperate, spluttering puff, at last choked completely to silence. Over in the corner, Charles Pinder blinked against the spray of water and continued to clutch his laptop to his chest.

"I won't surrender without a fight," the waterlogged bastard bravely announced.

"Good," I replied. "After all of this I am, frankly, very much looking forward to beating the holy living shit out of you."

23

As satisfying as it would have been to knock into the middle of next week the bastard who was the cause of all the chaos in everybody's night life around town and, more importantly, in mine, Charles Pinder's solemn promise to go down swinging was about as good as a vending machine meatloaf sandwich six months past its sell-by date.

One raised fist out of yours truly and the fearless grand duchess of the Internet was blubbering for mercy behind his laptop shield.

Two minutes later, I was hauling the godless SOB (who, it turned out, was not so without a god as he let on) out the front door of Sleep-Tite Pillows, LLC. We emerged into the sunlight at the precise moment my backup plan was racing through the front gates, sirens blaring and lights flashing.

My hope that I'd save my ass by programming one of my captor's phones with an alarm clock ring tone was a demonstrable stroke of genius, but I believe in not only bringing a gun to a knife fight but, if available, an atomic bomb as well.

After fiddling with the phone's alarm, I'd placed a quick call to Mannix, instructing my assistant to hold off for a half hour before calling in the cavalry.

The first police cruiser screeched to a stop a foot away from crushing my toes. Detective Daniel Jenkins rolled out of the passenger seat.

Jenkins ignored the sopping wet SOB with the water-logged laptop computer, whose collar I was ringing out as he stood squirming, and whose right eye was growing darker from a mysterious shiner he'd somehow acquired when I was absolutely sure nobody was looking.

"Where's the Sandman, Banyon?" the flatfoot demanded without preamble, which even the Constitution has and which, frankly, I richly deserved given the high profile case I'd dropped in the incompetent copper's lap.

"Mr. M. Sandan is currently a pile of melting sludge on the carpet of his third floor office," I said. "I would recommend shoveling him into a couple of airtight plastic containers before he dries out. I don't know if he needs oxygen to survive. Hopefully he does, which means you and the good people at Tupperware would be doing the taxpayers an enormous favor. It would also offset the municipal waste that is your weekly salary."

There were a half dozen cop wagons squealing in behind that of Dan Jenkins. They were followed into the lot by an army of eczema-red firehouse contraptions, including a hook-and-ladder and three rescue squad trucks.

The firemen ran to attach hoses to douse the blaze I'd pyromaniacally started and heroically extinguished before they'd even donned their rubber pants.

Jenkins hustled to retrieve a shovel from the back of his cruiser. He handed it off to some of the boys in blue and waved them inside.

"Look in the kitchenette for plastic containers!" the flatfoot hollered at the backs of his men.

Jenkins exercised assiduous care to wipe any trace of

gratitude or, indeed, acknowledgement for and of, respectively, my suggestion before he turned to me. "Who's this?" the moron ace detective finally asked, nodding to Pinder.

"The Sandman's primary supplier of angel feathers," I replied. "The king of dreams wouldn't have had feather one if not for Pinder and his guardian angel."

Pinder desperately wanted to plug his fingers in his ears and *la-la* his way out of the conversation, but I had one of his arms pinned behind his back. His free hand still clutched his waterlogged laptop, which appeared to be weeping tears of joy for a five minute break from being stabbed at by Pinder's angry, calloused fingers.

"You believe in *angels*," Pinder snorted. He also said "LOL" aloud. The bastard was so far gone up his own URL-hole that his fingertips instinctively twitched, keying the letters in the air on an imaginary keyboard. "*I* believe in science and reason," he insisted. "Nothing exists that you can't see with your own two eyes."

Embarrassing irony and exquisite bad timing have as much to do with the function of the universe as science and reason, a fact that can be attested to by any ex-cop P.I. who, for instance, runs home unexpectedly to grab the evidence file from a planetarium murder, only to find his wife discovering the joys of binary pulsars on the living room couch with the tenured astronomy professor from down the hall.

At that precise moment of maximum universal mockery, the angel Invictus stepped out from behind a nearby subatomic particle in all his glory, manifesting pretty goddamned spectacularly unto us.

When Invictus beheld Pinder's ugly mug, the days of tension drained from his rounded shoulders. His magnificent wings sagged with weary relief.

"Oh, *finally*, Mr. Banyon," the angel said. "I hope you'll forgive me for doubting you, but I almost couldn't believe it when your assistant told me you'd actually have Mr. Pinder here. Thank you. Thank you so very, very much. I promise I will not let him out of my sight this time."

"Who the hell is this?" Jenkins demanded.

"That this is clearly Pinder's guardian angel, who I mentioned to you all of thirty seconds ago, is evidence enough that the police academy should be shut down and go back to making movies starring Bubba Smith. Also," I said to Invictus, "I never told Mannix that Pinder would be here, just that I was hoping to wrap things up, assuming I didn't get killed. He was being his normal overly optimistic self. And he never should have told you anything in the first place, since he was supposed to keep you at his place."

"I'm sorry, Mr. Banyon," Invictus said. "It's just, well, I couldn't help myself."

Jenkins was having his usual hard time wrapping his brain around the situation, which wouldn't have come as a shock to anybody who knew him. As far as the flatfoot's brain being able to wrap around anything went, a zombie mall wrapping station would run out of a roll of Jenkins' brain on Black Friday after wrapping only the first Yuletide thimble of the jolly goddamn season.

"That's it," Jenkins said, whipping out a pair of handcuffs. "I'm taking the whole lot of you in. We'll sort this out down at the station. You," he said, pointing at Invictus. "Hands against the car, assume the position."

As hilarious a torpedo to the *Bismark* of his career as it would have been to arrest and perp-walk into the squad room an honest to God-ness angel, Kamikaze Jenkins didn't get the chance to slap the cuffs on Invictus.

I felt intense pressure in my ears, the air around us was suddenly zapped with electricity, the sky flashed brilliant white, and in the next instant Jenkins would have needed a million more sets of handcuffs to take into custody the vast heavenly host of robed bastards who had appeared out of the ether all around us.

"*Aha!*" the Angel Greg, who stood at the front of the newly arrived crowd, announced victoriously. "Aha!" he repeated. "You were right, Angel Boris! Your fascination with these shiny red water chariots paid off!"

"Thank you, sir," a nasal angelic voice responded from out the multitude.

The sheer number of angels crammed into the parking lot made it impossible to locate the one angel who apparently wanted to be a fireman when he grew up. The Sleep-Tite Pillow factory parking lot was a subway platform at rush hour. It was the men's room at halftime on Super Bowl Sunday. It was the line to my ex-wife's bedroom when I was working the night shift. The firemen who hadn't raced into the building were immobile, pinned shoulder to wing amongst the angelic throng. Cops were trapped in their cruisers, unable to open their doors. Angels not on the ground were perched like pigeons on emergency vehicle roofs and lined up on window sills and building ledges.

The vast number of the Angel Greg's horde wasn't satisfied merely to flood the immediate area and to extend out into the street and around the block. As had been the case the first night I'd met the hovering bastards, an uncountable number of them were parked in the sky, somberly passing airborne judgment on everybody below who wasn't wearing a Clorox bathrobe.

With, that is, the exception of one poor heavenly schmuck.

The Angel Greg smiled with, frankly, far too much B.C. malevolence for those of us in the parking lot with an A.D. perspective on goddamn angels.

"*Invictus!*" the Angel Greg boomed.

The chubby little cherub aimed an accusing finger at Invictus, who was standing too far away this time to grab onto me and disappear us the hell out of there.

"Manifesting *again*, I see," intoned the Angel Greg. "That's it. Both you and your charge, Mr. Charles Pinder, will have to go."

"N-no," Pinder stammered. "Angels aren't real. Things that aren't real can't kill you. Cars can kill you. Alcohol can. Too much steak can definitely kill you. If you believe in angels, you might as well believe in the FSM, FSM, FSM, FSM…"

The Pinder brain train had taken a hike off the sanity tracks. He was so far gone that I didn't even bother to waste my breath defending innocent booze and, to a lesser degree, blameless and delicious cows against the slander he'd just leveled against them. The psycho bastard just stood there, water streaming from both eye holes, as well as from the cracks in his shuttered laptop, repeating the same three letters over and over.

For Pinder, the three letters were an abbreviated mantra. They were the same three letters that he and his angry pals had typed a million times to mock in shorthand strangers they would never meet all around the globe. The same three letters that had, with such frequent use and the confidence of blind faith to back them up, produced a result that Pinder and the rest of his Internet bully buddies had not intended.

I was pretty sure Pinder and I were the only ones who heard the distant roar. It was lost to everybody else's ears over the nearby flap of restless angel wings and the white noise hum that was the daytime pulse of a living city. Pinder stopped babbling, only aware in that too-late instant that he'd said the letters aloud. His sick gaze raked the sky just above the uneven rooftops of the dilapidated buildings across the street.

The Angel Greg certainly didn't hear the far-off roar. A moment later he also missed the nearer bloodcurdling howl that succeeded it, which noise indicated that the beast that had made both cries was getting closer. The boss of the ethereal firing squad was too busy redirecting his reproving digit at me to turn an ear to the sky.

"And *you*, Mr. Crag Banyon. Aiding and abetting the aforementioned illegal manifestation," the Angel Greg solemnly sibilated all over the immediate area.

"Illegal?" Dan Jenkins demanded. "Listen, pal, *I'm* the law around here. Show me a badge and a warrant, or I'm hauling all of you in with the rest of these guys."

The Angel Greg pointed his overworked index finger at Detective Daniel Jenkins, who was hiking up his belt defiantly.

"You," the Angel Greg angrily intoned. He tipped his halo and gave Jenkins a good, hard look. "I don't know you," he admitted, unknowingly expressing a sentiment to which everyone who did know Dan Jenkins wished they could lay claim. The booming fled his voice, and he looked over his shoulder for guidance. "He's not a witness, is he?"

The pair of angels with trumpet and scrolls were, as usual, shadowing their boss, and Greg consulted with the papyrus SOB, who checked his scroll and shook his head.

"No, apparently you haven't been involved in these events, at least as far as we're able to determine," the Angel Greg informed Jenkins. "Still, we'll have to smite you, too, just to be on the safe side. Nothing personal. All right, people, line up. No pushing."

The magnificent silver sword appeared out of nowhere in the Angel Greg's soft hands. The nearest otherworldly apparitions in his posse took a few cautious steps in reverse in order to give their leader enough room to swing for the fences.

The angelic bastard had singled out me, Invictus, Charles Pinder (dripping wet and hapless), and a suddenly terrified and more confused than normal Dan Jenkins, who in his panic had evidently forgotten that the gun under his armpit was a mandatory trinket that came with his tin badge. Lucky for all of we who were about to die, I wasn't a moron like Jenkins. Before the Angel Greg could strike a blow for Old Testament justice, I reached under my trench coat and whipped out my piece.

"Let's just hold off the mass execution for one minute," I suggested.

No more horrible animal roars echoed off the distant buildings. Maybe the beast had lost its way. I thought I heard the great leathery *whump* of pumping wings, but it came simultaneous with a car backfiring a block away, so I couldn't be sure.

Sunlight glinted off the silver blade in the Angel Greg's hands. He held the sword back over his shoulder in a frozen batting stance. My wannabe murderer issued an impatient sigh.

"Oh, spit, you're making this difficult, Mr. Banyon," Greg groused. "Can't you just take your medicine like everyone else?"

"My bartender has a very different opinion on what constitutes medicine," I informed him. "And just so you know, his brand of homeopathy won't cure a bullet to the forehead, which is what you're looking at if you don't hand over the sword."

A troubled crease formed in his soft, pale brow. "I can't do that," the angel executioner insisted. His voice was tight, like a plucked guitar string that had been tuned within an inch of snapping. "This is bigger than you can imagine."

The eyes always give it away, even with angels. His baby blues darted not to Invictus, the alleged malefactor on whose ass he was supposedly meant to mete out cosmic justice, but to cowering, drenched Charles Pinder.

"Yeah, I figured it out," I said. "This was never about Invictus revealing himself to Pinder. It was always about Pinder himself, and what he and his boneheaded buddies unwittingly brought into reality." It was clear from the glance Greg shot the angel with the parchment that I was right. "So what's your mandate? Limit the faiths to an acceptable number? Some Shakers show up on the scene, make sure they're a blip that only lasts a couple of generations before they go out of style like hula hoops? But you missed the ball entirely on this one. No surprise, since you're a bunch of Luddites. If somebody melted down a pile of bling into a golden calf, you'd be right on it. But you didn't see this one because it rose from the Internet. By the time you became aware of it, you could only try to wipe out the guy who brought it forth and his eyewitness guardian angel, who's such an innocent that he doesn't even know what he may have seen. You're just covering your own ass. It wasn't Invictus manifesting to Pinder you've been worried about all along, it's your own screw up. It's what *you* allowed to manifest because none of you ever got so much as a goddamn AOL account."

Invictus frowned confusion. "I don't understand, Mr. Banyon."

An ominous flap of leathery wings. Unmistakable. This time not concealed by a backfiring car. All eyes — human and ethereal — were trained on me, and so mine were the only peepers to see the shadow that passed across the burning white sun.

I took a very careful step backwards.

"Neither did Pinder," I informed Invictus. "All his FSM bullshit, over and over, for years. Repetition became ritual. That's how it always starts. Believe in the omnipotence of the rock, and before you know it you're building an altar and sacrificing your first born to it. Pinder and the rest of them fell into the same million-year-old pattern, even as they attacked everybody else who didn't buy into their one, true faith. They couldn't see they were zealots. He and his asshole pals spread arrogance like it was goddamn Skippy peanut butter and the Internet was a loaf of Wonder Bread. They didn't see their proselytizing was every bit as big a pain in the ass as the Watchtower fanatic pounding on the back door when you're on the john. They'd be the first to tell you that unshakable faith absent rational thought leads to unintended consequence. Like, for instance, so."

I'm a mesmerizing proselytizer myself when I get a good tailwind. The Angel Greg was enthralled by my dissection of the true mission of his cherub army. His chubby face grew more appalled as I laid bare the truth of what he was really up to.

Invictus and Detective Daniel Jenkins were watching both me and Greg, their eyes darting back and forth between the two of us. Dimwit Jenkins didn't get it, of course, but Invictus did. As I spoke, a look of confused but reluctant comprehension slowly bloomed into horror on the mush of the guardian angel.

Of all the crowd within earshot of my sermon on the

asphalt, only Charles Pinder was doing his best to pretend not to hear.

Pinder got tired of staring at the ground pretending he couldn't hear me, and decided to pretend not to hear me while staring at the sky, and in thus doing was the first in the crowd other than me to see the massive, swooping, fanged and tentacled body of the horrible creature his utter faith in himself had summoned into existence.

"*RAAWWWRRR!!!!*"

The sound seemed to screech from every direction at once. The small shadow I'd seen cross the sun was suddenly a total solar eclipse.

The blood had drained from Pinder's face. "*FSM!*" he screamed. The son of a bitch promptly dropped to his knees in supplication to the thing which, unlike everything else that wasn't NASA approved, he apparently suddenly unreservedly believed in.

"You're giving a mixed nihilistic message here," I hollered at the quivering bastard, whose hands were clapped over the back of his head and who actually had the nerve in his next breath to pray out loud for deliverance.

The thing had grown since the last time I'd encountered it. Its body alone was now the size of an airborne freight car. Wings and other limbs were extra, jutting out in every direction from the slimy, lumpy main body.

Angels ducked and fell away as the monster strafed the ground. It soared across the parking lot, snatching up a dozen wriggling winged figures in its slippery white limbs. The angels in its grip struggled to free themselves as it took to the air once more.

I caught sight of a pair of massive, crooked legs and clawed feet that I hadn't spotted back in Pinder's dingy apartment. Back then they weren't visible, although I couldn't swear to it in a court of law. Not that anybody could blame me, since during my first encounter with the creature back at Pinder's place I'd just seen the thing bite the head off a little old lady, so my powers of observation weren't exactly daisy fresh.

In the harsh light of day in the parking lot outside the Sleep-Tite Pillow factory, the claws were clearly visible as busted chunks of sharpened lasagna. The legs that attached the feet to the pulsing underside of the beast were enormous, jointed manicotti shells. Judging from the scent it left in its wake, the wings that were currently lifting it to the roof ledge of the pillow factory were huge, leathery basil leaves.

The Angel Greg looked sick to his holy stomach. His blue eyes watched the beast rise to the roof, clamp onto the brick with its lasagna claws, then twist and fling mightily. One after another the dozen angels that were wrapped up tight at the ends of its spaghetti arms were hoisted up and sent with audible snaps back down to the ground.

Apparently angels have no natural defense against a newly born god. The flapping bastards were paralyzed in the creature's grip until the moment they were released. The speed at which they hurtled earthward was too great for them to have time to dematerialize their asses someplace safer which, for them, was anywhere but here.

The twelve angels rocketed to the ground at a million miles an hour. Some struck pavement with ugly, meaty slaps. Others wiped out other angels in the air and on the ground. One unlucky SOB got launched through the extended ladder on the fire truck, popping through the far side in bloody chunks more neatly sliced than a hundred and fifty pounds of bologna in an otherworldly deli.

"That's the same thing that attacked the wake at Pierson's Funeral Parlor!" Dan Jenkins yelled. "What the hell is it, Banyon?"

The worthless cop had finally located his gun. He had it trained on the creature, which had just raised high above its head one last angel that it had been clutching in a hidden tentacle behind its back.

I recognized the bastard. Angel Greg's horn-blowing herald squirmed for all he was worth which, a moment later, was the cost of the bucket and sponge they'd need to clean him off what I assumed was the Sandman's Porsche, which was parked in a space with a sign that read "Reserved for Mr. Sandan" in front of the building.

A tentacle cracked like a whip, and both the angel and his bent horn, which the beast had scooped up on its dive bomb run over the parking lot, were a grisly mess that not even a drum of Princess Di grade Armor All would have been able to clean off M. Sandam's crushed front seat.

"What is it, Banyon!" Jenkins repeated as one of the Sandman's front radials bounced between the two of us. We both had to duck to avoid a hail of shattered glass from the squashed Porsche.

"FSM for short," I informed the cop. "Flying Spaghetti Monster for long. It was a hilariously derisive term up until relentless overuse summoned the bastard monster into existence. Blame Charles Pinder, who no doubt ran it into the ground more than anybody else in the world. If I had to guess, I'd say the thing looks at him like its personal pope. That's why it was living in the walls at his place. Pinder, if you care, is the cowering bastard lying on the ground at your feet who suddenly knows every parochial school prayer by heart and is currently screaming them at top volume at the pavement."

The thing on the roof roared, and all the third floor windows in the pillow factory beneath it obediently exploded. Glass shards rained down on the upturned faces below. Jenkins and I barely had time to leap through a nearby open cruiser door. Busted glass broke into smaller shards of jagged hail on the roof of the cop car.

Jenkins grunted on the floorboards, and when I nudged him all he could manage was a long groan.

"Naturally, you'd knock yourself out doing something as simple as jumping into a squad car, Jenkins," I told the semi-unconscious flatfoot.

Oblivion at that moment might not have been such a bad idea. Lying supine on the back seat, I could see in a single snapshot the whole megillah Barilla horror show.

The Flying Spaghetti Monster reared up on pasta claws in preparation to take a flying leap.

Its body was a mass of gigantic meatballs that were stitched together with strands of ugly white spaghetti shoelaces. It looked as if a plate of the daily special at Il Duce's Italian Paradise had caught the mumps and simultaneously got a radioactive bread stick shoved up its ass. Some of the strands of pasta stretched out beyond the main body, forming the flailing, sloppy wet tendrils that had just killed a dozen angels and which had previously attempted to al dente me to death in Pinder's apartment. When it opened its mouth to bare fangs, bloody Ragu drooled out.

"Sound the attack!" a quavering nearby voice cried out.

The Angel Greg was mustering his remaining forces which, despite early losses, still outnumbered the Flying Spaghetti Monster by about a zillion to one.

"Oh, darn it all to heck," Greg said, remembering that the poor slob who would have signaled the order to charge to his troops was currently an angelic shit smear on the seat of the parked Porsche. "Just…oh, just everybody kill that thing!" he yelled.

Anybody who's ever walked through a flock of suddenly airborne pigeons knows what it's like to be abruptly surrounded on all sides by a thousand desperately flapping wings. In a flash, I was goddamn Tippi Hedren trapped in a phone booth.

It was a blizzard, a whiteout, a blinding squall. Yet through the feathered snowstorm broke flashes of sunlight. Yellow rays bounced with blinding brilliance off of the blades of thousands of swords that had appeared in the hands of the Angel Greg's army of charging seraphs.

Swords swung, slashing meatballs. Francesco Rinaldi sauce exploded with Tarantino delight from marinara gashes in the beast's sides.

The Flying Spaghetti Monster threw back its head and roared not in pain or fear, but in unbridled rage. Pasta tendrils lashed out with accompanying horrible whipping sounds, like the snapping of living power lines.

The Flying Spaghetti Monster wrapped powerful limbs around ankles, waists, throats and whatever else it could grab. Some angels were hurled to their deaths. Others were shoved deep into the creature's open mouth. Sauce-smeared angel wings flapped desperately, only to be forever silenced with a violent snap of the Spaghetti Monster's strong jaws.

The creature snagged two more angels and raised them above its head, slamming them together with eternal life-ending force. Before the limp bodies could slip from its tendrils, the flash of a slicing sword separated both offending limbs from its body with a single, mighty swipe. My neck felt an unintentional sympathetic twinge for the monster when I realized it was the Angel Greg who'd delivered the crippling blow.

The detached linguini octopus limbs plunged to the ground still clutching their dead angel cargo. High above, the brilliant white robes of the Angel Greg were spattered with Ragu that blasted like water from a hose from the flailing stubs on what I guessed — without great confidence — was the newly minted god's meatball thorax.

The enraged Flying Spaghetti Monster was suddenly airborne. Whole chunks of the factory's ledge were torn away as it launched itself skyward, showering the ground with broken brick debris. Angels flapped back as the great god of the Internet age soared out over the parking lot on basil leaf wings. The sky directly above me opened up a circle of blue with the dark, pulsing meatball mass of the Spaghetti Monster at its center, and around which the angel army regrouped.

The beast was a snorting Prince spaghetti bull in the middle of a ring, with thousands of sword-wielding matadors circling for the kill. The entire passion play was taking place two hundred feet directly above my upturned face.

Jenkins chose that moment of calm before the insanity to groan once more from the floor of the cop car. I'd forgotten the flatfoot was even there, and the shock of a voice so nearby caused my heart and bowels to momentarily trade places.

The Angel Greg was issuing another order to charge as I tore my eyes off the horror show. I sat up in the back seat of the cop car. The Flying Spaghetti Monster roared like a sonic boom directly above my head. Angels screamed. Robed bodies fell. A chunk of severed meatball ass cracked the cruiser's windshield.

"Well, it seems like everything's under control here," I calmly told the semi-conscious cop. "What say we get the goddamn hell out of here?"

The keys were in the ignition. Unfortunately, the steering wheel was on the other side of the scratched Plexiglass cage that was placed between the front and rear seats in order to keep people like me from homicidally volunteering to drive.

Screwing up the last vestiges of courage I hoped I'd ever squander in this life, I took one giant, reluctant step outside.

A shower of freshly excavated pesto splashed down ten feet away, followed by a thudding severed spaghetti limb. The detached appendage slapped around the ground in its death throes like a frenzied albino python.

I jumped back just in time to keep from being crushed flat by the falling angel corpse that accompanied the limb, and I promptly stumbled and nearly fell over Charles Pinder. The bastard lunatic had sought partial refuge under the police car from which I'd just emerged. Only his head was hidden under the cruiser, while his ass remained outside praying to Mecca. It would have been satisfying to just hop in behind the wheel and roll right over his neck, but it'd be my goddamn luck if while I was driving over him he made a very cutting skeptic's point and popped a tire.

I grabbed the SOB by the ankles and hauled him out from under the cruiser.

No sooner had I done so than I became aware of somebody standing beside me.

I had been studiously ignoring the battle raging up above. As far as I was concerned, the screams of horror and the steady wet thump of bodies and parts thereof were all in my head. The ugly storm cloud of a shadow that was painting a mural of silhouette devastation across the Sleep-Tite parking lot was just an interesting trick of the goddamn light. Divorcing myself from reality, I realized, was easier than divorcing myself from my ex-wife, who ten years past the joyous date of our un-marriage still clung to my wallet like the last bobbing survivor of the HMS *Alimony*.

When the figure appeared immediately beside me, I had no choice but to acknowledge the realness of reality. My gat was already in my hand as I wheeled around and aimed the cold barrel at the forehead of whoever had snuck up to kill me.

Invictus, my guardian angel client, didn't even react to the gun aimed at his brain box. He was gazing down with deep sadness at the pathetic figure of Charles Pinder.

"I'm going to buy you a cow bell so you don't get your head blown off," I snapped at the angel. I shoved my roscoe back in its holster.

"*You* did all this," Invictus said.

He wasn't talking to me, which was pretty goddamn impolite since out of all the assholes in the immediate vicinity, I was the only one who wasn't crazy, stupid or dead.

Invictus shook his haloed head as he sighed at Pinder, his AWOL charge whose zany Internet hijinks had, in part, ushered in the present and maybe final apocalypse.

The guardian angel tsked in deep disappointment. With a sigh, he reached down and took cowering Charles Pinder by the arm.

As an afterthought, he grabbed onto me with his spare hand, and I was suddenly a human missile launched from an ethereal catapult. The invisible snapping rubber band flung me out from under the battle raging in the sky above the pillow factory parking lot. Suddenly the thousands of fighting angels and the single giant spaghetti-and-meatball god were dots on a rapidly receding horizon. And then they were gone.

Or maybe it was me that was gone.

I hoped I hadn't left the gas on in my apartment. Or, if I had, I hoped my building superintendent No Thumbs Hooligan had taken up smoking again. There's never enough time in your life to settle all the petty scores that pile up on your doorstep, and it would've been nice to get revenge on at least one of the assholes on my list, because a moment after I was gone from the pillow factory parking lot it was clear that I might be gone in the permanent sense.

When my head cleared, I found myself in the last place I or anybody who knew me — with the possible exception of a thoroughly virtuous elf with great, misplaced faith in my basic human decency — expected me to go when I finally kicked le goddamn buckette. That was, assuming the clouds, the gentle distant plucking of harps, and the Pearly Gates were any indication of where my post-post-mortem ass had landed.

24

It turned out that Three Stooges director Jules White had a firmer grasp on what Heaven looked like than most of your major religions.

I stood before a giant gate without a wall. A pair of polished marble pillars stretched seventy feet in the air. The golden gates were moored to the white pillars. One gate was partially open. A small, tasteful sign like you'd find on the door of an exclusive snobby gentlemen's club read: **HEAVEN, Est. 0**.

Another hand-painted sign hanging at eye level below the Heaven sign advised: *Wipe Your Feet Before Entering (Sikhs and Cavemen, this means YOU.)*

The ground was solid underfoot, which was strange because as far as I could tell it was constructed entirely from clouds. The cumulonimbus terrain was exceedingly difficult to stand, walk and (until I got used to the standing and walking part) fall over onto.

Falling face first into a pile of clouds didn't hurt in the least. In fact, stubbing your toe on a cloud, pitching forward into a cloud, scraping your knees and palms on a cloud, and accidentally swallowing a mouthful of cloud as you hit your chin on a cloud felt amazingly good, and infinitely better than anything experienced while drunk and staggering home late at night on Earth. Then again, most of every minute of life down below was wasted worrying if you put a stamp on the phone bill you just dropped in the mailbox, worrying if it would rain after you washed the car, or worrying if that freckle was always there and, if not, how you could stick your ex-wife with the funeral expenses.

A very old angel in a long, dazzling white beard sat at an ornately carved desk next to the partly open gate. He was writing on a yellow legal pad with a very long quill. The nameplate on the desk identified him as St. Peter, because it was vitally important that the goddamn obvious be stated to new arrivals right up front.

I got an eerie sense of the familiar from St. Peter's work area. A "Hang In There, Kitty!" poster was thumbtacked to the front of his desk, along with a plastic plaque that read, "You don't have to be without sin to get in here... but it helps!" There were little stuffed toys and molded plastic figures saying "I WUV YOU!" with their arms stretched wide. Little smiley face stickers were stuck all over every available surface, including a banker's lamp and an ancient 1980s-era home computer.

"Is my secretary dead and working as an interior decorator up here?" I asked St. Peter. "Because nobody told me she croaked, and I would have bought a jeroboam of champagne to smash over the prow of my liver to celebrate."

St. Peter, his head still bent over his legal pad, looked up with only his eyes.

"Take a seat, Banyon," the most famous nightclub bouncer in Christendom commanded. He stabbed his feathered pen in the direction of the left-hand pillar.

I hadn't seen it before, because it hadn't been there. There was a bench next to the gate, on which sat the old lady who I'd last seen being gnawed to death by the Flying Spaghetti Monster. Someone had located and reattached her missing head, which I decided was a pretty goddamn decent thing to do for someone who hadn't struck me as worth the effort.

The old bat was sipping a cup of tea. As I approached her, she raised the steaming cup to her wrinkled puss and slurped. She let out the most contented sigh I'd ever heard, and, after so doing, patted the open end of the bench beside her.

"Please, have a seat," she said. "I don't like to drink alone."

"You clearly aren't doing it right," I informed her. I accepted the invitation and rested my weary ass next to hers.

"Did that thing in Mr. Pinder's wall eat you, too?" the old dame asked.

She nodded down at a particularly puffy pile of cloud that was heaped on the cloud ground, which was immediately recognizable as Charles Pinder.

Invictus — my angel client who popped up all over the place where he wasn't supposed to, but had pulled a vanishing act on his home turf — had apparently dumped Pinder outside the gates with me. I don't know what kind of heavenly blinders had prevented me from seeing Pinder until the old bag pointed him out to me, but I wished it could be bottled. I saw more assholes in my life than a San Francisco proctologist, and it'd be heaven on earth to forever blot out people like Charles Pinder.

Heaven's waiting room had clearly overloaded Pinder's sensory apparatus.

Pinder was lying on his stomach with his head buried up to his neck in a cloud. The human ostrich was screaming "la-la!" repeatedly at the top of his lungs. Fortunately the cloud was absorbing most of his hollering on our end. I didn't, however, know what was coming out of the cloud's ass end. I figured the Weather Channel was probably going nuts right now covering the mysterious "la" storm that was currently blasting the Great Lakes region and was slowly moving east, closing highways and businesses, and which would eventually bury New England in a foot of "*la*s" over the weekend.

The old lady on the bench beside me gave me a nudge. "Hello?" she asked. "Did you hear me, young man?"

"I'm middle-aged, not young," I said. "Assuming I'm not dead, in which case, with eternity yawning open before me, I'm practically a newborn. That's an ugly thought, and if I think it any longer I'm going to stick my head in a cloud and help Pinder paralyze the entire East Coast with the 'la' storm of the century."

She glanced back at Pinder. "He never should have had that whatever-it-was in his wall. The building has a strict no pets policy."

"You had a cat," I reminded her.

"Oh, poor Mr. Dimples," she lamented. "My son won't look after him, the dirty little ingrate. I suppose if they gas him, he'll be up here with me."

"No cats," St. Peter called over from his desk.

"If I had any doubts this was Heaven, they've been dispelled," I said to the angel. "As long as you're listening now, what the hell am I doing here?"

"Top level conference, Banyon," St. Peter said. "Which *you* are not attending."

Heavenly conferences apparently move faster than their boardroom boredom-fest equivalents down on Earth. At that moment through the high, solid gold gates beside me stepped Invictus. Pinder's guardian angel was accompanied by a short, tubby angel. The fat angel gave a nod to the gatekeeper and his dancing feather quill.

"Hey, Pete," St. Fatso said. "They keeping you busy?"

"Every hour six thousand people die," St. Peter grunted. "That's on Earth *alone*, forget about Moon-Men and all the rest of the inhabited universe. I haven't had a break since the bubonic plague. How busy do you think I am?"

"Ah," St. Fatso the angel said. "I'll let them know over in personnel."

Invictus and St. Fatso bypassed St. Peter's desk and came over to the little park bench which I was sharing with the tea sipping old hag. The dame continued slurping away and watched with interest as the fat angel looked me up and down.

"Charles Pinder," St. Fatso said.

"No, but thanks for letting me know that Heaven's record keeping is as screwed up as every other bureaucracy in creation," I replied.

"No, this is Mr. Crag Banyon," Invictus said, interceding on my behalf before I could haul off and belt his boss over the insult. "He's the private detective I told you about. He was of invaluable help during all this. *That's* Mr. Pinder."

The tubby angel glanced down at the dumb bastard with his head in the clouds. Shaking his head and audibly sighing, he wisely gave up on Pinder and turned to me.

"We've pulled Angel Greg and his forces from the pillow factory," the management angel informed me. "Invictus here wasn't responsible for Pinder's endless blah-blah rhetoric dragging that new god into existence. That was Greg's responsibility. We've been encouraging him to modernize his department since Guttenberg, but he insisted movable type was a passing fad, like mood rings or the Roman Empire. He just kept using those darn scrolls, you'll pardon my French. And now, thanks to the fact Greg didn't have a clue about this Internet thing you people apparently came up with, there's a new god out there, with all the conversions and schisms and possible holy wars that seem to always go along with them. Means mountains and mountains of paperwork for us, I can tell you. And we were just now finally clearing the decks on the last of the Episcopalians. As punishment, Greg has been busted down in rank. He's now a tenth-level guardian angel, assigned to an as-yet undiscovered and endangered-species tree rat in the Indian subcontinent. He always looked down his nose at the guardian angel corps, so it's a fitting penalty. We'll reevaluate his position in a few hundred thousand years."

"Speaking of guardian angels, and before you find some other rat that needs spiritual babysitting, none of this was Invictus' fault," I said.

"No," St. Fatso said, nodding in agreement. "Guardian angels are there to prevent people from stepping in front of trains, not stop them from inadvertently birthing a new religion. Now, Invictus *did* lose sight of his charge, as a result of which he had to hire you—" (He shot my client an admonishing glance, and Invictus hung his halo in shame.) "—but him looking over Pinder's shoulder all day, every day wouldn't have prevented all this from happening."

"Thank you, sir," Invictus said. His grateful eyes were, naturally, welling up. If he turned on the waterworks here, we'd all wind up going over the side of the nearest cloud in a barrel.

"Not that I give an Indian tree rat's ass, but what happens to Pinder?" I asked.

"Human justice," St. Fatso said. "Whatever form that

takes. I supposed we could see a deathbed conversion out of him in a few decades, but frankly…"

We all looked down at the shouting maniac with his head tucked inside today's up-to-the-minute weather forecast.

"So, that is, as you people say, that," St. Fatso said, rubbing his tubby, tiny hands together. "The fighting's over. We'll be returning you home, safe and sound."

"Hold on," I said. "There have been so many *dei ex machinis* in the past half-hour alone that my head's spinning. You know, Invictus only had to drag me here against my will because your people dropped the ball on whatever deity non-proliferation program you've had going for the past millennium. And if not for Angel Greg and his army targeting my client here, the Sandman wouldn't have had enough feathers to put everyone in town in a deliriously happy and relaxing coma, thus putting the entire planet at risk of a decent night's sleep. I could lead a class action suit against you people."

"You'd have to represent yourself," St. Fatso replied, with a shrug of his wings. "This is Heaven. There are no lawyers here."

"No cats and no attorneys?" I said. "You are tempting me to spend the rest of my days being good. For now, let's settle out of court. How about I just pop inside for a minute or two? I'm thinking I could maybe get Michelangelo to scribble something on a napkin that I can turn around and sell for a couple million. I would definitely donate every penny to the poor. I'm broke, by the way, just to make sure there is no confusion that I would be the poor in this scenario."

The way St. Fatso frowned I knew I had him on the legal ropes and that he was ready to acquiesce to whatever demand I made.

The little old bat whose head I'd inadvertently gotten chomped off when she let me into Pinder's apartment had finished her tea. She sighed as she put the porcelain cup and saucer down on the bench between us.

Sometimes I hate being the absolutely terrific example of human decency that I am.

"Or," I said, "when this old bag's cat Mr. Dimples croaks, whether from natural causes, if her son gases it, or from whatever other mortal reason, you let her have it here for the rest of all eternity, until the end of time, forever and always."

St. Fatso's face brightened. "Done," he said.

Who needs a million bucks anyway? If I'd gotten it I'd just have blown it all on food and shelter and health care for me and my employees.

Before I could change my mind, the reverse rubber band effect grabbed me firmly by the back of my trench coat. I was suddenly hurtling backward from paradise into the abyss that was the ghastly reality of real life. My last glimpse of Heaven was the beatific smile on the wrinkled old puss of the newly re-headed, née headless, bag who, because this was Heaven and existed out of normal space-time, was already stroking a purring cat that she was joyously cradling in her arms. The ingrate cat took one look at me and hissed like I was a scratching post smeared with Friskies.

"I should've taken the goddamn cash!" I shouted into the thankless maw of eternity.

25

I awoke from a normal, crummy, terrific, non-feather-induced regular human sleep to find a very surprised elf in a tiny little business suit staring at me with wide eyes like a couple of bulging tennis balls.

"Mr. Crag!" Mannix exclaimed. "How long have you been here?"

"A minute. Forever. Who knows? Where's here, by the way?"

I sat up. Here was my office, which was horrible, as always, but not entirely unexpected given the presence of my shocked elf assistant, who was cradling a stack of manila file folders in his arms as he stood before me.

"I didn't know you'd come in," Mannix said, simultaneously elated and baffled. "I've been at my desk all day. Did you use the fire escape?"

I dispensed with the details of my miraculous arrival as quickly as possible, and ascertained that, since vanishing from the parking lot outside the Sleep-Tite Pillow factory, today had somehow become the day after tomorrow. Apparently my few minutes in Heaven had translated to more than forty-eight hours Earthside, and had resulted in Mannix filling out a missing person report with the cops downtown.

"Call up Dan Jenkins," I advised. "Tell him to pull the missing person report and redirect the resources to finding his head. Its last known location was up his ass. Also, tell him to hammer the cork back in the champagne bottle, because I am reasonably certain I'm not dead."

Mannix just stood there before me, an enormous smile plastered across his beaming little face.

"Welcome back, Mr. Crag," my assistant said.

"Thanks, kid." I suddenly remembered something vitally important that could have far-reaching consequences for the future of Banyon Investigations, Inc. "What's the latest news on Doris?"

"Good news," Mannix said. "Miss Doris is out of the hospital and in wig rehab."

"My internal copy of Webster's doesn't agree with your definition of 'good news,'" I told him.

So much for my secretary being dead and working a part-time job after life sticking inspirational crap all over St. Peter's desk.

Mannix had brightened to give the report about Doris, a woman who despised his cheerfulness and efficiency and who tried to get him fired for every one of her screw-ups. After the initial glow of being able to report that Doris' singed cue ball head was getting the Eva Gabor treatment it deserved, the joy quickly left his face.

"Her mother isn't nice any longer," the elf informed me. "When I called today to check on Miss Doris, she said some *very* not-nice things about me. She was not nice for twenty minutes before I could finally get a moment to tell her I had to get back to work."

"Yes, it's difficult to wedge a word in sideways when the old battleaxe gets on a rhetorical roll," I said.

I guessed it was late afternoon. The clock on my office wall agreed, informing me that it was half-past drunk. A hot sun burned low in the sky.

The angels had tucked me into bed without my fedora and trench coat. There would be hell to pay if my two most prized possessions had been lost in transit. I got up off my crummy office sofa to search the cherished items out, talking as I walked.

"When I was dating Doris, I found the best way to get through a conversation with her mother was to politely slam the phone down on her. Just a warning though, it doesn't work in person. She managed to crack a blender over my head once before I could get up to rip her old AT&T unit off the kitchen wall. Don't be fooled by the clogged arteries, marshmallow arms, cascading chins, or the total lack of anything remotely approaching exercise since Doris' conception at the bowling alley. That old hag is greased lightning in a paisley housecoat."

Mannix was surprised that I found my trench coat and hat hanging on the corner rack a few feet away from his little desk. He hadn't seen me hang them there, mainly for the simple fact that I hadn't. I shrugged on coat and dropped on hat.

"I'll be at O'Hale's reintroducing my system to the joys of oral anesthetic. By the way, Mannix, it's safe for you to return to the office. Don't think I didn't notice you weren't hiding out downstairs at your place like I explicitly ordered you to."

"Oh!" he announced, remembering something that he mistakenly thought was more important than my imminent, urgent inebriation.

The elf hustled back into my inner office and returned a moment later with two copies of the *Gazette*.

"The paper had some stories about what happened," he explained. "I figured it was safe to come back to work when Heaven released a statement saying those naughty angels wouldn't be around town anymore."

"Good news for us, bad news for the rats of the world who might want to reproduce in their trees without a peeping Tom staring in their knotholes."

I cracked open the first paper. The headline screamed so loud at me, I wished I was wearing earmuffs.

TOP COP: "SANDMAN HATH
MURDERED SLEEP!"

"They're laying on MacShit a little thick today," I said.

The gist of the story from the couple of paragraphs that managed to suck in their guts enough to squeeze in around the "World War Declared, See Story Page 2" -size font was that the Sleep-Tite factory had been shut down by the Feds, all angel feather pillows sold were being recalled, and happy consumers of said product had been informed that they were actually the miserable bastards they'd always been, they were all just victims of temporary sanity. The Sandman himself was being kept damp and separated inside a bunch of Rubbermaid containers until police consultants from Dirt Devil could rig up a special cell that could hold on to the nitty-gritty dirt bag.

"Even the personification of sleep isn't above the law," the District Attorney was quoted slurring on the sidewalk outside Caviar Emptor, the upscale drinkery where only the most upstanding legal minds in the city went to get completely shitfaced.

"Hopefully, they find the bastard guilty and divvy him up inside a million hourglasses," I said. "It will warm my heart to know he'll spend the rest of his life doing nothing but timing three-minute eggs and getting lost in the back of a kitchen drawer.""You weren't mentioned in any of the articles, Mr. Crag," Mannix said, an adorable little furrow of anger creasing his usually cheerful brow.

"What do you know? There *is* a God," I replied.

The last thing I needed was the *Gazette* giving me free advertising about how great I art, and the thousand phone calls from desperate clients that would have come along with it.

I noticed a small piece in the "Arts and Style" section about a new artist that had exploded on the local scene and was currently knocking them dead with his fabulous, unpretentious masterpieces. Apparently my building superintendent, Harry "No Thumbs" Hooligan, had taken my advice to heart. The beaming gorilla was staring out at me from the paper, decked out in a beret, an ascot and an idiot's grin. No Thumbs was surrounded by hot, skinny dames at an art opening in one of those chichi galleries in the artsy Riche Tableau section of town. The eight-fingered SOB was making a fortune selling the paint-splattered newspapers he'd been using as drop cloths in the lobby of my building

"I take it back," I informed Mannix. I folded up the newspapers and tucked them up under my arm.

I thanked Mannix for saving the papers and hightailed it out of the joint before he pulled a Tom Sawyer on me and somehow tricked me into working.

Before I could punch the button for the elevator, the doors opened and Myron Wasserbaum, D.D.S. stepped off and nearly plowed straight into me.

"Get out of my way, Banyon," the least competent dentist in a universe of neglected teeth snarled.

"Have I told you lately, Wasserbaum, that I love you?" I said. "Of course not. Because nobody does, has, or ever will. You are just that repugnant."

The speechless oral sadist was sputtering bad enough to overflow the banks of his own spit sink as the doors slid closed on my beatific mug.

Downstairs, an exhausted Vincetti, the fascist fish peddler, was setting a barrel of pike heads out in the hot sidewalk sun in the vain hope that anybody who didn't pass out from the stench might pick up a couple of pounds for what would certainly turn out to be their last supper. He wiped the sweat from his face on the hem of an apron that was an unwashed record of his first day in business and every pungent decade since.

"Congratulations, Vincetti," I said. "Even standing next to a barrel filled with antique fish heads that only seem nearer to life thanks to an army of animating maggots, you yourself still remain the biggest health code violation in your store."

The old buzzard tried to give me that universal Mafia flip-off of a snapped, angry thumbnail against his front teeth. Apparently of the two of us, I was the only one who recognized the perilous condition of his rotting choppers, and so I wasn't surprised when he inadvertently launched a couple of horror-show incisors at my ducking head.

"You're in luck, Vincetti," I said. "Wasserbaum was heading to his office two minutes ago, so he's probably already killed his latest patient. Just don't let your decomposing fish stench blow down my end of the hallway."

I happily dodged a dozen pike heads on my way out of range.

The people I encountered on the sidewalk were just as delightfully horrible as had been Wasserbaum and Vincetti, all shoving and swearing and acting every bit the assholes that city dwellers were entitled to be. If anybody was still under the goddamn peace, love and good night's sleep influence of a Sleep-Tite Pillow, I didn't see them on the street or on the city bus that hauled me across town. Everybody from here to there was an asshole. The world, for what it was worth, was back to normal.

I read most of the two papers on my way over to O'Hale's, and by the time I shoved open the grimy tavern door with its window beautifully filthy to the point of opacity, I was largely caught up on the news I'd missed while I was in Heaven.

Jaublowski had apparently given up wooing underage kids who'd body-switched with their parents.

The joint was crawling with little old stereotypical 1960s broads who looked like they'd been shipped over from the set of *Dragnet*. I found out why from a flyer on the table nearest the door: "ANGLES AMONG US!"

Naturally, Ed Jaublowski had misspelled "angels," unless his intention had been to draw in aficionados of geometric rights, acutes and obtuses.

The angel battle with the Flying Spaghetti Monster and subsequent official divine apology issued from a burning bush outside the *Gazette*'s offices had, naturally, been big news on both of my MIA days. If I had faith in one constant in this world, it was that Jaublowski was a contemptible opportunist. The reprehensible barkeep had printed up a Kinko's ad welcoming to O'Hale's everybody in the neighborhood who had, even before the mass angelic manifestations of late, spent their days peeking under their dust ruffles for cherubs frolicking amongst the dust bunnies.

My favorite watering hole was now hag central, and my nose had to pick its way through the eye-watering combined offenses of peppermint ribbon candy, Halls mentholated cough drops, and Gold Bond powder just to reach the bar.

At least a familiar, fleabag figure was sitting at the stool next to mine.

The D.A. sheepdog who I'd last seen chasing cars in downtown traffic was back lapping at a bowl of Jaublowski's distilled paint thinner.

"Hey, Banyon," the mutt said as I slid in beside him. He offered a noncommittal wag of just the tip of his shaggy sheepdog tail. "Your name came up downtown today. Were you tied up in that Sleep-Tite mess?"

"In no way whatsoever," I replied. "In fact, I don't know what you're talking about, and I will swear to that on a stack of pornographic magazines."

"Didn't think so," the mongrel assistant district attorney said. "Lucky me, I'm part of the dream team that got stuck prosecuting the Sandman. It's me, a parrot with a two-thousand-word vocabulary and a knack for getting his owner into trouble, and that mule that kicks field goals. He got his law license after he washed out of the NFL. Just what this world needs, another jackass with a law degree. The D.A. himself is taking point on this one. Although that could be trouble. He was recently cursed by a voodoo priestess who's made it so that he has a total inability to tell any lies whatsoever. Can't even tell a white lie if his girlfriend asks him if her dress makes her ass look too big or when that reporter asked if the mayor wears a wig. We've really got our hands full on this one. Well, paws, claws, hoofs and hands full. Anyway, some uniform said you were involved, but that cop...what's his name? Jenkins? He said no way, and that the Sandman collar was all his. That guy's the hero of the day. Saving two funeral parties from the Flying Spaghetti Monster like he did? He'll probably get the key to the city for all he's done the past few days. Although the vice mayor will have to pin it on him, since the parrot lawyer flew off with the mayor's wig. Anyway, lucky for you that you weren't involved. This case could drag on for years. It's a real nightmare."

The dog shyster went back to lapping at his bowl of booze while I quietly enjoyed the savage mockery of a universe that might turn over to my mortal enemy the key to a worthless city the ownership of which I had graciously declined.

Jaublowski the greedy, seedy, soulless bartender had spotted me coming and was grateful for the reprieve when the doggie D.A. started chatting at me. The bartender saw I was in no mood, and so reluctantly trudged over and slid a glass in front of my usual spot.

"I know what you's gonna say, Jinx," the barkeep warned. "But paying customers is paying customers. Them angels what was tearing up town the other day was a godsend. All these little old dames what usually sit around their parlors all day waitin' for their numbers to come up couldn't wait to get out and yap at each other. I have created a — whatcha call — a sociable environment for like-minded old biddies."

"Yes, Ed, I understand that a lot of people have found religion. In the case of some of those people, religion has found them, whether they like it or not."

I'd read the *Gazette*'s "Worship Shmorship" religion section on the bus. The paper only knew some of the real story. I'd been able to fill in the blanks.

Pinder and pals, not the Sandman, had the lease on the old church, which was their sacred home base for mocking total strangers online. The Flying Spaghetti Monster had only been seeking out what it mistakenly thought were its most faithful followers among the carpal tunnel bastards, which was why it had crashed the funerals of my bakery van kidnappers. While I was incommunicado in Heaven, it had collected the body of Manny Wescott, the last of my three kidnappers, graveside at

Sacred Pancreas Cemetery. The three martyrs were the first saints in its eponymous church. They hadn't been raised, battered body and bent soul, into Heaven — at least I hadn't bumped into them when I was there — but according to the *Gazette* they were currently rotting up the neighborhood on the roof of Holy Jumping Jehoshaphat Reformed Orthodox Temple.

Charles Pinder was its big prize. As the unintentional pope of the Church of the Flying Spaghetti Monster, Pinder was the reason the young god had zeroed in on the pillow factory two days ago. After Invictus had ascended mine and Pinder's asses up to Heaven, and once Invictus' report had gotten Greg and his heavenly host recalled and reassigned to rat patrol, the lonely Flying Spaghetti Monster had soared down the street to the belfry of the former Holy Jumping Jehoshaphat Reformed Orthodox Temple.

The Flying Spaghetti Monster had been pretty peaceful the past couple of days, other than the quick hit-and-run visit to Wescott's funeral. It was mostly licking its Ragu wounds and waiting to be prayed to on Sundays and TBA holy days. In a turn of events to rival Saul on the road to Damascus, half of Pinder's buddies had already converted. The other half were relentlessly mocking the converts online. There was a mass baptism scheduled at the Prego sauce factory next weekend. Life was grand.

I downed my belt and signaled Jaublowski for a refill. As the clinking bottle was making a joyful noise unto my glass, one of Ed's wrinkled prune patrons in an ancient black mourning dress slid in beside me. She set a porcelain statue of an angel at prayer on the scarred altar at which I worshipped nightly.

"Medicinal tea, please," she warbled to the barkeep.

Jaublowski snagged a boiling teapot from an orange

burner fire hazard on the back shelf. Beats me where he scraped up all the china teacups that were distributed to the nonagenarian bags around the dump, but after pouring the old bat some thin tea, he darkened the hot water with two fingers from a bottle of his most potent rheumatiz med'cine.

He passed her the cup on a clinking saucer, and she proceeded to get sauced.

"I see you're admiring my angel," she said to me after a couple of warm belts of polluted East India Company product.

"I was most definitely not," I said. "And the last tea-slurping old bat who talked to me had her head bitten off. I don't have a spaghetti monster to work with me on that anymore, but with a snap of my fingers I can have a rabid D.A. all over you."

"Bite her yourself, Banyon," the mutt on my other side replied. "I'm on my way to the little puppy's room. Although I might've had a little too much hair of the dog." He hopped down from his stool and promptly tripped over his own four feet. "Woof-woof," he muttered to himself, before staggering off in the direction of the men's john.

"I see angels *everywhere*, young man," the talkative old hag pleasantly persisted, as if I gave two shits about her D.T. hallucinations. "Most of us here did long before they showed up this past week. Except for Gladys over there. She's just a lush. You see, it's not as important to know *where* to look for them as it is to know *how* to look." She frowned. "Except right now. Right now there's one standing over by the jukebox."

Her finger was so crooked from arthritis that it managed to simultaneously point at the jukebox as well as the cigarette machine on the opposite side of the room.

In a spot that I was certain had been vacant just one second before now stood Invictus, the real-life guardian angel. In all his schlumpy ethereal glory he managed to look pretty much nothing like the old dame's porcelain statue.

My former client offered a little apologetic wave.

"Hello, Mr. Banyon?" Invictus asked. "Is this a bad time?"

I held up my glass that Jaublowski had just refilled. "It's the first good time in days," I said.

Invictus smiled angelically and disappeared, reappearing at once next to me on the stool that the dog D.A. had vacated.

"I know I shouldn't be manifesting unto you like this," the angel said. "But as long as I was here anyway, I wanted to thank you for all your help."

"What do you mean 'here anyway,'" I asked. "You get pulled off Pinder?"

"No guardian angels get assigned to people who are in jail. They're being punished, after all," Invictus said. "And Mr. Pinder will be in jail for a very long time. If he ever gets out, a new guardian angel will be assigned to him then."

He dropped his voice and glanced around to make sure nobody was listening. Jaublowski was. The barkeep was rubbing a dirty rag around the bottom of a mug that wouldn't have been getting any cleaner if he'd first soaked it in penicillin. He was trying not to be obvious while making sure he kept a hairy ear aimed in our direction. The old dame with the angel statue was very obviously eavesdropping as well. Her wrinkled puss was stretched into a grin that reached from ear to ear.

A couple other old hags who'd spotted the real-life angel through their cataracts were tiptoeing nearer. They were making such a racket of it, what with their cracking joints and plastic Kresge shoes, that it was only their own deaf ears that didn't hear their crunching, creaking, tap-dancing, deafening approach.

Invictus, ever trusting, didn't notice that he had become the center of attention for everybody in O'Hale's Bar.

"Mr. Pinder won't get out," the angel confided. He said it so softly that I doubted even Jaublowski, possessed of the only fully functioning ears in the joint, heard. "Three years from now. Exercise yard. Stabbed in the back with a piece of sharpened lasagna. Very sad."

"Only if you hate happy endings," I said. "So did you get assigned a rat as well? You've come to the right place. They are fruitful and multiplying the hell out of each other inside the rodent Lover's Lane that are the walls of O'Hale's."

Invictus only gave a smile and vanished from his stool.

For a horrifying second I thought the universe's perverted sense of humor had upped its game a thousand-fold and assigned the winged pest to watch over me.

A moment later, Jaublowski's elbow dislodged the red-hot coil on which he was burning tea water for the gaggle of old biddies. The burner nearly set fire to the barkeep's alcohol-soaked apron, which nearly engulfed him in flames, which nearly jumped to the bar, setting fire to same, which nearly lit up the entire establishment, from which I and maybe a D.A. dog would have been the only patrons to make it out alive.

Instead, some unseen force caught the pot and fiery hotplate and set them back to the shelf. Jaublowski gave them a puzzled look, muttered a mildly surprised, but not terribly interested, "shit," and went right on watering up his drinks.

I caught a glimpse of a beaming face in the grimy mirror on the back of the bar. One big, innocent, angelic eye offered me a delighted wink. And then it was gone.

"Where are you going, Jinx?" Jaublowski asked.

I had slipped off my stool and was halfway to the door.

"Back to bed," I said. "If I die before I wake, it'll be a week too late."

I shoved open the door and slid my exhausted derriere out into the baking, late afternoon sunlight.

Other books by Jim Mullaney

The Crag Banyon Mysteries series:

One Horse Open Slay
Devil May Care
Royal Flush
Sea No Evil
Bum Luck
Flying Blind
Shoot the Moonstone
The Butler Did I.T.
X is For Banyon
Sleep Tight, Wake Dead
Habeas a Nice Corpus
Banyon Investigations, Inc. (*Crag Banyon anthology*)

The Red Menace series:

Red and Buried
Drowning in Red Ink
Red the Riot Act
A Red Letter Day
Red on the Menu
Red Devil

A Note from Jim Mullaney

If you enjoyed this book, please take a minute to post a review on Amazon. Every review helps, even if it's only a sentence or two. Believe me, the elf would appreciate it. I'll appreciate it even more. Thanks.

— Jim Mullaney

About the author

James Mullaney is a Shamus Award-nominated author of over 40 books, as well as comics, short stories, novellas, and screenplays. His work has been published by New American Library, Gold Eagle/Harlequin, Marvel Comics, Tor, Moonstone Books, and Bold Venture Press. He was ghostwriter and later credited writer of 26 novels in *The Destroyer* series, and wrote the series companion guide *The Assassin's Handbook 2*. He is currently the author of *The Red Menace* action series as well as the comic-fantasy *Crag Banyon Mysteries* detective series.

He was born in Taxachusetts, and wishes he were an only child, save one.

Printed by Amazon Italia Logistica S.r.l.
Torrazza Piemonte (TO), Italy

62404677R00198